D0502254

# A Well-Known Secret

**Also by Jim Fusilli** ——————————| *Closing Time*

G. P. PUTNAM'S SONS | NEW YORK

# A Well-Known Secret

This is a work of fiction. Names, characters, places, and incidents either are the product of the author's imagination or are used fictitiously, and any resemblance to actual persons, living or dead, business establishments, events, or locales is entirely coincidental.

G. P. Putnam's Sons
Publishers Since 1838
a member of
Penguin Putnam Inc.
375 Hudson Street
New York, NY 10014

Copyright © 2002 by Jim Fusilli
All rights reserved. This book, or parts thereof, may not be reproduced in any form without permission.
Published simultaneously in Canada

Library of Congress Cataloging-in-Publication Data

Fusilli, Jim, date.
  A well-known secret / Jim Fusilli.
    p.   cm.
  ISBN 0-399-14931-7
    1. Private investigators—New York (State)—New York—Fiction.
  2. New York (N.Y.)—Fiction.   I. Title.
  PS3606.U85 W45     2002                      2002023709
  813'.6—dc21

Printed in the United States of America
10   9   8   7   6   5   4   3   2   1

This book is printed on acid-free paper.  ∞

BOOK DESIGN BY VICTORIA KUSKOWSKI

To the memory of David Rosenberg

*For know that there is nothing more tractable than the human soul. It needs but to* will, *and the thing is done; the soul is set upon the right path: As on the contrary it needs but to nod over the task, and all is lost. For ruin and recovery alike are from within.*

—EPICTETUS

## R. THOMAS COOMBS

Metro Matters

# Murder Statistics Mean Little to Two Who Know Better

MURDER, we realize, is not uncommon in this city. Nor has it ever been, as recent statistics hailed as encouraging serve to remind us. The latest figures announced Monday by the Mayor at a contentious press conference at City Hall show an 11-percent decline in murder in the five boroughs in the last year. (Acts of terror, it has been agreed, fall under the new, unsettling category of attempted genocide.) Despite the decline, we are still left with 809 murder victims during the past year, a figure that fails to suggest cause for celebration.

It is a short leap from those numbers to the story of Terry Orr. Unlike those of us for whom murder is a remote concept, Mr. Orr is among the many New Yorkers who know that "809 victims" is not merely a statistic. It cries out that 809 people have ceased to exist, and that at least as many families have been irreparably damaged.

Mr. Orr became acutely aware of the difference between statistics and reality when his wife, the artist Marina Fiorentino, and their infant son were killed. A man later identified as Raymond Montgomery Weisz is said to have thrown the infant onto the tracks at the 66th Street subway station near Lincoln Center. In trying to save the boy, Ms. Fiorentino was crushed along with young Davy Orr beneath the wheels of an express train.

For statisticians and reporters who routinely cover carnage, the deaths of Ms. Fiorentino and her son were merely numbers 19 and 20 among people killed that year on the tracks of the IRT, the IND and the BMT. A "12-9" is what motormen call death by subway train. It is a radio alert that no one wants to make or hear, and it usually leads to a home visit from a member of the New York City Police Department that no one wants to receive.

For Mr. Orr, when that visit came on a July afternoon four years ago, his life as he knew it was ended. And then a new life began, for him and for his daughter Gabriella.

For most of the last four years, Mr. Orr has worked as a private investigator, having put aside a promising career as a writer and historian. There is a large part of Mr. Orr that seeks to bring the killer of his wife and son to justice, but he has expanded his mission considerably according

to Sharon Knight, an executive assistant district attorney for New York County who has employed Mr. Orr, as well as other private investigators.

"Terry's very bright, very passionate," says Ms. Knight. "He's willing to help friends, to do whatever he can. He's looking to set things right."

Mr. Orr has been a valuable citizen indeed: he has solved the murder of a livery cab driver, uncovered an extortion ring at the Byron hotel, and exposed both a rapist-murderer from Bosnia who was hiding in plain sight at St. Nicholas of Bari Church in TriBeCa and the priest who chose to ignore his crimes.

Mr. Orr is also said to have tracked a black bear through TriBeCa streets, to have apprehended a man on the Bowery who assaulted passersby with a cast-iron skillet, and even to be in possession of previously unknown recordings by Frank Sinatra. Apocryphal stories, perhaps, but of the kind that spring to life when a quiet, resourceful man gets a reputation for doing good.

What is certain is that Edward T. Orr has come a long way from the day when, as a member of the

St. John's University basketball squad, he punched teammate Howard Apple in the locker room at Madison Square Garden. The seven-foot-plus Mr. Apple lost four teeth and was unable to play that night, the Johnnies lost to their Big East rivals Seton Hall by six points—a third of Mr. Apple's average per-game output—and Eddie Orr, as he was known, lost his basketball scholarship. To this day, a few Red Storm fans in Queens spit at the sound of his name. Those with more finely tuned memories recall that several teammates declined to criticise Mr. Orr, who refused to reveal what Mr. Apple had done to provoke him.

Today, Terry Orr is raising his daughter, by all accounts a bright, curious, well-adjusted 14-year-old who, not coincidentally, plays on the freshman basketball team at Walt Whitman High in TriBeCa. Perhaps she is comforted by the knowledge that her mother's paintings hang in homes, offices and galleries throughout the world. Perhaps she finds consolation in the considerable estate her

parents' talents have provided: It is estimated that the sale of Ms. Fiorentino's art has generated some $20 million, and Mr. Orr's *Slippery Dick* is perhaps the only nonfiction book about the Tweed Ring to be optioned by a major Hollywood studio.

But it is more likely that Gabriella Orr misses the comfort of her mother's embrace. She no doubt yearns to play with her baby brother. These things no amount of money can replace. And curious though she may be, about murder she need know only this: For her, the number that matters is not 809, nor is it 11 percent. It's two: her mother and brother.

For Terry Orr, his wife and son.

"What I admire most about Terry," says Ms. Knight, the executive A.D.A., "is that he never seems to forget that the victim was a person with a family, with loved ones. It's never a stranger. It's somebody's husband, wife, brother, sister, friend. And he always remembers how devastating it is to lose a child."

**1**

Her name was Dorotea Salgado. Our housekeeper called her a friend.

She was sitting in a two-seat booth with her long, crinkled hands folded on the tabletop, and as I approached her she looked blankly at me, then returned to staring into the distance, toward the dappled sunlight and budding trees in Union Square Park. Her hollow, angular face was scored with wrinkles and dark lines, and her skin sagged slightly from the jaw. She wore a modest dress, burgundy with a paisley print, over her thin frame. Strands of gray, standing in contrast to her black hair, rested above her ears. At her side near the window sat a square pocketbook that wasn't new. It matched her brown belt and sensible shoes.

The old, '40s-style clock above the entrance to the kitchen read DIAMONDS, but if that was the name of the place, no one used it: The red-neon sign out front said COFFEE SHOP and nothing more.

At 11 on a Monday morning, black stools waited for customers at the Formica counter, and the small dining room to my right was empty except for a man working a laptop, nursing a mug of coffee.

I was in here once on a Sunday morning at about eight and was the only one who hadn't been out all night.

5

"Mrs. Salgado?"

She looked at me and blinked her sad eyes and said, "Yes."

I told her I was Terry Orr. She slid out of the booth and stood. She was of average height and that made her much shorter than me.

She had a faint accent. Mrs. Maoli had said she was Cuban.

"Please," she said as she gestured to the booth.

I waited for her to sit. When she did, I squeezed in across from her, leaving my legs in the aisle.

"Thank you for coming," she said.

I nodded.

When the waitress appeared, I ordered coffee black.

"An espresso, Mrs. Salgado?" I asked.

"Yes, please."

In here, espresso was as close as we'd get to café Cubano, which had the viscosity of Brent crude and enough caffeine to jump-start a slug.

I waited for her to doctor her drink with sugar. Her teaspoon clinked the sides of the tiny cup.

She wore her gold wedding band on her right hand.

"You're looking for your daughter," I began.

"Yes," she said, "Sonia."

"Where did you last see her?"

"In Bedford Hills."

"You haven't seen her since her release?"

She shook her head.

"Do you know where she went?"

Again, no.

"I see." I went gently. "You're not close . . ."

She looked down into the cup. "It is difficult. Mistakes were made, and, no, she didn't want me to come see her."

"'Mistakes?'"

"I—I was very angry," she said, "and then maybe it was too late." She hesitated. "In time, I visited, but she preferred not. Maybe so I would not see my daughter grow old in prison."

Our housekeeper Mrs. Maoli told me Sonia Salgado had been in Bedford Hills, a maximum-security facility up in Westchester, but between her wobbly English and my poor Italian she hadn't been able to give me much more. Her friend Mrs. Salgado was "a good woman, not young now—she must not work at this age. She has many problems. Her grandson is not well." Urging her to tell me more, I learned the that Italian word for a woman who murdered is *assassina*.

Mrs. Maoli mimicked downward strokes with a knife.

"Even after thirty years, she is my daughter," the old Cuban woman said.

"Did she have any plans? A job?"

"I don't know," she answered. "I have no information."

I sipped the bland coffee. "Is it possible she wanted to disappear?"

"Possible, yes."

"Is there a reason you need to find her?"

She frowned quizzically. "Did Natalia tell— Do you know about Enrique?"

"Is he the grandson?"

"He's very sick. She should see him."

"Mrs. Maoli said the boy has never seen his grandmother. Is that—"

"No. We would not take him to prison."

"How old is the boy?"

"He is three."

I found myself sketching invisible flow charts with my finger on the tabletop, avoiding the coffee-cup rings. "I'm trying to understand: You haven't seen her since—"

"Not in five years. This Christmas, five years. For a few minutes only."

"Does she know she has a grandson?"

"I wrote to her, yes."

I leaned forward. "There's no easy way to say this—"

"I understand, Mr. Orr, that Sonia does not want to see me and she does not want to see Enrique. I understand. But the situation has changed."

"Perhaps not for Sonia, Mrs. Salgado."

She stopped, then she shook her head. "I cannot explain. She is my daughter. I am seventy years old. And Enrique is sick."

"Sure," I nodded, "and you want to make things right."

"I think it is too late to make things right. But she was my little girl," she said without a trace of sentiment, without anger. "Then she was lost to me. I cannot explain. The newspapers said she was a monster. No."

Thirty years in Bedford Hills made it Murder One for Sonia Salgado. There was no sense asking her mother why she'd done it. A premeditated killing meant money or revenge.

"Perhaps she's hiding, Mrs. Salgado. That may be why she can't be found."

"I have thought of this and this is why I ask you and I do not ask the police. You can find her and you can give me the information. No one will know."

"You expose her and you may put her—and yourself—in danger."

"Mr. Orr, I just want to see my little girl. I want her to see Enrique. I want to see what is possible now."

"I understand, but—"

"And you help children, Mr. Orr. We know this."

On the north side of Union Square Park, they were cleaning away the debris from the Farmers' Market: Rotted fruit that had escaped the homeless lay in a pile near the curb. A city dump-truck moaned and wheezed as it backed toward 17th Street.

"Sure, Mrs. Salgado. Why not?"

She smiled, not in triumph but as if to signal that a burden had been lifted, a milepost passed.

"Give me a call in a day or two," I added.

"Thank you."

"No thanks yet," I said. "Let's wait until something gets done."

She reached for her handbag, but I dug out a five before she could get her money to the table.

"No, Mr. Orr, I insist." She pulled out a small brown wallet and dropped two folded singles between our cups.

That wasn't enough to cover my coffee, but I said nothing. I shouldn't have asked the proud old woman to meet me at this place, whose high prices paid for a hip cachet rather than customer satisfaction.

But since Mrs. Maoli said she knew Dorotea Salgado from the Farmers' Market, I thought it might be convenient for her.

What kind of people charge $3 for coffee?

I told her I was going to have another cup. She thanked me again, and I waited until she was halfway to Lex before I asked for the check. I left her two singles as a tip.

The New York County District Attorney's office is about a two-mile walk from Union Square. The best way to get there on a mild April morning is to cut through the park and stay on Fourth until the Bowery meets up with Park Row; or just take Lafayette through Little Italy toward the construction near Paine Park. Either way was faster than a cab, especially today: Somebody'd been given a big enough bag of cash to let Tim Robbins take over Spring near Balthazar for his latest flick, and traffic on Broadway had slowed to a dribble. Or so said WNYC before I left the house.

I went toward Fourth, stopping briefly by the melted candles, weathered fliers and inexhaustible well of sadness at the makeshift tribute to the victims of the World Trade Center attacks that stood sentry to Brown's statue of Washington on horseback. As I walked along the wide avenue, passing a Salvation Army thrift store, a year-round costume shop dubbed the Masters of Masquerade and the elaborate and decidedly English architecture of the Grace Church School, I called Sharon Knight, the best known and perhaps the best of Morgenthau's army of assistant district attorneys. A secretary with a Jamaican accent told me she was in court, so I asked for Julie Giada and got her voice mail. The clock in the musical quarter note on Carl Fischer's building told me a lunch recess wasn't too far off, so I kept going and arrived at Hogan Place just short of 45 minutes later: If Julie got my message, she'd help.

If Sharon was the star in the D.A.'s office, Julie was its angel. Julie, Sharon once said, had "a big, big heart," and added that "it's too bad she's doesn't check with her head now and then." Julie was plenty smart, but I knew what her boss meant: She liked to dig through the system to find lost causes—a bag lady who didn't want to move off a grate in Sutton Place, a wizened old man set up to take a fall by his pinstriped nephew and trophy wife, a wide-eyed yet insolent kid caught playing lookout for the neighborhood drug dealer. Julie had interned in the Brooklyn D.A.'s, then joined full-time after graduation from Penn Law. She spent a year in private practice, but jumped at the chance to come into Sharon's small group. "She really should've joined the Legal Aid, ACLU, something," Sharon laughed. "If I didn't trust her with my soul, I'd think she was working us from the inside." Maybe Julie's compassion would extend to the mother and grandson of a murderer.

I breezed through the first metal detector, then another, and I took the elevator upstairs. The receptionist was a cop who long ago had been taken off the streets and given a job that kept him warm and relatively safe: He still carried a service revolver. His family name was Casey, and whenever I came up here, perhaps 50 times in the past four years, he reacted as if he'd never seen me before.

"Officer Casey," I said with a nod.

He pushed aside his copy of the *Post*. "What'll it be?" he asked blankly. The thin black man had pale blue eyes and a long chin.

"Julie Giada, please," I said.

"Are you somebody by the name of Terry Orr?"

"Terry Orr," I replied, surprised.

"You have some ID?"

I dug out my wallet and showed him my P.I. license.

He handed me a white envelope that bore the New York County crest. "Julie's still out."

I nodded.

"You can call later if you want."

"OK."

I tore open the envelope and slid out a single sheet of paper.

Sonia Salgado's address. St. Mark's Garden in the East Village.


I stopped at Bazzini's, grabbed a *salade niçoise* and a half-pound of raw pumpkin seeds for lunch and brought it in a sack across Greenwich Avenue to my house. As I punched in the security code, I looked west to the river and watched it roll by for a while, its narrow ripples undisturbed by ocean-bound boat traffic or heavy winds, its scent barely discernible in the warm spring air. But at that moment the light scent was as fragrant as the saltiest sea, because its presence meant that the oppressive odor of toxins and death had finally been vanquished.

With the door open a crack behind me, I sat on the front steps, a mere eight blocks from where the World Trade Center had stood, and looked up at the wooden water tanks and ornate acanthus leaves in the fading green copper edging high on the buildings on Greenwich and Hudson. Bathed in sunlight, they seemed fine now, crowns on vital, broad-shouldered homes brimming with activity—creativity, housework, children playing, music, laughter—or quiet, as people slept off long nights of work and pleasure. But I knew that tomorrow these buildings might once again seem fragile repositories of gloom and sorrow, sagging remnants of a once-thriving neighborhood hit by an inglorious attack, by a stunning loss of life and the overwhelming aftermath: police sirens, a din of whirling helicopter blades, panic, crippling fear, brilliant klieg lights, expressionless soldiers in high boots and khaki carrying M16s, firemen in uniform staggering away from their 12-hour shifts (opposite raccoons, Bella called them, their faces black with soot and their eye sockets unmarked thanks to protective goggles), horrified tourists slowly approaching the burning chasm in the city, the nation. Neighbors lost in grief. The smell of death, the eerie silence.

Everywhere, every day, I see signs of hope, and of distress and defeat. A new restaurant opens on Harrison to rave reviews, Windows on the World is gone forever. A bustling crowd at a five-and-dime on Chambers, a shuttered storefront on Reade. A red carnation in a flower bed high on a ledge on Warren, and sidewalks still covered in a gray sheet of ash. American flags that have fallen from cars are now soiled rags in black water pooled in the gutter. ("Bella, I'm not sure you're supposed to put a flag in the washing machine.") On Duane, a Champagne party celebrating the anniversary of a shop that sells *tchotchkes* from England. On Duane, a man sitting on the steel steps of an old egg depot, his head buried in his hands as he sobs uncontrollably.

I believe we will be all right. We are resilient. We are strong.

We will never be the same. Something in us has been altered forever.

I've heard both sentiments expressed by the same people, unaware they had said the opposite moments earlier.

What can I say? I know what it's like to be caught between echoes of death and the possibility of recovery.

It takes a boundless courage to hope.

I mean, why should we bother?

Because we are inexorably driven toward life, even in the darkest hours. We must accept this. Failing to do so, we are fighting our best angels. We are defeating ourselves.

And when we smile, we are asking the dead to forgive us. When we laugh, we know they have.

That's what I say. Now, regarding what I believe . . .

I stood up. Under white streams of light, thin branches of trees on Harrison had spawned delicate yellow-green leaves. Someone—not me; Bella?—had sprinkled potting soil in the small squares of earth amidst the concrete and slate, as if store-bought nutrients would ward off ash, asbestos and fiberglass particles to help these slender trees grow strong. Nice gesture, I thought; futile? Who knows? Things continue to grow here and no one can explain it.

I went inside, dropped the lunch sack on the kitchen table and bent down to pick up the mail that had scattered after a short fall through the slot. The copy of a music magazine from the UK, a Janus statement and three junk fliers went on the table near Bella's neatly stacked manuscript.

As I slid out of my jacket, I noticed a note on the refrigerator, pinned under a rubber magnet from Sam Flax. *M. Orr, I speak to Dorotea. Grazie tante. Natalia Maoli.*

On the stove, my reward: two jumbo artichokes, spiked with garlic cloves, expertly trimmed, were in the steamer. I'd bet rolled thin slices of veal were in Tupperware in the refrigerator to complete the meal.

Neither Bella nor I could convince our housekeeper that artichokes and *messicani di vitello* constituted not one but two meals for us.

I hung my coat on the back of the laundry-room door and went to the phone. Since Mrs. Maoli wouldn't make a call without permission—a formality she insisted upon despite her years of service and Bella's unconditional, if occasionally bemused, love—I knew Dorotea Salgado had contacted her. I tapped *69 and was given a 10-digit number; since all of Bella's friends were in school, I figured the number belonged to Mrs. Maoli's Cuban friend.

Outside, it was mild enough to eat in the backyard, to linger over the *Times* book review, to listen to Sheila Yannick, who lived behind us, run endless scales on her Amati cello. But I wanted to wrap up the favor to Mrs.

Maoli, so I washed my hands in the kitchen sink, picked up the sack and took it and a small bottle of Badoit to the back of the house.

Mrs. Maoli had expressed her gratitude by feather-dusting Marina's scene of Lake Occhito. I stopped, tapped the frame and centered it on the brick wall.

As I sat behind my desk, I tore open the lunch sack and inadvertently toggled the mouse. With a shudder, the screen saver, a quote from Poe, kicked in: "All that we see is but a dream within a dream." I watched it scroll by as I dialed Julie Giada's number and used a paper napkin to wipe off a plastic fork.

On the third ring, I got voice mail again.

"Julie. Terry. Thanks for the address," I said, talking to the tape. "I'm thinking maybe you'd better give Salgado's parole officer a heads-up, just in case. She ought to know someone's looking for her, even if it's just her mother."

I thanked her again and cut the line. I logged on as I picked a plump caper from the salad.


"It's up to you," Bella said coyly as she dipped an artichoke leaf into the garlic butter I'd prepared.

She dragged the leaf against her bottom front teeth. One of what she calls her "trance mixes" played from the laptop at the other end of the table; something rehashed from the '70s, I think. With little regard for copyright law, my daughter pillaged MP3 files from the Web for our nightly entertainment. She's burned me a few CDs that aren't half bad.

"If you didn't want me to look at it, you wouldn't have left it there for me to ask you if I could. That's obvious." I pointed with my fork. "It's been there since Friday."

"Thursday." Then she muttered, "Obvious."

She was right. It was on the table the night before we went uptown to see Elizabeth Harteveld, Bella's twice-a-month shrink. The two of them probably agreed it was time for me to read it, that I was finally ready to give it its due.

Two years ago, I learned from Harteveld that Bella was putting together a chronology for, and biography of, a fictional detective named Mordecai

Foxx, who was supposed to have worked here in the 1870s. Her idea: She'd turn it over to me and I'd write a novel, as if a man who'd written nonfiction about Tammany could snap his fingers and become a novelist. When she was 12, what Bella wanted most, I thought, was a return to the life she'd known, which included me at the library or the computer keyboard 10–12 hours a day. I thought she was embarrassed that I'd put all that away to become a P.I. A lot of listening to her and Harteveld convinced me that what she wanted was for me to stay alive, for me to, as she once put it, "stand where a Dad is supposed to stand. Which is not digging through the trash for used condoms." She wanted me to hold her when she puts on her brave face: Her lips flatten, then quiver as her eyes brim with tears and her cheeks go to red. Bella's brave face: It tears me open. It reminds me that my heart is not the cold stone I'd convinced myself it had become.

I told her I wasn't going to write again—and as far as I've come, I can still say that unequivocally—and I challenged her to write the novel herself.

"Mr. Orr," said Mary Gottschalk, the librarian at Bella's Montessori school, "I'm not supposed to tell you anything about what Gabriella is up to. She made us all promise." The cranelike, silver-haired librarian looked left and right and then leaned over books stacked hastily on the long check-out desk to whisper to me. I bent down as she said, "It is the single most amazing thing I've seen in my seventeen years here. She's written an *entire* book."

"Yes, I—"

"No, you don't understand," Mrs. Gottschalk insisted. "It's really a *book*."

Now I took a sip of the red, a '97 Il Sodaccio that Leo had scored for me. "So . . . ?"

"So it's there," Bella said, without looking at me. "There it is."

She had butter on her dimpled chin. A girl who was obsessively neat in many ways—*House Beautiful* could do a piece on her closets—had abysmal table manners: She now had a bare foot on the chair and her knee up by her ear. A ridiculously large hoop earring lay flat on one of the patches on her jeans.

"You want me to read it or what?" I asked. "Just say so." I looked at the title page. *Nursery of Crime* was what she called it.

"Oh, I don't know . . ."

"Bella . . ."

She suddenly asked, "When did McSorley's open?"

"In 1855. Why?"

"Fifty-four."

"Fifty–" I stopped; I felt myself frown. "Are you sure?"

Her earring rattled as she gestured toward her manuscript. "The man who wrote *Slippery Dick* doesn't know when McSorley's opened. He-he."

I wiped my slippery fingers on a paper napkin. "What is your—"

"Fraunces Tavern?" she challenged.

I cut into a piece of juicy tomato. "It opened in 1719. Samuel Fraunces bought it in 1762. Does Mordecai Foxx have some sort of drinking problem?"

"No, not at all," she said aggressively as she defended her creation.

"So your point is . . ."

"My point is that I don't need a fact-checker. Or a proofreader. To read is to read only. For pleasure."

I looked at her as she toyed with a ring of purple onion. I couldn't tell if my daughter was outgrowing her looks or growing into them: She walks into my study and I see what will soon pass for a young woman. She walks into my study and I see a little girl. Tonight, she's a precocious 14-year-old. No: Tonight, with her long brown hair bunched on top of her head with a big pink clip, she looks like a Dr. Seuss character with a couple of freckles sprinkled about her nose. A nose which didn't resemble her mother's. Nor did it resemble mine. Since I'd had mine broken four times, I was glad of that.

Every time Bella leaves the house with her basketball tucked under her arm, I can see Marina shaking her head in disapproval, looking at my nose, and the scars and knots on my knees and elbows, before looking at Bella's sweet perfection. "Is this what you want for your daughter?" she'd ask, her Italian accent a bit thicker than when she was less nettled.

"What?" Bella asked. She caught me staring.

I changed the subject. "Is Glo-Bug's mom still helping you find a dress?"

"Sure." She put down her fork. "Everyone knows it's a big thing."

"Everybody," I repeated.

"*Everybody* wants to go to the Rock Critics' dinner."

We sat in silence for a moment. Not silence—electronic beeping and bleating and Bella whisper-singing absently into her cup of cranberry juice: "And for a minute there, I lost myself. I lost myself."

She looked at me. "Remember, Dad, it's 'rock 'n' roll black tie.' "

"Got it." Maybe she'd explain later.

"He's going to win."

"If Diddio wins, I will be very happy." I stood and grabbed my plate. "What about Mordecai Foxx?"

"What about him?" She dipped another leaf into the garlic butter.

"Bella . . ."

She made a sound that seemed like a snort.

I scraped scraps into the garbage pail and put the plate in the sink. "I'll be fair."

She took a deep breath. "Go ahead."

## 2

I felt the warmth of the early-morning sun, despite the chill off the river, and I paused for a moment on cobblestone, went back to my front steps to stretch again, then headed off to West Street, away from grinding bulldozers, groaning cranes and the caravan of dump trucks and containers on flatbeds at Ground Zero. I crossed the highway and ran south, then passed Point Thank You at Christopher, where handmade posters, bouquets and men and women with grateful hearts and generous smiles paid tribute to weary workers as they passed in Humvees, city-owned buses and blue Chevy Suburbans wearing NYPD shields.

I got in a quick three miles and was back on Greenwich by 8:15. After a stop at the refrigerator for bottled water, I went to the cabinet, remembered I was out of vitamins and took one of Bella's Flintstones chewables. Seconds later, I washed Dino out of my back teeth with *l'eau minérale naturelle gazeuse.*

Upstairs, I sat on the edge of my unmade bed for a moment to cool down, flipping on the radio on my nightstand for company. Unlacing my running shoes, I half-listened to a report on the corn grown near a nuclear plant in central France.

By the time I got out of the shower, NPR had moved on from mutant corn to something that involved Aldous Huxley. I missed most of what a giddy Brit commentator had to say as I towel-dried my hair. I tossed the towel in the general direction of the steamed bathroom and called Julie Giada.

"Well, this is a coincidence," she said, her voice clear and characteristically bright.

"You had your finger on the nine?"

"Not quite."

I went toward my chest of drawers and cradled the phone between my ear and shoulder as I started to dress.

"This Sonia is not for you, Terry. Terry?"

"I'm here."

"She robbed and killed a sixty-seven-year-old man. Asher Glatzer. At the station at Chrystie and Grand."

I knew that station. It was a block from the Bowery, near the downtown diamond district.

"Vicious, Terry. Cut his chest, chin, throat. Arms, hands." She made a guttural sound. "Not pretty."

"You call her P. O.?" I asked.

"Left messages. He was out by the time I got back last night and he's not in yet."

"Damn."

"Why? Something wrong?"

"Well, something's not quite right," I said. "Mom stays away at least five years, then suddenly wants to visit." I got my black loafers from the other side of the bed. "I mean, the kid's sick, but—"

"Kid? What kid?"

"Sonia's grandson, Enrique."

I could hear her ruffle pages. "Sonia Salgado doesn't have a child. She never gave birth."

"Are you sure?"

"They can tell these things, Terry," she replied. "And she was too young to adopt before she went inside." She paused as she shuffled through the file. "No, there's nothing in here. No child."

"No child, no grandchild."

She said, "The mother's story—"

"—is bullshit."

"I was going to say questionable," she laughed. "Did you give her the address?"

"Not yet."

"Well?"

I tucked my blue Oxford shirt into my jeans. "Can you keep trying her parole officer?"

"Of course."

I grabbed my money clip from the top of my chest of drawers. Sixteen dollars.

"I'll go see Sonia," I said.

"Terry, remember: She's not for you."

Falling in with the stream of subdued, almost indifferent men and women in light coats and suits pouring toward Travelers' huge red umbrella logo, I went north along Greenwich until I saw a cab roll to a stop on Hubert. After waiting for the passenger to adjust bills in her crowded wallet, I avoided the pale silt where the cobblestone met the curb and jumped in. Too much sweet perfume and a high-pitched interpretation of a song from India greeted me.

"Saint Mark's Place," I said.

The Sikh driver wore a beige turban and had a thick, perfectly groomed beard. He waggled over to Broadway and, as if to remind me why I was in the cab, headed east on Canal to the Bowery: Less than a half mile over my left shoulder was the subway station where 67-year-old Asher Glatzer was killed, the knife tearing his throat as he struggled in vain to protect himself.

People die in subway stations here, I thought, as we caught a red on Houston. They enter, perhaps warily; but they have a destination in mind. They're thinking not of the journey, but where they will be, and they expect to be delivered. . . .

A Madman, orange hair done up Rasta-style, ragged rips in his soiled pants, dirt crusted around his ankles. He approaches a beautiful woman and her baby boy who, in his stroller and his blue jumper with its rubber soles, pedals his tiny legs, who flexes his tiny fists—

"Radio OK for you?"

"I'm sor— Excuse me?"

"Radio," the driver repeated, his voice a terse bark.

"Radio, sure. It's your cab."

I remember everything: I had a habit, which I started in college, of keeping a journal. To exercise my ability to observe, to refine my craft (such as it was), to remember everything.

I destroyed all my journals. But I can't purge my mind. It's all there for easy referral. And it's easily triggered: passing a subway station, for example, on a sunny morning.

I use the good now to block out the bad. I'd spent a good portion of the past four years trying to use the bad to push away the good, only allowing in the light when I wrote love letters sent toward the heavens, where Marina resides, Davy sitting in her lap. Obsession? Can anyone know? When I wasn't among burning suns in distant galaxies, I was in the squalor here, wallowing in self-pity, in self-loathing, rummaging through my ragged mind for what was wrong, beginning with bad, racing toward worse.

Of course, even I could recognize the futility of my obsession, the absurdity of my self-absorption, when two 110-story towers collapsed and some 3,000 of us were killed and countless families shattered by another type of madman, by many madmen.

Forty-six kids at Walt Whitman High School lost parents in the World Trade Center attacks. Even though we could not return to our home for nearly a month, Bella and I went to funerals, memorial services, in TriBeCa, the West Village, Chelsea, for 13 consecutive days. Sometimes we went to two in the same morning.

Bella's brave face. Bella holding my hand.

A happy thought, please. A good thought.

That summer Marina and I visited the Tremiti Islands, the Lesina and Varano lakes, the Castel del Monte built by Frederick II, the amphitheater in Lecce. We rested under the late-afternoon sky in her sister Rafaela's fragrant garden behind the small stone house. We shared a hearty *Squinzano,* olive-stuffed bread and chestnuts her father had roasted.

"Terry, you like?" Benedicto asked. The old man eased himself onto the bench on the other side of the weather-worn table.

Smiling, Marina said something in Italian to her father. I understood only *"Papà"* and "New York."

Benedicto repeated, "Terry, you like?"

*"Si,"* I replied. *"Mi piace."*

Rafaela shrugged, unimpressed. "It's a beginning."

The cabbie entered the East Village at Third and went to St. Mark's Place, where I hopped out, tossing him a five.

I went east along the wide, lumpy thoroughfare that's part bazaar, part hackneyed backlot. Here reside the last vestiges of hippiedom and free-flowing sexual ambiguity, the Village longing for the days when Lindsay let his hair go over his ears and wore double-breasted jackets with wide lapels and shirts with fat pinstripes. Squint (to blur the Internet ads stapled to telephone poles) and you see what you saw then: scrawny men with scraggly beards and bleary eyes, squat women with cropped hair, heavy boots and thick chains looping from front pocket of their stiff Levis to rear, and odd specialty shops that cannot survive and yet there they are, all in a mismatched row. I looked at the boutique on my left; Religious Sex was its name. Maybe they called it Purple Peace or Leary's Lair 35 years ago.

On my right, a church bore the history of East Village immigration on its façade. Up on the brownstone was carved FIRST GERMAN METHODIST EPISCOPAL CHURCH; below, a blue backlit sign in Korean and English— MANHATTAN CENTRAL UNITED METHODIST CHURCH. In between, black block letters on whiteboard: a sign in Spanish promising daily services. Luisa C. Martinez was the pastor.

I continued toward Second Avenue. Near the corner, the soiled, off-black awning of the dusty Holiday Cocktail Lounge gave way to a regulation-issue Gap, which, I guessed, represented a halfhearted attempt at gentrification. In between was an old three-story building. Its bricks were closer to brown than red, and in the glass above the door, gold letters painted before the days when the Fillmore thrived said that it was St. Mark's Gardens.

The front door opened easily and I went inside. On the wall to my left were six buzzers above a speaker. All of the name slots were empty.

A bare bulb burned overhead and, beneath my shoes, the old terrazzo floor was chipped and soiled. Junk mail held together by thin green rubber bands was collecting in a corner near the vestibule door.

Hastily painted a charmless brown some time ago, the inside door had a dented knob and a lock reinforced with a steel plate. It seemed deliberately uninviting, and yet a porthole of cracked beveled glass at its center permitted a look inside. I leaned down to peer in and I put my hand against the door, and it opened. I hesitated, then left the boxlike entryway.

A staircase stood to my left, and to my right was a door to the front apartment. There was another brown door toward the back.

Despite the mild weather outside, a radiator supplied dry heat. It hissed low and steady, as if imitating a snake.

I knocked on the door to my right. There was no answer. I knocked again. I could hear no one inside: no footsteps stopping suddenly, no radio or TV being eased toward silence, no labored breathing from someone waiting for whoever had knocked to disappear.

I heard only the hissing heat.

I went past the staircase to the apartment in the rear and knocked on the door. It swung back slowly. I hesitated, then offered a polite greeting. Then I shouted her name.

She was in a pink robe and white socks and someone had snapped her neck. And before he'd done that, he'd punched her in the left eye and blood had flowed onto the robe, her splayed hair and the bare wood of the living-room floor.

And all seemed to be as it had been before he had come in and crushed her orbit bones and straightened her up and snapped her neck. None of the furniture in the room had been damaged or overturned. Several books and what appeared to be a photo album rested on a low coffee table. A half-empty espresso cup sat undisturbed on the cracked and flaking table near the worn couch. The furniture, supplied by the city, the state, was cheap, and the end table didn't match the coffee table, nor did the sofa match the lumpy chair near the old TV. But Sonia Salgado had kept the oblong room neat and clean and this is where she sipped her coffee. Until someone came in and killed her.

I leaned down and pressed the tip of my index finger to the espresso cup. Cold.

Before he had arrived, Sonia had been reading a book, and she'd placed it on the coffee table when he'd entered. The book lay open, words facing the ceiling.

I squatted and put the back of my hand to her forehead. Natural warmth had left her.

But the blood on the floorboards had yet to dry.

And as I studied her, I saw a resemblance to the woman who claimed to be her mother: the shape of the long face; the deep, dark eyes accompanied by narrow wrinkles; a nose that was thick now but might have been altered by time, as Dorotea's had; full, contoured lips; and the beginnings of jowls under the chin. As I stood, I saw that Sonia was tall, and her bare legs were long, thin at the ankles, round where her thighs met at her white panties.

I decided to look around the apartment and, as I headed toward the back, I passed a small, eat-in kitchen where a faint trace of adobo, coriander and cooking oil hung in the air, wrinkled limes collected in a small wooden bowl and green bananas in a bunch rested on a counter. In the bedroom, the sagging bed had been made, and behind pale curtains, the window was open. I went around the bed and looked outside. A six-foot drop led to a concrete courtyard that funneled into an alley no more than 100 feet long. At the end of the narrow strip was a spiked fence topped with razor wire.

I left the bedroom, stuck my head into the bathroom and found more neatness applied to the humble surroundings. The sink and bathtub were scrubbed clean, though Sonia could do little with old rust stains from her dripping faucets. The water in the toilet was a bright, unnatural blue.

Passing the kitchen again, I returned to the front of the apartment. On a small table near the door, surrounded by candle flames in tall red jars, a black saint stood sentry, oblivious to violence, to death. She wore a silver crown and a long red cape and held a silver sword. I stepped closer and noticed a $10 bill tucked under the statue. A shot glass contained sweet dark rum.

I pulled the cell phone from my belt.

They arrived ten minutes later: four uniforms and a detective—Tommy Mangionella. On the way over to St. Mark's, they let the sirens wail. In my mind's eye, I saw the gathering crowd and imagined the buzz as they craned and strained against the fresh yellow tape strung across the front steps, angling for a look inside. A chance to ogle a dead neighbor might take someone out of his routine, at least for a few minutes. Even now.

I was sitting in the kitchen, rolling a soft lime under my hand. Mango came in and gestured for me to lean forward, to slide my chair closer to the table. In the corridor, the uniforms, waiting for the team from the medical examiner's, paced toward the back of the apartment. They spoke in respectful hushed tones.

"So, Terry P.I.," Tommy the Cop said as he sat. He took the lime from me and returned it to the bowl. "Here you are and there she is."

He wore a knee-length black leather coat, maybe not the best choice for a man of his short, sturdy build. As he put his hands on the table, I saw that he had on a meticulously tailored suit that may have been sharkskin. Over his thick chest he wore a white patterned shirt and a white tie.

His silver toupee matched the color of his suit.

"Well, it's more like she was there and then I was here."

"And you got in how?" he asked. He kept his voice soft, but his phrasing retained its customary snap.

"The door was open."

"You don't climb in windows, Terry P.I.? Beneath you, maybe?"

I said, "Nobody climbed in the window, Tommy. The guy came in the front door. She let him in."

"This you know how?"

"If he came through the window and surprised her, she wouldn't just lay the book on the table," I answered. "She'd drop it on the floor."

"Or you put the book back on the table."

"And I made the bed."

"Could be you did," he nodded.

I shook my head and held back a smile.

"Don't be a pain in the ass now, Terry P.I.," he warned.

"OK," I replied, holding up my hands in surrender. *"Whither wilt thou lead me?"*

He wasn't amused. Tommy the Cop, the swinging dick among lawmen below Canal, apparently wasn't a Shakespeare man.

"Tommy, I was here for about ten seconds before I called you."

"And you called me why, Terry? I don't work the East Village. You know that."

I knew two cops worth knowing in Manhattan. Tommy was the one who worked downtown.

"Shorter ride," I said finally.

He looked at me. Then he said, "Yeah, maybe so."

He told me to repeat what I'd said on the phone about Dorotea Salgado, the sick grandson and the information I got from the D.A.'s.

After I finished, he said, "So how are we going to talk to this old broad?"

"I may have a number," I said as he stepped away from the table. "She called the house."

A big red-haired uniform knocked on the door frame. He looked not much older than Bella. "Detective Mangionella, you got a minute?" he asked.

"What is it, McDowell?"

"Voodoo." The young cop rocked proudly on his rounded black heels. He had small, pearl-like teeth. "The statue. By the door."

"Voodoo," Mango repeated tiredly.

McDowell's confidence began to waver. "A sword—"

"A ritual neck-snapping," Mango muttered. He looked at me. "Terry?"

"It's Saint Barbara," I told McDowell. "For Cubans who follow Santería, she's kind of a front for Shango, who's a spirit, a deity. For Catholics, she's a saint."

"I'm Catholic," McDowell huffed, "and I never heard of no Saint Barbara."

"They didn't have any black saints in my parish either," I told him.

"This Santería. I'll bet it's—"

"It's been around forever, as long as Roman Catholicism. Longer. It's no cult, unless they all are."

"'A spirit, deity.' 'Shango.' See Terry is very smart, kid," Mango said, "though I don't know when somebody's got millions in his pocket and can write books why he wants to be a cop."

Already deflated, McDowell now frowned in confusion.

"Could be . . ." Mango shrugged. "Something."

With his small, firm hand, he now gestured for me to stand and then he turned to the young patrolman. "Find him a ride home."

"Yes, sir."

"And you, Terry, you get me the number of that woman who sent you here."

I nodded.

He reached up and slapped me on the back as I went by.

McDowell followed me as I walked along the corridor. In the living room, in a sleeveless white shirt under her blue overalls, a photographer snapped shots of the body as a heavyset man in thick glasses and an ill-fitting gray suit supervised.

Rather than continue toward the door, I decided on a last look at the small room. When no one stopped me, I went in, inched past Sonia Salgado's vacant eyes, hard lines on her sagging face. Her head lay awkwardly on the wood floor.

"Excuse me, fella."

I turned to the round man. He adjusted his glasses, tugged on his belt and pointed to my bare hands.

McDowell watched.

"Oh, right," I said as I tapped my pockets, as if I misplaced what I needed.

The man squinted his face impatiently, then dug a clean pair of latex gloves from his suit jacket. He passed them to me over the prone body.

"Thanks." I pulled them on.

I went to the sofa and sat to examine Salgado's photo album and old, well-worn book. As I leaned in, I saw she'd been reading a play: Dialogue filled the pages and the lines of one part were underscored in yellow marker. I turned to the cover: *Cuban Theater in the United States: A Critical Anthology.*

I returned to the page the book had been open to and reached for the album. Behind its green faux-leather cover were clippings from newspapers and magazines.

The clips pasted to the black pages were faded and yellowed, and the tape at the corners had dried and shifted. The first and oldest clip was from a Spanish-language newspaper. The headline—TEATRO PRESENTARÁ LA EXPE-RIENCIA CUBANA—announced the opening of a cooperative theater, the Gertrudis Gómez de Avellaneda.

I gingerly turned to the center of the album. All the clips, in English or Spanish, were about Cuban theater and Cuban playwrights. Many, if not most, were about the Avellaneda. The publicity stills in the first few clippings were almost all the same: black-and-white shots of a theater. There was one shot of a thin man in a dark suit and a long scarf. He had a pencil-thin mustache and the glow of someone who was proud of what he had done.

I went back to the front of the album. The first clip was dated August 16, 1984, and on the next page, a feature from the old *Village Voice* about the cooperative carried a—

"*Terry*. God damn it." Mango slammed his hand against the door frame.

I looked up, then eased the album back on the table. The photographer stopped her repetitive click-*whirr*.

Mango had turned to McDowell. He shouted harshly, urgently, "What the fuck are you doing?"

I stood.

McDowell managed, "I thought . . ."

Mango spun and glared at the fat man from the M.E.'s. "Aaron, what is wrong with you, you let him back in like this?"

"The kid let him—" He stopped and he tried to reason. "Tommy, now . . ."

I stepped directly over the body and landed in front of Mango. He grabbed me by the arm and he held it hard by the elbow, his thumb digging into bone. I had to yank twice to get free.

"All right, Tommy," I said calmly. "All right."

The uniforms had the front door open and they'd gathered in the hall and were staring at Mango and me.

I knew if I challenged him now, I'd lose him.

"You're right, Tommy. I'm out of line."

He glared up at me, couldn't find anything else to say, then snapped back to the young cop.

"McDowell, can you do what the fuck I tell you?" he roared.

"Yes. Yes, sir," the red-haired kid muttered.

Mango stared up at him until he jumped.

I said, "There are a few books missing from the bookcase."

"Go, Terry," Mango seethed. "Now."

I went out in the narrow hallway, passing Sonia's tribute to Saint Barbara, passing the gaggle of uniforms.

McDowell put his hand on my back.

"Keep going," he said angrily.

I spoke low. "Don't push it, kid."

We went across the terrazzo tiles. In front of St. Mark's Garden, a blue-and-white idled, its front bumper inches from a yellow hydrant.

# 3

His Chiclet teeth shining as he flashed an insincere smile, McDowell insisted I sit in back, behind the screen, where they put bad guys wearing cuffs, not a witness who called in the find.

The milling crowd watched us with a curiosity that waned to boredom, and then they went back to looking at the Garden's front door, at a window that belonged to another apartment. A stocky, crewcut news photographer who'd snapped frantically when the uniform and I started down the old concrete steps turned away and resumed negotiations with a big blond sergeant in blue who I'd bet had little tolerance for whining.

"What's the point of driving me through TriBeCa like I just got caught snatching a purse?"

"Procedure."

Bullshit. I'd ridden shotgun with Luther Addison a dozen times. I'd even been in the front passenger seat with Mango. "No cuffs?" I asked.

"In."

He pulled back the door and waited for me to slide onto vinyl. At least he didn't put his hand on my head.

He went around the front of the car, got in. As he backed away from the hydrant with an unnecessary squeal, he said, "I heard you got a wise mouth. You do. A wise mouth. Somebody should shut it."

He went to Second, where he made a sharp, squealing right.

"You know where you're going?" I asked.

"Zip it, asshole."

His ears were bright red.

A Volvo with Connecticut plates hung on the right side of the avenue to turn onto Houston. McDowell couldn't wait: He pumped the siren. The woman behind the gray station wagon's wheel jumped, froze in fear, then started to get out of the car. Doing what he could've all along, McDowell went around her.

"You showed me up back there," he said, looking in the rearview as we went west, passing Lafayette. "With that Santería bullshit."

I looked north on Mercer and I saw the purple flags of NYU fluttering modestly in the soft breeze. Students in frayed denim and dark hoodies, in tight blouses and funky skirts, ambled along the street, not quite moved to urgency by the pounding drums and clanking cowbells that rose from amid robust, leafless trees in Washington Square Park.

I pulled my cell from my belt. "I'll make it up to you, McDowell. Report back to Tommy. He'll think you're an ace spy."

I held up the small phone so he could see the number I'd punched in.

"D.A.'s," I told him.

I got her answering machine, which disappointed me: Her questions might've solicited an answer McDowell would've taken back to Mango.

"Julie," I began, "I wanted you to know that we're going someplace else on this," I said. "Sonia Salgado's dead. Tommy Mangionella is at the apartment now."

I looked at my watch and gave her the time as we crossed Sixth.

"I'll be in touch," I added. "Thanks."

I put the phone away and held on as McDowell made a left onto Varick, then slid to the right to zip around the tunnel traffic. Four lanes were trying to melt into one, with the help of two Port Authority cops. A military transport sat closer to the tunnel's mouth, and a guy in camouflage khakis with a sidearm kept a diligent eye on the end of the funnel.

A graffiti-covered Strick wanted to inch its way into the crawl, but Mc-Dowell wouldn't go for it.

"Punch him," I said. "See if he jumps higher than that housewife from Trumbull."

"Shut up," he replied, as he grabbed the mike.

I watched the truck driver as McDowell's voice boomed through the speaker. The gaunt, tired man in a torn red-plaid jacket was shocked when he heard it—"Keep it moving. You. *Now!*"—and he slumped in disappointment as he twisted the black wheel and kept moving south. I figured it would take him 45 minutes to circle back and get in the queue to his New Jersey home.

Meanwhile, we went easily along Canal. A pudgy old man in suspenders that kept his pants over his belly tried to cajole his bulldog to pick up the pace as they crossed gingerly on round cobblestone.

*All My Sons* was playing at the Screening Room.

"You think you're hot shit because you're connected," McDowell ventured.

I'm so connected I'm riding where the flashers and nickel-and-dimers go.

He added, "Don't need to know somebody to call the D.A."

"Maybe I should've told her I know you," I said.

"You don't know me," he scoffed.

"Sure I do," I replied. "You're a cop but you're not sure why. Maybe it's the twenty-and-out. The OT at Yankee Stadium, the easy parking with NYPD plates, the free fries at Nathan's. Or maybe it's the way that girl who wouldn't go to the prom with you looks at you now when your uniform is pressed right and your hat is blocked the way it ought to be."

He tried to laugh it off, but I saw him stiffen.

"You live in Queens in a neat little mother/daughter with a patch of grass out front," I went on. "You're proud of that house and you should be because your Mom and Dad worked hard to float you the money for the down payment. For fun you like to tool down to Atlantic City in your used Caddy, blow two hundred, two-fifty bucks on blackjack, flirt with the help, chase Chivas with good ol' domestic beer. On the other hand, you're thinking maybe next week you'll go up to Foxwoods because you heard they'll comp you if you tell them you're on the job. How am I doing so far?"

"You're not even close, asshole," he sneered.

"Then let's try this: You've begun to think the straight way with the good blue isn't for you. You're not going to be digging through rubble the next time some building goes down. Not you. That's for a different kind of guy. You, you want to hook up with Tommy Mangionella because you think it's a shortcut to where you deserve to be. You want him to notice you so you take a shot with that dumb play about voodoo. Voodoo, Christ."

"That's enough, Orr."

"I could've told you. I know Tommy a long time, kid. He's not going to mess up his good thing for anyone."

"I said slam it shut."

"Fine," I said. "But when you tell Tommy I tried to call the D.A. before he could, tell him it wasn't because you treated me like a perp. Or because you flexed your biceps for that terrified woman in the Volvo and that worn-down guy in the Strick."

"Listen, wise mouth—"

"Tell him it was because you swiped the ten-dollar bill from under the rum glass Sonia Salgado had under the statue."

He let his glowering frown slip and his green-brown eyes went wide for a second. "Bull—"

"Nobody but you. I saw it before Tommy came in and the other uniforms were in back when you were at the altar whipping up your theory."

We were across White and were coming up on Finn Square. McDowell checked the sideview on the right, passed an old Plymouth, then, slowing down the blue-and-white, pushed over to the curb to let me out.

I stepped onto West Broadway.

He leaned across and rolled down the passenger-side window. "You're off about that ten-spot, Orr," he said. He couldn't have been less convincing.

"Fine. Lay it on one of your partners. Lay it on Tommy," I said.

McDowell took his foot off the brake and let the squad car move. He was thinking of the best way to tell me to go fuck myself, but he knew he took off with the $10 bill so he let it slide. Or perhaps he was already thinking Mango saw that bill when he arrived and had come to the same conclusion I had.

I walked toward Greenwich, toward the river.

———

I had McDowell out of my head by the time I hit the front door.

Upstairs, Mrs. Maoli was banging the old Hoover against the baseboard heating vents.

I went straight to the back of the house. The phone number was on the Post-It note I'd stuck to the corner of the computer monitor.

The phone rang and rang and then I heard a jarring sound, as the handset banged when the line came alive.

Then there was the whirling sound of open air, the rush of public space, the rumble of city traffic.

"Hello?" I said.

"Yes?" A woman, young, no accent. Not Dorotea Salgado.

I heard a harsh, disruptive beep-beep, a mechanical squeal: A big vehicle, likely a wide-ass garbage truck, was backing up.

She said, shouting, "Hello?"

"It's a pay phone, isn't it?"

"Yes, a pay phone. No one's here. If you're expecting someone, that is." A sweet voice, flat, unhurried.

"But you. Nobody's there but you," I said.

"Yes, but we're only passing by."

"'We'?"

"My family and me," she said. "We're going to Ground Zero."

She was downtown, I figured. Maybe Dorotea Salgado lived near the quarter-a-call phone booth somewhere on the way to Vesey or Church Street from Union Square.

As the coarse beeping grew louder, I asked, "Where are you?"

"Iowa."

"No," I hollered, "where are you now?"

"I'm on West Broadway and Duane," she said, shouting her reply. "Between Thomas and Duane, actually."

In front of the Odeon. About three blocks from here. If I asked Mrs. Maoli to cut the vacuum cleaner, I could hear the garbage truck from here.

McDowell probably passed the booth as he circled back to St. Mark's.

"I have to go," she said. "My family is waiting."

"Thanks."

"Sure. God bless," she added as she hung up.

I left my study and went into the living room as Mrs. Maoli began to lug the vacuum cleaner down the stairs. Though I heard her struggle as the machine clanged on the steps, I knew well enough that she'd refuse help: Since Marina hired her shortly after Bella's third birthday, Mrs. Maoli had insisted on bearing her load, on doing her job as if merely a hired hand. It was more a statement of pride, of honor, than stubbornness, though she could be damned obstinate. I appreciated her diligence, dedication, reliability. More importantly, she loved my daughter and my daughter loved her.

Throw-pillows were gathered in a bunch on the sofa, where I'd lain the night before and watched a turnover-plagued NBA playoff game in Boston. On the coffee table was an old copy of *American Heritage* with water rings on its cover. A well-worn paperback of *Arrowsmith,* its binding held together more by hope than glue, lay on the floor where it had fallen from my hand as I'd drifted off.

I was still standing near the couch when Mrs. Maoli entered the room. She smiled politely, hopefully.

"Mrs. Maoli," I began gingerly.

"Good morning, Mr. Orr," she said. She let the vacuum stand and came over to fuss with the pillows.

"Mrs. Maoli, I need to talk with you. If you have a minute . . ."

"Yes. I have a minute." She eased into the soft, patterned sofa.

I sat at the other end.

She folded her hands in her lap. The front of her black skirt was pulled tight across her lap. Her perpetual apron, with red trim and tiny red-and-yellow flowers, lay over her skirt. She wore gray, rubber-soled clogs that Bella thought would do her better than the old slippers she used to scuffle around in.

"Did you hear from Dorotea today?"

"No," she said cheerfully.

"Can you call her?" For some reason, I brought my right fist to my ear, mimicking the use of a telephone handset.

"Call her?" She shook her head. "No . . ."

"You don't have the number."

"No."

"How do you contact her?"

"I don't und—"

"How do you meet?"

"Meet? I meet at the market." She still had a heavy accent, still spoke simply, directly, despite more than half a century in New York City.

"At Union Square?"

She nodded. "I enjoy to walk," she smiled.

"I think you said she lived near the market."

"No, I see her *at* the market. Where she lives, I don't . . ." She shrugged. "I don't know."

"I see."

She inched forward and the smile began to drift from her plump face. "What has happened?"

I looked away and saw her reflection in the green-gray TV screen. Her tattered dust cloth was in her apron pocket.

I hesitated. "Mrs. Maoli, I have to tell you that . . . Mrs. Maoli, yes, something has happened."

"To Dorotea?"

"No. It's about her daughter, Sonia," I said. "Sonia never had a child. Your friend's story, it's not true."

"I see."

"No child, no grandchild," I added, quoting Julie.

She nodded as her trepidation grew. "There is something more. . . ."

"I'm afraid there is."

"You must tell me."

"Yes, I know," I replied. "Mrs. Maoli, somebody killed Sonia. I went to her apartment and I found the body."

She sat motionless, and then tears welled in her dark eyes.

"I'm sorry," I said.

She turned away and made a low disturbing sound. "It's terrible."

"Yes. Yes it is."

She ran a small, thick finger under her baggy eyes. "What can you do, Mr. Orr?"

"Not much," I said, "unless you want to go to the market and see if she's around. I'll take you—"

"No, no. What can you do about who has killed Sonia?"

"Me?"

"I am thinking—"

"—that your friend wanted to warn her daughter," I said, finishing her sentence. "That she knew someone wanted to hurt her."

"Yes. A mother would do that," she said firmly. "Warn her child."

"I think we have to see what the police can do, Mrs. Maoli."

"The police, they won't help find a woman who they say killed a man."

I wanted to tell her it doesn't work like that, but I couldn't.

She pointed at me. "Do you know, Mr. Orr, that Sonia did not kill that man?"

"Who told you this?" I asked.

"Dorotea."

"Yes, but don't you—"

"And," she continued sharply, "many people know this. Very many."

She sat back on the sofa, defiant now, as sorrow turned suddenly to anger, as tragedy aroused her sense of injustice. She may not have known Dorotea Salgado all that well, but she couldn't tolerate the death of her daughter, a woman who, to her mind, had already suffered too much for too long.

"Dorotea does not have a child now."

Nor does she have a grandson. Or a great-grandson.

"That's not right, Mr. Orr, you know . . . It's not very—It's not very right."

She folded her arms under her bosom and nodded knowingly.

"All right," I said finally. "I'll make a few calls and I'll try to find out what's up."

She pushed her round frame off the sofa. "Yes. Thank you, Mr. Orr."

"Stay here," I offered. "Let me get you something. A glass of water. You should take it easy."

"No, Mr. Orr." She walked past me and reached for the vacuum cleaner. "We have work we must do."

As she went by, I tapped my hands on my thighs. "OK, Mrs. Maoli."


I thought about heading to the Tilt for a bowl of Leo's andouille gumbo, but, with memories of Sonia's last act nipping at me, I set out instead for a bookstore. My gut was to go to the Strand on 12th, since they have everything, and at unbeatable prices. But no, not the anthology *Cuban Theater in the United States,* I was told. Seemingly sensible advice followed and, with a reviewer's copy of Habegger's bio of Emily Dickinson for Bella in a Strand bag, I set out for Lectorum, a shop on 14th that specialized in Spanish-language books and the works of Spanish-language writers.

As I went north, I walked along a line of people, almost all men, that snaked out of Forbidden Plant, a comics emporium on 13th. Most in the queue were grown kids, in their 30s with jeans too tattered to be merely old, threadbare denim and Army surplus jackets, potbellies straining dark T-shirts with faded slogans, glasses with heavy frames, unkempt hair; all seemed happy enough in the cocoon with fellow members of a distinct class. Diddio would've fit in, I thought, as I crossed Broadway on 13th, where the New School's green-and-white banners were tossed gently by the meek breeze.

As I passed a restaurant specializing in sweet potatoes, a health club, the Quad Cinema and a guy who looked like Nicolas Cage entering the 13th Street Rep, my mind wandered back to D and then I let myself hear his voice. His is one of the voices I hear clearly, his tone, inflections.

"Terry, man," I heard him say, "you know how embarrassing it is to not have a date, man, to, like, my own thing? I'm sitting next to an empty seat, everybody else paired off."

"Not so embarrassing, D," I'd reply. "Things happen."

"Yeah. To me." He'd tap his chest. Or twirl his shoulder-length, too-black hair. "Just what is it, T, with me and these women?"

"You haven't met anyone who understands your charm. That's it. Nothing more."

"You think?"

"Sure."

"I got charm?"

"Absolutely," I'd say.

"And women think this?"

"Marina did."

"Ah, Marina, man." I could hear him sigh. I could see him smile.

Actually, Marina said this: "Terry, he is following you like a puppy."

I told her no. D and I are friends. For real.

(Do daydreams require full disclosure? If so, back then I used to call him 3D and he called me Eeyore, his take on my given initials E.O.)

"Are you sure you are equal?" Marina asked. We had just left the Bottom Line and we were going to walk for a while in the late-summer air. Diddio had decided to stay behind for the second set. Marina wore a thin black sweater over a simple pale-blue blouse, a black skirt and leather sandals, and I suggested biscotti on Cornelia Street and she agreed.

"Friends are equals, no?"

"No. I think you are not equal," she said. "I think you have resources he does not."

As I turned on Sixth, I realized I'd passed at least a dozen college students, girls who seemed not much older than Bella, who might've been happy to accompany D to the dinner, if they knew him as I did, as Bella did. But, since they didn't, they'd probably think he was no different than any other guy who felt fine when he was in his own world and thoroughly uncertain when he wasn't. Poor D. He never was much good with women, a very bad thing for a guy who wants so bad to be loved.

The play Sonia Salgado was reading in the moments before she was killed was written by Isolina Leyva and it was called *Obligación*. I read it as I picked at salt-cod cakes at Pico, a first-class Portuguese restaurant across from my home on Greenwich. Since mid-October, five weeks after 9/11, I've eaten at least once a week in a TriBeCa restaurant. I was going to do that until the neighborhood either regained the bounce in its step or disappeared.

As I took a bite of lemon-and-grapefruit side salad, I reviewed Levya's play. It's the story of young love, battered by circumstance and manipulated by an industrialist father, told through Marta, who, as a teenager in 1959, fled Cuba with her wealthy family to Little Havana in Miami. She pines for her boyfriend Juanito, never believing he's abandoned his promise to join her until the end of Act I, when she's told by her father that Juanito died trying to reach her.

In the second act, it's years later, and we learn that Juanito has been laboring all the while as a groundskeeper at the Biltmore Hotel, not far from Calle Ocho where he and Marta were to rendezvous. He didn't come to her, we learn, because Marta's father threatened to harm his family if he did. ("What is the love of a poor boy worth?" the father sneers.) Marta, a mother now, lives in luxury on Brickell Avenue, not very far from the small apartment occupied by Juanito, now known as Juan. Of course, neither knows of the other's presence.

In the third act, Marta and Juan finally reunite; *deus ex machina*: Marta's daughter is to have her 16th birthday party at the Biltmore, where Marta, a widow, sees Juan toiling amid the eucalyptus and salal.

She returns to meet secretly with him and the life that could have been is revealed, with revelry and tears. But the ending is bittersweet: Affluent now, a success in her new homeland, Marta cannot join Juan, though she is free to do so. He is a poor man, a laborer; her father's daughter, she is a woman of standing in her community, of responsibility. They must be satisfied with their memories, with dreams of what might have been.

Christ. What tripe.

At least it wouldn't be expensive to mount, I thought as I flagged down the waitress for my check. It required three pairs of actors—each progressively older than the last—to play Marta and Juanito in the three acts; another for the father; and a bunch of people who'd try to make their parts sound better than third guy/waiter on their résumé. Leyva demanded that the staging be sparse, almost Spartan, which ought to hold down costs: In the directions, he had written, "It is a story of emotion, of aspiration, not of possessions and details."

It was also a story of people who didn't get to live the life they believed they would, who might've had a chance to reconnect with a lost dream.

The Avellaneda had a Web site, of course, and the theater's founder was listed as Safi Majorelle. A cute alias, I thought. He had invoked the New Yorker's prerogative to reinvent himself, and I wondered if he was signaling his ethnic background with the new name. Was he French, as Jacques Majorelle had been? Or, as the name Safi suggested, did he have family in Morocco where Majorelle painted the kasbahs of Irounen and built his gardens in

Marrakesh? As I scrolled, learning he still ran the place as president and artistic director, I found a photo that was probably taken 20 years ago: Majorelle had black, brushed-back hair, an immaculate pencil-thin mustache, a knowing smile on his angular face. He wore a bright yellow scarf and what appeared to be a black smoking jacket. He seemed neither particularly French nor Moroccan, but a sort of nonspecific southern European or North African. And to add to the ethnic confusion, the mission of the Avellaneda, the site said, was to present exclusively the works of Cuban-American playwrights.

After that, the site would only have been useful if I'd been interested in its forthcoming events—*No Direction Home* by Edwina Acuñar-Gonzalez was up now, through May 15—or if I wanted a hyperlink to TicketCharge. I wondered briefly if Majorelle had mounted *Obligación.* When I saw that the brief history section was but a few paragraphs long, one of which was a list of renowned Hispanic actors who had played the Avellaneda, I moved on.

I went next on a search for information on Asher Glatzer, the man Sonia Salgado had killed some 30 years before. Fifty-nine hits but, remarkably, there wasn't a single site that mentioned the murder. I did find an HTML site thrown up by a young boy in Haifa, Israel; Abba Glatzer's father's name was Asher. Abba was a good student and he wanted to be a pilot. He liked American music. Or he did in 1999, when he put up the site.

"Hey."

I turned to find Bella in the door frame. She had a chubby pen stuck behind her ear, and over a rock-band T she wore a big, long denim shirt that she had bleached to a near-white. On her left wrist, she had a rainbow of perhaps 30 plastic bracelets. She had kicked off her shoes. One sock was yellow, the other a bright pink.

"Do you remember that play we saw at the Public by that Cuban guy?"

*"Two Sisters and a Piano,"* she replied. "At the little place."

"The Shiva, yes," I confirmed. "What's up?"

"The checks."

She handed me a small batch of checks to sign.

I lifted a pen from the off-kilter cup she'd made four years ago for my 32nd birthday and started quickly scribbling my signature on the line on the front right.

"You're not even looking at them," she groaned.

"I trust you." I let her keep the family checkbook. Why not?

"You know, you should be more serious about money."

"I don't care about money, Bella. You know that."

"That's not too difficult, Dad, when you're a millionaire."

I craned my neck to look at her. Millionaire? We tried to live on $700 a week. I'd paid off the mortgage—against advice, but who in their right mind wants to wangle and worry to save a few hundred bucks in taxes?—and put my advance aside and set up her trust. Marina's money is Bella's now. One day I'll tell her, but not yet: She's already too interested in the stuff.

"What's on your mind?" I asked.

She paused, then she said, "Mrs. Maoli is upset."

"I know."

She gestured with her head. "What did you do?"

"What did *I* do?" I said, as I reached for the mouse to log off.

She pointed to the computer monitor. "I'm not going to look."

"No?" I asked as I swung around in the chair to face her.

"I learned my lesson."

I came home one wintry evening to find that Bella, hungry to know what was in her father's mind, to know what had happened to her father's spirit, had cracked the password on my Word program and read 18 months' worth of diary entries. Not exactly diary entries: letters to her mother, often profoundly personal, certainly private. When I entered the study, her eyes were ringed in red and her nose was raw and balls of tissues were scattered on the floor. "You are heartsick," she cried as she leapt into my arms.

That night, I read what I had written. It was all sophistry, all self-indulgence: the spouting of a man seeking sustenance, solace, counsel from the dead. A man hiding in his own misery, an act of egoism absolutely unacceptable in a father.

I believe Bella has forgiven me.

But I haven't written to Marina since.

Why bother the stars?

"We agreed not to speak about that," I shrugged. "Now, about Mrs. Maoli . . ."

"Yes . . ."

"You know her friend asked me to find where her daughter lived."

She nodded.

"I found it. And when I got there Sonia Salgado was dead. Someone had killed her." I punched my hand, I put my hand on my throat. "Strangled."

"Wow."

"Yes, 'wow,'" I said. "Now Mrs. Maoli wants me to find who did it."

She shifted.

"This is a coincidence, Bella? The mother wants the address and the next day the daughter is dead?"

"Maybe she wanted to warn her."

"Sure. Yes."

"Did you give her the address?" she asked.

"No."

"Then how can she be involved?"

"I don't know. But, Bella, one thing you've got to realize is that Sonia Salgado is . . . is not *admirable.* I mean, she killed an old man. I mean, *really* killed him. Slashed him, savagely."

She nodded solemnly.

"You know, these people who are killed, Bella, they just don't close their eyes and they're dead. It's painful, it's degrading; and then they're gone. And their dreams die with them."

"I know, Dad."

"This complicates things. I mean, just because Mrs. Maoli believes that her friend is a nice old lady doesn't make it so. And just because the nice old lady says her daughter is innocent . . . What else is she going to say?"

"OK," she said abruptly. "I got it." Then she began to toy with the colorful array of bracelets on her forearm. "I got it. Geez, I'm trying to understand, that's all."

"Understand what?"

"If you said no to Mrs. M."

"No," I replied, "I told her I'd look into it."

"Will you?"

"Bella . . ."

"Despite what she did?"

"What Sonia did . . . It seems to start there."

She didn't reply.

I said, "OK?"

She shrugged. "Dead bodies. But you've got to help Mrs. M."

"I think we agree on that."

I turned back to the checks. I'd let Bella choose the pattern: white sails on a lake, the horizon visible through pine-covered mountains.


I was searching the soapy water for the last fork from our quick dinner when the doorbell rang.

Bella yelled from upstairs. "Who is it?"

"Don't know." I grabbed the dish towel and cut the radio on top of the refrigerator. Sibelius's Concerto in D Minor came to an abrupt end.

"If it's for me, I'm here," Bella added.

I looked into the peephole.

"It's not for you," I shouted, then I opened the door.

Mango made a laconic gesture and told me to come out onto Harrison.

"You can come in, Tommy," I said.

He stepped aside so I could go down the steps.

I had the dish towel in my hands and no shoes on my feet as I went into the evening chill.

Mango's black Town Car was running. Steam rose from the tailpipe.

He let the front of his black-leather coat hang open. The knot of his white tie was undone; now the tie made an X that was held together with a silver bar.

The concrete was cold and the street was dark. The violet streetlight on Greenwich flickered unevenly.

"You didn't call," he said.

"The number wasn't hers. Dead end."

"You tell the D.A. that?"

I didn't bite. "No. I didn't get a callback."

He thrust his hands into the pockets of his long coat. "McDowell says you're a pain in the ass."

"Who doesn't?"

"Listen, Terry," he began. He looked at his buffed shoes and he looked up at me. "You're out now. You got me?"

"How do you figure that, Tommy?"

"I don't see a role for you is what I'm saying."

He was starting slow, but I knew him well enough to understand he could ramp it up fast.

"I've got to close my end," I said. "I got the mother to talk to."

"The mother's been talked to," he replied sharply. "And the D.A.'s been talked to, an A.D.A., and not Knight, that *melanzana* friend you got."

"'*Melanzana*,' Tommy?" The word, Italian for eggplant, was a nasty pejorative for successful blacks among people like Mango. "Where's that coming from?"

"Don't be cute, Terry. I told you I don't want you fuckin' up this thing. It's a B-and-E gone bad and I'll close it like *that*." He snapped his fingers.

"B-and-E? What did she have to steal?"

He pressed on. "Building full of ex-cons. They steal anything, these guys."

I kept quiet.

"What do you think?" He stepped closer to me. "You and me, we play nice, Terry. Let's leave it that way."

I looked down at him. "Long day, Tommy?"

He started to come back at me, then he stopped. He smiled and he shook his head. "Maybe that's it. Long day." He chuckled. "Maybe you ain't the only pain in the ass."

A cab took the yellow on the broad avenue behind the cop.

He patted me on the arm. "Look, we all got responsibilities"—he nodded toward the house—"and you're trying to find this guy Weisz. What I'm saying is maybe you keep your concentration here, where it ought to be, and I'm with you."

There was no need to ask the question. The implication was clear.

"You're right, Tommy. Responsibilities."

"Good, Terry." He started toward the car. "Maybe I'll see you at the Delphi, huh? Buy you some French toast, something."

I left the street and was back inside before he drove off.

## 4

With Julie Giada, it couldn't be just warmed-over, 25-cents-a-pop machine-made coffee in paper cups. It had to be fresh-brewed in matching mugs with plump bagels, low-fat cream cheese, glistening fruit—strawberries, juicy purple grapes, slices of fresh peaches. No way the D.A. caters this quality stuff.

"Julie," I said as I inched into a chair in the conference room, "you are unbelievable."

"What?" She sat with her back to the floor-to-ceiling rack of West reporters, case summaries that were referenced often and had to be back on the shelf before the borrower left for the night. "You have to eat."

"I don't know that we have to eat this well," I said. "You shouldn't spend your—"

"It's not all that much. See?" She smiled as she pushed a small paper plate and a plastic knife and fork toward me. "Go ahead."

I put a few strawberries and peach slices on the plate. I usually don't eat breakfast, but I didn't want to disappoint her. I had the impression she'd begun working on this spread shortly after we cut the line last night.

She put the top half of a sesame bagel next to the fruit.

"Go crazy," she said, as she dabbed her fingers on a paper napkin. "How's Gabriella?"

"Fine, great. You know. A wonder. Who knows?"

Julie nodded and smiled. She had a pleasant face, not unappealing, the kind that emitted a sense of hope, of openness, despite dark brown eyes that drooped a bit at the corners; in fact, in a certain light, Julie glowed. She kept her immaculately groomed brown hair pulled back, clipped tight and parted on the right, which, along with a cute, short chin, served to make her face seem rounder than it was. She was a little shorter than Bella; with her serious business heels on, she might be about the same height.

She usually dressed conservatively. Today, she wore a collarless black jacket, a matching knee-length skirt and black flats. I figured she was due back in court at ten.

"Is that a new blazer?"

She gestured to the brown tweed thing I'd put on over my jeans and a white button-down.

"I haven't bought a new blazer since the last century, Jule," I told her. "That the file?"

She said yes. "I've got to get it back to Sharon."

"She know what happened yesterday?"

"Of course." She tapped her fingernail on the file. "It's my job to tell her what may come in before it does."

"And?"

She took a sip of her coffee. "It's as I said. Sonia Salgado Arroyo was a bad puppy, Terry. The life of that old man meant nothing. He had the diamonds and she wanted them."

Julie put down her cup, picked up a plastic knife and, with a backhand jab, gave a terse demonstration.

"Diamonds?" I took a bite of a peach slice; Christ, it was soft, sweet, fresh.

"Glatzer was carrying a cache of diamonds."

"Really?"

"Not so unusual back then," she said, "to barter with another merchant, repay a loan. Probably not now, though. I don't believe anyone's walking along the Bowery with six hundred thousand dollars in uncut diamonds under his shirt."

"Are you telling me Sonia Salgado killed Asher Glatzer to rip off six hundred K in diamonds?"

"I'm saying they found the old man's wallet in Sonia's room and they found the paper sheath Glatzer and his sons used to hold the diamonds buried in the trash in the basement. With Glatzer's blood on it."

"And no diamonds."

No, she said with a shake of the head. No diamonds.

"She say where the diamonds went?"

"She claimed she lifted Glatzer's wallet on the Bowery but knew nothing about the diamonds or the killing."

"The knife turned up?"

Julie said no.

"Anyone else implicated?"

She shrugged. "She passed off the diamonds, that's for sure, unless they're still hidden in a drainpipe somewhere. So she had a partner, but she wouldn't give him up."

"You find out anything about the mother?" I asked.

"Nothing much."

"You got a photo?"

She nudged aside the file to reveal a standard letter envelope that bore the New York County crest. When she shook it, out slid an old black-and-white head shot. I spun it toward me. It was Dorotea Salgado.

"That's her," I said. "When was this—"

She gave me the date. Twenty-eight years ago.

"Any idea where she was going?" I asked.

"She never went anywhere and she let the passport expire."

"Her maiden name is Arroyo?"

Julie nodded. That's why she called her daughter Sonia Salgado Arroyo. Many Hispanics took their mother's maiden name as their surname. Sonia probably dropped it to Americanize her name. Or because her father insisted.

"What about Mr. Salgado?" I asked. "Any word on him?"

"Died when Sonia was eight or nine, I believe. Working on the Triborough Bridge. Landed on Ward's Island. Arturo Salgado." She picked up a strawberry and took a slow bite. I put the photo back into the white envelope.

"Well," I said as I pushed back my chair, "we'll see where it takes us."

" 'Us.' "

"The royal 'us.' "

"I see," she answered. She dropped the tiny green leaves from the top of the strawberry onto a plate. "But it's taking you somewhere. . . ."

"Mother asks me to find daughter. Daughter is killed the next morning. Tommy Mango tells me to stay home." I shrugged. "It is what it will be."

She leaned forward, placing her arms on the table. "Terry, you understand we're not in this. Not yet, anyway. Not until Sharon says."

Since Sharon was the executive A.D.A. who ran the homicide bureau, she'd be in it soon enough. "When do you—"

A slim man in an impeccable blue suit with a black alligator briefcase at the end of his arm went by. He stopped, backed up his long stride and peered into the conference room.

He looked only at the fruit. He sang, *"Julie . . ."* He had sky-blue eyes and sharp features and he wore a cologne that blended licorice and sandalwood.

"There will be leftovers, Chad," she said tersely.

"You angel, you," he said, smiling as he resumed his stroll down the corridor.

"Good friend?" I asked as I stood.

"He's all right," she replied.

"He interested in you?"

"It's more likely that he'd be interested in you," she nodded. "Isn't that the way?"

I let her pass and we went out, leaving behind the scent of peach and sesame.

"Where are you off to?" she asked. At the end of the long corridor, a photocopy machine hummed and churned.

"I'm going to look for a way to go back thirty years."

She tilted her head in confusion.

I said, "This girl is clever enough to ditch the knife and pass off the diamonds, but not smart enough to get rid of the wallet. And she brings the victim's blood into her home."

"And that doesn't work for you?" she asked.

"We'll see."

I thanked her and told her I'd be in touch. "And the breakfast was great, Julie."

"You patronize," she chided. "You ate less than half of a peach and two strawberries."

"I was leaving the rest for Chad," I replied.

"Poo," she said.

"Well, there's no rebuttal for that, Jule."

We shook hands. Julie had a good, firm handshake.


Who knew *The Daily News* was no longer in the Daily News building?

The giant globe still spun slowly in the lobby of 220 East 42nd, but the Art Deco edifice, put up in 1930 and a landmark now, was home no longer to the tabloid's editorial staff and printing plant. It cost me 50 cents to buy a copy at a deli and learn from the masthead that it'd gone across town.

I grabbed another cab in front of the Pfizer building and told the driver to head toward 11th.

"You know the News isn't there anymore?" I asked as we left the curb.

When the man laughed, the skin on his face crinkled like parchment paper. "Of course. Ain't been there for a good long while."

"Oh." It had taken them two years after the News building opened to discover that the globe was turning the wrong way. Dumb bastards.

He said, "Hey, you heard about that old Pfizer building back there?"

The cabbie had turned to face me, then spun back as we came up on Grand Central.

"Grew eight new stories on top since they started making that Viagra in there."

He let out a howling laugh and slapped the steering wheel with his palm.

"Building got bigger!" he bellowed. "Oh man, I'll tell you. Ain't that something?"

"Yes," I said dryly, "very good. Topical."

"Getting bigger," he cackled.

He caught his breath at Fifth.

"Pull over," I told him. I saw the main branch of the Public Library to my left.

"What?"

"This is good enough."

He was sputtering as I got out. "I ain't moved *The Daily* god-damned *News.*"

I decided to enter the library via the main entrance, to pass by the stoic lions, head up white marble toward Bartlett's portico. With the sun sitting high above the avenue, the steps were crowded with tourists, their backs arched, palms flat on stone, faces awash in the soothing rays as if they were lounging on the Piazza di Spagna. Midtown seemed fine now, with its customary business bustle—UPS trucks, delivery vans in front of upscale sandwich shops, a load-in at Pier 1, messengers scrambling, a few businessmen with briefcases chatting casually, the rush of taxis, their horns blaring. Meanwhile, around the corner, long concrete slabs protected Grand Central Terminal from suicide bombers. And downtown in TriBeCa, it was still as quiet as a hospital zone.

The air in Astor Hall was cool and I paused for a moment to let my eyes adjust to the sudden shade, though I could make my way to the Microform Room wearing a blindfold. I'd spent the better part of eight months there more than a decade ago digging through copies of the *New York Herald,* walking the long marble corridors, lost in thoughts of Tammany, Tweed, Connolly, my Marina and our little Gabriella, my suddenly bright life, my unexpected and promising future.

And, for much of the last 18 months, I'd spent Tuesday evenings, Thursday mornings and Saturday afternoons back with Bennett's breathless *Herald,* with Bella in her quest for an environment for Mordecai Foxx. Those journeys uptown provided a welcome respite from all the reality that surrounded us after September 11, all the damnable living history, and, before that, gave me a sense of how my daughter worked and how much she had grown. "Not yet, Dad," she'd say when I asked her if she needed help. But then I'd leave the security of the past to retrieve microfiche for her, buy her $15 credit cards for the printers, go to the bargain stores on 40th for strawberry bubblegum and another marble notebook—always a marble notebook, very precise. "Yes, thanks," she'd say before plunging back into a 130-year-old newspaper on a flat gray screen. Then, when my usefulness dwindled to uselessness, I'd go over to room 108 and read last week's glossy magazines, last month's *World War II, Allure, Cracked,* anything; tried my hand, unsuccessfully, at *Il Messaggero.* And I sat in every chair in the vast Rose reading room with nothing but my thoughts to haunt me, at least until the silver towers came down. ("Perhaps, Terry, quiet contemplation is an environment that connotes achievement, that recalls memories I would call 'action-oriented,' and is far more beneficial than you might have imagined." Harteveld, the shrink.)

"Bella, I'm not going to spend the summer staring at these murals," I complained, pointing at Haas's rendering of the old *Times* building. "I've memorized them, for Christ's sake."

I spent three hours one day in Nat Sherman's, and was the only man in there who didn't smoke cigars.

"Sir, might I interest you in a special?" asked a man who smelled of clove and impatience. "Leon Jimenes Number Five, natural wrap—"

"Beat it," I declined.

"Dad, while we're here," Bella said as we ate Thai, picnic-style, under the summer leaves of the Fifth Avenue trees, "why don't you start a project?"

"Beat it," I said to the hectoring pigeon. Tough guy looked me dead in the eye.

"You could've just said, 'No thanks,'" Bella huffed.

"I was talking to the pigeon."

"You were talking to the pigeon," she repeated. *"OK, then . . ."*

Eyes open, I passed the information desk. An ancient woman, dressed in a sea-green dress and a matching coral necklace, shone a charming smile. "Good morning to you, sir."

"Yes, good morning," I replied.

"And how is Gabriella?" she asked. Then she became serious, somber. "She is all right, I hope."

I stopped; *squeak,* as my sneakers caught on the hard floor. "Yes, she's fine, thanks." It was a question everyone who lived below Canal had to answer.

Relieved, she said, "Lovely girl."

"You bet."

I reached Room 100 a minute later. Behind the counter was a woman who seemed familiar from every library I've ever been in: thin with flat, lifeless hair, perpetual turtleneck, eyeglasses on a handmade dope rope; patient smile, a seriousness that suggested her mission was to ensure learning with order.

She said, "Hey, where's Gabriella?"

These were the glory days of *The Daily News:* screaming headlines; stark, gory photos; punchy writing on deadline by an army of crime reporters; *Ching Chow,* the *Jumble,* Sally Joy Brown's *"A Friend in Need";* ads with pudgy, pouting sex kittens for X-rated films "you won't tell your neighbors about"; full-page spreads from Korvettes, Hearns, Alexander's; Dick Young, Gene Ward on sports; Ed Sullivan's *"Little Old New York";* the total mutuel handle from Aqueduct, which gave the Jersey bookies the night's number—all for 10 cents.

The April 11 edition carried photos from the previous night's Oscars on the front page—Hackman, Jane Fonda; and 82-year-old Charlie Chaplin's return from exile. The hed didn't match: GALLO BURIED, TWO OTHERS CUT DOWN. And underneath it, in smaller, italicized type: JEWISH LEADER SLAIN; DIAMONDS GONE.

Page two had a big piece on the Vietnam War—B-52S STRIKE THEIR DEEPEST INTO THE NORTH—and on the opposing side, I learned that, after six mobsters had been ventilated during the past two weeks, Carlo Gambino was "seeking peace." And I learned about Asher Glatzer.

Or maybe not: The two reporters on the story had gone immediately into overdrive, nearly turning a man who was the respected leader of the downtown diamond district, a beloved family man, into a one-dimensional stock character in his own story. They wrote as if they wanted to impress Spillane, and only the emotional outbursts of his friends saved Glatzer from vanishing amid the pumping adrenaline, the requirement to shock. The scent of fresh plasma that emanated from their prose couldn't hide what Glatzer's friends and colleagues felt.

"We've lost our father," cried one unidentified man.

Nice summary quote, I thought. Might've meant more if we knew who said it.

"I cannot imagine what we will do now," said Marion Rosenbloom, a clerk at Tri-County Jewelers. "He was everything to us. Everything."

Much better.

The photo: Glatzer's body in the litter-strewn, concrete stairwell of a subway station on Chrystie, under a sheet, near a crumpled brown paper bag, gum wrappers, cigarette butts.

"I blame myself," said Ralph Glatzer, the victim's son.

"He had not an enemy in the world," commented Asa Dieskau, a fellow Bowery-based diamond merchant. "He could walk anywhere in this neighborhood without protection. It's outrageous."

I sat back. Glatzer was killed at about 5 P.M., the *News* said, before the day had faded to darkness, as workers moved along the busy streets to the subway that ran through midtown on its way up toward Harlem. Yet the *News*'s Night Owl edition, which hit the streets by 9 P.M., had enough on the diamond angle to run with it.

The lead: "At Chrystie Street near the Bowery, where the B and D lines end their journey through Manhattan, diamond merchant Asher Glatzer found death under a sharp blade. What likely began as robbery concluded in murder."

I turned the plastic handle to advance the film, stopping to read *Dondi*, then to see what the Knicks had done, and then I found the front page of the next morning's paper.

SOLDIERS LAND IN PHU BAI NEAR DMZ was the headline; in itals below: *"Teen Girl Quizzed in Glatzer Slaying."*

I spun to page three. TEEN QUESTIONED AS GLATZER IS MOURNED ran across the top, above a four-inch photo of two plainclothes cops hurrying a young girl toward the precinct house. Or so the caption said: One of the cops had thrown his raincoat over the girl's head. She had on old-style high-top Converse sneakers, jeans and handcuffs.

"A female student at a Hell's Kitchen high school was questioned today by police about the April 10 slaying of civic leader and diamond merchant Asher Glatzer.

"The student, whose name was not released by police, was brought into custody following a tip received early this morning."

Had to be, I thought. They found Sonia less than 24 hours after Glatzer had been killed. But the cops didn't know yet that she was 18 or the *News* wouldn't have kept her name under wraps.

I followed the story to the inside of the tabloid. It shifted to a summary of the service at Riverside, and it carried the obligatory list of attending dignitaries: Lindsay stayed away, but two of his successors were there—then–City Controller Abraham Beame and Congressman Edward I. Koch.

A photo of Asher Glatzer with then-Senator Jacob Javits accompanied the piece. Both men wore tuxedos and confident if stoical smiles. A B'nai B'rith banquet in 1967, the caption informed, at the Plaza. Below, another photo: a woman in her late sixties wearing black, sobbing profoundly, supported by two men. The widow Glatzer, following the service.

I went back to the photo of Glatzer. A round man with gray hair, he seemed hardy for his age, with clear eyes and a broad chest.

With a flick of the wrist, I returned to page three. Sonia Salgado was as tall as one of the detectives who had her under the arms, but her legs were slender beneath floppy jeans and the alloy cuffs floated on her thin wrists. And when I closed my eyes, I saw her more than 30 years later on the floor of her apartment. I imagined she might have added a few inches to her waist during the decades in Bedford Hills, but she wasn't particularly robust. I wondered if she could've wrestled Glatzer to the Chrystie Street station floor to rob him, if she could've ripped him open with those slight wrists and skinny arms.

Somebody thought she did. Twelve somebodies.

I went looking in Thursday's paper for the commentary by a columnist, whoever the *News* had who ran with Breslin and Kempton—men who covered New York City as living history, whose 750-word pieces sang with wit, passion and a sense of justice. Surely, somebody was going to let the *News* readers know more about the high school senior who had been brought in, the girl who ditched more than a half-million in diamonds but forgot to toss the wallet.

Someone would have a snappy line about how quick the tip had come in.

The *News* was down on doves and peaceniks. They gave Agnew room on page two. They weren't going to find balance in a story that had a dead rich man on one side, an immigrant teen on the other. This was great stuff. No need for temperance here.

But why should there be? Glatzer was a man of faith, a man who did his job, made friends, served his community. A man who struggled to make something of himself, who raised a family, built a business. Now he is forever remembered as victim, as a man who died as he lay in a pool of his own blood.

Somebody called in a tip. The cops moved fast. The wallet in her bedroom. In the basement, the bloody wrapper.

But the columnists—

There were no columnists. No Murray Kempton, Jimmy Breslin. *Dream Street* by Bob Sylvester, *Monique in Paris*, yes. But no one on Asher Glatzer's death. Crime was handled on deadline by 25 hard-nosed reporters, masters of the declarative sentence.

HOODLUMS, NY was the hed above their story on page three: Two more gangsters had been gunned down, they told us. Somebody, they said, dumped Gennaro Ciprio in Brooklyn, Frank Ferriano in Manhattan. This gang war was sweet butter on hot toast for these guys. WE KNOW GALLO KILLER, COPS SAY. (Christ, Gallo got it in front of his kids.) And there'd been a gunfight at Grand Central; the brief caption ended with the phrase "the cop who shot him was wounded."

I came to New York as a kid with my Uncle Eddie. I don't remember the hail of bullets, the river of blood. I remember Jerry Lucas and Earl Monroe, Radio City and Prometheus at Rockefeller Center. The Checker cabs. Hot dogs at Gray's Papaya. The sense of excitement, and my sense of wanting to be part of whatever it was that made this vital, energetic place so spectacularly unique, so relentlessly appealing.

In the world depicted by the *News*, someone had to pay and pay fast. Maybe it didn't matter who.

GANG GIRL ARRAIGNED IN GLATZER SLAY.

The story had moved to page four.

"Police today said 18-year-old Sonia Salgado, a senior at DeWitt Clinton

High School, was arraigned and charged with the first-degree murder of diamond merchant and civic leader Asher Glatzer."

A photo from the DeWitt Clinton yearbook.

A sweet, bewildered girl, her black hair flipped up above her gangly shoulders. Simple flowered dress. A forced smile. Uneasy eyes.

The *News* found a teacher who claimed Sonia "ran with the wrong crowd."

The gang.

"The smell of marijuana cigarettes was ripe as the police raided the girl's tenement apartment at 572 West 36th Street."

I put my finger on the screen. That's interesting, I thought. Balance: Sonia Salgado was in the Drama Club.

Her mother, the *News* said, worked in the garment district.

Somehow they made it seem sordid.

I had my fill of it now. There was even a holdup in *Moon Mullins*.

"We're grateful to the members of the New York Police Department who worked so diligently to bring our father's killer to justice," said Ralph Glatzer.

Guilty as charged.


I got back downtown by 1 P.M., hoping Leo had some warmed-over etouffée, crawfish gumbo, backbone stew, anything he could reheat on the old hot plate, its frayed wire stretched across the desk in his musty office. Living alone now, Leo still cooked the kind of meals he had enjoyed as a child in Louisiana, once served with a confident glee in his Cajun-Creole restaurant and now made for Diddio and me, while Leo pretended that what was in an old plastic container in the leaky beer cooler was left over from a meal he'd concocted for someone else. Someone who filled his hours away from his ramshackle bar with laughter, tenderness, possibility. Someone who could gently nudge him to manage his weight, which had ballooned to nearly 380 pounds; who would take his arm when he wheezed, coughed, grew red and then pale after the mildest exertion and tell him he was too important to her to settle for that kind of life. Diddio and I tried to help: dragged him to the doctor's, invited him out, chided him, threatened him, told him we cared and didn't want to see him go this way.

"I guess it's not the same, D," I said one evening. "You and me doing this."

"Ain't that a fact," replied Diddio, running his fingers through his long hair.

As I approached the Tilt, I heard music, a romantic aria, resonating clearly despite the thickness of the reinforced green door. It was unmistakably Italian. Verdi, Donizetti? Bellini? I stopped, I put my hands on the door, I listened and I could feel the door vibrate with the power of the tenor's tremulous voice. Accompanied by the faintest instrumentation—warm woods, the plucking of violin strings—he conveyed bravado, tenderness and a profound sadness within a phrase. I was captured.

To follow the motion of the music, I closed my eyes and leaned my weight against the door; if there was traffic behind me on Hudson, pedestrians crossing from shade to sunlight, another John Deere backhoe on its way to Vesey, I was oblivious to their presence, their mission. I was lost as strings rose up like feathers on a peacock, then receded mysteriously, as the tenor's voice—Pavarotti, undoubtedly—broached, then shattered, the silence. I could feel the aria build confidently to its peak yet never abandon its epic sense of tragedy. Silence again, and Pavarotti rose above the zenith—a new pinnacle of sorrow, of loss. He made his final, powerful declaration, but there was no crashing crescendo from the orchestra. Instead, woodwinds and strings entered solemnly, as if to carry the moment forward rather than abruptly end it.

I waited, I waited: I knew Leo was lost in memory, and I knew well that no one wanted to be pulled from that sacred space, at least not before it was time to move on, time to let go.

Leo's memories were different than mine. I recalled what was. He remembered his dreams of what might have been.

Eleven years ago, I was awakened by a knock on the front door. Turning over, I looked to the clock on the nightstand, the red light in the deep darkness: 3:22.

"Terry?" Marina wore long nightgowns. This one was a pale yellow and it felt like silk. "It is your turn."

I threw my bare legs over the side of the bed. "It's not the baby," I said, my voice cracking after hours of silence. "Not unless she snuck out."

It was Leo.

The big man—going 275 then, with muscles across the shoulders, at the biceps—hung back at the bottom of the steps. He still had on his kitchen whites, an apron, his white, size 16EEE shoes. Under the stark streetlight, his uniform seemed illuminated.

"Loretta's gone," he said plainly.

"What?" I threw my arms together in front of me in a feeble attempt to ward off the February cold.

"The money's gone," he said. "Loretta's gone."

"Christ."

"And listen here, I don't want to talk about it with nobody," he continued, his Louisiana singsong evident despite the harsh message. "You tell Marina, you tell Diddio. You tell whoever you want. Me, I'm leaving."

"Leo, come in," I said quickly. "Come in and sit down."

He waved his big, wide hand and he shook his head. "I'm fucked," he said. "The city is gonna take Big Chief's. I found papers. . . ."

I went down the cold steps in my bare feet and I reached for him. But he backed away.

"If nobody is upstairs," he spit, gesturing toward the restaurant with his empty eyes, his head, "I burn down the motherfucker now. Right now."

I looked across Greenwich. Maybe 12, 14 families lived above Big Chief's.

Leo had been suffering. I'd known that. The Cajun-Creole cooking thing died fast; even Prudhomme had started pushing low-fat. Loretta, a tough cookie who'd always been hard to read, seemed to have grown even more distant, though she managed a dry smile for Bella, who waddled into Big Chief's expecting a strand of purple, green and gold beads.

So, Loretta had run off with the cash box, which couldn't have held enough to get her a ticket back to New Orleans. But he hadn't said she took the cash box. He said the money was gone, and that the tax man was at his door. Loretta would've drawn a fat stake by holding back from the IRS. She could do it: She kept Big Chief's books.

"Leo, please."

"Fuck all," he said with a diffident wave. "I'm gone. I'm going back home."

And he turned and left. I didn't see him, didn't hear from him, for five years.

Now, as I entered the bar, I was greeted by the scent of stale beer, by a sense of timelessness, of enduring melancholy, of absence.

I let the door swing closed behind me.

He sat perched on his stool in his usual spot under the TV; his cane, a gift from Diddio, rested on his massive thighs. Amid dark rings, his eyes were closed and his head tilted back, as if he had been thinking about something very far away.

"All right," he said. "So?"

I tossed the spoon back into the empty cup. Jambalaya with chicken and tasso, a bit on the spicy side; jalapeños in with the green bell peppers. I took a long pull on the Badoit.

" 'So . . .' " I shrugged. "That's what is."

"Dead man. Dead woman. Thirty-something years apart. Mango," he summarized.

"Not entirely unrelated," I said.

"Only Tommy the Cop telling you to stay home makes it like that. Connects the dots."

I eased off the stool. Streaks of sunlight came through the window above Diddio's jukebox, silent now in his absence. Cobwebs coated a red neon Bud sign. Somewhere in the distance, a siren wailed, moving away. An all-too-familiar sound; still.

"I thought that. Sure," I said.

"You don't need me to tell you again Mango is somebody you can't trust," Leo sneered.

"Refresh my memory, Leo: Tommy or Jimmy?"

"Either. None. They're no fuckin' good. Tommy, I seen hundreds like him, dirty to his bones. A criminal with a badge. And Jimmy can't control himself, thinks it's smart to run his mouth."

When Leo ran his restaurant, Big Chief's, Tommy squeezed him for a tab he never cleared. His brother Jimmy ran one up too, on Tommy's say-so. Maybe it was more than that; if it was, I knew nothing about it.

I stretched high, then leaned down to crack my back.

"Two scumbags," he muttered, "from a bad, bad seed."

I straightened up, then started for the water bottle as the phone rang.

With a grunt, Leo turned, reached behind him, and grabbed the heavy black handset.

"Tilt," he barked. Then he looked at me. "For you."

The cord couldn't reach so I went around and came over to the business side of the bar, passing through a waitress station that hadn't been used in decades.

I took the handset.

"Yes?"

"Terry Orr?" A man's voice.

I told him yes.

"This is Danilo Villa," he announced. "I think we should have a conversation."

He had hit his name hard, proudly releasing his Spanish accent. *Vee-ya,* he said. I knew who he was.

"Go on."

He continued, "There are things you should know about Sonia Salgado."

"How do you figure that?" I asked.

I looked at the CD case near the '50s-style telephone. *L'Elisir D'Amore* by Donizetti. Pavarotti, Sutherland, the English Chamber Orchestra. A young, bearded Pavarotti held a robin's-egg-blue vase to his cheek.

"We can say I am aware of your interest," Villa replied.

"How?"

He answered by giving me an address, an act that supported my impression of Villa as imperial, arrogant. Of course, I'd have to go to him.

"You are going to arrive at the conclusion that Sonia Salgado is innocent."

"And you're going to talk me out of it."

"No," he replied. "I am, in fact, going to agree with your conclusion. Sonia Salgado did not kill Asher Glatzer."

"How do you know this?" The pause button held the CD at track 11: *Una Furtiva Lagrima.* One Secret Tear.

"I close my office at four o'clock," Villa said. Then he hung up.

I pushed the handset toward Leo and I went back around the bar.

"Guy says he knows Sonia Salgado is innocent," I told Leo as I settled back on the wobbling stool.

"Innocent?" Leo grinned mischievously.

"That's what he said. Danny Villa. You've heard of this guy. *'El Caballero,'* the *Post* calls—"

"Hey," Leo waved. "I already know too much, if you catch my meaning."

"All right." I finished the bottle of Badoit, leaned across the bar and tossed the empty into the black bag that coated the trash can.

He nodded, but said nothing, and in the silence, the sense of melancholy returned; and I suddenly felt uncomfortable in a place that at other times felt like a second home. Leo closed his eyes and raised his head as if to peer at the ceiling. I knew he was ready to go back to Pavarotti, to the tale behind a secret tear, where, despite sorrow, there was warmth, affection, desire.

"Where you going?" he asked without opening his eyes.

I repeated the address Villa gave me. "I might learn something. Who knows?" Then, as I dusted off my hands, I added, "Be my fifth ride in a cab today."

"You ought to buy a car," he proposed.

"I had a car. Piece of shit Jimmy Mango sold me."

"See?" he said, shaking his head, now looking across at me. "I told you you can't never trust a Mango. Bad seed."

**5**

Spanish Harlem began east of Lexington Avenue and north of 96th Street, having been nudged farther uptown by Upper East Side gentrification in the 1980s. Puerto Ricans had long been the biggest group among the Latin Americans and Caribbeans in the neighborhood, which sprang up after the first world war. Though prevalent in the area in the '20s and '30s, Cubans had become increasingly scarce as at least some parts of their native country flourished under the flow of U.S. dollars and mob activity after World War II.

When Castro ousted Batista in 1959, Cubans who fled north beyond Miami settled in Union City, a few miles across the Hudson in New Jersey. Today, there were more Cubans in Union City than in Miami or Havana. The city, which intrepid Cubans saved from commercial and social collapse, was their political, economic and cultural base in the U.S.

But Danny Villa kept his storefront office not in Union City but at 89th and Third, amid the soiled awnings on aluminum skeletons above a nail salon; a locksmith; a one-stop, all-purpose medical center that offered chiropractics, weight loss and footcare; and, not surprisingly, an awning manufacturer. As the obligatory talking head when anything involving Cuba found space in New York media, Villa needed to be but a brief limo ride to the TV news bureaus in midtown or on the other side of the river in Fort Lee. During the Elián González flap, he broke nationwide: Villa was everywhere. I think he might've made his way to *Larry King Live.* Seemingly reasonable, always gracious and well trained to issue sound bites rather than ideas, he had made his way into the press/politics cycle, where a kind of twisted synergy reigned. An appearance on TV, in the *Times, The Wall Street Journal, The Washington Post* led to an invitation to address some politically active group, be it a small civic association or guests at a retreat sponsored by a Fortune 100 firm, which led to media coverage. What changed as the cycle spun was the amount a man like Villa could charge per speech.

What also distinguished Villa, and what made him palatable to conservative business leaders, was his reserved, almost fastidious approach to social protest: While Al Sharpton and other community leaders seemed to wind up in handcuffs and a cell at least once a month as part of their street-level public demonstrations, not Villa, not *"El Caballero"*—the Gentleman— who the *Post* painted as a man who let others do his heavy lifting. It seemed to me a fact that never would Villa be seen in a sweatsuit, bullhorn in hand, at the center of a raucous rally, surrounded by angry supporters, handmade signs and police on horseback. He worked behind the scenes, mobilizing his followers in the Cuban community, or appearing, regal bearing in full bloom, to give the keynote address at an orderly rally. As I entered his office, I recalled that even the *Times,* more tolerant than the *Post* when it came to the peculiar habits of the Left, had dubbed him "an orchestrator."

The *Times* also said he was quietly effective, that the influential Cuban business community supported him. And that gave him real clout.

"You have a powerful curiosity," he said as he shook my hand. "I imagine you find it very useful."

He went back to his desk and eased himself into his leather high-back. Villa's place was deliberately masculine: old club furniture in dark brown, worn but far from unattractive; an old Indian rug—burgundy and olive green were the predominant colors; a laptop computer; floor lamp and desk lamp, both gold; a credenza that matched the dark wood of his desk; a staged photo of Villa shaking hands with Giuliani near a carefully draped American flag.

He gestured for me to sit in one of two club chairs that faced him.

Villa reached into his desk and withdrew a wooden box that was polished to a high sheen. It had his name engraved on a small gold plaque on top.

"A cigar, Terry?"

The scent of his previous one hung in the air, despite the air-freshening device he kept on the side of the credenza.

He opened the box: hand-rolls, torpedoes, a few longer ones, carefully arranged.

"No, thanks."

"A modest vice," he said as he removed one.

"I don't suppose they're Cubans."

He shook his head as he reached for the clipper. "We support the embargo," he said as he snipped the pointed end of the cigar, "and we, more than anyone, are aware there is a price to pay."

Danilo Villa was, by anyone's account, a handsome man, though without any defining characteristics I could see. Among his flawless features: a strong, broad nose; eyes darker than brown; pearl-white teeth; his tight skin a rich light-brown, as if he'd been tanned thoroughly by a predictable sun. He wore his thick silver hair combed back and it lay on his ears, on the back of his white collar. His gray suit served to highlight his shock of hair, his brown-and-silver tie his skin and eyes. He wore silver studs in the French cuffs above his manicured fingers.

Villa was older than I was, maybe 15 years or more, though it was hard to tell with his impeccable appearance, and his face, which was remarkably free of wrinkles. I made him for a well-preserved 50.

He tossed back his head and blew a purple plume of cigar smoke toward the ceiling.

*"Ah, yo soy contento,"* he said.

"Sonia Salgado," I replied. When I stretched out my legs, my sneakers tapped against his desk.

"Of course. Sonia." He slid the cigar onto a gold ashtray near his cell phone.

"Who told you I was interested?"

He smiled. "If I tell you, how would you continue to trust me?"

"I don't trust you now."

He leaned forward, bringing his elbows onto the desk. "Excuse me, Mr. Orr," he said sharply, "but my reputation in this community is not questioned."

"Fine, but I don't know this community. And I don't know you," I said. "I've read about you, seen you on TV. You were on the City Council a few years ago, so you've got a few friends in City Hall."

"I served my people," he said with a curt nod, "and it pleases me that I can have many friends, and not only in City Hall."

"OK, you've got a lot of friends. Producers and reporters find you dependable. Everybody thinks you're terrific," I said. "But you're a stranger to me, and only an idiot trusts a stranger."

He stayed in place, but he let the aggression wither.

"Whoever told you about me looking into Sonia Salgado's murder knows I hang out at the Tilt-a-Whirl," I said. "That may limit it."

"You don't think I read *The New York Times*?" he smiled.

There was no mention of the Tilt in the *Times* piece, but I kept still.

He continued, "I would like to express my sympathy for the loss of your wife and son."

I nodded.

"And I would like to say that it is best if I proceed without revealing how I know about your interest. If you would like my assistance."

"The cops are working this, Mr. Villa—"

"Danny."

"—and I'm not sure they need any help. Danny."

"The police are trying to discover who killed Sonia," he said. "They will not be interested now in whether Sonia had been treated fairly so long ago."

"No," I said, "I guess not."

"And you will soon learn—and maybe you have already—that she was not." For emphasis, he tapped a finger on the desk. "I will suggest to you that there is a relationship between who killed the diamond man and who killed Sonia."

"I don't understand," I told him.

He reached for his cigar, sat back, and took a long drag, clasping the plump tube of tobacco with his index finger in a small circle. This time, no sensuous plume; just fragrant smoke.

"I know about Sonia," he said. "I will tell you about Sonia."

And he did. As a junior at DeWitt Clinton, Sonia Salgado fell in with a group of seniors. Petty criminals, Villa called them. Shoplifting, purse snatching; perhaps one or more had developed the skills of a pickpocket.

According to Villa, Sonia was the girlfriend of the group's leader Luis Sixto.

"He was the clever one," the lawyer said. "Very clever, very bold. If you check the records, you will see he is the one who showed the most promise."

"As what? A thief?"

Villa smiled.

"Where is he now?"

"It has been a long time since anyone has heard from Luis Sixto," he said. "Guatemala? Honduras? Panama? Colombia? Who knows where he is?"

"He leave for any particular reason?"

"A better life, perhaps."

In Guatemala in the '70s? In Colombia under the National Front?

"Then what about the others in this gang?" I asked.

"I would not call it a gang," he replied. "Friends who were bored, who perhaps did not have the guidance that is necessary to become more productive . . ."

"All right."

He put down the cigar and he counted on his fingers. "You have Sixto. Sonia. Bascomb, Alfie Bascomb. And Ahmed Hassan. Only four."

"And these three corrupted Sonia?"

"In a word, yes. Sonia was not the brightest girl. Simple, I would say. Perhaps there was something exciting about these boys. . . ." He shrugged.

"So she went off shoplifting with them. Picking pockets," I said. "Maybe they needed a girl to go places they couldn't."

He nodded. "I have been told that she could be very sweet. She had aspirations to be an actress. She played a role."

"Thief."

"Yes. In her pretty mind, by playing a part, she was becoming an actress. I am told Hassan encouraged her in this way." He touched his temple. "As I said to you, she was not . . . Perhaps the money is important; I don't know. But the sums, they had to be small. So some might call it only an indiscretion."

"Which becomes something much more," I said. "And not so forgivable."

"If you believe the official version, that's correct."

"I don't—"

Villa's cell phone buzzed.

"Excuse me," he said as he leaned forward, looked at the number of the caller, and pressed a button to send the call into voice mail.

He glanced at his wristwatch. "The question," he continued, "is 'how could this young Cuban girl of limited means arrange all this?'"

The tall, thin girl in sneakers and handcuffs in the *News* photo came to mind. "You think she was incapable of killing Glatzer."

"Of course," he smiled. "But you are missing an important point. The reason Sonia was convicted so quickly, so harshly, concerns more than the death of this man."

"How so?"

He leaned forward. "I suggest you examine the records, Terry."

"They had a pretty solid case for Murder One." I shifted in the leather seat. "If the intention was to kill Glatzer for the diamonds, you have clear premeditation."

"Ah, if there were diamonds . . ."

"You're saying there were no diamonds?"

"We know these people," he said with a shrug.

"'These people,'" I repeated.

"Don't be sentimental, Terry. No one disputes whether this man Glatzer was killed, and this was very unfortunate. And perhaps there were diamonds," Villa declared. "But the Jewish community brought tremendous pressure on the mayor, the police commissioner, everyone in city government. And there was Sonia, a dumb *Cubanita,* who was foolishly picking pockets on the Bowery. She took Glatzer's wallet and she brought it back to her apartment—this was the level of her intelligence. That is all they needed. She was not completely innocent, but . . ."

I found myself standing next to the chair I'd been in. "You're saying that Sonia ripped off Glatzer for his wallet," I recounted, "and someone else killed him."

"What else could have happened?" he shrugged.

"And the diamonds . . ."

"*If* there were diamonds . . . If there were diamonds, someone took them and then planted the evidence on Sonia. Obviously."

"And who took the diamonds?"

"The killer," he replied. "Obviously."

"And you think Glatzer was killed by his own people. For political reasons."

"No, I didn't say that," Villa replied. "I don't know who killed Glatzer. I don't know if Glatzer had diamonds."

He reached for his cigar.

"What's the motive if there are no diamonds?" I asked.

"I have no idea. But," he added, "I have established reasonable doubt."

I went behind the chair. "And what about these other guys? Her gang?"

"If you think about it, there can be no doubt that Sixto told Sonia to go down to that part of the Bowery," he replied. "He must have understood they'd find more in the wallets down there than in Hell's Kitchen or by those old tracks near 30th Street. But who among them was smart enough to plan to kill a man for the diamonds he carried, to fence the diamonds and plant evidence on Sonia? I say none."

He again glanced at his watch. He stood and came around the desk, bringing the cigar with him.

I said, "So your theory is whoever killed Glatzer needed to kill Sonia to keep her quiet. Thirty years later."

"I would think so."

He reached to shake my hand. Then he put his left hand on my back, as if to signal it was time for me to go.

"My customary consultation fee is $350 per hour, Mr. Orr," he said, "and we have been together—"

I stopped. "You're charging me?"

He paused and looked at me. Then he said, "Let's leave the account open, shall we?"

I didn't reply and tried hard to hide my incredulity.

"Can I give you a ride someplace, Terry?" he continued effortlessly. "I'm not going as far downtown as TriBeCa, but to midtown, if you're in a hurry."

I was tempted to take the lift: I wanted to ask him a few more questions. But I feared it'd cost me another 350 bucks.

"No," I said. "I've got no place in particular I've got to be. But," I added, "I'd like to ask you something."

"Of course." He slipped into the camel's-hair coat that had hung on the back of his door.

"What's your interest in this? Fee aside."

He pulled on his lapels to adjust the lie of the coat, then he tugged at the sleeves of his shirt, revealing the silver studs. Now it was perfect.

"I am an advocate for my people," he replied. "What happened more than thirty years ago was a travesty. This you know. We cannot allow what happened to Sonia now be the final injustice. The police will not do what they should. With your help, Sonia will be vindicated."

I waited outside on Third trying to decide whether to go down to the Bowery to see if the Glatzers were still in business, visit the Avellaneda or go home to check in with Julie at the D.A.'s. Home sounded best for now: Spend some time with Bella; learn whether Mrs. Maoli had heard from her friend Dorotea Salgado, who might've been the one who told Villa about me; and try to figure out why a man like Danny Villa, who never did anything that wouldn't benefit him, was so forthcoming with me. As I said, only an idiot trusts a stranger, and I'd never heard anyone say Villa was an idiot.

But as I went to the corner to flag a cab, I knew I'd have to scrap those plans. McDowell was sitting behind the wheel of a city-issued car and he reached out to adjust the side-view to watch me as I crossed 89th. If I hadn't turned away quickly, he would've caught me staring at him.

Sitting between 89th and 90th on an avenue that ran north, he was in the wrong spot for a tail if I went west. As I walked to the southwest side of the crosstown street, he saw his mistake and pulled his black car away from the curb, waited, and drove hard over to the west side of the avenue as I threw my hand in the air to hail a cab. He started inching toward 89th, white taillights signaling he was in reverse.

"I could do no worse than that," I told myself as a mustard-yellow Ford pulled up next to me. New York City plainclothes cops were astonishing. When they went into action, it was as if they materialized, spirits taking form. This guy: backing up on Third, car dovetailing, wobbling as he went to ease behind a beer truck.

I slid in and told the cabbie to go west on 89th and take a left onto Lexington Avenue.

The round, slouching man in the driver's seat had a fat, drooping bottom lip, hair only above his large ears, and he'd had a rough time shaving this morning. His short-sleeved cotton shirt was off-white, and he'd thrown over it a maroon sleeveless vest. Joe Moran was his name, according to his license. He looked tired in the photo and he looked tired behind the wheel.

"Joe," I said as I leaned forward, "we're being followed."

As he turned onto Lex, he raised his head to look in the rearview. "The ex?"

"No. Somebody I don't want to talk to."

I dug out a business card and slid it to him through the murky Plexiglas via the money cup, as we sped past the Lutheran Church at 88th.

"Private eye?" he asked.

As it says. I bought 500. I have maybe 480 left.

"They need anybody?" he asked.

The light was going yellow on 83rd. "Hang a right, Joe."

He did, cutting the corner near the austere brick of the Loyola School. There was an oil truck up ahead, but enough of it was near the hydrant for us to ease by.

He asked the question another way. "They got any openings at your place? I mean, they could use a guy like me. I got people skills, you know, doing this."

"Joe, get on Fifth," I said, "and go into the park at 79th. We'll figure out what to do when we hit the West Side."

I dug into my pocket and pushed $30 toward him.

"And we've got nothing for you, Joe," I said.

"You ain't asked around."

"No, not yet."

"You got to, 'cause I've got to quit hacking, I told the wife," Joe Moran said. "The kidneys, they're shot."

"That's no good." I inched back in the long seat.

"Potholes," he explained, "and six hours you wait to take a leak. I got that prostrate thing going on someplace."

"Joe, what's back there?" I didn't want to turn around to let McDowell know I'd spotted him.

"Crown Victoria," he said. "Black."

"Redhead behind the wheel," I added.

Joe Moran nodded, then looked a second time. "But a guy, though."

"He's a cop, Joe. Don't risk the medallion."

"You want, I could lose him if I go seventy-second."

"No wheelies, Joe. No three-sixties. We'll be all right."

We made it to Fifth, then started south, running alongside the Met, passing the errant spray from its oblong fountain, a curious crowd that milled near the charcoal and easels of streetside artists. Joe thought about timing the light at 80th until it was ready to leave yellow, but he realized the young cop would jump the red. I could've told him we weren't going to shake McDowell now. His determination made up for the smarts he might've lacked.

We went right on 79th into Central Park. Young leaves were growing cautiously on the branches over the transverse and, as we passed under stone arches, I saw that the black cobblestone walls were damp with remnants of winter ice that had turned to water and seeped into the thawing ground. Old blue wooden police sawhorses were stacked near a narrow path that led to Belvedere Castle. We swung right as the road curved north and, out of the corner of my eye, I caught a glimpse of a small, enthusiastic group of teenaged girls playing soccer near The Ramble, using orange traffic cones to form their goal. They were oblivious to the pale, ornate towers of the Beresford that hovered nearby, stoic against the gray, late-afternoon sky.

We came out on Central Park West at 81st Street, near the Natural History museum. A left would soon put us where the traffic grew thick as taxis and limos that had picked up their passengers at the Dakota, the Majestic and other stately apartment buildings were caught in the logjam caused by Columbus Circle. I told Joe to stay on 81st.

We passed the glass cube and Hayden Sphere at the Rose Center. School buses were queued on the wide, two-way street, new takes on the old yellow school bus alongside sleek, bullet-like models. "When you get to Columbus,"

I said, "stay in the center lane until sixty-sixth and tap your blinker like you're going to get on Broadway."

"Broadway. Got it," Joe agreed.

"But stay on Columbus. You with me?"

"You really want to lose this guy, I drop you at sixty-sixth, you grab the subway," Joe advised. "He won't leave his car there. By Lincoln Center, they tow in two minutes." For emphasis, Joe Moran held up two fingers.

Not the subway, Joe. Not for me.

"We'll drive it," I said.

"So you want him to think I'm going Broadway but I'm going Ninth."

"That's it, Joe." McDowell would only ease up if he thought we tried to lose him but couldn't: The sense self-satisfaction would bring a moment of complacency. That might be my chance to break free.


But the zealous young cop was still on our tail when we made it back to TriBeCa. According to Joe Moran, McDowell was never more than a block behind us, even when we snaked onto Hudson, instead of Greenwich, at 14th.

"We square, Joe?" I asked as I stepped out in the front of the Tilt's green door.

"You put in a good word, right?"

"I think you're better off where you are," I told him, as he rolled down the shotgun-side window. "But if you want to do this, call one of the big guys. Maybe they could use somebody like you."

"What about you?"

"There's no money in obsession, Joe," I said. I patted the cab as if it were a palomino on the Ponderosa. Frowning, Joe Moran restarted the meter, his hood light went on, and he headed toward the bottleneck on Canal.

McDowell was waiting near the corner of Harrison, a block south of the Tilt; I could see his front end as it jutted onto Hudson. When we'd gone down Greenwich, he probably figured I was heading home. When we'd circled back north after using Chambers for the huey, he probably guessed I'd go to the bar. I'd bet he thought I'd sit for awhile and muse over a few drinks, none the wiser.

Leo had Monday's *Times–Picayune* spread on the bar and he was using his bifocals to decipher the small print of the classifieds. Crying fiddles of sad old country music poured from the jukebox. Now Diddio was scoring Leo's life.

"Changing careers?" I asked him. The door banged behind me.

"Killing time," he replied. He threw his thumb in the air. "In back."

"Leo, in 15, 20 minutes a cop's going to come in here looking for me."

"You ain't looking for D?"

"Sure. D," I said. "But later. Leo, this cop—"

"One of Mango's boys?"

I nodded.

"Fuck him."

I drummed my fingers on the hardwood.

"Sorry," Leo muttered. Above him, a channel dedicated to animals in the wild showed a lithe gazelle bouncing, springing across a green field.

"When he comes in, tell him I left," I said. "Tell him I probably went home."

"Yeah."

"Mind if I use the bathroom window?"

He shook his head. "Get D to lock it on up," he replied. "Don't want nobody ripping off my urinal cakes."

I went past the pool table to Leo's rumpled office. Diddio was on the phone. He had his big, fat Rolodex with him, the old-fashioned kind with the rectangular cards. He looked like he was at the back of the rack.

"Don't hang up," I told him.

"Aw, she's not there." I noticed the plastic letters on his old black T-shirt had nearly peeled away. "Her company went out of business. There's no more Woolworth's?"

"D—"

He groaned, "Terry, I am dateless. I am dateless for my own coronation."

Stoned again, I thought.

"Don't get desperate," I advised, looking over my shoulder.

"I passed desperate three exits before the last rest stop," he said as he eased out of the hard chair. "Terry, I'm calling record-company flacks here next. Tonight, I'm digging out my high school yearbook." He hitched up his black jeans. Apparently, he'd been at it for awhile: His black boots were under Leo's messy desk.

"D, I'd like to commiserate with you later, but now I—"

"N-G to later, T," he said. "Marianne Faithfull at BAM, Beth Orton at Roseland, Angie Stone at Irving Plaza."

"There," I said quickly, "three possibilities."

"Don't joke. I'm fantasizing I walk in with somebody like that on my arm. I'm thinking Chrissie Hynde. That'd be sweet. Can you imagine the look on—"

"D," I interrupted, "come lock the window behind me."

"But I love Thora Birch too—"

"D."

"You ditching who?"

I stepped aside so he could pass. His stringy hair smelled of Herbal Essence and pungent pot.

He slid on his old sweat socks across the cracked green-and-black linoleum squares and squeezed past the tower of long-necks. Red, orange and blue wires hung from the wall where Leo had pulled the pay phone.

"Listen, when it starts getting busy a cop's going be looking for me," I said. "Don't say anything. Let Leo do the talking."

" 'Getting busy.' You mean, like, the same three Wall Street guys, yellow suspenders, mousse heads, shooting pool? The final Gekkos?"

"Them," I said as we entered the bathroom. To kill time before their evening cruise, the three guys dropped in and shot $100 a game. Money meant everything to them, but they started counting at 100K. A $100 bill was toilet paper, even now, with the Trade Center gone. Another sign that downtown might recover: the reemergence, if only sporadically, of the unconscionable spender.

I went over to the sink, climbed up and withdrew from the frame the long nails Leo used as security. I handed them to Diddio.

I opened the window. The air cut the scent of mothballs, memories of Lysol.

"Ask the Wall Street guys if they have sisters," I told Diddio as I got ready to boost up.

"They don't," he replied.

Ninety minutes later, and I'd reached the corner of 40th and Eighth. On the walk uptown, I made two calls: one to Bella, who was unimpressed with the news that a cop would be staring at the front door for the next few hours; and to directory assistance to learn that Glatzer & Sons was no longer in business, on the Bowery or anywhere else in New York City.

Glancing occasionally for signs of McDowell, I started out with school kids and shopkeepers in the West Village and Chelsea, then fell in with people from the warehouses and drab buildings at the edge of the Garment District who were headed happily for the A, E and C trains. Pushing aside memories, entirely spawned by media, of McKim, Mead and White's old Pennsylvania Station, I thought about Villa, who either clued me in on Sonia's old running crew or tried to send me off to a dark corner. And I wondered when McDowell had picked me up: at Hogan Place early this morning; as I moved from the News building to the Public Library; to Leo's; at the Cuban lawyer's; or at Leo's for the second time. I hadn't given him much of a day, but if he was on the clock, he was pulling in easy overtime. His report to Mango might've seemed tedious to him—"He didn't do nothing, Lieutenant, basically"—but Tommy would know what the seemingly empty motion meant: I hadn't heeded his warning. In fact, I'd visited the D.A.'s, dug up the old news on the Glatzer murder, and met with the leading, anointed-by-media Cuban advocate in Manhattan. Mango was too smart to lean on me hard—he didn't need the pressure a call to Police Commissioner Kelly's office from Sharon Knight might bring—but he'd take my snub as personal. His thinking: I spoke nice to you and you insult me with your actions. (Injured expression, shoulders hunched, palms to the sky.) Your offense has made you an enemy.

But who gives a shit? A threat, I thought as I entered the jostling wave of commuters that poured toward Port Authority, is an incentive. Especially from those fuckin' morons.

I made it through the masses, ignored the Vegas-style displays on 42nd and pushed past the stretch that once held porno parlors and 25-cents-a-woody peep shows and approached the theater district.

In the creeping twilight, beyond the blank expressions on the faces of the people moving toward the bus terminal, I could see a half-mile up ahead Russo's marble statue of Columbus on its nearly 80-foot-high granite pedestal near the park, and I realized I'd made a 10-mile lap around the center of Manhattan island, just to ditch Mango's boy. That made it hours without digging into Bella's manuscript, without time to sit with lonesome Diddio, to find Marina and Davy in my mind.

But, you see, I told myself, there's this dead woman . . .

At the corner of 45th, workers were fixing up an old Beefsteak Charlie's.


The Martin Beck Theater was the only big-time Broadway house on the west side of Eighth on 45th. Behind me, the glittering marquees of the Minskoff, the Royale, the Plymouth, the Imperial. In front of me, past the Beck, shadows and what seemed to be a block of old brownstones, refurbished cold-water flats and parking garages. None of the crowd that had been on Eighth were on this side street.

As I headed west, I felt the evening's chill, tugged at the front of my blazer and went under the glow of Beck's lights. The Avellaneda was farther up the block—362 West 45th made it closer to the corner of Ninth. Since there were no other marquees in front of me, I knew Majorelle's place would be a shoebox-sized theater, more than likely tucked into a basement, offering no amenities beyond Equity actors in worthy plays. As a U-Haul van bounced down the street, its headlights shone on a patch of the sidewalk up ahead that had been washed down with a hose. I figured that was the Avellaneda, getting ready for its 8 P.M. curtain. I kept moving, passing a square patch of cracked tarmac whose proprietor charged theatergoers $48 to park for the evening. On the other side of the street was the Aladdin Hotel, which seemed new. Or at least its gray façade and nameplate did. The three young men and two women out front in jeans and sweaters, sandals and socks, their backpacks lying on the cold concrete, suggested it was a youth hostel, which meant a bed and a charge of less than $100 a night. Meanwhile, big-chain hotels two blocks east on Broadway got $300 per, for not much more.

I was looking into the darkness beyond Ninth when I saw him out of the corner of my left eye, coming hard up the scoop of another underground garage. He was a big man with a big head and he lumbered: a bull in a field, moving, gaining momentum, his body shaking on its rumbling frame. The dark-haired man had on the kind of short blue jacket that mechanics wear, soiled with grease; a gray sweatshirt under it, blue pants and heavy work boots. He had something in his hand, and without warning, without changing his dull expression, he lifted his arm over his head to bring that thick wrench down on me.

I turned and moved hard toward him and he caught me across the shoulder with his wrist and forearm, and he tried to grab me with his left arm, but I got underneath him. But as I stepped back to square up, he slammed me in the left shoulder with the flat side of the wrench and I went to my right, stumbling, and I hit the post of a street sign hard and it snapped against my back and scraped the side of my face. He came at me, this imposing man; his purposeful scowl chilled me, and when I came away from the sign, I threw a right at his stomach. It hurt him and he stopped but he didn't quit.

And there was my shot and I took it, springing at him and driving my right to the center of his face. And I knew I got him. The blood flowed hard, across his lips, his broad chin.

He quickly gathered himself, but his nose was hurt bad and he was confused. He swung the wrench again, but he missed and his right flank was exposed. I drove a left into his ribs, then another.

The wrench flew out of his hand and smacked the cold sidewalk with a sharp clang. He looked down, he looked up at me. And then he lunged at me. His move was awkward—he seemed to want to grab my head with his two big hands. I ducked, but then he surprised me: He brought his right hand back quickly and I raised my hands, but he looped an uppercut into my stomach. And I went down hard, landing on my knees. And there was the wrench, inches from my left hand.

Gasping for air, I threw up my right forearm to protect the side of my face against a blow and, at the same time groped for the wrench. But the blow didn't come and when I risked peering up, I saw he was running toward Ninth. He had a cumbersome gait, as if he had to throw his legs forward to keep moving: Karloff running, an unexpected image in my hazy head. As I tried to rise to catch him, I realized I was hurt. My wind was gone and there was something wrong where I'd hit the metal street sign. For no reason now, I reached for the wrench, brought it toward me, then collapsed onto the pavement. I brought my legs toward my chest and I saw the jutting cornices of the brownstones below the night's first stars before I turned my head and felt the cold concrete on my face.

A gangly garage attendant helped me to my feet, but he wasn't really interested.

"I heard, but I ain't seen," he explained.

"He came from your place," I said. "Did—"

"I ain't—"

"Did he park with you?"

"No one's come in since I went on at four o'clock," he said. "Out, but not in."

The students from the Aladdin, who were speaking what sounded like Dutch, were more curious than frightened.

A pretty blond girl in a pink sweater looked at me with sympathy. She had a round head and pale eyes.

"Taxi," I said.

The wrench dangled at the end of my arm. A thin stream of blood trickled down the side of my face from the wound near the edge of my right eyebrow.

The blood on the sidewalk came from the big man's shattered nose.

"Taxi?" she repeated.

The attendant turned away.

*"Ja,"* I said, *"bitte."*

She smiled.

I knew two words in German. Amazing that they would both be useful now.

"I want to go home," I added as I dabbed at the small wound near my eye.

# 6

Stravinsky's Concertino for String Quartet was playing on WNYC. The Tokyo String Quartet, recorded in Prague. The work of a Russian-born composer played by Japanese musicians in the Czech Republic. How about that? Small world.

"Dad, stop fidgeting."

I was at the dining room table, shirt off, and my daughter was applying peroxide to my right shoulder. That damned sign had caught me good: gash at the eyebrow, slice at the shoulder, bruising near both wounds. The welt on my left flank hurt only half as much.

The first-aid kit rested atop Bella's manuscript. *Zuppa di vongole* burbled on the stove and the scent of clams, garlic and fresh tomatoes wafted around the room.

"What time did the cop leave?" I asked, checking on McDowell, who was trying to check on me.

"I looked out at about five-fifteen and he was gone," she replied as she tore open a Band-Aid. With her teeth.

"Did he see you?"

"Peephole," she uttered impatiently. "*Dad,* I'm trying to concentrate here."

"Sorry."

I'd had the cabbie drop me off at North Moore and, to get the long view, I came up the west side of Greenwich. If McDowell was out front of our house, I was going to go back to the Tilt to clean up before I headed home. I didn't want Mango to know about the assault, which was not random, which was planned by someone who expected me to visit the Avellaneda, which was executed by a cretinous son of a bitch who was due a first-class ass-kicking.

Tearing at a second Band-Aid, Bella asked, "How are you going to get the handkerchief back to that girl?"

My daughter, who bought Bobbie Brown eyeliner and asked if her weekend curfew could be midnight, still said "hankachiff."

"I think she considers it lost," I replied.

"It's pretty. I mean, without the blood. It matches my dress for Saturday night, kind of."

"You got something? Good."

"Mrs. Figueroa was no help, but the people at Ancient Artifacts are so incredible. . . ."

A used-clothes shop on Broadway near NYU. "And it's pink?"

"You'll see." She tapped me on the shoulder, away from the wound. "We're done," she said, with pride.

I stood. I ached.

"You sure you don't want me to do your eye?"

"It's all right." A scab had begun to form.

"Get dressed," she instructed as she took the handle of the first-aid kit. "I'll get dinner."


Bella slid a clamshell into the communal bowl between us.

As I showered, she'd decided we'd forgo the pasta and have the clams with chunks of the round loaf of bread Mrs. Maoli had scored in Little Italy and an escarole salad Bella had made. My daughter likes escarole; the sweet girl likes a bitter leaf.

She poured me another glass of Il Sodaccio, a signal that it was time to leave our discussion, such as it was, of her Global homework. "Global" in the sense that the class was designed to contemplate a basic tenet of human existence. Bella and her classmates were spending the year mulling a question posed as the first semester opened: "When did people start to want more than they need?" Thus far, the discussion had encompassed Proverbs, Quintilian's *Institutio Oratoria,* the stories of the *Panchatantra,* the *Tao Te Ching* and *The Canterbury Tales.* The question was superfluous, since the answer preceded recorded history, but the class introduced Bella and the others to the idea that a fundamental moral precept—*Crudelitatis mater est avaritia*—transcends race, language, geography, time. I thought it was a great idea for a class; I loved it. I loved it so much that Bella told me to butt out.

Remembering the curriculum, I asked if *Hamlet* or *Great Expectations* was next.

"*Hamlet,*" Bella said, as she sent a shell clattering into the bowl.

"I know *Hamlet.*"

"Yes," she replied dryly. "I know."

I tried to lighten things by suggesting she invite her Global Studies teacher's aide to be Diddio's date. "Why don't you see if you can fix him up with Ms. Reynoldo?"

You are a dunce, Bella's sidelong glance told me. A high school teacher, no matter how extraordinary, wasn't for her Diddio.

"He's going to win, you know," she added.

She watched as I took a bite of the bread, rich with olive oil, basil and a delicate trace of clams.

"Watch the love handles, Dad."

"Love handles? I think not."

She smiled wryly, then said, "Do you even know why Dennis was nominated?"

"What is your nightly quota on insults, Bella?"

"Er, no more?"

Of course, I knew why the New York Rock Critics Association had nominated Diddio for Best Feature article. He'd covered last January's reunion of the surviving Beatles, the $500-million benefit at the Garden[1] that turned

---

[1] See page 276.

out to be George Harrison's last public performance, and had written a piece for the Sunday *Times*'s Arts & Leisure section. His hook: He sat in the pit with security, faced the audience and described their reaction to the show. I had to admit it was a terrific story, one of expectation and dedication, of the transforming power of pop music. And, mid-story, he found in the crowd Harrison's wife and son, who knew full well that he was critically ill with the cancer that would kill him 11 months later. Each time the fragile Harrison approached the microphone to sing or stepped into the spotlight to play a guitar solo, his wife and son seemed to hold their breath in fearful anticipation. But by the show's end, they were cheering joyfully, as were the adoring Beatles fans who surrounded them.

"Maybe I ought to change the subject," I said. "You want to hear about my day? Pretty interesting."

"There something more interesting than almost getting your head taken off?"

"In fact, I had a real *This is Your Life* afternoon."

"Before my time." She taunted me with a pretty smile.

"Bella, why are you so damned chipper tonight?"

She shrugged. "I don't know. The dinner with Dennis. Friends. Stuff." She used the tongs to put lettuce leaves, glistening with red-wine vinegar and olive oil, and rings of red onion in her bowl. "Just stuff."

"As I was saying, I went past the Garden—"

"Site of past glories."

"And I was by Lincoln Center."

She stopped, put down the tongs. "You went there?"

"No, I mean I was *by* Lincoln Center," I amended. "A man suggested I take the subway."

"Did you?" Then she quickly answered her own question. "No."

"I'm just saying I was there. That's all."

She sensed an opportunity. "Maybe you should, you know," she said, as conviviality shifted to forced informality. "I was thinking maybe we should."

She turned to face me, brought up her leg, and placed her foot on the chair. Her baby blue socks had ducks on them.

"Oh, Bella. They're not there."

"We don't know that, Dad."

I shook my head. "I know."

"Maybe we would have a very, very clear sense of them."

I disagreed. "I think you're more likely to find them here than where they were killed," I said.

"But they're not here. Not much." She looked down. "Not often."

"Bella, we'd be like those people, you know, who come down here to stare up at the empty sky, up where the towers used to be."

"That's bad?"

"I suppose not. But it's not very practical."

She turned to me. "Dr. Harteveld says—"

"I'm sure she does," I said. "Of course she does."

"Dad, she's right. We should go. We should."

"Maybe so. Probably we should."

The concession seemed to please her. Or she wanted to stop it before I began to slide. She is a very astute girl, acutely aware. Compassionate, ever thoughtful. And we'd done this many times before. I don't know why I start, and yet I do. It is always on my mind.

"And it would be practical, Dad," she added as she returned to her meal. "You spend $100 a day on taxis now. Get a Metrocard. Fifteen bucks."

I wasn't going underground. My wife and son aren't there. But bad, bad things are. I don't want to confront bad, bad things I cannot see. I've had enough of that.

Threaten me with a hulking, fire-breathing man swinging a wrench. I'll make him scramble.

A subway platform, the muck near the tracks. A baby cries. A woman screams. A man who could save them is not there.

"Dad, you're bleeding." She pointed to the corner of my eye.


I treated Bella to a strawberry waffle cone for dessert and we came back along Greenwich, quietly enjoying the purple streaks of clouds, the narrow sliver of moon, the unexpected serenity that, for the moment, brought a sense of optimism. "Look," Bella said, her young voice suddenly full of wonder as she pointed toward the TriBeCa Grill, "limos. They're back."

"You think it's going to be OK, Bella?" I asked her. I noticed The Red Curry, a once-popular Thai place, had closed early.

"I know it's going to be OK," she replied.

"Really?" I handed her another paper napkin.

"We're going to make it OK," she said confidently.

I didn't ask her who "we" were. But I wasn't unaware that Bella, despite the loss of her mother and brother and the death of hundreds of neighbors, their families and friends, insisted on believing that willing something could make it so.

"You still want to go to basketball camp this summer?"

Strawberry ice cream against her lips, she looked up at me and nodded.

I owed it to her to let her get out of here, to get away from death and obsession, from a city still uncertain, still struggling to recover.

"I'll miss you," I said.

"So that means I can go?"

We crossed Jay. "Let's see how your report card turns out."

She smiled. Only disinterest would keep her grades from perfection, even at Walt Whitman, a challenging school for so-called gifted kids.

"Maybe I'll see if I can get a job up there as a counselor," I added.

"Dad—"

"Just kidding."

When we returned home we went our separate ways. I took my running shoes and padded toward the living room sofa while my daughter bounded upstairs to her on-line chat rooms, her e-mails, her CDs that seemed to sprout like weeds. No, an inept metaphor: Her CD collection may seem to grow inexplicably—the not-so-hidden hand of Diddio, explicably—but it is immaculately arranged. J&R Music World should be so well organized.

I was too worn out to give Sinclair Lewis his due, so I stretched out on the couch and clicked to search for the NBA playoffs. The next sound I heard was Bella's quick, almost perfunctory " 'Night, Dad." Waking, shifting to stand, I managed a guttural reply and, with my shoulder screaming and temple thumping, I cut the TV, stood up and went past Marina's work to the kitchen to shut down the house. I reset the first-floor alarm and, after grabbing a cold bottle of Badoit, told myself it was only my imagination;

that the kitchen nightlight wasn't casting a spot on Bella's pages. Moving through dull gray, I grabbed the creaking banister to climb toward my bedroom.

I had awakened from my short sleep on the sofa in a melancholy mood brought on, I concluded, by that simple sentence—"I'll miss you." And as I reached the top step, I realized, once again, that time had been lost and no longer was I needed to tuck her in, to check up on her after she's fallen asleep, to retrieve her stuffed animal Moose and slip it back under her arm or return her book to her nightstand, wipe off her brow on a warm night, adjust her Phish throw when it's cold.

I came to a stop outside her closed door.

She has her own life now, her own sphere, confidences. Neither child nor woman, my daughter lives in a netherworld by choice, by circumstance. But not alone: She is with friends, schoolmates, teachers, teammates, coaches, shopkeepers in the neighborhood who remember her preferences, thin librarians in turtlenecks, women who take her to buy party dresses, Harteveld, Mrs. Maoli. She has her satisfying memories of Papa in Foggia, her aunt Rafaela amid her cut peonies, sunflowers and African daisies, her cousin Nino. Sweet, melodic lullabies sung in whispers by her mother. Her baby brother in an old-fashioned woven bassinet.

"Why is he wearing a dress?" she asked, on her bare toes to peer in to see him.

I know she's taken the subway. She took it with Diddio to see some band at Roseland. He wasn't supposed to tell me. It slipped, "Oops. Oh, shit. T, *man.*" Now I'm not supposed to tell her.

Bella and I share secrets, sometimes. Sometimes not.

Here's one of mine: I regret every time in those lost years when she looked at me with wide, inviting little-girl eyes that said, I need somebody now, Dad, I need you.

If I had held her then, if I had brushed aside her tears by kissing her soft cheeks, stroking her hair, taking her small hands in mine, simply holding her . . .

I mean, there is something between us now, something real but unseen, something immutable, that keeps us apart, even when she is tending to me, patching my wounds, listening to my stories and deciding what they really reveal. Even when she is at my side, eating strawberry ice cream or trying to spin a basketball on her index finger.

I stood outside her bedroom door. All was quiet in our house.

There was a handmade sign, PLEASE KNOCK, on the door, the letters surrounded by stickers of butterflies, hearts, puppies.

"Hey, Bella," I whispered. "You awake?"

"Just about."

I put my hand on the wood. "Thanks for helping me before. You know."

"No prob."

"OK," I said. "Good night, little angel."

"'Night, Dad."

I waited. I went toward my room.

It's my job to make sure the nightlight in the bathroom is on.

He was in front of my house when I returned from my three-mile run, vapors spewing from his tailpipe violating the morning mist, the V-8 growling as if it needed attention.

Why couldn't one of the state troopers who patrol TriBeCa's streets come and drag him away?

McDowell rolled down the passenger's-side window and called to me. "Nice shiner."

My right eye had taken on a purple ring, but it no longer pulsed with pain. "Think so?" I had a good sweat going, my heart rate was up to 132; under the listless sun, the slow run up to the Joltin' Joe and uptempo run back along Washington had loosened the stiffness in my shoulders. I was doing all right. Until now.

He was wearing his uniform, not the navy-blue hooded sweatshirt he'd had on the day before.

"Maybe that shiner says you're not going to give me any of your Jack Webb speeches today." His little teeth sparkled behind a forced smile.

"Aren't you a little young for *Dragnet*?"

"We get *TV Land* in Queens, P.I.," he said with a short shake of his head.

"It must be tough sitting out here, McDowell, when you could be home watching the tube, washing down the aluminum siding, buffing the lawn jockey."

The chill off the river was cooling me down faster than I'd wanted. I turned toward my house.

"Where you going, P.I.?"

I pointed to my white front door.

"And after that?" he asked.

"Big day," I said as I walked away.

"Then it's a big day for me too," he shouted.

I stopped. "You're going to tail me again?"

"It's fun. Libraries, bars, *El Caballero.* Where we going today?"

I was staring at his teeth when I replied. "Dentist. On 68th, off Fifth." There had to a dentist on 68th. "Then Dario Fo at the 92nd Street Y."

He frowned and I could hear him thinking. The Fo part sounded plausible, at least to me. I used Jimmy Mango on a tail job last year. When I relieved him, I had a copy of Fo's *Accidental Death of an Anarchist* in my back pocket. Crazy Jimmy made a big deal of it, laughing like a hyena on ecstasy.

"Sounds fabulous," McDowell said sarcastically. "I'll give you a lift."

"Thanks," I told him as I backpedaled toward my front steps.

"You're not going to invite me in?"

"I would," I said, "but I've got some loose change in a cup in the kitchen."

When I shrugged, I felt my shoulder ache.


Answering machine. Again.

"Julie, Terry," I told the tape. "I've got three names for you: Luis Sixto, Ahmed Hassan—"

"Hello," she blurted as she picked up the handset. "Terry, hi."

"Not in court?"

"Not yet," she said.

I sat on the edge of the bed and slipped into my loafers. "You get the first two names?"

"No. I only knew it was you."

"I met with a guy yesterday who said he knew about Sonia Salgado—"

"You're staying with this?" she asked.

I stood and started to slide my belt into the loops of my gray cords. "Sure."

"Sharon said you would."

"I'm nothing if not persistent," I told her.

"Me too."

I went to the closet for a shirt.

"I looked at Salgado's file again last night," she said.

"You come across the names Sixto, Hassan and Bascomb?"

"Her little gang. Yes."

I took a white Oxford from a wire hanger. "What did you get on Hassan?"

"Not much. In fact, not much on any of them," she said. "Bascomb went to Spofford for pushing a cop. Sixto liked to drive a little too fast, ignore red lights. He got picked up in a sweep near the train yards, sniffing glue. They walked, but it put them both into the system."

I redid the belt, finding a hole and putting in the gold prong. A jacket and I'd be ready to go.

"Julie, this Hassan. Where's he from?"

"They all went to DeWitt Clinton together."

"No, I mean, by any chance is he Moroccan?"

She said yes. "Is it Argana?"

"Argana. The capital under the French."

"Why?" she asked.

"A hunch." I put my wallet in my back pocket. I was ready to go. "Julie, listen. Thanks for all your help, OK?"

"It's useful?" Her voice lifted.

"Sure." I'd grab my short leather jacket from the laundry-room door and head out back toward Sheila Yannick's cello, away from McDowell's dull wit, raw ambition. "You know you can call any time, Terry," Julie said warmly. "I mean, I took these files home with me."

"That's great," I said, as I went to put the handset in the cradle. "It says a lot about you, Jule."

"Yes. Yes it does."

This time I went to Ninth. At 45th, the lanky driver of a white Econoline van was sneaking a mid-morning egg sandwich, its ketchup dripping onto the bag in his lap. On the other side of the avenue, a short guy with a squeegee on a pole was washing Zanzibar's windows with soapy water. A wobbling woman in a tattered housecoat and a pale-green parka supervised. The half-empty bottle of Colt 45 in her hand suggested she wasn't on the restaurant's payroll.

I shielded my eyes from the sun and went west toward the Avellaneda.

The black door of the old theater was locked. I rang the small, rectangular buzzer in the intercom. As I waited for a reply, I looked at the glass panel next to the door. It held reviews for the current run: photocopies held by thumbtacks to a plywood sheet. *"No Direction Home,"* said *Newsday,* "is a gritty slice of reality." The *Post* called it "a *Romeo and Juliet* for modern times." "As the disheartened teacher, Hector Elizondo is terrific," reported *Vanity Fair.* I stepped closer. "By Edwina Acuñar-Gonzalez, *No Direction Home* is about the painful travails of a troubled teenager who must choose between the promising path his late father chose for him and what seems an inevitable journey to destruction." "Acuñar-Gonzalez," said the *Post* review, "worked in an advertising agency before—"

"Yes?" The intercom. A man's voice: weak, wavering.

"I'm looking for Mr. Majorelle," I said, bending at the waist to use the plastic speaker.

"You are?"

"I'm a friend of Sonia Salgado."

He seemed to sigh. Several seconds later, I heard a metallic buzz, which let me push back the door.


He was waiting for me at the bottom of the steep stairwell, hunched, faded into his oversized wheat-and-black djellaba worn over black slacks, tilting his head to shield his face under the shadow of his tarboosh, which covered the top of his head but did a poor job of hiding the sporadic tufts of his graying hair. Behind him was a heavy black curtain; when I reached the last step, I saw that behind the curtain was the auditorium of the Avellaneda theater: perhaps 20 rows of seats, no more than 10 across in a semicircle.

I looked at the man before me. Even in the dull light of the landing, I could see he wasn't well. His sickly gray-yellow skin clung to his skull and his eyes seemed sunken in large, oval pits. His lips were cracked and dry, and as he leaned his left elbow on the ticket-taker's station, he let out a soft groan, as if trying to conceal the pain of his muscles raking against his bones.

"Safi Majorelle?" I asked.

He nodded softly and looked down at his embroidered slippers.

He kept his hands under the djellaba.

I reached across quickly and lifted the garment, as if I expected he was concealing a scimitar. Instead, I found thin, spotted hands folded against a black turtleneck that hung limply on his frame.

"Sorry," I told him. "I had a little bad luck here last night."

He looked at the wound at the side of my eye.

"You're the one," he said.

And when he spoke, I saw the vague, distant resemblance to the photo on his theater's Web site.

Chemotherapy, radiation: Safi Majorelle had cancer and it had been a rough go, a brutal fight. He was no more than 50 years old. He looked 25 years older.

"Sonia . . ."

He turned to push back the curtain.

I followed him as he took a seat. I sat in the row behind him, on the aisle.

On the stage, a subway-station platform: a black sign, its white letters announcing 168TH STREET, hung on white tile; thick, square pillars, dotted with rivets, that disappeared into the rafters; a neglected bench, hosting a discarded tabloid newspaper and a cloth bag filled with textbooks and notepads; and, at stage left, the exit—the tall, gate-style turnstiles that swung but one way.

He turned slowly to face me. "Sonia Salgado," he said, as he adjusted his striped pullover. "How can I help you?"

I handed him a business card. He looked at it and nodded slowly, thoughtfully, as he covered his hands with the front of the warm djellaba.

He said, "I don't see you as police. Your hair . . . No; even with that eye, you have . . . But how do you know Sonia?"

"Her mother hired me to track her down," I told him. "I found the body."

"I see."

"And you knew her," I led.

"I can't say I knew her," he replied, his voice weak, raspy. "We had a correspondence. She came to appreciate the work of the writers."

"When did she first contact you?"

He said, "I would say at least fifteen years ago."

"Why you?"

He managed a shrug. "She is Cuban. We are Cuban."

"So Majorelle is not your name?"

"I don't mean I am Cuban," he replied. "The Avellaneda . . . In that sense, I say 'we.'"

"I see." I unzipped my jacket. Majorelle kept it warm in here; the djellaba, turtleneck, hat, and yet he shivered. "What was your reaction when you heard—"

"That she had been murdered?" he asked. "It is unfortunate. I did not know her well: letters, requests for material, manuscripts—apparently she had tried to create a cooperative among the prisoners to mount . . ." He shook his head. "Unfortunate."

"Who notified you?"

"The police. They found some of the materials I had sent her."

I told him she'd had books about Cuban theater in her living room. I didn't mention the clippings. If he knew I'd seen them, he'd also know I was aware that his relationship with Sonia had gone on for much longer than 15 years. He might've guessed that I already suspected he could be Ahmed Hassan, the only Moroccan in young Sonia's clique.

"I have been told they can have a sort of fixation," he said, "these people in prison."

"I guess."

"But to have a passion . . ." Removing a mottled hand from under his cloak, he gestured toward the stage.

"Yes," I agreed.

He closed his eyes as if to request a moment's rest.

I waited, then I asked, "When was the last time you spoke to her?"

He moved his head but kept his eyes shut. "Last time? At no time."

"Was there anything in your correspondence that might've suggested she was worried about what might happen after she was released?"

"It could be so many things, so many possibilities," he sighed. "Someone from prison. Or just someone . . . In her letters, she was like a child. A dreamer, I would say." He opened his eyes to look at me. "When someone is naïve, they will answer the door for anyone."

I shifted in the small seat, the narrow aisle. "When you say she was a dreamer . . . I don't understand."

"She sent a list—Prida, Machado, Ariza, Huidobro. She wanted to perform their work in Bedford." He frowned. "Later she suggested she wanted to perform here. Here, without experience. Here, at the Avellaneda."

"Not possible?"

For a moment, he seemed insulted, and he drew up in his indignation. But he let it go. "Impractical," he allowed. "You can start a new career at forty-eight years of age, but it will not be easy."

"So you think it could've been random," I said. "A break-in, a thief—"

"They will steal anything to buy their drugs."

"Do you know if she had any contact from the family of the man she is said to have killed?" I asked. "The Glatzers."

"I wouldn't know," he replied.

He turned from me and, with much effort, lifted himself from the seat.

As I waited for him to gather himself, I looked to the uptown subway platform on the stage. An artful facsimile, I told myself. Well executed. But not real. Though we are underground, encased in cement, in timeless stone, with death hovering nearby, perhaps as close to us as the black pipes clinging to the ceiling: not real.

I stood to join him in the aisle, thinking it would've been too easy if he'd been putting on *My Fair Lady, Oklahoma!, Rent* even.

"I notice that you say 'said to have killed,'" Majorelle said, nodding, his voice still a pained whisper. "You are saying, then, that you don't believe she killed this man."

I said, "I don't know. Someone did. Someone took the diamonds and killed an old man."

"Diamonds," he repeated. "Yes, interesting."

"Why?"

"Do you think someone came to Sonia for the diamonds?" he asked.

"I don't think she kept six hundred thousand dollars in diamonds in a flat in the East Village, no."

"So many possibilities."

I said, "You think it's possible she kept the diamonds hidden for thirty years?"

"So many possibilities," he repeated.

He brought his left hand from under the djellaba. His gesture told me it was time to leave.

Who, I asked myself as I looked down at him, is this sick man, this suddenly old man, with his ethnic affectations, artificial gestures, ludicrous theories, bald-faced lies? A man who was, from a distance, kind to Sonia Salgado. Who may have been involved in the crime for which she gave 30 years of her life.

Did he first tell these lies to whomever Mango sent? Or did Mango tell them to him?

"You have to pull the door behind you," he instructed as he looked toward the black stairwell that led up to the air, the light, the street where I'd been beaten. "I ask you to make sure it is locked."

I told him I would.


I went to the slope of the parking garage east of the Avellaneda and stared at the spot where the lumbering man had attacked me. There were no blood-stains on the cracked sidewalk, but the damned NO PARKING sign was there, unbent, triumphant. I thought about kicking it, but didn't. Old loafers and I had a lot of walking to do. I headed west.

Up ahead, a bus was idling outside the Aladdin Hotel. The kids were go-ing somewhere beyond midtown: the Cloisters, maybe, or down to White-hall Street, which might appeal to history-minded kids from Denmark. (Sure. Knud comes 4,000 miles to New York City, wants to see where Peter Stuy-vesant lived in the New World some 350 years ago. When MTV's studios are up the block. When 16 empty acres sit where the World Trade Center used to be. Sure he does.)

As I reached Eighth, I decided to walk over to the Diamond District on 47th Street. There were about 2,500 jewelers on a crowded stretch between Fifth and Sixth. I had a naïve notion that an old man in one of the shops would remember the paternal, politically connected victim, Asher Glatzer, or his sons.

The sun was bright up ahead on Broadway, but the crosstown wind repudiated its warmth and in the shadows that fell beneath the marquee of the Minskoff, a group of city workers in green overalls shuffled as they gossiped, laughed, leaned on push brooms or against gray trash cans on wheels, grateful, perhaps, that they hadn't drawn duty in the cheerless streets downtown. On 45th heading to Broadway, as cars and taxis swerved dramatically to pass them, two Middle-Eastern men in heavy coats and long beards pushed hotdog carts toward the bright light; to put heft into the effort, they angled their bodies until they were nearly horizontal to the blacktop. As I caught up, I could see the sweat on their brows, the effort in the sinew of their necks.

The Loew's on the north side was playing a revival of Scorsese's *The Age of Innocence.* As I reached the crowd of middle-aged tourists outside the Marriott Marquis, I noticed an electronics store over on the west side of Broadway. It bore the requisite GOING OUT OF BUSINESS sign, and I knew its prices were marked up 20 percent to grab out-of-towners made ebullient and unwary by the noise, the lights, by sympathy for the city's plight. I could almost hear the disdainful pitchmen who used guile disguised with rudeness and impatience as a selling technique, as if they were in the open-air *souks* of Marrakesh. As I crossed past the blue wooden horses set up to manage the queue at the TKTS booth, I shoved my hands into my pockets.

I went to the window of the electronics store, which also carried faux Fabergé eggs, alabaster Buddhas and a chess set made of characters from *The Simpsons.* On a clear shelf, below a row of digital cameras, the subject of Diddio's prayer: a portable, anti-shock DAT player/recorder with built-in microphone. These guys were offering it for $999, which meant you could get it for $300 less within a short walk from here.

The New York Rock Critics Association was giving it to award-winners on Saturday night.

"Terry, man, do you know what I could do with this?" Diddio said, as we lounged in a sticky booth at the Tilt one afternoon before September 11 in the winter that was 1,000 days long.

He jabbed his finger onto the pages of a Sam Ash catalogue.

"Bootleg concerts?"

"Abso-freakin'-lootly, T."

When I looked up, I saw behind the electronics store's glass-top counter a rail-thin man in a short-sleeved shirt who was simultaneously sneering at me and cajoling me to venture inside. That, I told myself, is an amazing skill: the ability to make someone feel valueless and valuable at the same time. It came from reducing people to the amount of money they had in their pockets.

I went along Seventh, passing through the scent of baking pizza in Sbarro's. At the curb stood a well-built man in sunglasses, a sweatshirt and a long leather coat. When he saw me over the heads of the bustling crowd that ignored him, he smiled to show me his gold teeth, then quickly pulled open one flap of his jacket to reveal dozens of wristwatches secured to the lining. When I pointed to the watch I was wearing, he switched flaps and presented a collection of cell phones. I pushed my finger toward the phone in my pocket and he dismissed me by turning his shoulder and closing his coat.

I was at 46th, wondering if Gold Teeth had a portable DAT player hooked to his back, when I heard someone call my name.

Tommy Mango had his foot up on the fire hydrant, catching the sun on his patent-leather shoes. He wore a perfect dark-blue suit.

# 7

He waited for me to come to him. I did. I couldn't do him like McDowell.

"What's up?" I asked.

He stepped away from the hydrant.

"What I tell you, Terry?" he began, aggressively. "I told you to play house. Didn't I?"

"I don't play house, Tommy," I told him.

He reached up to touch the gash at the corner of my eye. Instinctively, I brushed aside his hand.

Before I could react, he grabbed my wrist and gripped it tight. With his other hand, he snapped a finger against the wound.

Then he let go.

"What's your point, Tommy?" The quick jolt to the scab brought a tear to my right eye. "It's the badge that lets you guys smack whoever you want."

"Maybe," he said, "but you ain't got one."

"I want to smack somebody, Tommy, I don't need a badge."

He stopped. I pulled back. Under that suit, that white-on-white shirt, Mango had short arms. I wasn't going to let him grab me again.

Suddenly, he smiled. "Terry, you always have to do it the hard way. That's you."

I said, "What's up, Tommy?"

"I guess I got to talk to you myself." With a wave of his hand, he said, "Come on. There's a gin mill up the street."

"It's 11 o'clock."

"We're talking, kid. Not drinking. Though maybe a little Jim Beam might do us both nice, slow us down. What do you think?"

I wasn't going into a dark bar with Tommy Mango. Not when he was in a mood to muscle up.

"Espresso."


He used his shield to get us into La Cucina on 44th. He took a double espresso and had them toss in a spoonful of Sambucca. L'Acqua Minerale for me. And a lemon biscotti.

We were alone among the white linen tablecloths in the long room.

"Terry, you're smart enough to lose the kid—"

"The hydrant you were standing on's got more going for it than that kid, Tommy. You can do better."

"He's what we've got." He took a sip of the hot coffee. As he returned the cup to the saucer, I caught a whiff of the anise liqueur and I recalled, without trying to, that Marina's father kept a bottle made by a friend. Benedicto watched as I sipped the thick licorice drink. He made a gesture with the side of his fist. *"Forte."* As the warmth spread across my chest, the old man seemed pleased: His future son-in-law had respected his tradition, accepted his courtesy.

Mango said, "Terry, it's not— Terry, over here."

"I'm with you, Tommy."

"Terry, it's not like I don't see what you're doing. You find this woman dead on the floor and you want to know. You got to know. But I'm telling you you're way off."

"How do you figure?"

"It's a B-and-E. Or some bitch fight going on since Bedford, I don't know."

I looked down at the crumbs on the tablecloth.

"What?" he said. "That don't add up for you?"

I'd already told him it didn't.

"She's in a halfway house with four other cons," he said, filling the silence. "Her place looks like a fuckin' palace next to what they got."

"All right," I said, "but what did they take?"

"Who knows? A little cash, maybe."

I thought of the $10 bill McDowell had lifted from Santa Barbara, but I kept quiet.

"You, I know." He pointed at me. "You're going to stir up all sorts of shit."

I shook my head. "That explains what, Tommy?"

"So I tell the kid to follow you, see where you're nosing around. I'm thinking maybe you'll hook up with the old broad who hired you. You do that, Terry, and we find out something new about her."

"I haven't seen her," I said, shaking my head lightly.

"She didn't put you together with Villa?"

"No," I told him. "Villa called me."

"He called you," he repeated flatly, with a sudden flash of fire in his eyes. "And he said what?"

"There were no diamonds."

"Thirty years ago, there were no diamonds," Mango said. "Then why did she kill him?"

"He says she didn't."

"Not a peep out of this broad for thirty years." Mango reached across and broke off a piece of the cookie. "Soon he'll be on *Live at Five* telling everybody she was set up. You know, everybody gets along, spics and the whites, and this Villa's out of a fuckin' job."

He dusted his hands over the table.

"And what about the guy at the theater?" he asked. "What's his name?"

"Tommy, you know his name. Your guys were there."

He nodded. "He's got nothing. We both know that."

"Except he may be the only friend she had," I added. "And he's dying."

"That's how it works, kid. You stick your neck out, you get cancer."

I leaned forward. "So it's a B-and-E, nobody knows anything, but yet I've got this," I said as I gestured to the cut near my eye.

He laughed. "It's a conspiracy."

"Yeah, well, it wasn't too funny, Tommy, when he was swinging his wrench over my head."

"A wrench did that? No, a wrench and you lose your eye. A dent in your face forever." He inspected the bottom of his sky-blue necktie. "Terry Orr goes walking through midtown, thinking about his wife, his boy, off in space thinking about better days five, ten years ago, and he's a mark. You keep doing that you should wear a neon sign says, 'Mug me.'"

A six-foot-four, 225-pound mark. Me.

I took a sip of the water. Fine, crisp. But not Badoit.

At the bar, a young waitress stacked hard-boiled eggs in a silver receptacle.

"Listen, Terry, I don't want to hurt you. You're doing this P.I. thing, that's your business. You throw my brother Jimmy a little work, that's fine. But I want you to keep your nose out of this."

"Look, Tommy—"

"I'm fuckin' serious, Terry," he said firmly, without raising his voice. "You're going to find your ass is exposed you keep this up. And the last person you want to piss off is me. And you know that. I don't fuck around, D.A. or no D.A."

I pushed the remainder of the cookie toward him.

"It's not so much being an enemy, Terry," he continued as he went to take the last bite. "It's not being a friend."

"I'm glad to hear that," I said. "For a few seconds there, I almost thought you were threatening me."

He swallowed, then brought the linen napkin to his lips. "An example, Terry, one you'll appreciate. Do you know a drug company in Indianapolis, one of the big ones?"

I shrugged.

He said, "They had this guy come in, he wants a job."

"All right."

"A job in what they call the Animal Conduct unit," Mango said. "He's got no experience but it's a menial job, sweeping up monkey shit, so it's OK."

"Tommy, what—"

"This guy, he gives them a name, a Social Security number. They've got to run a sheet on him," he said. "You got to be bonded if you want to work there."

"And?"

"And turns out the guy is dead."

"Phony papers," I said.

"Sure. This guy, this *redheaded* guy, can't give his real name."

Red hair.

"The company calls the local police and they tell them to string him along, invite him back in," Mango continued. "But the guy doesn't show. He catches on."

"All right."

"The cops in Indianapolis, they go to the address the guy gave, some kind of Midwest version of a flop, and he's gone."

"He's gone?" I repeated.

Mango nodded. "But they found some interesting things."

"Like what?"

"Like an empty bottle of a prescription drug, Zoloft."

"With his real name on it," I said, too eagerly.

Mango shook his head. "He gave the clinic the fake papers too."

"And what else?"

"Out in the garbage, scraps of paper with some kind of music written on it. Notes. Some cop out there claims it's by Bach. The Goldstein—"

"The Goldberg Variations." I could feel my pulse quicken.

"Might be," he shrugged. "My point is, Terry—"

"Your point is that they found Raymond Montgomery Weisz in Indianapolis."

After four years, confirmation that he still exists. The shadow in my dreams, the ever-present specter in the life Bella and I had cobbled together: The Madman is alive. He is real. The redheaded former child prodigy of the piano, the psychotic misfit who, after becoming unhinged, was found living in the Bronx Zoo, scaling fences and climbing into the landscaped forests and open meadows where the animals resided. The homeless man, dirt caked on his ankles, hands and face, who raced across the platform and tossed Davy and his stroller onto the subway tracks and watched as Marina scrambled in vain to save him. The murderer who vanished and remained so. Until he turned up in Indianapolis.

The air had leaped from my lungs. The muscles in my neck and across my shoulders had tightened.

"Terry. Yo, *Terry.*"

Returning, I muttered, "Weisz."

"My point is that a friend is a friend."

"When did this happen?"

"Over the winter," Mango replied. "November, December. After the World Trade Center."

"Tommy, why didn't you tell me?" I asked.

"Your question should be 'Why didn't my friend Luther Addison tell me?'"

Addison had been the investigating officer when Weisz killed Marina and Davy. For the past four years, he'd spent a lot of time trying to jerk me back, telling me Weisz was merely a suspect. When they couldn't find him, Addison's men started telling me that maybe the witnesses had it wrong. That they'd made the wrong guy.

I am irrational, says Luther Addison. I am obsessed. Though he concedes I'm no longer an amateur, he says my methods are crude and naïve. He tells this to Sharon Knight. He tells this to me. "You disappoint me, Terry," says Lieutenant Addison, husband, father, a man who claimed he understood. I think: *I* disappoint *you?* As I groped in the darkness, oblivious, half alive, ignorant even of the responsibilities I had to my own child, never did I consider that you would conceal vital information from me, that you wouldn't understand. "Terry, you are corrupting what little we have," he charged. I have corrupted witnesses, with unannounced visits, with late-night phone calls, with articles in *The New York Times.* "Now they don't know what they saw, Terry," Addison told me, "because they feel sorry for Gabriella and for you."

Pity? For Bella, perhaps. For me? Absolutely not.

I wrote this in a letter to Marina, a year after she'd gone: "I am never without you, *mei carissima,* as I am never without this thought: Had I been with you, holding your hand, listening to your tales, learning to be more; had I been holding Davy, tickling him under his chin, running my finger across his glistening lips to provoke a smile; had I . . ."

I heard a voice: "Terry, whoa. Terry."

I focused on the cop as he returned the espresso cup to the saucer.

He said, "Man, when you do that . . ."

"Yeah, well . . ." I sipped the sparkling water.

"Terry, nobody's saying you ought to fall back into your funk," he said. "Nobody wants to see you walking around TriBeCa like a zombie again, your daughter looking up at you."

"But . . ."

"'But,'" he repeated sarcastically. "What did you tell Jimmy? 'Nothing matters 'til this nut fuck is torn down.'"

"Something like that."

"Which means you take advice from a friend who can help with what's important," he said sharply. "And my advice— Once again, my advice is for you to stay away from Salgado, Villa, Hassan and all the other people you think are in this fuckin' thing. You got me?"

"I hear you," I told him.

"And when Sharon Knight asks you what happened, you tell her something that says, 'Nothing. A B-and-E gone south.' And you walk away."

He stood, tossing the linen napkin on the table.

"Shake my hand," he said.

I did.

"I'm going back downtown," he said as he adjusted his suit jacket. "You want a lift?"

I said no.

"Go to the movies, Terry. Or a museum. You like museums, right? Pictures?"

"All right, Tommy."

He put a finger to his temple. "Everybody says you got good brains. Use them."

He patted me on the shoulder, buttoned his jacket and went to say good-bye to the lean, silver-haired maître d'. On his way to the door, he lifted a hard-boiled egg, looked at it, then returned it to the waitress.

I refilled the glass with sparkling water and took a long drink.

I wasn't unaware that Tommy the Cop had said Hassan, not Majorelle.

I got a good brain.

As I leaned forward to ease out of the chair, I caught a whiff of the anise.

I tossed a $10 bill on the table and pulled out my cell phone.

I said, "Lieutenant Addison, please."

And on the way uptown, walking toward the park, I couldn't make it work, no matter how many times I tossed it around. I couldn't make it fit. Why would Addison deliberately deceive me, intentionally mislead me? To preserve his supremacy, status as the lead dog, alpha male? Promote his perception that Weisz is not the killer; no, merely a suspect? "Luther, can you tell me he didn't do it?" I asked him, last winter, at Virgil's, over pulled pork and unsweetened iced tea.

"No, Terry," he said solemnly. "I can't do that. But—"

"No buts, Luther, all right? No."

Addison knows where Weisz is, I thought now, as I crossed Sixth, Radio City up ahead and budding green trees in the distance. Addison knows where he is and he won't tell me because . . .

Because why?

He conceals what?

No. Even I know that Luther Addison cannot stand accused of false behavior.

Of excessive patience, yes. Of an occasional lack of focus, sure. ("T, I'm not, you know, defending him or nothing, but he's probably got 50, 100 murder cases to solve," Diddio explained. "I mean, he ain't Columbo.") Of moral corruption? No, though there were times when I would take comfort in the thought that he too didn't care whether the Madman would be pulled by his matted red hair from the dark, urine-soaked maze in which he hid, to be brought down, hard and forever.

Luther Addison is a good man.

I was running on West on the river's side, having hung a 180 up by the Intrepid, and I was coming back fast. No pain in my knee, no stitch in my side. The weather was perfect, a slight breeze off the Hudson, flawless pale-blue skies, and perhaps it was this prelude to a beautiful September day, the definition of Indian summer in New York City, that cleared my mind and I wasn't thinking, I was running, and my mind was clear.

And I saw it: The big silver plane was far too low, this I knew immediately. But I tried to understand—maybe my angle is wrong, my eyesight off, maybe the plane is farther south than it seems and, for some reason, it's taking an odd flight path to LaGuardia. An emergency, perhaps; a mechanical failure of a sort. But there was no smoke, no flames; and the plane seemed to hold its lane in the sweet sky.

I didn't stop: the mental equivalent of a shrug, and the quick thought, Maybe I'll keep an eye on that as it continues to bank to the east. I was really running now, and my heart was racing, and my skin was warm and moist with perspiration that caught the breeze off the river, and the silver plane slammed into the north tower of the World Trade Center, about three-quarters of the way up, maybe higher. And I saw it, I absolutely saw it. And I knew, because it had moved, glided, with such confidence, resolution. Though I was confused: a malevolent plane? No, a crazy man. A pilot gone mad. But the copilot . . .

Christ.

I pivoted, a hard left, and crossed West, and I was on 14th, running harder now, dodging cars, hearing sirens, and I made it to Greenwich Avenue and took that, not Washington, to get to Carmine. And to my surprise there were a few parents outside the school, not many, but they seemed calm as they looked at me with tilted heads, bizarre expressions, and I ran up the steps, two, three at a time, and I looked in classrooms, classrooms, class— And there she was, and it was clear she didn't know, no one knew, and as I tried to open the door, my damp hand slid off the knob, but I grabbed it a second time and I got it. By now, Bella was standing, and as I yanked open the door, I heard her say "Dad" in a voice that encompassed fear, embarrassment, amazement, wonder.

I reached for her, clumsily—I missed her hand and caught her wrist.

"Dad, what?" She groped for a notebook, a pen, on her desk.

I heard another voice, "You—" Man or woman?

"Come on," I insisted, shouted. "Bella, let's go."

And as she surrendered to my urgency, another voice, sporadic, crackling from the speakers in the ceiling.

Something about an explosion at the World Trade Center.

Bella's classmates, I saw them, they were looking at each other, trying to stay cool. (They must be cool, detached. They're *teenagers*. It's high school.) But they could not. So many of them had one parent, two parents, among the 30,000 or so employees in the towers.

Bella and I were back on Carmine.

*"Dad!"*

"Bella, a plane hit the World Trade Center," I said, gasping.

She didn't speak. She looked up at me.

"On purpose," I added. "I know it."

And then we heard it, and later we learned it was a second plane. This one hit the south tower, on the side facing south. We couldn't have seen it from Carmine. Maybe I would've seen it from West, gliding beautifully, horribly, toward the tower, toward the parents in the tower, the people.

"We can't go home," Bella said. She'd started to cry. (No brave face this time. No attempt to hold it back.) She was clicking the top of her pen, repeatedly, without rhythm.

By then we were in a hotel, sitting crosslegged on a king-sized bed, staring at CNN, at BBC, watching on TV what was happening less than two miles from where we sat. Bella punched numbers on the phone on the nightstand. She couldn't reach her friends, all of whom had been in school with her. Except one.

Diddio.

But I knew he was safe, I knew. He would've stumbled into bed only a few hours earlier, after dragging himself home from a late show at a club, a long hang-out bullshit session backstage or out by the band's bus, then would've stopped at the Delphi or another greasy spoon for a meal.

Maybe he would've gone up to the roof of his building to watch it after the first attack.

"Oh, man," he'd moan sadly, as the shock started to settle in. "Oh, man."

I knew what he'd do.

No, I didn't.

He threw back on the clothes he'd worn the night before and he ran over to Harrison to save me, to help me find Bella.

And when the north tower collapsed he was at my back door, trying to warn me. He figured I was in my office, deep in my haze, searching online for Weisz, for knowledge that would help me locate the Madman, something.

Then he came around on Harrison, passing my front door, and he was on Greenwich when the cloud of debris and smoke and ash came and he fell back as frantic people scrambled to avoid the terrible gray wave, to find safety, and someone fell over him, and then someone else. Finally, he crawled to the side of my home and rolled up in a ball, where he stayed, he told us, until he no longer saw, no longer heard, the pounding, scraping shoes of desperate people trying to outrace wreckage, trying to escape. Until he no longer heard the shouting, the screams, cries.

Covered in white ash, his eyes stinging, his throat raw, he stumbled to my front steps.

Which is where he was sitting, sobbing, when Luther Addison arrived.

Addison came to find Bella and me, just as our closest friend had done.

After determining that we weren't home, he drove Diddio to St. Vincent's.

Diddio was fine, the doctors told him. Sprained wrist.

Around 4 P.M., still in my running outfit, I walked over to Midtown North. They called up and Luther came down the stairs and he threw his arms around me. When he stepped back, he said, "Nobody could find you."

"We're all right," I told him. "I got Bella and kept going."

He insisted we come to his place. Giselle, he said, would set us up: dinner, a place to sleep. Clothes for Bella.

I pulled my ATM card from my pocket. I took it with me when I set out to run. On the way to the hotel, as empty-eyed people marched silently toward ferries to New Jersey, trains to Westchester, the 7 line to Queens, I found what might have been the last working ATM in the city.

"We're going to ride this out," I told him. "But thanks anyway."

"Man," Diddio said later, "that guy came for you, T."

"Lucky he did," I told him as I patted his knee, the black denim of his jeans. Early October and we were on Greenwich, leaning against a police van, watching a yellow crane do its business, looking up at something that was no longer there, listening to the sad neighborhood, the sounds of shock, grief, loss, an uncertain future.

"All the world is falling apart and he came for you," Diddio repeated. "You live to be eight hundred and you can't doubt him."

"No, you're right, D."

"Ain't that a man," Diddio added, shaking his head as he adjusted the bandage on his wrist.


I found him on Madison at 58th, at the ass-end of FAO Schwarz, a world away from downtown and its plight, its uncertainty.

A pair of blue-and-whites were cutting off traffic on the west side of the avenue, and cars, taxis and buses were jockeying for room over in the right lane. A lunchtime crowd of business suits had gathered in the pale light on the east side, white paper bags filled with sandwiches and Snapple at their sides. It seemed the action behind the yellow tape had been going on for a while: Some of the suits were easing away, shuffling back to the brick buildings off the avenue.

As I crossed 58th, I saw that Addison's men were focusing on a tin trash can near the corner. The dented can, with a black plastic sack tucked inside, had been removed from its red-and-white station and, from where I stood, it seemed empty. But apparently it wasn't, since two cops, badges clipped to their baggy nylon jackets, were staring at it, and in it, with dark looks, firm, furrowed brows.

In a corner, with bright, whimsical posters from the toy store surrounding him, a scruffy homeless man sat on the damp concrete near a shopping cart and a clear industrial-sized trash bag filled with empty soda cans and bottles. A battered American flag was taped to the front of the cart. The old man had his head in his hands and he was muttering to himself, loud enough for me to catch the sound but not the words.

When I found Addison, he was already looking at me, and while he didn't smile, he seemed glad to see me, if only to get away from what was going on behind him.

Up the block, toward Fifth, the cops were intent on keeping tourists and their kids away from the crime scene.

I stayed on the citizen's side of the yellow barrier.

Addison came toward me, unmistakable confidence in his large, powerful frame. He wore his perpetual uni: black suit, white shirt, black tie with a diamond pattern woven into the fabric. As he drew closer, I saw in his pale-green eyes that he didn't know why I'd had him paged, and that perhaps he thought we were just going to go have lunch and everything was going to be all right, like he was going to invite me over for his annual Kwanzaa celebration again and this time I'd say yes.

"Good to see you, Terry," he said as we shook hands over the tape.

"Been a while."

He bent down, slid under the tape and came to my side. "How's Gabriella?"

"Great. Yours?"

"Everyone is fine," he said.

"What's this?" I asked, gesturing toward the trash can, the homeless man and his stash.

"He was working, gathering empties," Addison said. "He digs in and comes up with a hand full of red."

"Cut himself?"

"Not unless he's overflowing with the stuff. There's about ten gallons of blood at the bottom of the can."

There was a blood center up on 67th, off Third. But Addison knew that. There wasn't much I knew that he didn't.

"Man keeps saying a name," Addison said, nodding over his shoulder. "Audia. Audia." He shrugged.

"Anything else in that can?" I asked.

"We'll soon find out."

I gestured with my head, asking Addison to follow me back across 58th, to the shadows on the south side of the street. To my left, a block away, was the Plaza, the Pulitzer Fountain, Sherman in gold.

"Luther, why didn't you tell me they found Weisz in Indianapolis?"

It took a second to sink in, then it did and I watched as the goodwill drained from his face.

"That's what this is about?" he asked. "Couldn't be just catching up."

"We're not going to do much catching up until Weisz is in a cage."

"I have told—"

I cut him off. "It's not what you told me. It's what you haven't."

"You want to hear from me every time I get a call about Weisz."

"Damned right I do," I replied.

"All right," he said, as he edged away from the curb, "I heard from Los Angeles. A security guard at the Hollywood Bowl hears piano playing at three o'clock in the morning, looks down on the stage and there's a naked man sitting there. Guy's got his head shaved, arms, legs, everything. The old guard calls his buddies in the LAPD. When they arrive, the naked man is playing Prokofiev, one of the cops says. As they come toward the stage, he runs off and they can't keep up with him and they can't track him down. He's quick, they say, like an animal."

"Weisz," I told him. It's all there: The Russians, his forte, the core of his repertoire. And the escape: quick like an animal.

Wait. Weisz earned a silver medal at the Van Cliburn competition by performing Tchaikovsky's Piano Concerto No. 1, Opus 23 and Rachmaninoff's Concerto No. 2 in C Minor, Opus 18. But Prokofiev? Yes, of course. The—

"It's our man?" Addison asked, his eyes fixed on mine.

I nodded.

"That was one day before he applied for the job at Eli Lilly," he told me. "The same day, in fact. It was about six o'clock in the morning in Indianapolis when he took off toward Cahuenga."

"So he was in L.A. or Indianapolis," I said as he ran his hand along his thin tie. "Either."

"Maybe, but I've also been told he's been in Grand Forks, North Dakota; Green Bay, Wisconsin; Peoria, Illinois; Orlando, Florida—that's a big one, Orlando. He's been seen there a few times. Las Vegas, that's another big one. Did you know he applied for a job at the Venetian? Yes, he did. Used the name Scarlatti. That guy, a redhead, by the way, had all kinds of fake ID. Turns out three years ago he was a she."

"The one in Indianapolis, Luther, wasn't a guy who had a sex-change operation," I said, as I shifted in the seat. "He was taking antipsychotic medication, wanted to work with animals. He was transcribing the Goldberg Variations on scraps of pap—"

Now Addison cut me off. "Who told you this?"

"Tommy Mangionella."

Addison smiled wryly and, as he looked away toward the east side, scratched the top of his head amid his close-cropped salt-and-pepper hair. "Tommy Mangionella," he chuckled. "Tommy Mango."

I tried to recall whether Addison had ever told me how he felt about Mango. Even if he didn't, I wouldn't have to ask. Son of a sanitation worker, a John Jay graduate who worked his way up after starting on foot north of 125th when Malcolm X Boulevard was still known as Lenox Avenue, Luther Addison wouldn't go for an angles guy like Tommy Mango.

"Is it true?"

As if exasperated, the lieutenant let out a long breath. "All right," he began, "the guy seemed to like animals. Bach? More like doodling. Nothing about antipsychosis medication. Indiana state police think he was a plant from PETA or one of those animal-rights groups." He leaned forward. "By the way, I thought you said Weisz preferred the Russians, not the German, Johann Sebastian."

"Russians," I repeated meekly. The Pulitzer Memorial is known as the "Fountain of Abundance."

"Mango's mistaken," Addison said. "And so are you if you think I'm in the business of keeping you in the dark."

"Well, like you said, it's been a while."

He pointed to the center of his chest, to his heart. "The case is open."

"And Weisz—"

"Weisz is a suspect. For you, he's guilty. Period," he said. "For me, I need to talk to him and it's going to be a good, long, productive conversation."

"If we find him," I added.

"'We,'" he said, without rancor. "We're back to that."

I started to reply, but he held up his hand.

"Never mind," he said. "I know your ways." He added, "And, yeah, nice eye. I don't suppose that's from an elbow under the boards."

He turned and started back to the yellow tape. One of his guys in nylon was trying in vain to talk to the homeless man, who had pulled his ratty coat over his head.

Addison asked, "Just what are you doing with Mango?"

I filled him in, telling him about Dorotea and Sonia Salgado before moving on to the conversation Tommy the Cop and I had had less than an hour earlier.

"So he's trying to buy you off," Addison said.

"I wouldn't— Yeah, sure. That's him, yes."

"Pretty low price for a man's integrity," he said softly.

"A man's integrity might be worth knowing how to find who killed his wife and son," I told him.

"There's a right way to do this," Addison continued. "Getting in bed with Mango isn't it. Not by a long shot. This guy is bad. He was bad in the cradle."

A willful man, Addison was coming at me with force, and his patient whisper had more power than Mango's threats. He knew I'd listen, though I'd rejected his counsel, crossed him—putting him in a hard place with Sharon for a while—and challenged his passion for his work. Sharon and I agreed: Here was an honorable man.

"You started out with an obsession," he said, "and you turned it into something good, something fine—"

"There's a 'but' coming. . . ."

He waved a finger at me. "Now you want to help this woman who lost her daughter—for the second time. Fine."

"Good," I said. "We don't disagree."

"I told you a while ago, Terry, if you do this, always do it for the right reason."

"All right, Luther," I said. "I've got you."

"Let me finish."

"No need."

"You help the mother, it's a good thing," he said, as he lifted the yellow tape, straining it. "You go off trying to solve a thirty-year-old murder case, you're drifting."

Two young women in neat business suits, short skirts under efficient tops, crossed between us. Each carried a thin cell phone and a Palm Pilot bearing the stylized logo of a company I'd never heard of.

"But I've got to ask—even if I'm only talking to myself, Luther—why is Tommy Mango interested in a simple B-and-E that's outside his jurisdiction?"

He slid under the tape. When he stood tall, he said, "You have never taken advice, Terry. You won't start now."

"That never stopped you from giving it, Luther. You might as well go on."

"I will," he laughed. "You know I will."

I nodded. We let it get lighter. But I could tell he had something he wanted to say. Probably something about my stubbornness, my recklessness, though I was neither stubborn nor reckless. Resolute, maybe. Determined. And inexperienced, still; too inexperienced to take down the Madman who—

"Terry," he began, as he leaned closer to me, "that question about Mango, it's a good one. And there's a question of whether you'll deliberately sit on something just to get next to him. Whether you'll compromise who you are for what Mango says he can deliver."

"I hear you," I said.

"We're not much but what we stand for."

"Luther . . ."

"What we've got doesn't say who we are," he went on.

"Luther."

"What am I saying?" he asked.

"You're saying you'll tell me every time you get anything on Weisz."

He understood. "No matter how ridiculous."

"Right," I affirmed.

Then he said, "Who's watching your back on this one?"

I pointed to the scab near my right eye. "No one."

"You want me to call somebody downtown?"

"No," I said. "Everything's coming at me straight on now."

He let out a low chuckle.

"What?"

As he shook his head, he murmured, " 'The Goldberg Variations.' Jesus."

# 8

Hogan Place was about three miles from midtown. It seemed about the right distance to go to burn off a couple of lectures from a pair of cops who worked opposite ends of the same alley. I brought a gyro-and-rice plate I picked up from a cart on 44th into Bryant Park and ate quickly, surrounded by the late-lunch crowd gathered on white pebbles, on the dull-green lawn, craning their pale faces toward the April sun in hope of a glowing tan. After dropping the Styrofoam container into the trash and leaving the park, I tossed around thoughts of how to define pragmatism, and I considered how two men about the same age and drawn to the same profession, two lifelong New Yorkers, men who understood conflict and the nature of life beyond civility and reason, could each conclude that theirs was the best way to play it. Addison, head of the Black Patrolmen's Benevolent Association. Tommy Mango, the Pope of TriBeCa. Luther Addison, who followed the book so closely he may have been a contributor. Mango, who made it up, then changed it when he needed to. Addison, who, with sobriety, with genuine gravitas, says, "We're not much but what we stand for." Mango, who smirks and says, "That's how it works, kid. You stick your neck out, you get cancer."

As I reached the dependable swirl and rush on the west side of Fifth, as I fell in and quickened my pace to head south, I found myself wondering how Addison could believe idealism had any place in this world. This world of blood, collapsing steel and stone, of greed and justification, zealots attack the innocent, where the young die before they've had a chance to live, where mothers scream in horror as they see their babies . . . Where a self-satisfied father, lost in his own ignorance, knows nothing of what is about to happen, nothing. Where a father cannot help before the threat is enacted and life is no more. Where a father has to hold his young daughter as she sobs uncontrollably, longing for her mother's embrace, for a father who did what he was supposed to do.

Tommy, no idealist, might've had Weisz by now. In pieces, maybe, or beaten down to paste. Or in cuffs. And Tommy ushers me into the cage and he leaves to get coffee, a notepad, a stenographer . . .

I'd like to think I'd get him to remove the cuffs before he goes.

There are times when all I want is to look into Weisz's eyes and watch the light go out, to see in them the fear that was in Marina's eyes when she saw Davy in the rat piss and sludge between the tracks, and the train was roaring toward the station and I was not there.

Christ.

Look at me: I'm doing it again. I'm stoking my anger, the perpetual fire. For my own gratification. For my own gratification, I'm doing it again, walking along Fifth Avenue, engulfed by purposeful strangers, patriotic tourists, office workers, beggars, pitchmen, women and men of means. On a sunny day, four years later. Because a red-haired man applied for a job in Indianapolis, because a naked man played Prokofiev at 4 A.M. in the Hollywood Bowl.

It will never stop. I'll always do it.

Let's not kid ourselves.


By the time I reached 35th and Fifth, I'd found a better place to be: I was thinking about Marina and me in the Delphi, a booth in the back. We had just learned that her agent had sold her "Blue Boats of Gallipoli" to the wife of the chairman of Banca Popolare di Bergamo for $800,000 and still we were sharing a $6 turkey club sandwich.

But that memory brought another: "Noci," her painting of the church of St. Maria del Barsento, had been in Credit Suisse First Boston's offices at 5 World Trade Center.

I was trying to recall the whitewashed brick, the bell in the tower, the simple cross in the keystone, when my cell phone rang.

"Hello."

"Where are you?" Bella asked.

I told her.

"Look up at the Empire State Building."

"Bella, it's easier to see the Empire State Building from 135th and Fifth than it is from here."

"There's no 135th and Fifth."

There is—Fifth wraps around Mount Morris Park before it vanishes at 141st—but why argue?

She asked, "Where are you going?"

"The D.A.'s," I said. I'd left a message for Julie: I wanted to see the files on Hassan, Bascomb and the leader Sixto and, I told her machine, I could justify the request to her boss, if necessary.

"Say hello to Ms. Knight for me."

"Bella, why are you home now?"

"No sixth and seventh period on Thursdays, Dad."

"You don't—"

"Because of my book. The extra frees to write. Remember?"

No. "That's right," I said. I waited for the light to go green. Most of the crowd that had surrounded me had disappeared into office buildings or had turned on 34th. For them, the dull, reassuring routine continued. "What's up, Bella?"

"Oh, not much," she said, her sweet voice trailing off.

"Just ask."

"How did you—"

"Bella . . ."

"Can Glo-Bug and Eleanor and maybe another kid come over tonight?"

Now I was next to the Empire State, a building I admired. Its existence suggested an audacity, its design a blend of strength and beauty, the impossible speed with which it was built a fervor and confidence, that defined New York in the early 1930s. And it, like the Chrysler Building and the Woolworth Building closer to my home, suggested a New York bent but unbowed, rattled but never defeated.

"Three kids. What for?"

"Global project," she said. "And to hang out."

I couldn't deny her when she was forthright. Who doesn't admire directness?

"Sure," I told her.

"Are you going to be here?"

"Where would I go?" I asked.

"What I'm saying is if you want to do something you can."

"What do the other parents say?"

She said, "I'm the only one who's not allowed to be home alone after dark."

"We'll see."

"Maybe you could go find Dennis a date," she offered. "He called."

"He did." As Fifth continued its downward slope, I could see the bare, sturdy trees of Madison Square Park, the gray stone of the Flatiron Building up ahead and, in the distance, the empty sky. "I thought you were his date."

"He needs a real date, Dad. He's *pining*. To *me*."

Is he ever not stoned? "I'll call him."

"Better hurry," she advised. "You've got two days."

I decided I'd go behind the Flatiron, covered in lean, midday shadows now, and continue on Broadway to Union Square. To give Julie time to pull the files, I thought maybe I'd drop in on the coffee shop off the park and see if Dorotea Salgado had returned. Or ask around the neighborhood: She might have been anonymous a week ago, another of the hardworking immigrants who toiled in the heart of town. But now she was a woman whose daughter had been killed. That sad fact would lift her from anonymity, if only temporarily.

"Bella, how's Mrs. Maoli doing?" I asked.

"Good. She's got a lot of energy, I think. She's doing all her chores in, like, record time. I think she goes someplace after she leaves here."

"What's for dinner?"

"I think it's chicken," she answered. "It's in the oven, spitting and hissing. With garlic. Lots."

I told her I'd see her for dinner, that I had to move on.

"OK, Dad," she said. "How's your head?"

"Same as always."

"Who knows what that means?"

"I didn't hear you, Bella. Static."

"See you tonight."

We said good-bye.


Julie was standing with her hands on the hard chair, back to the rows of books. She wore a gray-tweed suit with an off-white blouse that was open at the neck.

"Where's your crucifix?" I asked, pointing at the space above the breastbone where the thin gold cross usually rested.

"No overt display of religious symbols in court, Mr. Orr," she replied with a warm, subtle smile. "It's in my pocket."

"This them?"

I nodded toward the files on the table.

"Hassan, Bascomb and Sixto."

She came around the chair and put her hand on the top file.

"Sharon is OK with you looking through these in here," she said. "No photocopying." She pointed to a yellow legal pad and Bic pen on the table. "You can take notes."

"Fair enough." I started to slip out of my soft leather jacket.

"I'll be in my office," she said as she came out from behind the chair.

I told her thanks. I tossed my jacket on the table and, jostling the chair in under me, I reached across for the top folder—Hassan—and started to flip through forms, pink and goldenrod copies, Xeroxed pages, transcripts, typed, handwritten, disorder that somehow seemed orderly. All sorts of seals: city, state, INS. And official rubber stamps and florid signatures.

"Terry."

I looked up. Julie handed me a small San Pellegrino. Droplets ran along the green bottle, across the pale-blue label.

She had snapped the silver cap.

"Thanks."

She smiled. Then she added, "As I said, I'll be in my office."

"Julie."

"Yes?"

"Julie, you and Sharon understand that there's something going on here."

She shook her head slightly, gently. "I think what we understand is that you have an interest."

I leaned across the table, grabbed the yellow pad and pushed it toward her.

"Since I found Sonia Salgado's body, I've been threatened, assaulted—"

"I saw that. Your eye," she said, as she sat next to me. "Are you all right?"

"I'm fine," I replied.

She was facing me, pen in hand on the pad. "'Threatened, assaulted' . . ."

"Assaulted, lied to, trailed by at least one cop," I said.

"Why 'at least one'?"

"Somebody knew where I was headed when I got this," I replied, pointing to my eye.

"And where were you going?"

"To the Avellaneda. I don't think there's much doubt the guy who runs it, Safi Majorelle, is actually Ahmed Hassan." I tapped the open file.

She wrote on the yellow pad.

"And," I told her, "I got called up to Danilo Villa's office."

"I might have guessed," she smiled. "What did he say?"

"That Sonia didn't kill Glatzer."

"Of course."

I looked away.

"Terry . . . What?"

"People tell me she was a susceptible, somewhat slow-witted girl who couldn't have pulled off the theft and fenced six hundred K in diamonds."

"Maybe not, Terry," she said. "But the bloody envelope was found in her possession—"

"Not exactly."

"—and a jury of her peers, Terry, declared she killed this old man."

"Her peers? Thirty years ago?" I asked, without rancor. "Jule, I can't believe the jury was anything but twelve men who read the papers, knew Glatzer's good name, his influential friends—"

"That's not really fair, Terry," she replied calmly, reasonably, as she tapped the plastic pen on the pad.

"Sonia Salgado was a patsy. A dreamer, who for thirty years held on to a fantasy that she'd be an actress when she was let out."

"A patsy? That I find hard to believe," she said. But her inquisitive expression, the way she had changed her posture in the chair, the way she spun the pen as she held my gaze, told me she wasn't as resolute as her reply suggested.

"Why?" I asked.

"I find it hard to believe that she would sit for thirty years in Bedford Hills and tell no one what you say really happened."

"I don't know what happened," I said. "But I can imagine this girl, this girl who *might've* been strong enough to cut paper with scissors, is overwhelmed, scared, confused, *used,* and promises that have been made are all she has to hold on to."

"But thirty years, Terry . . ."

"I don't know. I suppose a fantasy can sustain someone for a long time," I said. "Things change, Jule. Eighteen months, two years, three: shock, anger, confusion. And then it changes again. There is some acceptance. What's happening seems inevitable. And then five, ten years have gone by and what's left is the new life, the fantasy."

"You believe she was told if she kept quiet she'd be able to be an actress?" she asked.

"An actress on Broadway," I replied. "Maybe. Or maybe it was something more fundamental. Maybe she was waiting for Sixto to return."

She frowned. "What do you mean?"

"Villa suggested that Sixto and Sonia had something going," I told her. "After the robbery, the killing of Glatzer, he said Sixto disappeared."

"So she gave up thirty years of her life for love? Oh, my."

I tapped Hassan's file, then pointed to the short stack on the other side of the table.

"I'm looking through these," I said, "because I don't know. Now I got this"—I pointed to the purple skin at the corner of my eye—"and I've got

Tommy Mango out of his jurisdiction and I get called by Danny Villa. Doesn't sound right to me."

"I see."

She said those two words with such earnestness that I believed her: She was opening her mind, looking at the other side without partisanship. An admirable trait. An enviable one.

"You know, Julie," I said. "I think if you were here thirty years ago, you would've been asking the questions no one back then seemed to ask."

She shifted. I thought I noticed a blush touch her round cheeks.

I said, "But Sharon once told me something, Jule: 'Prosecutors prosecute.' After all the old movies I watched in which lawyers played cop before they went to trial, I needed to know that."

"She likes that one," she smiled. "A favorite expression, for sure."

"I'm just saying we ought to see where this goes before the prosecutors prosecute."

"Fair enough."

I tapped Hassan's file.

She understood and she nudged the pad toward me, tearing away the sheet she'd written on.

"I'll come by later," she said.

I turned in the chair.


If she returned, I didn't notice. I dove into the files and stayed there and I felt fine doing it, scratching out notes on the legal pad, pausing only to see if what I'd written revealed anything that might not have been clear before. After reading through the three files as if they were chapters of an awkwardly constructed epistolary novel, I went through them again and again. And then I focused on the years immediately following when Hassan, Bascomb and Sixto met in high school and started making foolish, immature mistakes that might've turned into something that's as bad as it can be. The files were kept in reverse chronological order, so I saw them at their worst before I learned how they got that way. Hassan was the least problematic of the small gang: petty crime that never escalated to felony; or at least he was never caught at it. Bascomb, a big guy born and raised in Hell's Kitchen, was the worst of the bunch on paper: He did 39 months for assault when he was 26. He was picked up a half-dozen times before that, always strong-arm stuff. And loitering, down on Tenth Avenue or in the old trainyards. Which didn't mean he liked to hang around. It meant he had a big mouth and couldn't keep from yapping at a cop who tried to get him to move on.

Or maybe not: Sixto had the same two loitering raps. Maybe the big goon stood there with his huge arms folded when Sixto played streetcorner lawyer and had them both run in.

Sixto looked like the kind of cocky kid who'd think he was smart. And the kind who might be able to get his way with young, impressionable girls: straight black hair, deep-set eyes, a jutting jawline, flat nose, an affected sneer. Back then, at least a decade after it went out of fashion, Luis Sixto looked like he'd been one of the Sharks in *West Side Story*. Which might've been why he looked familiar. I felt like I might've seen him flicking a switchblade at Riff, just before they did a pirouette in tight jeans.

He had his mug shot snapped after getting caught shoplifting. "Said perpetrator was observed . . ." Sixto's M.O.: grabbing gold jewelry and slipping it under his tongue. What might've worked in Gimbel's got him probation when he tried it at Van Cleef & Arpels on Fifth. But nothing violent. Nothing with a knife. Same with Hassan. And with Bascomb, who preferred his fists and a blackjack.

I flipped the page on the yellow pad, then started digging though the files again, looking hard this time for any link that might rise above coincidence, writing down my observations as if doing so made them interesting. Bascomb was born to the neighborhood, but Sixto came to it when he was 11 months old from Cienfuegos after a brief stop in Kendall outside of Miami. Hassan arrived when he was three. They all went to DeWitt Clinton with mixed results: Bascomb dropped out, Sixto made National Honor Society as a sophomore (though never again) and Hassan put three years into the drama club where, it was safe to guess, he met Sonia.

It all seemed to confirm what Villa had said. And he was right about their life of petty crime. Bascomb and Sixto had a few motor-vehicle violations in their files. Tedious stuff: busted taillight, failure to stop. Bascomb got a ticket for turning right on a red, something that's legal almost everywhere today, the kind of thing that was usually waved off with a warning.

Sixto was probably riding shotgun, I thought. Probably tried to tell off the cop. Streetcorner lawyer becomes front-seat mouthpiece.

If Sixto came up with the robbery of Glatzer, made off with the diamonds, then disappeared, as Villa suggested, he'd learned to keep his yap shut.

I didn't have to write that down.

I was back in Sixto's file, combing through the traffic sheet, when I noticed something that made me shift in the chair and bring my sporadic pen-slapping to an abrupt halt.

On a December night, coming across town, Sixto ran a red light on Houston in Alphabet City. Actually, he ran two lights: on Clinton and, three blocks later, on Essex. A cop on patrol saw him, threw on the siren and cherry top, and pulled him over across from Katz's on Ludlow, citing him for both violations on a single ticket.

The cop who signed it 33 years ago: Ernest Mangionella.

As I stared at the signature, barely legible on the carbon copy of the ticket, I realized I knew nothing about Tommy Mango's family, other than that he had a brother, Jimmy, who had a 14-year-old son. I didn't know, or couldn't remember, if Tommy was married, had been married, had kids. I knew nothing about their father.

And then I heard Addison's voice again: "Bad from the cradle."

What was it Leo had said? "Bad seed."

Jimmy was a neighborhood wiseguy, a spry punk with a narrow streak of charm and a lot of kinetic vitality he wasted on the short end. He hustled pool, snarked dime bags of pot, sold DVD players out of the trunk of his car, did a little work for me when I needed a body with a pair of eyes and quick legs. Mostly he hid in the broad shadow of his brother. Before the Madman appeared, I had little need for the Mangionella brothers. I didn't play pool, didn't smoke weed, and now I had a DVD player. And Tommy was the ball of muscle in gray toupee, an almost tasteful suit and buffed, pointed shoes, who looked hard at my Marina and understood he had no chance, whether she was with me or whether she was not.

And none of that told me whether their old man had been a cop.

"Terry."

Julie had a long, stylish raincoat over her suit and a leather briefcase at her side.

I flipped over the cover of Sixto's file, sealing in the apparent link between Tommy the Cop and Sixto. "Julie, why is Alfie Bascomb's photo missing from his jacket?"

"I don't know," she replied quickly, "but I've been assigned the task of tossing you out."

"By Sharon?" I tore sheets from the pad.

"By everyone who's left. The interns, security. It's six-thirty. They want to go home."

I looked at my watch. She was right: I'd been at it for almost four hours.

"We've got to put those away and—"

"I understand," I said as I stood and put the folded sheets in my back pocket. "I didn't mean to hang you up, Jule."

She waved. "It's all right. I was catching up on paperwork. You find anything interesting in there?"

"Sure," I told her as I popped a kink in my neck. "Sonia Salgado hung with a bunch of punks." I leaned over to gather the files.

"I'll take care of that," she said as she came closer to me. Getting ready for the evening, she'd sprayed on perfume and I caught the scent: plum, an earthy wood.

"You have a date," I said.

She grabbed the files and looked at me with appealing bemusement. "Maybe I do."

I squeezed by her, taking the empty water bottle to the trash. "Well, you're looking good, Jule. Good luck."

"Good luck?" she laughed. "What if it's my boyfriend? A guy I've been seeing for three years?"

The bottle hit the bottom of the barrel with a dull thud. "Everybody needs a little luck, right?"

"Or what if I'm meeting my girlfriend for drinks?"

I went for my jacket, edging near her, carefully avoiding the briefcase near her slim ankles, her black shoes. "So you don't have a boyfriend for three years?"

"No, Terry," she huffed. "Not presently."

I slipped into my coat and felt for the cell phone. It was on and the battery was still good: No one had called. Not Bella, not Dorotea Salgado, not McDowell asking for cooperation on his badly drawn tail job.

I looked at her and I asked, "You doing anything Saturday night?"

She stared at me as if my eyebrows had burst into flames.

"Not that I can think of," she replied finally.

"I'm going to this dinner at Vanderbilt Hall in Grand Central. Some thing for rock critics, believe it or not. A friend of mine is up for an award. Good guy," I said, "you'll like him. You want to go?"

Whatever had shocked her seemed to have worn off. Now she seemed merely astonished.

"Yes," she said.

" 'Yes' as in you want to go?"

"Yes, I'd like to go."

"Great. I think we've got to be there at eight, so seven-thirty, all right?" I zipped up my jacket and absently tapped the folded paper in my back pocket.

"Great, yes."

She lifted her briefcase and started toward the corridor and I followed, flipping down the light switch and pulling the door behind me.

This end of the D.A.'s was quiet, and as we headed down the hall toward the elevator, she looked up at me and said, "What do I wear to something like this?"

"I don't know," I shrugged. "Ask Bella. She knows everything about this stuff."

"Is she coming?"

I nodded. "Though that may not be the word for it. She will be *arriving* at Grand Central. For her, this is the event of the season."

"I've never met your daughter," she said as we passed an empty office lit only by a generic screen saver.

God help us if Diddio doesn't win, I thought, nudging aside the mental picture of Sixto I'd been framing. "Call her," I repeated. "Ask her a question. She'll tell you her life story."

She touched my arm. "Thank you, Terry," she said, smiling broadly. "I'm going to enjoy this."

"Yeah," I replied, as thoughts of the Mango family returned in a rush. "Could be interesting."

## 9

Ernest T. Mangionella, retired cop, lived at 200 Elizabeth Street in Little Italy. I was going to 200 Elizabeth Street.

By now the sun was long gone and it had taken its heat with it. Cold, wet, I had my hands buried in my coat pockets, black-leather collar turned up to my ears, and I hunched forward whenever I went east and had to fight the wind from the river. The sonorous-voiced announcer on WNYC merely said it was going to rain tonight; "rain overnight" was how he put it, without mentioning that the temperature would plunge into the 20s. I had no idea when "overnight" began, but, at least aware of the rain, I tried but couldn't figure out how to work an umbrella into this thing. And a trenchcoat didn't go with running shoes and jeans.

"At least take a hat, Dad," Bella shouted. She and Eleanor, the sneering, scowling Grumpy E, were in the living room when I came down the creaking stairs, checking for wallet, cell phone, thinking about Leo's .38 in the cabinet in my office.

The "another kid" turned out to be a boy. Bella left it to her little friend Gloria Figueroa to make the introduction.

"Mr. Orr," said Glo-Bug. "Gabriella says you have never met Daniel Wu."

An enormously pudgy boy stood next to little Glo-Bug, who seemed as tiny as a doll next to him. His features were mushed to the center of his rotund head, and his glistening mop of black hair, sort of parted in the center, lay limp over his ears. If he was 14, he looked younger: I imagined his features hadn't changed much since he was a baby. But when he stuck out his plump hand, his black eyes sparkled with confidence.

"Hello," he said.

"Hello, Daniel Wu."

Under a black vinyl zip-up he wore an old hockey jersey, pale blue with black-and-white piping. FUBU, it said across the chest. For Us, By Us. I don't think so, unless "us" had taken a new, more inclusive meaning.

"Your daughter has told me much about you," young Wu said.

"*Daniel.*" Bella's voice, in a tone that demonstrated the precision of her hearing, despite the spacy, oscillating music from her laptop now with her in the other side of the house.

As if to dissociate herself from the conversation, Glo-Bug edged away from the smiling boy. Apparently, Bella has a level of authority in her little clique.

But Daniel Wu wasn't deterred. "You are a private investigator."

Little Glo-Bug looked away, looked down at her shoes, pursed her lips as if she would whistle, then walked off toward the vestibule that opened to the living room.

"That's it, Daniel," I said. "You got it."

"Perhaps it is challenging," he suggested with an agreeable nod.

"You bet."

"Are you at work—"

I snapped my thumb toward the door. "I'm going to do some private investigating now."

"Can I ask—"

"Oh, no, Daniel."

Pressed by his clear, globular cheeks, his eyes twinkled. "That is why it's called 'private' investigating."

"I like that, Daniel," I told him.

"O*K,* Daniel," sang Bella as she returned to the kitchen. "TV time."

Daniel nodded politely and started to leave us. For some reason, I patted him on his broad back.

He stopped when he reached the archway of the vestibule. "So this is one of your mother's paintings," he said to Bella as he looked up at "The Cliffs of Gargano." His chubby finger hovered near tranquil blue-green waters, near limestone softened by Aleppo pines.

*"Daniel."*

"Very beautiful," he commented. Then he looked at us and made a sad face as he turned to go toward the pulsing music, his untied high-tops slapping the hardwood as he moved away.

My daughter shook her head as she went to the cabinet for a flat bag of unpopped corn. She rattled it and tossed it into the microwave.

"Bella, you said homework. Yet no one has a book, a pencil, a calculator . . ."

"Dad, *Hamlet,* remember?" she said as she punched in the time code. "We're watching the disk."

I went to the back of the laundry room closet for my coat. "Olivier or Branagh. Gibson. Burton?"

"Branagh. Mrs. Crommyda says it's definitive."

Branagh, I thought now as the raw beams of the headlights on Lafayette cut across my frigid face, sending red starbursts into my line of sight. He embodied Lavater's observation: *"Melancholic persons and mad men imagine many things which in very deed are not."*

You bet they do.

I zigzagged through Little Italy to escape the biting wind, passing few things Italian. Instead I saw upscale boutiques and shoe stores, French patisseries, organic-food restaurants and scores of Chinese businesses that once would've been stationed on the other side of Canal. Little Italy once filled a space from Broadway as far east as the Bowery, from Houston south to Franklin. Now it had been squeezed to less than half its size by SoHo edging east and Chinatown pushing north, by tenements cleared for condos in the area the travel magazines call NoLIta (Christ). The remaining Italians who lived now on quiet streets in contented anonymity were nestled in a much smaller area, perhaps no more than 25 blocks in total, with very few given exclusively to *salumeria, pantetteria,* quiet espresso dens, shops for tailors, barbers and other Old World craftsmen. Perhaps the Italians in New

York City didn't mind. They no longer required their own district: Fourth-, third-, even second-generation Italians refused to be confined to an area once populated by their ancestors who neither knew nor could afford better. "Yeah, well, we assimilated pretty fuckin' good" was how I once heard a gravel-throated guy in a skin-tight black sweater put it moments before a brush-up at Leo's old joint, Big Chief's. The guy, so edgy that he seemed to dance in place when he spoke, may have lacked the eloquence of a Mario Cuomo, but he got it right.

I'd had my head down against the cold and went back to Elsinore to entertain thoughts of Claudius's boundless greed, and then I found myself in the bright lights and bustle of Broome Street at Mulberry, the small, bustling quarter of Little Italy that tourists come to see. I wanted to keep moving, but I had to stop as grinding traffic came together at the intersection as if trying to fight out of the end of a funnel, black cars and yellow taxis lurching to within inches of each other as they jockeyed to get ahead. I finally shuffled between rubber bumpers and protruding fenders until I reached the curb under the white lights and blue signage of Umberto's Clam House. As I continued away from the tourists on Broome, I eased through a surprisingly subtle cloud of white clam sauce heady with fried garlic.

They tell the tourists that the ghost of Joey Gallo hovers above Umberto's, I knew. Tourists from Tennessee, from the UK, from Helsingör, Denmark, even, they want to believe. They find this appealing; the cult of personality extends to criminal-as-celebrity now. It's thrilling, the tourists say, to move through the aura of evil. They come to see the Ravenite Social Club, made famous in grainy, black-and-white footage shot by the FBI. Gone now: no John Gotti, no Sammy the Bull. And it's so damned hard now to spot a regular old made man on the street if his picture hasn't been on CNN or *Entertainment Tonight*. So, to get their fix, these tourists pass by Umberto's, oblivious to the tender calamari (*Squid?* No thank *you*), the Seafood *Marechiaro* over handmade linguini, to see where a member of the Colombo family was shot and killed. "He died here," they say, whispering, pointing, as if the pool of blood still lay on the sidewalk. They stand tall and have their photos taken with disposable cameras.

I moved on until I was alone again, under thin, leafless trees, under violet lights, under vanishing stars.

What is Bella doing? I could call. . . .

I told her not to call me unless she had to. I didn't want to have the phone buzz if I was hanging in jagged shadows near the old cop's place on Elizabeth.

"Not even if Dennis calls back?" she asked.

I'd told Diddio we'd be a foursome for the critics' bacchanalia. He said, "Yippee." He meant it. "I am fulfilled. Man, I spell relief T–E–R—"

I told him I'd see him Saturday.

Leaning against the frame of my office door, Bella watched as I cut the line and dropped the handset onto the cradle.

"Everybody's happy?" she asked. She was wearing a lime-and-black bowling shirt with the name "Donnie" on the breast, over khaki parachute pants.

"He is. Are you?"

She nodded.

"Then me too," I told her

She handed me the *Nursery of Crime* manuscript. "Stash this in here for me, please?"

I took the neatly stacked pile, which was held together with a red rubber band, a thicker brand than Bella wore on her wrist.

"I don't want it on the table when my friends get here."

"Any of them read it?"

"Daniel."

"And?"

She smiled.

"And you're OK with Julie and Saturday night?"

She ran her hand through her hair. "I'll still have plenty of face time with Dennis."

"Sure," I said. "Of course."

"I have faith, Dad," she nodded. "I'm a serious believer."


At its core, Little Italy was still a closed enclave that would be reluctant to give up one of its own, so I reached Elizabeth Street expecting no help and intending to ask for none. To me, the whole place was a storefront social club where silent old men with gnarled cheroots and bitter espresso would look up from their penny-a-point gin game only to give me the *mal occhio*. I had to go right at it.

Long, narrow Elizabeth Street was empty, except for parked cars and the diffused glow of the streetlamps. White light came through the glass windows of a store on the west side, and then the light went dead and, a moment later, a young woman in a smart black coat came from the store, locked its front door and, without looking behind her, went north on clicking heels, adjusting her oversized handbag, bringing up her pink Pashmina wrap to cover her ears. I edged toward the darkness she'd left behind.

Translucent clouds drifted high above me, tracing across the pale moon.

The center of the east side of the street was occupied by a stoic row of plain tenements, their once-golden bricks now soiled to brown. Their five-story façades wore rusted fire escapes that were home to struggling houseplants and sturdy flowers in large crocks. And Italian flags, standing tall, flapping hard in the night wind. Two plastic geese were tied to one railing, yellow ribbons painted on their necks. Behind the fire escapes, the snapping flags, fat plastic geese, old-fashioned window shades had been pulled shut, revealing only the occasional flickering blue glow of a TV.

The rush of traffic came from the distance now. From inside a seafood warehouse on the corner behind me, a dog growled, barked sharply, then went silent, leaving only the disturbing sound of the thrashing wind. To my left, dangling in the haze off in the distance, were stark lights from the massive skyscrapers that dominated the ever-changing midtown skyline.

The rain started to fall again, thin streaks crossing the streetlamps' lights like speeding comets before some far-off star. Chilled to the bone, I took my hands from my pockets, wiped the raindrops off my face, and started toward 200 Elizabeth.

But before I reached the front door, I heard a familiar voice echoing down the quiet street.

Up ahead, at the middle of the next block, was a bar, a bullet-and-beer joint for neighborhood guys. At its front door, a thin man with frizzy hair, an orange V-neck sweater and blue jeans had his hand out to confirm what his eyes told him.

When he caught the rain, Jimmy Mango wiped his hand on his jeans.

"What'd I say?" he spit bitterly over his shoulder. "Yeah, Pop, it's still fuckin' raining."

I made a quiet bet: "Memories Are Made of This" on the jukebox. A black-and-white shot of Michael in his Army uniform, with Sonny, Fredo and the Don smiling proudly, arms hung on each other's shoulders.

He saw me as soon as I walked in.

Besides the young bartender, there were three men in the place: a guy in a UPS uniform with the *Post* folded under his elbow at the bar, and two at the only table in the small, square room. One was Jimmy, the other, with his back to the wall, had to be his old man. The guy looked like Tommy shrunken down by age, by life, by memory's echo voices. He wore a red flannel shirt that swam on him and a gray sweater-vest and dark blue slacks. He was drunk.

Jimmy came out of the chair.

I turned down my collar. Rain beads ran off my shoulders.

"Forty-four," he said loudly, as if he was glad to see me. "Forty-four comes to Little Italy. What a surprise."

He stuck out his hand and I shook it and held it, keeping an eye on his left. Jimmy was quick, but he wasn't as strong as he might've thought.

He stepped back.

"Nice eye," he said, looking up.

"So I'm told."

"That's what happens you go to Broadway. Crazy people, they go to plays and shit. Fantasy."

"Jimmy, you know, I've never met your dad."

"My *dad?*" the incredulous Jimmy repeated. "What he is, like, Tom fuckin' Bradford? There's no dads here, Four." He looked at the bartender. "Lil' M, you got a dad?"

Lil' Marco ignored him. But the UPS man, apparently an *Eight Is Enough* fan, chuckled.

The radio prattled. *These jerks in Washington . . .*

"Jimmy, I'm here," I said. "We don't have to fuck around."

"You ain't talkin' to the old man, Terry."

I put my back against the bar. I could see Lil' M and UPS out of the corner of my eye.

"Somebody's going to do it, Jimmy."

"No, they ain't."

He moved his right hand slowly to the front of his old jeans, then he started to slide it toward his back pocket.

"Jimmy, you come up with something besides five fingers, you won't walk home," I said plainly.

Mango lifted his empty hands. He smiled darkly. "Not tonight, no. Not after you handled that big guy in midtown, Four."

"You saw that, Jimmy?"

The worm shrugged.

"What happened to Sixto?"

"I don't know what you're talking about," he said.

The old man called him. "Sonny, *dove siete?*" he muttered.

Jimmy turned. "Pop, I'm right here."

I reached and snapped the railroad spike out of his back pocket. It clanked when it hit the floor.

I kicked it and it slid across the room, banging against the bar, then scooting toward what had once been a fireplace.

Jimmy watched it go. Then he looked hard at me.

*"Sonny?"* I asked.

"You're in over your head, Four," Mango said bitterly. "This ain't St. John's, this ain't the fuckin' NBA. Throwing elbows under the boards ain't near enough."

"You being here, Jimmy, and following me to midtown tells me that," I said. "Tommy hounding my ass tells me that."

"You made me a few large, Terry, I like you. But Tommy, he don't give a shit. You and your whole thing, your *woes* or whatever, it don't mean a fuckin' thing."

"There's a dead woman and your father's name on a ticket. Why is this a big deal?"

Jimmy shifted and he ran a thumb across his eyebrow.

"My old man wrote a lot of tickets in his twenty years, Terry."

"Maybe that's all it is," I nodded.

"I always said you were smart, Terry. I always said that."

I looked past Mango to his old man. He was muttering to himself, muttering into a glass of dark brown liquor as his eyes slowly closed, slowly opened again. He needed a shave.

Either that guy ran recklessly through his cut of the 600K long ago or he never collected a dime.

"I guess I don't have to ask you to tell Tommy I was here," I said.

Mango shook his head. "He already knows, Terry, you know what I mean?"

*"Figlio,"* the old man mumbled. Son.

"He talking to you or Tommy?" I asked.

"Who the fuck knows? Only time he talks Italian is when he's stewed."

"Probably has a lot on his mind."

"The back door ain't open either, Four," he smiled. "Drop it."

I stepped away from the bar. "You want a hand getting him home?" I asked.

Jimmy said no. "Lil' M, he's done this before."

"All right," I said as I turned up my collar.

Which meant that Jimmy was going to walk away from his old man before the bar shut down for the night. And that meant Lil' Marco was only going to take Ernest Mangionella as far as his front door. A bartender usually doesn't undress a drunk, tuck him in, kiss him on the forehead. Even if the drunk is Tommy the Cop's father.

That's Jimmy, I told myself. Doing a half-assed job even when it's his own father.

Stepping out of the cold rain, I stationed myself in the shadows of the tenements on the west side of Elizabeth, finding a spot under a cornice in an unlit doorway.

The Empire State Building wore a crown of blue and orange lights. Airplanes headed to LaGuardia grew larger as they descended.

I blew into my hands, rubbed them together.

I was in place for more than a half-hour when the first car passed, raindrops glittering in its headlights. If the driver saw me, she didn't let on. A few seconds later, she slid to a stop in front of Marco's and tapped the horn. Jimmy came out of the bar, jumped in and the young woman with dark pulled-back hair and the twirling CD tied to her rearview eased out to head uptown.

In case she'd spotted me, I went south, looking for another place to hide. As I reached the end of the block, the warehouse dog started up again: This time he leapt and crashed against the front doors, stressing the heavy chain, the padlock. Then he did it again, growling and snarling.

Hands in my pockets, I went back up the street, the rattling of the doors following me. I stopped at the chic boutique, with the thought that the woman in pink Pashmina wasn't going to return until tomorrow at noon.

About the hour the damned dog would stop barking.

There was a time when you would've found a god-damned dog that could wake up this neighborhood with a slug from a .25 between its eyes, permanently shut down.

Unless the dog was protected.

Christ, a mobbed-up dog. Why not?

I was still thinking about it when I noticed the silence.

If Jimmy's girl had seen me, she hadn't told him. I knew him well enough to be sure he wouldn't hang back and let Tommy step in. Or even tip off Lil' Marco. Jimmy would've had to make like a tough guy in front of his woman. It was in his DNA, on the double helix of all cocky guys his size: Never pass up a chance to go hard against a big guy, to take a big guy down. Especially if shouting out a few words in Italian might bring three guys with Glocks out of the building behind me.

I stepped back against the shop's door. Maybe Pashmina had left the heat on.

No, but I was out of the wind.

*"For this relief much thanks: 'tis bitter cold."*

Francisco or Marcellus. Bernardo? One of the sentries.

I looked to my left, through the glass. Lil' M was walking a wobbling Ernie Mango along Elizabeth.

The UPS man was heading the other way.

I moved away from the shop and slid to where I had been: under the shelter of the cornice, directly across from old man Mango's front door.

He stopped and seemed to want to argue with the dull-eyed bartender, who gestured as Mango began to shout incoherently. Lil' M's good deed wasn't about to go unpunished.

I couldn't hear what they were saying, but old Mango suddenly pushed the young man. The ex-cop came off the curb and tottered across the side street.

Lil' M hung back. The old man went a few, uncertain steps forward. And then I understood what he and the bartender had scuffled about: Ernie Mango reached down, whipped out his sorry old cock and started pissing on Elizabeth Street.

"Shit," Lil' M spit. "Ernie . . ." He skidded, came up behind the old man, took him by the elbows and steered him toward a building until the arching flow hit brick instead of concrete.

As Lil' M steadied Mango, trying to give the ex-cop at least a shred of dignity, I cut across the narrow street and crouched behind a car in front of the old man's tenement.

Mango crammed his cock back in his pants, but didn't bother to zip up. As Lil' M avoided the piss puddle and wiped the rain from his face, the old man went ahead and stumbled to his building.

I shifted behind the parked car and watched as the bartender found the old man's keys and opened the inside door. As he held back the door and nudged old Mango in, I rose up and saw I'd get my chance.

As Lil' M steered the old man to the stairs, the inside door stayed open.

I waited until they were out of view, then came around the parked car and dashed into the building. Once inside, I went easy, careful not to let my wet shoes squeak on the floor. I walked slowly, noiselessly, to the back of the first floor and found a niche under the stairs. I turned, squatted and fit in nicely.

After about 10 minutes, I began to wonder if Lil' M *was* tucking him in. Or maybe Jimmy had asked the kid to stay with the old man.

But then I heard a door right above me open, then close.

Lil' M pounded down the stairs and he pulled the inside door shut as he went out into the cold mist.

I waited, then eased myself from the darkness and shook the stiffness out of my knees.

I came around and went up the stairs.

I knocked once. The old man came to the door.

I saw he thought Lil' M had returned. I could see he didn't recognize me.

The bartender had helped him undress. Ernie Mangionella was in a sleeveless undershirt and his suspenders hung limply on the legs of his damp slacks. His feet were bare.

Though he was drunk, he knew something wasn't right, and he stood in the door frame, drawing himself up the best he could.

"Tell me about Sonia Salgado," I said.

"Who the fuck are you?" he slurred.

"McDowell. I work with Tommy."

He cocked an eyebrow and glared at me.

"You're full of shit," he said finally, as his eyelids bobbed.

Then the old man looked up at me and with as much defiance as he could muster, tried to stare me down.

So that's where they get it from, I thought.

"You ain't coming in my house," he added. "Nobody comes—"

"Sonia Salgado," I said.

He stopped.

I repeated her name. "Sonia Salgado."

"Listen, you, McDonald—"

"McDowell."

"You, you fuckin' Mick fuck, you *Irlandese* . . ." He came closer. His chin was at my chest.

I could smell the bourbon. I could see the gray stubble on his drooping cheeks.

"I got nothin', you hear me?"

"Yes, sir," I said.

"Never did." He jabbed me with his finger. "Never."

He started to totter again. I grabbed him by his shoulders. He went to push me off, but it got worse and he went backward. Luckily, he hit the door frame. Otherwise he would've crashed to the floor.

"OK," I said softly, "steady."

He looked at me, frowning harshly.

"You work with my Tommy?"

"Sure," I lied. "McDowell. You tell him I was here."

I said it loud enough for the neighbors to hear over the 10 o'clock news.

"Yeah and you tell him . . ." He inched forward again. "You . . ."

Then he took a deep breath and his shoulder sagged.

There'd be no confrontation now. Ernie Mango, bourbon in his blood, wanted to confide.

"I'm asking you," he said. "Listen, I'm asking you: A man with scratch, what? He lives here? He don't take his family to Florida, over to Jersey, some place? He don't take his wife some place nice, Miami Beach, the mountains? Give her what she wants . . ."

His heavy eyelids drooped as his head sank toward his chest.

Then he looked up at me. "I told Tommy. I got nothing." Gesturing with the back of his hand, he repeated, "Nothing. You got me?"

I had what I needed now. When you ask a man about murder and he answers by talking about money, about a big prize he never got, he's telling you more than he ought to.

"A cruise," he continued, slurring. "All Rosa wanted: Go on a cruise."

"OK, Mr. Mango," I said. "You'd better go in. You get some sleep."

He hung his head. "My little Rose," he mumbled.

What a sorry old man.

He looked at me and he wanted to tell me something to clinch it, in case I hadn't understood that he never had a slice of the 600K cache.

But all he came up with was a lazy, looping wave of the hand.

"Bah," he said.

I watched as he turned slowly, steadied himself and went inside.

I reached and pulled the door toward me until it clicked.

## 10

The rain clouds had moved on by the time I woke up and went out for a morning run. I'd intended to take it north past Point Thank You and soon-to-rattle-and-quake construction on Canal up to the lip of the Joltin' Joe before coming back along Ninth to Greenwich. But with the numbing wind off the Hudson stinging and slapping me, I couldn't get my knee loose and I cut the run short, looping back at 14th. It was a good call: In the shower, I saw that the knot of skin from when I'd had my right knee scoped had gone bright red. Probably didn't mean much to an orthopedic surgeon, but to me it meant I pushed it too hard. Running too frequently on blacktop, on unyielding concrete. Standing in the rain, the winterlike chill. Or crouching under old Mango's stairs.

Walking never bothered me. "The best medicine, man. Natural mystic," said Diddio, who walked nowhere. I'd walked once from the Cloisters to Battery Park and my knee felt fine.

So I couldn't blame it on last night's short hike back from Elizabeth Street. I'd kept it simple: Dodging Mulberry, I carried my thoughts along Centre and, with a quiet Criminal Court Building, site of the original Tombs, to my left, fought the night wind off the East River as I moved across town on Franklin. By the time I reached Finn Square, I had it sorted out. It all started with that ticket Ernie Mangionella had hung on Luis Sixto. That was the night they met: No cop cites someone he knows for running a red—a moving violation, points.

"And now you have a cold," Bella said as we stood on the sidewalk, the morning sun not yet above the buildings on the east side. "Because you never dress right."

This is an old song. When the temperature dropped below freezing, Bella dressed as if she expected Peary and Henson to ask her to fetch the huskies for a side trip across the Nares to Greenland.

"I don't—"

"And you still have a tendency toward melodrama, Dad," Bella said.

She hates it when we leave the house at the same time. Someone might think I was walking her to school, the pink handle of her Barbie lunchbox in my big hand.

I'd simply pointed to the patch of ice on the front steps. Maybe "fall and break your neck" was a bit over the top. But "slip and skin your knee" didn't seem like much to fear.

She had a royal-blue beret pulled down to her eyebrows, and a red scarf covered everything to her bottom eyelashes. My daughter, whose head had become the flag of France.

"They say it's going to hit forty today," I smiled. If only there were a graceful way to go back in and throw on a sweater. . . .

"'*They.*' Ha."

Glo-Bug had nodded off last night, her head on a throw pillow as she lay on the sofa, but Daniel Wu, Grumpy E and Bella were in front of the TV as Branagh glowered.

"Hello, Mr. Orr," said Daniel Wu, who was sitting against the sofa, his sneakers tucked under the coffee table.

The popcorn bowl was empty except for a few plump kernels at the bottom.

Bella and Eleanor were stretched out on the floor: Grumpy E rested on Daniel's down coat while my daughter used her laptop as a pillow.

Bella pointed to the TV. "T. S. Eliot says this is an artistic failure."

"He's right," grumped E, a frown reducing her dark eyebrows to a single line.

"Yes," I replied. "But Goethe and Coleridge—"

"Shhh," Bella said gently, with a nod toward the screen. "More swords."

I wonder what happened to that Barbie lunchbox.

On the first day of school, Bella charged confidently into the kindergarten classroom, took the desk squarely in front of the teacher's, whipped out a marble notebook and a fat pencil. By her fourth birthday, she could read the *Times* editorial page. A year earlier, while watching *Pinky and the Brain,* she turned to me and said, "Brain sounds like Orson Welles." And, to prepare for the first day of school, she spent the summer memorizing the multiplication table, not to 12, but to 13. Why? "To see if I could. That's all. I wouldn't tell anybody."

I wonder if Davy would've been as clever as Bella. He had bright eyes and he seemed alert as he watched the mobile his sister made turn above his crib, groping at the air with little fists, kicking his feet to his own rhythm.

*A double blessing is a double grace.*

I looked at Bella, barely visible now under layers of winter clothing, yellow galoshes over shoes, flannel-lined jeans over long johns, big Michelin-man coat. And still I can feel the light that radiates from within her.

Under that blob of clothes is our very good kid. No need for Polonius's double-edged speech to Laertes: Here is a child who by instinct is true.

Marina, I know, would be proud. (Eighteen months ago, I might've said "is proud." I don't do that anymore.)

"Dad, don't look at me like that," she said. "You're, like, kind of creeping me out." I got a kiss on the cheek last night.


It looked like I'd made it to 89th before Villa. The blinds of his storefront office were down and *The New York Times* in a blue plastic sack was jammed into the ornate door handle. As I stepped out of the warm cab, I looked at my watch. Nice life, being a community leader, an ethnic activist at $350 an hour. I'd have to wait a while to learn what he'd heard about Sonia's murder, to probe him on what else he knew about Sixto, Bascomb and the man who now was Safi Majorelle.

I dodged shallow puddles and walked up the block to the Stargate Diner to kill 15 minutes over a cup of black coffee. I kept my jacket on as I sat at the end of the counter near the glass door. Staring at the revolving coconut cakes, meringue mountains and bear claws, I wondered how long it was taking McDowell to convince Tommy the Cop he'd never left Queens last night. Might be amusing; probably not. Once he knew it hadn't been the young cop at his father's door, Tommy would know it was me and he'd start wondering what the drunken old man had said.

And, I asked myself as I sipped the hot coffee, how slick was young Sixto back then? Not yet 30 years ago, he takes a ticket from a cop and turns it into a partnership that brings him a good portion of 600K in diamonds.

Or maybe the operator was old man Mango, back when he was young, before he started leaning on the sauce. He gets his hooks into an eager kid and builds a scheme around that ambition, around his willingness to do bad.

Did he have to work to turn Sixto's eagerness to ruthlessness?

What did Villa say about Sixto? "Very clever, very bold."

I saw it playing like this: Ernie Mangionella's beat includes the Bowery. He knows Asher Glatzer carries gems between stores. He tells Sixto, who rips off the old man.

But the armed robbery goes wrong as Asher Glatzer is killed, savagely. The merchant's political connections bring heat down in waves on Police Plaza. It gets crazy on the Bowery: protests; shop owners demanding protection; Beame and Koch in the neighborhood. Media, the icy glow of TV lights. And Mango, a blue who is working the beat and can't peel off to find Sixto and finish their business together.

And Luis Sixto, opportunist and maybe the smarter of the two, takes off with the diamonds.

"A man with scratch, what? He lives here?"

Ernie Mango didn't get his slice. Maybe he used to look like Tommy does now, square, compact and strong, but maybe his head was like Jimmy's, a head that would make him capable of seeing only what benefits him, regardless of what it did to the people around him, including family. Maybe Sixto knew the Bowery cop could be played, that he wouldn't have thought it through, that he'd carelessly leave a gaping crack in his plan.

Bitter, outmaneuvered by a kid, does Ernie Mango set up Sixto's girlfriend?

Or does Sixto kill Glatzer so Mango can't make a move on the diamonds? Does he set up Sonia himself so he can disappear?

Even if Sonia manages to find a lawyer who can shake her out of the frame, the time it takes gives Sixto a chance to flee to— Where did Villa say? Anywhere in Central or South America where his native language was spoken. Or did he vanish into the discouraging, city-run projects in Spanish Harlem, lying low in one of thousands of apartments that seem to run together north of 116th? Villa was right when he said $600,000 could make a man disappear. Especially a daring young man, clever and bold.

I looked up at the waitress. She had tired green eyes and a tracheotomy scar across her throat.

I put my hand over the cup.

She went away and slid the steaming pot back on the heater.

I dug two singles out of my pocket.

Where does Majorelle fit in?

Tommy knew I'd go to see him. He had Jimmy tail me to midtown. Or he had Jimmy on 45th, waiting for me to show up.

He didn't have a whole lot of confidence in McDowell.

But if he used Jimmy instead of a cop he could trust, what did it mean?

As I left the diner, stepping back onto windy Third, I asked myself if Tommy would send in muscle before he asked for a sit.

To cover up grand larceny and murder? Yes. Sure.

I turned toward Villa's office.

And up the block, leaving Villa's, was the guy who came at me on 45th. He wore the same outfit he'd had on the other night outside the Avellaneda: short, soiled jacket, a gray sweatshirt under it; blue slacks; heavy, grease-stained work boots. One difference: His eyes were ringed in purple and yellow and his nose was swollen across the bridge. As he pulled the handle on Villa's door, the blue bag holding the *Times* fell and landed on the slate threshold. The big guy looked at it, then he walked away, his back to me as I stood, exposed, on Third.

As I backpedaled toward the diner, he scuttled awkwardly as he waited for cars to pass, and then he lumbered across the avenue, dug for his keys and jumped in a tow truck that once had been fire-engine red. He kicked over the heavy motor and pulled away from the curb. I caught a good glimpse: That nose looked like it had given him some trouble. Good.

He hung his left arm out of the truck as if to signal he was going to cut across Third. But the light was about to change and he stopped, staying on the east side. His big hand came to rest on the side of the truck, where painted lettering said AB TOWING AND REPAIR.

When he looked to his rearview, I left the diner and went south, away from the truck, and kept moving until I saw a cab come to a stop on the other side of 89th. I trotted to it and nodded at the driver who, without looking at me, acknowledged I was going to jump in. Holding open the driver's-side back door, I waited as a pert brunette, bundled in a chunky turtleneck under a long wool coat, gathered her change and stepped into the whipping crosstown wind.

"Oooh," she moaned as she shivered and looked at me for sympathy.

I nodded politely and squeezed by to ease into the cab as the light went to green.

The driver, a black man with almond-shaped eyes who might've been all of 25 years old, punched the meter and peered without expression into the rearview.

"A tow truck just hung a left at 91st," I told him. "We want to follow it."

We caught up at Lex and 89th, then fell in right behind it as the big guy had to stop to let midmorning jaywalkers, fresh from the 86th Street subway station, amble by.

"Don't let him know," I said.

The driver sighed as if bored, then gunned it, passing the tow truck. He pulled to a stop by a hydrant in the middle of the southbound avenue between 83rd and 84th.

He waited until the big guy made it to 82nd, then left the fire pump and fell in behind a frog-green VW Beetle. I could see the tow truck's hook over the little car's roof.

He'd done this before.

"I apologize," I said.

The clever driver tried to conceal his smile as torrents of yellow cabs went by us.

————

The big guy with the bruised nose made a right at 49th. He wasn't pushing it hard.

"He's going to 45th and way west," I said.

We both caught the red at Park. Limos were stacked side by side in front of the Waldorf; huge U.S. and Japanese flags flapped aggressively above the avenue. We were deep in the glass-and-steel jungle now, small amid the prominent towers.

At this rate, he was going to run into Rockefeller Center. That meant a left on Fifth, waiting for the school kids wading from NBC toward St. Patrick's.

We pulled away and got onto Fifth Avenue, moving from shadows to bright sunlight. At 45th, he headed to the west side. I knew we'd run into crowds of eager tourists, delivery vans and messengers on bikes as they darted recklessly through traffic.

"This man does not know midtown," the driver said in a soft voice.

Twenty-five minutes later, we arrived at Eighth Avenue, rolling under pulsing red neon arrows for parking garages and Broadway marquees, dark now but on call for tonight's curtain. I could've walked from 45th and Fifth to the Avellaneda in less time, but time wasn't what was important. The big guy didn't seem to know we'd been on his ass for more than three miles.

When the light changed, the tow truck went past the Aladdin Hotel and, to my surprise, Majorelle's theater. It continued to Ninth, went left, then pulled in front of a deli.

"Stay on 45th," I told the cab driver, "then pull over."

We pushed past the white, triangular marquee of a Seventh-Day Adventist church and eased next to a row of old, unkempt brownstones. Lids of plastic garbage cans littered the sidewalk, tossed aside by the wind. A page from a tabloid was caught in a puddle.

"He got out," the driver said. "He's going east."

"Do me a favor," I told him as I turned around. "Stay here for a minute or so."

I sat in the heated cab and watched through the rear window as the big guy, hands buried in the pockets of his dark slacks, crossed Ninth and trudged toward the center of the block, pounding his work shoes through standing water, past bits of swirling debris.

"See? He's going into the theater," I said.

The driver was using the sideview mirror. "Yes he is."

We both watched as he waited for the buzzer to open the front door of the Avellaneda.

"Let's stay with this for a while," I suggested.

He didn't reply.

"Go to Tenth, then let's come around and hang on 45th," I said. "On the west side of Eighth, but up the block."

The cabbie threw it back into drive. We left the curb.


The theater door of the Avellaneda swung open 28 minutes later and the big guy emerged.

As the tow-truck driver went toward Ninth, the cabbie asked me if I wanted to move on to follow him.

"No, I got enough," I replied.

He gave me a quizzical expression, raising his shoulders, bringing his eyebrows over his dark eyes.

I said, "What do think that man just did?"

"I couldn't say."

"He's troubled, right? Looking over his shoulder . . ."

"I guess. Yeah."

"But he doesn't look like he just smacked someone around," I said. "He looks like he had a conversation. Nothing more."

The cabbie agreed.

I gave him two twenties and told him to keep the change.


This time Majorelle didn't wait for me at the bottom of the long, steep stairwell.

When I entered the theater, he was again in one of the seats, a few rows closer to the lip of the stage. Now the curtain was drawn, closing the subway station behind crushed velvet.

"Your name is Terry Orr," he said as I began walking toward him, wondering if I'd find myself where the big guy had sat.

Majorelle wasn't wearing a djellaba now, but he still had on his curious hat. A long, black sleeveless sweater covered a thin black turtleneck.

He had the heat on high, and yet, as I drew closer, I saw he shivered.

"And yours is Ahmed Hassan," I said. "And you just had a visit from your old pal, Alfie Bascomb."

As I eased into the aisle behind him, I saw he had a thick wool blanket on his lap.

"Do I have to pull that?"

He moved his head from side to side. "I prefer that you do not."

His skin still bore a dull yellow pallor and the skin on his flat lips was drawn and dry.

As I sat, he asked, "How do you know Alfie?"

I kept still. I'd taken a guess on the AB in AB TOWING AND REPAIR. It wasn't a long stretch: His jacket down at the D.A.'s said he liked to play rough. Someone brought him in to beat me into scurrying home.

"You ought to cast yourself in one of these," I said, gesturing toward the curtain that hid the stage. "You had me fooled, playing innocent: 'That was you?' You knew Bascomb tried to take me apart."

"I did not."

"The murder of Asher Glatzer," I began as I settled into the seat, "you, Sixto, Bascomb, you ripped off Glatzer and you killed him to do it."

"I remind you that the police think differently, Terry Orr," he said softly.

"Let's forget about what the police think."

"What the police think has made all the difference."

I said, nodding, "All right, I'll take that for what it is: You were involved."

"I was involved in nothing."

"And now she's gone," I said. "You needed to be sure her secrets went with her."

"Sonia wanted to be an actress," he said tiredly.

"Yes, I know. You only knew her from her correspondence," I said. "You forget you went to DeWitt Clinton with her. That she dated your friend Luis Sixto."

"By the time Luis was dating Sonia I was working at the Broadhurst Theater, removing chewing gum from the bottoms of seats, running for coffee . . ." He wheezed as he sighed. "I am not a criminal. I resent . . . I resent your implication."

"Loitering. Sniffing a little airplane glue. Shoplifting," I recounted. "You were a good boy, all right."

"I made something of myself," he said, evincing as much pride as he could muster.

"So did Bascomb. He's got his own business too."

Exasperated but unable to protest, he merely shook his head. "This is much more than a business."

He was right, of course, but now was not the time for consolation.

"And what about Sixto?"

"Gone."

"With the diamonds?"

"Perhaps, but I do not know where he is," Hassan said.

"So we'll agree there were diamonds and Sixto made off with them. Is that right?"

He said, wistfully, "*If* there were diamonds . . ."

"Sixto cashed in and took off. But not before setting you and Bascomb up well enough so you'd keep your mouths shut."

Slowly, he closed his eyes and, with a quiet groan, he turned his back to me.

I waited, then stood and walked onto the carpet to face him.

"Mr. Hassan, can it be that all this, the Avellaneda, is because Asher Glatzer was killed and Sonia Salgado took the fall?"

He kept his eyes closed, but he ran his spotted, skeleton-like hand along the side of his black collar.

"Sonia gets to spend thirty years in prison so you can have this," I repeated. "But it's not enough. She has to die, too?"

He looked at me, holding me the best he could with his rheumy eyes. "Don't be a hypocrite, Terry Orr," he said sharply. "Don't you now play the innocent."

He lifted his hand from atop the coarse blanket and pointed at me.

"It is you who should be on the stage," he said.

"I'm here for the truth, Mr. Hassan."

He stared at me and, slowly, deliberately, he smiled. "You are here because you were sent by your friends in the police to pressure Sonia," he said. "When she could not tell you what you wish to know, you killed her."

I started to reply, to wave off his outlandish accusation.

But I saw that he was serious. He nodded knowingly, as if the secret he revealed not only halted all discussion of Sonia's death, but explained all that had happened 30 years ago and earlier this week.

"Who in the name of Christ told you that?" I snorted. My voice rose in disbelief.

"This I know," he said, nodding still. "You were sent to Sonia by the police, the Mangionellas, to do their work. You failed, it seems. Because here you are. Here you stand, with your lies, your manipulation."

"The Mangos sent me to kill Sonia?"

"You know that is correct."

"Old man," I said, "you are cracked."

He turned.

I walked into the aisle in front of him, my back to the curtain that shielded the stage.

"One, I am no killer," I said. "Two, I work for nobody but myself."

"Oh, dear man, you have forgotten Sonia's mother, which was your story. . . ."

"What I do I do for me," I repeated. "When I help someone it is for me. For mine. Is that clear?"

"As you say," he replied, as if bored now.

I nodded. "As I say."

Hassan eased himself to the back of the chair. "You were counting, Terry Orr."

"The autopsy report will show I arrived at Sonia's after she was dead."

"Returned, perhaps. Not arrived."

The debate had given him a boost, and Hassan was showing the wit and bite that the impresario Majorelle must have had before the cancer had taken hold. With what he thought was truth on his side, he clearly enjoyed the interplay.

"Ask the cops," I told him.

"The cops who know the Mangionellas."

"And how do you know the Mangos, Mr. Hassan?"

"If you had only arrived before Alfie," he said, "I would have known none of this."

"If he told you I killed Sonia, your friend Alfie Bascomb is full of shit."

"Now you are here to do precisely what, Terry Orr? To kill me?" he asked bitterly, defiantly. "You will be killing a dead man."

"No. What I want you to do is tell me the truth about Sonia, Glatzer, the diamonds."

"You know the truth. Sonia robbed Glatzer. Did she kill him? For the police, for the world, the answer is yes. Did she take diamonds? She said she did not." He smiled. "No one with six hundred thousand dollars goes to prison in America, Mr. Terry Orr, friend of the police, seeker of truth."

"She wanted to be an actress and you were going to help her," I led.

"That is not unbelievable."

"If she kept quiet for thirty years . . ."

"That is," he said.

"Did you see her since her release?"

"No. I tell you what I told Alfie and the police: I did not see her."

"You didn't see her," I repeated, "but you sent her books in prison, encouraged her—"

"Why not?"

"Why?"

"You ask me to explain why I chose to be kind?" he replied.

"Absolutely," I said. "A few books, some encouragement. The least you could do in exchange for thirty years and a cut of the six hundred thousand, the cash to get this place up and running."

"That is the second time you said this," Hassan replied sharply. "The Gertrudis Gómez de Avellaneda Theater owes it existence to no one. No one but Safi Majorelle."

"Yes, Safi Majorelle. Very clever. But you play your audience cheap. I mean, did you think no one who came here would know Jacques Majorelle? The Majorelle Gardens? It's not very far to Marrakesh from Argana, is it?"

"Once you cross Tizi Maachou," he said cryptically.

"When this—"

"Thorough research, Terry Orr. Congratulations."

"When this is done with," I continued, "when we know what happened with Sonia, with the diamonds, with Glatzer, all anyone will remember about you is that you helped kill a good man, a family man, so you could have a place to put on your plays."

He waved at me. "If that is what—"

"You're dying, Mr. Hassan," I interrupted, "and your legacy is on your mind. You want it to be this great theater you've built, this home for Cuban writers, Latin writers. And maybe it ought to be. But it's going to be this: You helped kill Asher Glatzer and ruined the life of a girl who trusted you. And you profited from that. This good place, Mr. Hassan, you built it on blood."

Hassan reacted as if I had slapped him, opening his eyes wide, then stiffening. The sick man, suddenly weak again, tried to draw himself up tall, to call on his self-regard to give him strength. But he could not.

"Who killed Sonia?" I asked rhetorically. "Me? No. You? No, but we're a lot closer to it now, aren't we?"

He looked at the velvet curtain. "I don't know . . . I don't know who killed Sonia, if it is not you," he said quietly.

"Bascomb lies."

"Alfie cannot." He slowly lifted the blanket from his lap and lay it over the back of the seat in front of him. "On his own, Alfie cannot think of a lie. He was never creative."

"Past tense," I commented. "You said 'was never' . . ."

"Perhaps he has changed," Hassan replied. "It has been a very long time."

"So where does it come from, this wild tale?"

He shrugged, then he hoisted himself from the seat. To steady himself, he paused for a moment, his bony hands on the arch of the seat. He closed his eyes and he trembled, as if suddenly stung with pain.

"You haven't seen Bascomb for years," I led.

He didn't reply.

"Sonia is dead and now Bascomb visits you."

He nodded.

I waited. Then I asked, "Is Sixto here? Has he returned?"

He looked at me. "Luis Sixto is no more."

Moving sideways, Hassan inched his way into the carpeted aisle.

"And the Mangos. Have any of them visited you?"

The steep pitch of the aisle as it sloped toward the stage caused him to lose his balance and he grabbed at me. I caught his frail arm, then held him by the wrist, the shoulder, until he was stable.

"I do not know the Mangionellas," he replied. "I never did."

I stepped back and watched him teeter slowly down the aisle, his hand on the black wall.

I could feel the heat from the steam pipes.

"I tried to be kind," he said as he reached a door to the right of the stage. He turned to me. "What happened . . . I was not involved. Not thirty years ago, not now."

I looked at him. He was groping for an exit line.

"I have been a good man," he said finally.

**11**

I half-expected the young cabbie with the dark, memorable eyes to be perched up by the Marriott, his off-duty sign stubbornly aglow to turn away the eager or the exasperated caught in the discouraging task of flagging a taxi in the booming heart of Times Square.

Or maybe McDowell would be outside the Aladdin Hotel, behind the wheel of a black Ford, nightstick at the ready, his ruddy face made redder by memories of the ass-blistering that Tommy the Cop gave him echoing above the radio blare.

Alfie Bascomb? Not yet, not again.

I went toward Seventh.

And I started south, moving more purposefully than the crawling crowd of wide-eyed yet cautious tourists around me, though without the scowl of a typical New Yorker caught behind a crawling crowd, some of whom had traveled 1,000 miles to stare up at a giant TV that was showing the same thing they could see at home. As I passed Father and Sons Shoes, I stopped short to avoid bashing into a stout, silver-haired woman with oversized glasses who, for some inexplicable reason, had decided to open her handbag and withdraw her wallet. Then

I noticed a young man on the island that separated Broadway and Seventh who had pulled down his video camera to focus in on the handbag lady. With all there is to shoot here in the new electronic circus, in Tokyo West— giant stock symbols swirling overhead and underfoot, reflected in murky puddles; billboards of perfect models, sullen in fresh underwear; familiar labels and slogans on rippling banners affixed to the faces of the towers and buildings, on moving billboards mounted on flatbed trucks; flashing, dazzling lights; manipulation—and he decides to videotape a woman—

She withdrew a snapshot, the kind they take at Sears, at elementary schools, and held it high for the camera.

"We're thinking of you, Wendell," she shouted. "Happy birthday, sweetheart."

She held it high until the man on the island held up his thumb, turned the bill of his baseball cap to the front and started across Broadway, camera at his side.

She looked up at me as she tucked the photo back into her wallet.

"My grandson," she smiled. She wore a red, white and blue ribbon on her green, fuzzy-collared coat.

"And him?" I asked, gesturing with my head toward the young man with the video camera and the NY Fire Department logo on his hat.

"The other one," she said as she snapped the clasp of her bag.


The April sun had returned, but I lost its rays as I moved under a block-long construction scaffold in Chelsea.

I hadn't worked it out yet. Bascomb resurfaced to visit an old friend. The first time, he waited near the friend's theater, then came at me with a wrench to leave me splayed in a pool of blood that would've run to the stage door. The next time he told his friend I'd been hired to kill Sonia. In between, he called on Danny Villa, counselor to the disenfranchised, media star.

Resurfaced? No, he'd been running a junkyard in Queens. He probably advertised under his own name in *Newsday*.

And Bascomb had told Hassan it was Tommy Mango who hired me.

Actually, Hassan hadn't specified which Mango. Maybe it was old man Ernie. Maybe he was the one who had resurfaced. Maybe Tommy didn't know.

Yeah. Sure.

"I do not know the Mangionellas," Hassan had said. "I never did."

Had he confirmed that Sixto knew the old man? Or was he telling me Bascomb knew Tommy?

Jimmy knew Bascomb had come at me.

Christ. My head was spinning.

I needed paper, a pencil, a desk. I needed to work it out, to look it over, to ruminate.

Addison once said, "You're best in a library, Terry. In front of a computer screen. Or playing ball, banging under the boards. But putting that together, young man, isn't going to make you a cop."

I told him he was wrong. A man can develop instincts, intuition.

Back at the Avellaneda, I didn't even bother to look behind the curtain. Who was hiding there, crouched behind velvet on the wood-and-Styrofoam subway platform?

McDowell? He would've stumbled, kicked over the scenery.

Sixto? Like Leroux's Erik the Opera Ghost, hiding in the dank sub-basement of a small theater, struggling—

No.

Other ghosts? Like who?


I closed the door behind me, and as I entered the kitchen, I heard voices from the living room.

I hesitated.

My daughter's manuscript was back on the table. It hadn't been there this morning when we'd left the house.

"Mr. Orr . . ." She doesn't usually greet me. But she didn't sound alarmed.

"I'll be right there, Mrs. Maoli," I shouted.

I hung my jacket on the back of Bella's chair and went to grab a bottle of Badoit from the refrigerator. I took a drink as I passed through the brick alcove.

Mrs. Maoli was sitting on the sofa, facing me. Next to her was Dorotea Salgado, pink tissues in her hands as they rested in the lap of her black-and-burgundy dress. She had been crying and so had our housekeeper.

"Mrs. Salgado," I said.

"She apologizes, Mr. Orr," Mrs. Maoli replied quickly, as she dabbed at her own red nose with a man's handkerchief. "She did not want to lie."

"The newspaper," Dorotea Salgado began, her accent a faint trace, "it said you help children. And Natalia said also."

"She is ill, Mr. Orr."

"You are?"

Mrs. Salgado nodded sadly, solemnly. As she bent her head to avert her eyes, I looked at Mrs. Maoli, who discreetly touched her temple, then slowly shook her head.

Looking up at me, Mrs. Salgado whispered, "I *am* sorry."

"No, I understand," I said, "but I couldn't reach you."

"Mr. Orr," Mrs. Maoli said. "Her daughter . . ."

"Of course," I replied. When I came across the body in the St. Mark's Place apartment, Dorotea Salgado had found her Sonia. As I looked at her, I knew she would have preferred not to. "I'm very sorry."

She had on black shoes as fashionable as her finances would allow. Mrs. Maoli wore her customary support hose and clogs.

"My Sonia . . ." She began to weep.

As Mrs. Salgado dabbed her brimming eyes with the tissues, I silently told Mrs. Maoli that I wanted to speak to her friend.

"I will make coffee, Dorotea," she said, nodding to me as she pushed off the soft cushions.

As Mrs. Maoli left the living room, I crossed over to where she'd been seated.

Mrs. Salgado looked at me and absently tugged at the black scarf she had pinned to her dress with a brooch. I put the bottle of water on the coffee table, next to the rented *Hamlet* DVD.

"Mrs. Salgado," I said, turning to her, "I wonder if you're up to answering a few questions."

"Natalia says you will find who killed my Sonia. Do you have ideas?"

"Well, I can tell you I believe now that your daughter did not kill Asher Glatzer."

"Yes," she said hesitantly.

"And I believe whoever . . . Well, this has to do with what happened back then."

"I am sure," she said, nodding. She tucked the tissue under the buttons of her long sleeve.

"Tell me about the police. When did they notify you?"

"Tuesday," she said. "At the showroom. When I saw them . . ." Remembering, she started to cry, but fought hard to hold it back. Tears welled, then tumbled onto her face. She ran her fingers along her cheek. "I saw her body. They took me to the medical examiner's office."

"Do you remember the name of the policeman who came to see you?"

"No," she said, "but he was, what is the word?" She suddenly snapped her fingers. "I don't know the word in English. Yes, compact. Strong, but he was not too tall."

"Silver hair?"

"Yes."

"Mangionella."

"Perhaps," she said. "I believe so."

Tommy the Cop goes to Union Square. "Did you mention me?"

"I didn't, no."

"Why not?"

"Oh," she sighed, "I was not thinking. I only answered his questions."

"Did you tell him you were looking for her?"

"No. Is it important?"

"It's probably best if we said the same thing. And I told him you hired me," I said. "Did he ask you when was the last time you spoke to her?"

"Yes. Not for many years. I said this."

"I imagine he asked you about enemies. . . ."

"Yes."

"And I imagine you told him what you told me, that Sonia didn't kill Asher Glatzer."

"Yes, I did."

"What did he say?" I asked.

"It was not important to him."

"He said that?"

"No," she replied, "but I know. I saw."

I took a sip of the sparkling water.

I said, "I guess I still don't understand why you wanted to see her now."

She let out a long breath. "What Natalia said is so," she said finally, without explanation. "I am not well."

"And you didn't want to tell her while she was in Bedford Hills?"

She said, "I only know then for a few weeks. Maybe two months."

"Mrs. Salgado . . ."

"I have the Alzheimer's, Mr. Orr."

"Oh." I sat back. "I see."

She paused, groping for words. "It is coming—"

"Yes, progressing," I said. "Are you taking medication?"

"Yes," she replied.

She reached into her purse and withdrew a small orange pill container. She handed it to me.

Tacrine, the label said. Four times a day, 10 milligrams.

"And you wanted to see her—"

"When we both could understand, yes," she said, as she returned the container to her purse.

"To make peace."

"It could be possible." She stopped, closed her eyes tight. "It could have been possible." She opened her eyes and looked at me. "We could have helped each other."

I nodded.

"And now I want to help her while I can."

I kept quiet. The old woman had tried a different approach in the diner and she'd been lying. She might be telling the truth now, but I'd check out the Tacrine online. If it wasn't indicated for early-stage Alzheimer's, she'd have other questions to answer.

But I believed her now; or I was starting to. If she'd lied, she'd given me a lot of data to play with. I had her address from the pill jar—she lived up in Morningside Heights, about a six-mile subway ride to Union Square— and she knew I could get her work address from Mango.

"You met Mrs. Maoli," I said. "A coincidence?"

"She became my friend. But yes. We talk about your daughter. In the market. I said to her about Sonia."

"She told you I was a private investigator?"

"She said you would help." She tilted her head. "But I have made trouble for you."

"No."

"Your eye . . ."

I said, "It happens."

"And the police?"

"They know I wasn't there," I replied. "Until after."

The rich scent of coffee wafted toward us. I heard Mrs. Maoli at work in the kitchen: the clatter of cups, saucers, spoons; the bustle of service. She'd had a busy morning: resurrecting Bella's manuscript, cleaning up the modest disarray left by my daughter's little clique. Even my copy of *Arrowsmith* was neatly in place and not on the floor, where it had fallen once again as I'd dozed off on the sofa the night before.

"Mrs. Salgado, does the name Luis Sixto mean anything to you?"

"Yes. Oh, yes," she said, wagging a finger at me. "He is the one who changed my Sonia. She was a good girl."

"After Sonia was arrested, did you ever hear from him?"

"No."

"Not once," I led, "in any way? A letter, postcard . . ."

"It was not true," she said, as she shook her head. "She was not his girlfriend. I know this. She was too young for that."

"I understand."

"But this Sixto was not good. I told Sonia."

"What did she say?"

She held up her hands. "She had changed."

"So she continued to see him . . ."

She nodded her reply. "But not in that way," she added, defensively.

"Did she have other friends?"

"The one who was her true friend was the Arab boy."

"Ahmed Hassan."

"Yes. He was a funny boy. Very lively. He wanted to be an actor and my Sonia wanted to be an actress."

"Did Hassan contact you after Sonia went to jail?"

"In the beginning, yes. I think he was different. He came to my house."

I felt a twinge in my knee and rubbed it. Mrs. Salgado looked at my jeans, then turned her eyes back to me.

"You have hurt yourself?"

I shook my head. "Old injury."

She pointed to my eye. "Old one, new one," she said, smiling.


Mrs. Maoli was carefully pouring the espresso into small white cups.

"None for me," I said as I entered the kitchen.

She removed a cup and saucer from the floral tray.

On the counter between the sink and the stove was a small box from a bakery on Bleecker, on the cusp between Little Italy and the West Village.

"You knew she was coming." She nodded, but didn't turn toward me. "How?"

She filled a second cup. "Because I ask her."

"She called?"

"I find her," she said curtly.

"You found her? Where?"

"At the cemetery. Yesterday."

"The funeral. Right."

Pulling aside the thin red-and-white string, she opened the box and removed bow-tie cookies dusted with powdered sugar.

"Mrs. Maoli . . ."

She didn't reply and continued to place cookies on a small plate.

"Mrs. Maoli."

She lifted the tray and turned.

"What's on your mind?" I asked.

She made a face, pressing her lips together and inverting a smile, creating an expression that purported to show apathy, but instead said she was vaguely displeased.

I reached over and took the tray by the handles and slid it onto the kitchen table. Deep-brown coffee rippled in the tiny cups.

"You don't like that I have to ask your friend those questions?" I suggested.

"You have to," she said, shrugging.

"What is it?" I reached over and took a cookie.

"Your friend, the policeman. Mangionella." Her voice dripped with scorn. "He calls you today. He says you know what it is about. I ask and he says you are helping him. To find out who killed Sonia."

"And?"

"So you are not trying to help Dorotea."

"Why isn't it possible to help Mango *and* Dorotea?"

"You know," she said. "You know."

I could not be impatient with this small woman who stood before me, this surrogate grandmother to my daughter, this source of continuity, of tenderness, for our little family.

"You think he's against Dorotea?"

"He is like the father: *un ladro.* A thief who helps no one, only himself."

"A thief? What does he steal? What has he stolen?"

"He's no good. *Sporcato e corrotto. E piccolo.*"

She was wrong. There's nothing small about 600K in diamonds.

"And how do you know this?" I asked.

"Ah," she exclaimed, waving her hand at me in dismissal. "Everyone knows this. Everyone in Little Italy. You forget," she added, "I knew the mother."

"Rosa."

"Rosa. They made her sick. All of them."

"Mrs. Maoli . . ."

"And you know this. That they are not good people. The men."

"I've heard it said—"

"But the son is your friend," she charged.

She's at least a foot shorter than I am, but, as resentment simmered to anger, she now controlled the room.

"He's not my friend. He's not *not* my friend. He's a cop. He's helped. I found the body and I called him. That's it."

" 'That's it.' But nobody can say who kills Sonia."

"No," I sighed, "not yet."

"I don't know why you don't call the good one. Addison."

"He works uptown—"

"Him, you don't like and he is your friend. He is thinking about your wife and—"

I was slowly shaking my head. *"Basta, signora. Prego,"* I said softly, my eyes closed. "Don't mention her. Don't mention— You can't. *Per favore, dire nient'altro."*

Knowing she had violated an unspoken trust, she stopped, and as the anger dropped from her plump face, she stepped back and looked away before slowly turning to me. *"Io sono spiacente."*

*"Io so,"* I nodded, *"Io so.* You want to help your friend."

"I'm sorry, Mr. Orr," she repeated. "I don't wish to hurt you."

"Forget it," I said. "Go have coffee with Dorotea. It's all right."

She nodded and lifted the tray. The cookies shifted on the plate.

I stepped aside to let her pass.

"Mr. Orr."

I turned to face her. Marina's pale limestone cliffs were visible over her shoulder.

"Don't forget to read the book of your daughter," she said. "Gabriella, she worries."

A moment later, I heard the clatter of small spoons stirring espresso.

## 12

I hailed a cab outside the video store after dropping off Bella's *Hamlet.* "If you wouldn't mind, Dad . . ."

A dance tonight at Walt Whitman; a rave, it's called. A theme, even: "The Body Electric." Not bad. "Hokey," Bella says, frowning. A rave requires preparation, apparently: silver-and-purple glitter around the eyes. And a pre-event warmup: pounding, pulsing, throbbing music that had all the charm of the warning klaxons at a power plant. It started before dinner began. My protest drew a smirk, but we ate to Schubert's Fantasie in F minor for two pianos.

Then the electronica boom tick-pulse, whir-whirl, click-click returned, grating from two rooms away.

"Good-bye," I shouted. Dishes away; damp checkerboard towel on the faucet.

She had her laptop hooked up to the TV speakers. Windows rattled, mortar chips between bricks fell to the floor. (Not really.)

"Good-bye," I screamed. I understood now why Eva Figueroa let them get ready here.

Bella and little Glo-Bug bounded into the kitchen. My daughter looked like a teenager all set to attend Mardi Gras, Glo-Bug like a hood ornament. I glanced at their fingernails: purple, suddenly four inches long. Baby talons.

Bella wore black Converse sneakers. High-tops.

"You're dressed right," Bella said approvingly. "Finally."

I had on a black sweatshirt under my peacoat, the hood hanging in back over the collar, and thick gray cords.

I had Leo's .38 in the sweatshirt pouch.

"Gloria, tell your Mom I said thanks, OK?" I said as I hooked the cell phone to my belt.

Eva was chaperoning the rave. I'd be covered until midnight.

"Why are you going to Queens?" Bella asked.

The music was relentless. Somewhere, Robert Moog cringed.

"I told you," I said. "I've got to talk to a guy."

"In the auto graveyards."

"In the auto graveyards."

"I think," she said, "you're going to buy a car."

Glo-Bug nodded. Leo and Glo-Bug want me to buy a car. Bella does, too. I guess I don't have a choice.

"I'm not buying a car."

The scent of Mrs. Maoli's chicken cacciatore, particularly splendid tonight, remained pungent, alluring.

"If you do," Bella pressed, "remember I'll be driving in three years."

I smiled. "Have fun. Rave well," I said as I went for the front door, *Hamlet* tucked under my arm.

"You got gloves?"

I tapped my coat pockets. "Gloves. Yes."


Now, as the cabbie slid his two right-side wheels around a death turn that took us to the Triborough Bridge, I ran my hands over the pockets again. Gloves.

The night sky was a deep indigo, with a sprinkling of stars beyond thin, translucent clouds.

"You don't get many people go to Shea by taxi," said Edwin Salida, cabbie. The meter was already at $18.50. $19.25. "Limos, maybe, for these fuckin' guys, they pay $65 a ticket. Them."

We bumped hard over a swelling in the blacktop. My hatless head barely missed the dome light. My hair bristled.

"Or the number seven, out of midtown," the cabbie amended, as I settled back into the vinyl seat.

Signs on the Grand Central Parkway warned of La Guardia up ahead. Cars started drifting right.

"I was here last year. The first game after, you know? When Liza sang 'New York, New York,' Diana Ross, *mi hombre* Marc Anthony, and Piazza hit the home run," Salida said.

"I saw it on the news." Bella was sitting on the hotel-room floor, working her new journal, clipping and pasting, cataloging with a new set of coloring pencils, and I was up on the bed, on my stomach, legs out, my chin and forearms on a small mound of pillows. When Mike Piazza hit the ball, the crowd at Shea let out a cheer unlike any I've ever heard. More than a cry of joy, it was a spontaneous burst of unbridled relief, a collective explosion in which something familiar and elemental triumphed over the sudden sense of uncertainty and fear that gripped New York. It was as if Piazza's home run told the fans that everything could be all right again, that the old feelings, all the old things, would someday return and be all they were before.

"Did you see that?" I said.

Short on clothes, Bella was lounging in one of my wrinkled blue Oxfords. She started to cry, and I did too.

After a minute, as the crowd continued to roar, I said, "When you were a baby, you would sit on my back when we watched TV."

"I'm too big," she said as she sniffled.

"We could hold hands. . . ."

"Who they playing?" Salida, I noticed, had an unusually large head and the beginning of a bald spot, no bigger than a silver dollar now, but threatening to expand to monk-like dimensions before the decade closed.

He repeated, "Who they playing?"

"I don't know," I said.

He shook his head. "You go to the game you don't know who's playing?"

"I like a good surprise," I told him.

I got Salida to let me out on Northern Boulevard, past Shea, and with the bright lights that rimmed the stadium to my back, I walked east to 127th Street. The Yellow Pages on *Yahoo!* told me that AB Towing and Repair was at 1213 35th Avenue. Which could've been right near Shea, on Flushing Bay or way over at the edge of Rego Park. I thought I'd start out in the area close to the stadium, then circle back toward the water, where the harsh wind blew, and I'd do it with my head up. A rough place here: dark, grease-stained alleys walked by hard men who had to hustle to apply their skills, to compete with neighbors of circumstance who might be friends, to fight off wise guys who wanted to muscle in.

Made uneven by the thick roots of trees and the abuse of heavy equipment, the sidewalk beneath the Northern Boulevard overpass jutted and sank, peaked and sagged. As I went by a car wash that had shut down for the night, my shoes crackling on the broken glass that had been shoved toward the gutter, a pink van bearing the legend FORDHAM BEAUTY SUPPLY drove by quickly, confidently, and turned right up ahead, as the road bent away from the underpass. Behind me, faint cries, a muffled roar. For now, the home team was doing all right.

I went south on 127th toward 35th Avenue.

Auto graveyard, I realized, wasn't really an apt name for this part of the strip. While there were short stacks of flattened auto bodies, racks of mismatched doors, transmissions standing as sentries in orderly rows behind barbed fences and corrugated sheet metal, 34th Avenue was a long block buzzing with scores of services to bring cars back to life: signs advertised rebuilt engines, electrical systems, door regulators, steering columns, manyforts. (Manyforts? Manifolds, maybe.) Men in soiled unis not unlike the one Bascomb wore were still at work, pulling shattered windshields, carrying bulky batteries, hosing down the clumps of oily soil around mottled sidewalks in front of the shops.

Logic dictated that AB Towing and Repair was still open and boss Bascomb would be on hand.

I looked west as I shuffled in place to ward off the wind from Flushing Bay. At the far end of the street, orange sparks rose like fireflies from the flames at the bottom of a charred garbage can. Workers appeared, disappeared: Ignoring flickering stars, they moved with intent as they went back into the shops. A lean man in a brown hat with earflaps rolled a tire toward an open bay.

I heard the roar of a jet plane and looked up to see its silver underbelly. It seemed no farther away than the end of the street, where old pallets burned. Its wheels were down, its landing gear ready for impact on a runway about two miles away.

I kept moving on 127th, walking past a multicolored yet somehow gray tower of crushed bodies. As I reached the corner, the lively, cluttered work areas scarred only by the effects of heavy labor suddenly gave way to a place that felt abandoned, abused. To my right, once-small cracks in the blacktop were now vast, odd-shaped potholes and craters worthy of the moon.

Bascomb's street was as eerily lifeless as 34th had been bustling with industry. Garage doors were locked and cars were parked behind gates and graffiti-stained cinderblocks. Fluttering tubes in the streetlamps cast unreliable light on the shredded mudflaps, soiled pizza boxes and crushed aluminum cans on the battered sidewalk, its concrete so thoroughly chipped away that a fire hydrant seemed suspended above ground level. As I stared at the empty street, at the translucent halo cast by the stadium lights in the distance, I heard a low, rattling noise to my left: a rat scurrying along the cinderblocks, over broken glass, sniffing, its long, pink tail slinking behind it as it padded on small paws.

Another plane thundered overhead. By the time I looked back down, the rat was lost in darkness.

I started down 35th, passing a pile of old, treadless tires that surrounded the corpse of a mid-'70s LeSabre, its front hood open, its brown body marked with handwritten yellow numbers, arrows and lines.

Up ahead, light from a window. As I drew closer, I saw it was a storefront diner, competition for the Stadium Deli a block over. Chubby's was its name, according to an old sign hung over its front door. It offered falafel, gyros, souvlaki. French fries. Tomatoes—Fresh! Hamburgers. Coke *and* Pepsi.

I listened to the wind, the rush of cars on Northern Boulevard, the sudden whirr of a hand tool from over on 34th.

Have to be the best souvlaki in Queens, in the five boroughs, from here to Athens, to make me come to this bombed-out hellhole of a block to eat.

A little bell attempted to ring when I pushed open the front door, but instead it made a dull, tired *ting*. It let out the same dead sound when I let the door close.

Chubby's had four red seats, cracked vinyl on tarnished silver bases, at a counter that was more for storage than service: flattened cartons that once held generic brands of pita bread and juice were stacked on its top. To the rear, beyond the round seats, were more crushed cartons tied with hemp, and a cigarette vending machine; on the business side of the counter, a griddle, a well for deep-frying and, under the small TV, a dried stake of gyro meat kept warm by orange-red coils. Near a tower of take-out containers, three pots of coffee sat warming on silver rings: Chubby's *raison d'être* at this time of night.

On the TV, the Mets were playing the Phillies. The Mets pitcher looked as if his ears were frozen to the sides of his head. In the dugout they wore parkas and ski masks.

Behind the glass counter that held boxes of Life Savers, gum and antacids, stood a tall, very thin black man who seemed to be approaching retirement age after a hard stretch. He had scar tissue above his eyes and a crude rip that ran from below his ear through the flecks of stubble toward his lips. He wore a soiled white apron over an oversized green-and-black flannel shirt that had a tear in its left sleeve. With his elbow on the cash register, his head cradled in the palm of his hand, he was either staring at the TV, planning to get back at the guy who sliced him years ago or reviewing what he'd done to end up stationed in the armpit of Queens behind an eye-level row of yellow mustard jars, ketchup bottles with crusted tops and a lifetime supply of cheap Louisiana hot sauce.

I took in the diner's scent and figured they changed the frying oil on Mondays. At least it was warm in here.

"I guess you're not Chubby," I said as I opened my coat. The man didn't move.

The license on the face of the cash register gave the address of the place as 12-12 35th Avenue. Which meant Bascomb's place should've been on the other side of the street.

I shifted to look out the front window and I saw a black door next to a wide steel gate that had been pulled tight to the splintered sidewalk and was held shut by a thick padlock.

"AB Towing over there?" I asked, pointing.

The man didn't answer.

"Excuse me," I said. "Is that—"

"I don't know what you want," he said tiredly. "But I ain't got it."

"Why not?"

"Man breaks in your window, your steering lock, busts up your bumper, your front end, it ain't my business." He still hadn't looked at me. "I heard it before."

"I've got no complaints," I told him. "I'm out here to talk."

"Yeah," he scoffed.

I didn't reply. The man was right. I was out here to talk, but I also came for payback. I was going to kick Bascomb's ass and I was going to like it.

"Will he be back tonight?"

"Man with a tow truck don't need no office."

I said, "What, he just sits on the highway and waits for triple-A to call?" He blinked.

"You mind if I hang here awhile?" I asked. "I'll order something."

"No need," he replied. "Go sit if you want."

I nursed a club soda for three innings. Bascomb didn't show and the thin man who wasn't Chubby stayed silent, mostly: Out at frigid Shea, one of the Phillies hitters took a hard, stingy fastball off his bare elbow. As he hopped and hollered in anguish, not-Chubby laughed.

Outside, a few cars rolled by, going slow to slip around the craters. I turned to watch.

"Forget it," the man said.

"Yeah?" The gyro meat on the stake hissed and spat.

"He do his office in the morning, then he go."

"What time?"

"Morning," he repeated.

I was about to ask him why he hadn't told me about Bascomb's office hours when I first came in, but I let it slide. He'd saved me the trouble of having to rent a car and have it break down on the Throgs Neck Bridge.

I took another sip of the flat, salt-laced club soda and decided to stretch my legs. As I swung around, accompanied by a metallic squeak from the springs beneath the seat, I saw a car ease to a stop in front of Bascomb's door.

The driver stepped out of the black Ford and into the dull light, onto the splintered sidewalk, his heavy shoes crunching loose cement.

McDowell, wearing a black stocking cap and, over a dark, long-sleeved sweatshirt, a navy-blue down vest.

"Cop," said the man behind the counter.

McDowell went through white headlight beams past the front of the car as, from the passenger's side, Jimmy Mango appeared. Mango watched as his brother's errand boy tugged the dented knob on Bascomb's black door.

Mango had to try for himself, and he nudged aside the taller, redheaded cop. Steam rose from his mouth as he muttered.

I watched through the thin frost on the diner's window as Jimmy Mango skipped past McDowell and tried in vain to lift Bascomb's locked gate.

Mango stood in the rays of the headlights. He wore a purple V-neck sweater, a gray T-shirt, black jeans and sneakers. Though he'd been out of the car for less than 30 seconds, he began to shudder in the cold.

McDowell said something that Mango discounted with a shake of the head and a condescending grimace. Mango gestured toward the door. Dutifully, McDowell went over and knocked, first rapping easily, then pounding with a flat palm.

When McDowell stopped his banging, Mango gave him a hard glare and I watched as the young cop waited to be told what to do next.

Jimmy Mango went back to the car. I could see him say "Fuck it," with a quick, desultory wave. He pulled the car door hard and I heard it bang and echo along the alleyway.

McDowell gave Bascomb's damaged knob one last pull, then returned to the driver's seat. He and Mango consulted briefly and then they ripped away, tires slipping on black mud. A moment later, the thin spiral of blue vapors they'd left behind wafted away.

"That it?" the man asked.

"More or less."

As I tossed a five-spot on the countertop, he answered my last question by telling me I could grab a cab at Shea. Livery drivers circled, he said, like carrion crows. He said that: like carrion crows.

I was home before the game ended. Out of curiosity, I watched the top of the ninth and the Mets' modest celebration near the pitcher's mound. I cut the TV before they were back in the clubhouse.

I called Julie and left a message on her machine at the D.A.'s.

I picked up *Arrowsmith,* fumbled through a long passage and, knowing I was cheating the story of Martin's frustrating plight with the Tozers, I put the book back on the coffee table.

I dug through the cabinets above the sink, then decided against making myself a cup of hot tea.

This house is empty when she's not home.

I thought this at 10:30 and again at 11:15.

*Nursery of Crime* was still on the table where Mrs. Maoli had placed it, its pages perfectly aligned.

I went back to my study and reviewed my notes in Word, with WNYC streaming through the tiny, tinny speakers.

Sixto, Hassan and Bascomb knew Sonia; old man Mango knew Sixto; and now the old man's son Tommy was trying to work the edges around Sonia's murder. And now Tommy wanted Bascomb. Brother Jimmy and McDowell were going to bring Bascomb where Tommy wanted him. Bascomb, who told Hassan I had killed Sonia.

Tommy knew it all: He knew who killed Sonia. And he didn't want it to circle back to his old man. He needed Bascomb, who ran with Sixto. Who might've been Sixto's muscle.

Who might've been the one who sliced Glatzer open.

Takes a strong man to drag a blade through another man, through thick muscle.

I heard the front door open. I heard Bella's voice.

She had been sweating and she'd had a good time. Look at that smile.

"Hey."

"My ears are ringing," she said as she tossed her fanny pack on the table. The glitter had run down to her cheeks. She sparkled.

"I'd better say good-night to Eva," I said. As I passed by, I helped my daughter wriggle out of her heavy coat and stuck it on the newel post. She wore a black, long-sleeved T-shirt with a big red star on its front. The shirt was soaked through.

When I opened the door, I saw neither Eva Figueroa nor little Glo-Bug. Instead, there was Daniel Wu.

"Hello, Mr. Orr," he said. The pudgy boy was on the sidewalk, by the frail tree, and he tilted back his head to look up at me.

Harrison was silent. The streetlights reflected on the damp cobblestone and I could hear the river run. On Greenwich, traffic rolled on: taxis, mostly; cars with Jersey plates, a 4 × 4. No military Jeeps, no backhoes on flatbeds. No black Ford easing to the curb, a redheaded cop at the wheel.

"Enjoy the dance, Daniel?"

"Oh, yes."

"You want to come in, warm up?" I asked. I was wearing red sweats cut off above the knee, loose sweat socks and the Oxford I'd had on all day. Its wrinkled tail hung free.

"No, I have a curfew," he smiled. "I have to go."

"OK," I said, turning to get my cold legs back inside.

"Good-night," he waved.

I stopped. "Hey, Daniel," I said, "where do you live?"

"Over on Walker." He pointed east.

"You want me to walk you home?"

"Oh, no. I'll be fine." He puffed up his chest under his black vinyl jacket. "I like to walk at night. You know, with my own thoughts."

My thought: This is some kid.

I said good-bye again, and off Daniel Wu went toward Walker Street, accompanied by what was inside his own head.

"No Mrs. Figueroa," I said, sealing the door.

"Gloria got sick. Dizzy."

My daughter had been escorted home from a party by a boy. A milestone? She danced over to the sink. "What kind of car did you buy?"

"No car," I said.

"Couldn't find anything?" She turned on the cold water and got her jelly-jar glass from a cupboard.

"Bella, I hope you plan to sleep your customary twelve hours tonight."

She took a long drink. Then she wiped her mouth on her black sleeve. "Why?"

"I'm out of here very early," I said.

"As long as you're back in time."

"For?"

*"Dad."*

"Kidding."

Another gulp. And she turned, drizzled dish-soap into the jelly jar, washed it and rinsed it and put it in the drainer to dry.

"Did you get a tuxedo?" she asked as she bounded around the table.

"I'm not wearing a tux, Bella."

"If he was winning the Nobel—"

"If Diddio wins the Nobel Prize, I'll wear a tux."

She went to the stairs.

"Bella, dry your hair before you get into bed."

"I'm going to take a shower," she replied. "I won't sleep now: too much energy. All that music, dancing. All of us in a big, perfect circle."

"Good time?"

"Great time." She smiled as I grabbed her coat to hang it up. "Thanks, Dad."

I nodded and watched as she went up the stairs. She was humming. A sweet voice, all over the place.

"Bella, don't open the door tomorrow for anybody."

She made the turn toward her room. I couldn't see her.

She shouted, "OK. I won't."

I'd leave a note for her. I'd stick it on the back of the front door.

Even if it's Tommy Mango, I'd write. Especially if it's Tommy Mango.

## 13

Back in black with Leo's .38 against my belt, I got to chilly 35th Avenue before six, before the planes blasted overhead, and in the silence, I posted up by the abandoned brown LeSabre. Hiding in plain sight, I was stationed on a sheet of old concrete that had been poured ineptly into a flat clump, surrounded by thick, ruddy mud coated with a thin sheen of ice. In the silver light of a cold morning, the street was no less coarse and unattractive: Huge potholes remained, and loose trash was everywhere, surrounded by oil slicks and black dirt. Every 10 minutes or so, a car would use 126th to make its way to Northern Boulevard or the Van Wyck. Otherwise, this part of Flushing was Saturday-morning quiet. Even Chubby's had yet to open its doors.

Bascomb rolled up the street at 6:50 and, as I ducked down behind the Buick, he pulled up in front of his shop. Leaving the motor of his tow truck idling, the lumbering big man with the swollen nose withdrew a key from his pocket and opened his front door. As he went inside, he shut the door behind him.

I came around the car carcass and moved toward Bascomb's shop.

When I reached the tow truck, I stuck my arm inside, cut the engine and took the key. Then I hit the horn.

I shifted quickly to the side of the door.

He was one step onto 35th when I hit him. A hard solid right to his sore, tender nose.

Bascomb stumbled backward and I came in after him. Before he could recover, I hit him again, a right cross to the left temple, and he was hurt. As he fell back against his desk, his arm smacked against a wire basket that held receipts and other paperwork. The sheets fluttered and fell.

I grabbed him by the collar of his work jacket and hit him a third time, again to the nose. Blood spurted: I'd probably broken it again.

"Listen, motherfucker," I told him, spittle dribbling into his face as I hovered over him. "I'm going to bust you up for coming at me, then you're going to tell me about Sonia."

I pushed his head hard onto the concrete floor.

The blood ran both ways down his cheeks. He tried to focus, but couldn't.

"It's me, you fuckin' loser," I said. "Terry Orr."

"Mango's man," he managed.

I had my knee on his chest now and I had my right hand cocked by my ear. "Don't feed me that shit," I said. "I'm not your friend Hassan."

"You're supposed to kill me," he said, his voice steadier. "Get it done."

"You. You and your fuckin' wrench. You're the killer."

"Fuck you," he barked.

I reached into my sweatshirt pouch and pulled the .38. I rammed the barrel against his nose.

He closed his eyes tight.

"Enough of this," I spit. "Enough jerking me around. You're going to tell me what went on and you're going to do it now, you piece of shit."

I jumped off. I felt good, I felt strong. Alive.

There was a red mark where the barrel of the gun had been jammed against his skin.

"Up," I said. "Park your ass in that seat and start talking."

Bascomb rolled over, pressed his big palms on the ground and wobbled to his feet, then dumped himself into the wooden chair.

"Go," I said, trying to catch my breath.

I leaned over and, with the gun, pushed a stack of paper towels toward him. He grabbed one and dabbed at his nose.

"Shit," he moaned.

"Don't complain," I said. "You're breathing. Unlike Sonia, your friend from DeWitt Clinton."

He tossed the red ball of paper on the floor.

The office was long and narrow and completely utilitarian: desk, coil-neck lamp, chair, paper, cup of pencils and pens spilled now on the desk, phone. Behind Bascomb was the entry to the bay where he stuck his truck when he had to. In the back of the room, an open door revealed a toilet and sink.

Another blood-soaked towel fell to the floor.

"I don't know why you're after me," Bascomb began, as much in pity as in defiance. "I've got no business with you."

"You came at me on forty-fifth Street," I said, "by the Avellaneda. I'd—"

"A job," he nodded. "Nothing personal."

"A job? For who?"

"Don't," he said with a smirk. "We've got the same boss. That's fact."

I shook my head. "I don't have a boss."

"You know who hired me to keep you away from Ahmed," he said plainly, still pressing a towel against the center of his face.

The gun was growing heavy in my hand and I shifted it, and I let my hand rest on my thigh. Bascomb eyed the gun as it moved.

"Start with that," I said.

"Jimmy," he said, "all right?"

"Not Tommy."

"Jimmy," he repeated.

"How did he know I was going to see Hassan?"

"He followed you. When you got to midtown, he let me know."

"Where were you?" I asked. "You're a disaster in midtown."

He frowned.

I told him I'd followed him yesterday.

"Driving in midtown," he mumbled. "But I came in on the Seven train. I was at Port Authority when he called."

"Why is Jimmy on me?"

"You don't listen. Jimmy says."

I lifted the gun. "What the fuck does that mean?"

He managed a crass smile. "I'd say you don't listen at all."

"So," I said, "you work for the Mangos. You do what?"

"Same as you," he replied.

I'd started to catch my breath and the red flame of my fury had started to die down. But I wasn't yet ready for riddles.

"You think I kill for the Mangos," I said. "So you—"

The phone on Bascomb's desk rang. I looked at it.

And he was on me: The big man came off the swivel chair fast and hard. He knocked me back and I hit the door frame.

Before I could raise the gun, he grabbed my right arm with his thick left hand and he banged it against the frame, then again, again. But I didn't let go and I got my left hand onto his slippery face and I pressed hard against his cracked nose. He stopped as if shocked, but quickly stepped back, shoved me and, when I spun on the door frame, drove a right deep into my kidney. I fell hard to my knees.

Bascomb ran out and I could hear him go for his truck. When he saw that I'd taken the key, he slammed the door shut.

I gasped for air as I rose. When I made it outside, Bascomb was running toward 126th.

I set off after him, jamming the gun back into my sweatshirt pouch.

He had a long lead on me as he turned left on 126th, moving toward the sun. I was having a hard time catching my breath and I was running awkwardly, without speed. When I reached 126th, I saw him. Despite his strange gait, he was at least two blocks ahead of me and on the other side of the long, wide street. I sucked hard, took in as much air as I could and ran faster, the gun jiggling against my belt.

Above us, a plane leaving LaGuardia fought to gain altitude, to rise toward the strips of cloud. Roaring as it rose, it ripped the uneasy silence.

Bascomb kept tilting to the right as he passed the gates that let the cars into Shea.

The big man surprised me. He moved well now, despite his bulk, his work boots. But I was drawing up on him as my legs found their rhythm, my sneakers pounding hard on the asphalt.

We were running through the vast lot, with its 25,000 or so empty lanes, cutting across faint yellow lines, careening past green Parks Department trash cans. Bascomb was now beyond the center-field side of the horseshoe-shaped stadium and I was coming up on him. To my right: the empty stadium and a splash of color from its orange, red and blue plastic seats, gone as fast as it appeared. Pale brick on the stadium façade. Small puddles on the blacktop and the bottom of Bascomb's boots. Flat silver light and I felt fine.

The tracks of the elevated 7 line hung over Roosevelt Avenue. Beyond that, more asphalt, more emptiness, fences. I knew the Arthur Ashe Tennis Center was on the other side of the wide avenue. The old World's Fair—the Unisphere, the Hall of Science. If Bascomb ran to the park, I'd have him.

I'd have him if he kept going toward Roosevelt Avenue: four lanes of traffic under the elevated train tracks. He'd have to stop until he could barrel across.

I was getting closer, closer.

Bascomb suddenly zigzagged to his left, toward spiral steps inside a circular chain-link fence. As he left the lifeless light and ran toward the stairs, I followed. If he was going to cross the avenue from above, avoiding the rush of traffic below, I'd catch him before he made it to Flushing Meadows. A straight run had turned into an endurance contest. I knew my body was ready for it. I doubted his was.

I went through the gate of the rusted fence and onto the cement stairs. I'd lost sight of Bascomb, but I heard him: echoes of his heavy boots on the concrete overpass. He was above the highway, heading toward the old World's Fair. Despite the pain from his cracked nose, the big man hadn't stopped for air.

A killer was on him. He believed that. That's what was driving him. Jimmy Mango said so. Maybe Tommy said so too. And the killer had a .38 he might use.

When I reached the top of the stairs, snapping myself around on the cold handrail, I saw him at the end of a long, tile-lined corridor and he hesitated. He looked left, he looked right. He went right.

I followed. I hadn't stopped and I was drawing nearer.

Bascomb went for the light at the top of the high stairs.

As I reached the stairs, I heard a roar, an enormous rumbling sound, the rush of motion, energy, vigor.

Another plane?

I took the stairs two at a time.

When I reached the top, when I stepped into the silver light, I saw it.

A subway train.

Long rack of cars, rectangles in dark red. Doors open, people easing inside, moving indifferently, tabloids tucked under their arms, sauntering, as if it wasn't all wrong.

Bascomb jumped the turnstile, dodged along the platform, skidded into a car in the center. Panicking, he continued to move on the inside. I saw him. He stumbled past silver handrails, past outstretched legs, and he opened the door and went into the next car.

I stood still. With the pale, open sky above me, I did not move.

The conductor looked out. She looked at me. She went back inside and made the doors close.

The subway train grunted, it lurched slightly and then began to ease out of the station and I watched as it went, as it pulled away, gained speed, grew smaller. And I looked at the rails, the thick, splintered wood on which they rested.

And though there were taxis, vans, cars below, rushing along the avenue—sudden, colorful blurs catching the morning light—I did not see them. I was somewhere else.

Marina, leaping down into the mire surrounding the tracks, scrambling, crying out in horror. Davy screaming his baby scream, little hands groping at air, his perfect baby face coated by filth, by blood. The light of an incoming train growing brighter, stronger. Marina, realizing time is about to end, cannot lift her baby from the stroller, she grabs the stroller with Davy strapped inside and she turns and she thinks and what will be her thoughts are unmistakably obvious:

Terry, where are you?

*Terry. Terry!*—


"Where are you?"

"Queens," I said, "by Shea." I was walking along 126th, next to an empty lot.

"Hold on," he replied, keeping his voice soft, low. I heard the rustle of sheets, the groan of bed springs, the swing of a door: He was putting on a robe, moving away from his wife, taking the phone to the next room.

"All right," Luther Addison said.

"I lost him."

"Who?"

"He got on the train and I lost him."

"The subway?"

I nodded.

"Terry?"

"The subway."

Addison understood. He'd seen the bodies. Marina's, Davy's. The stroller, crushed, shredded.

"What's it all about?"

"A guy, Alfie Bascomb," I told him. "He's involved in this thing I'm working on."

"The Cuban woman."

"He told me he's a killer," I said. "Whether he's *the* killer . . ."

"Alfie Bascomb," Addison repeated.

I gave him a brief description that boiled down to a big guy with a rap sheet who now had a broken nose and blood on his soiled work shirt.

"He might still be on the Seven line," I added. Or he got off a few stops up on Roosevelt Avenue and was doubling back. He had another key for his truck somewhere in his shop. He'd take the truck and he'd go where he had to.

"All right."

I could've told him Sharon Knight knew all about it. But she didn't. I hadn't told Sharon or Julie about Sixto, Ernie Mango's involvement, about one of his sons telling Bascomb I'd been hired to kill him.

"Luther, what you want to do is grab him before he can get to anyone involved in this thing," I said.

"Why's that?"

I'd reached 35th Avenue. As I turned, I saw Bascomb's truck. It was still in front of the shop.

"It's kind of tangled up," I replied. "Maybe you'll get something out of this guy. Press him on Mango."

"Tommy Mango?"

"That's it," I said.

"And what are you going to do?"

"I've got to catch my breath," I said. There was no sense in telling him the truth. He'd only try to talk me out of it.

"Terry, are you OK?"

"Sure." I passed Chubby's. A fat man was wiping down the counter.

"Terry, let me get you a ride back."

I put my hand on the back of Bascomb's truck. "I got a ride."

"Go to the one-ten," he said. "I know the commanding officer. He'll—"

"Luther, I've got to go," I said as I went toward the black door. "Bascomb, OK?"

I turned off the cell phone.


It wasn't hard for me to guess that Addison would call his friend at the 1-10 as soon as he got off the line with the Transit Authority cops. I had to move fast.

The phone on Bascomb's desk had rung at about 7 A.M. It might've been somebody paging him for a tow, but I was betting the big man had a cell in his car for that kind of business. Maybe he'd come to the office at a predetermined time to take one special call.

I stepped over the scattered paper on Bascomb's floor, kicked aside a bloody towel and grabbed the phone. I tapped *69 and got the number. When a canned voice asked me if I wanted to connect with the number, I said yes and heard a series of beeps.

The phone rang and rang and then the call went to an answering machine.

*"Buenos días, esta es Danny Villa. Yo he dejado la oficina . . ."*

Villa had called Bascomb at 7 A.M., then shut down his cell phone.

Maybe he'd be in his office by the time I reached Manhattan.

I went outside and, pulling the key from my coat pocket, climbed into the cab of Bascomb's tow truck.

# 14

I took the Grand Central Parkway over Randall's Island to the Triborough, accompanied by new knowledge: A tow truck rides a hell of lot smoother than anyone might've imagined. Automatic transmission with the press of a button on the dash; cruise control, which I might've used if I'd once gotten the thing over 55; power brakes; power steering; the works. Finding guys stuck at midnight on 95 or 278 brought in good coin.

I was going to ask the guy at the tollbooth if I looked like I belonged behind the wheel of a 20,000-pound truck, but Bascomb had E-Z Pass and I slid through without having to stop.

So I made it from Queens to Manhattan without getting pulled over, without having to explain why I had stolen Bascomb's tow truck and why I was carrying Leo's hardware in my sweatshirt.

I thought about driving the truck to Little Italy, parking it on the curb in front of Marco's, the bar where Ernie Mango drank himself stupid.

Or up on the sidewalk in front of the Delphi, where Tommy held court.

Too melodramatic, I concluded. Besides, I needed the transportation to the Upper East Side.

The sun was to my left as I came off the Harlem River Lift to get onto the FDR going south. (Amazing how drivers with Hondas and Geos will yield during a center-lane merge when the other guy is driving a tow truck.) Yellow streaks looked like lightning on the choppy East River and bulging white steam rose from brick stacks on the Queens side. I wriggled out of stop-and-go traffic and eased over without incident to leave the highway at 96th. On the concrete island under the FDR, a scraggly man with a ratty beard and a big German shepherd held a sign that said his dog needed food. A good ploy, I thought, though it might've worked better with something smaller, something less able to fend for itself—an underweight Jack Russell terrier, maybe. I caught a red at 91st and York and watched a half-dozen kids, Bella's age, use the basketball court for a roller-hockey rink.

I had choked at the Willet's Point subway station. Choked. I ought to have Bascomb now, with Addison's friends from the 1-10 descending on 35th Avenue, an EMT ambulance at the door to tend to the big guy's nose.

I had choked. And I know damned well that by now I should—

Four years now and I still haven't worked it out. And I know it, even when I'm telling myself I have.

I can deal with the senselessness of it and the emptiness I feel. I've become accustomed to the lack of their sound, their ideas, the lack of their affection. I don't dwell on thoughts of their potential and I don't ponder the possibilities. I asked only the simplest questions, ones where an answer was imaginable. You know, like, what would Davy do today? Just today. What would a boy going on six years old be doing? And what would Marina say tonight over dinner? What would she be working on now? Would we be back in Italy with new subjects for her to commemorate, to celebrate? Or would she be exploring here, New York, the East Coast, where? She hinted: On a morning in May six weeks before she died, we took Davy to the Cloisters.

She hated the way I carried him: near my hip, his little round diapered ass in my big hand.

At the Cloisters, she had an epiphany, she said. (Same word in Italian, though I didn't understand at first.) Above the green cliffs that line the Hudson, on a hill in exquisite Fort Tryon Park, is a museum that's essentially a replica, a reconstruction, of French cloisters created with pale limestone and pink marble from Spain. It houses medieval art from the world over: a hand scroll from eighth-century China; a baldacchino from 12th-century Burgundy; a wing of a diptych depicting the crucifixion of Christ created in 14th-century Tuscany; a 16th-century ivory mask from Nigeria. All in a setting that is tranquil, secluded, seemingly secure. Created by men of industry and of unimaginable wealth—John D. Rockefeller, Jr. and J. P. Morgan.

"America," she said, with a knowing nod, a shake of a long, brown finger. "This is a metaphor for America."

We were in the flourishing green garden of the Cuxa Cloister, having left the shadows of the processional walkway to step under the stone arches into the courtyard's bright sunlight.

"That's pretty good, Marina," I said as I sat on a bench, shifting Davy and his rubber rattle to my lap. America, where the world comes together, still.

I watched a cardinal perched on the lip of the birdbath in the center of the yard.

"Yes," she said as she reached for the baby, "America. If you have enough money, you can recreate—is that the word, *fare qualche cosa sembrarlo era?*"

"Recreate. To create again, yes."

"If you have enough money, you can recreate something so lovely that the people will forget he could go home again maybe. That this is what he has at home."

I didn't respond, I think, because I wasn't sure I understood. Was she saying America is merely where we are until we return home? That we don't ever cease to be immigrants in whom memory doesn't exist separate from a longing that can't be satisfied? Or was Marina saying that we're lucky there is something lovely to remind us of home?

Now I was sitting in a tow truck on York Avenue, my hands gripping the wheel as if I were choking it, watching a man share a buttered roll with a dog. And I realized that my wife was telling me New York was not her home.

I heard a horn honk behind me; a bleat, a kind of "excuse me," rather than a "move your ass" sound. I proceeded steadily along York, aside the rush on the highway. At the curb at 90th, a young woman in a long navy-blue coat held a colorful bouquet of tall flowers. She squinted as the sun shone on her face and held up her hand to protect the flowers as they wobbled in the wind

We were happy here. Why wouldn't we have been?

I hit the blinker at 89th and turned right onto the narrow street, wondering if I could squeeze by that moving van up there.


I pulled over by a fire hydrant on the northeast corner of 89th and Third. Before I got out of the truck, I knew I'd arrived at the right time.

Looking through the dirty front windshield, I saw before Villa's storefront office high-tech vans from WABC News, Telemundo 47 and the local Fox affiliate. And two blue-and-white NYPD cars. In the shade on the west side of the street, a crowd gathered: people peering up the block from the hair salon—curious women still in black smocks, towels on their damp heads—the jewelers, the Stargate Diner customers. From the apartment building above Villa's, a couple in their sixties pointed at the scene below, narrating the budding action to each other.

I cut the engine, left the key in the ignition and scuffled across Third, waiting to weave through traffic that was held up by drivers rubbernecking at the scene.

On the sidewalk outside Villa's, a cameraman from ABC was struggling to get the right backdrop for his setup and, as he shifted, his middle-aged partner with the microphone kept eyeing the front door, as if ready to burst forward to pose his lone question. The young woman from Fox held back, standing with forced casualness by her station's van. Her camerawoman was doing the heavy work, jostling her way toward a good spot in the crowd. As she started to clear a path, I decided to follow.

As I squeezed past a burly man in a thick turtleneck, I felt a hand grab my shoulder. I turned fast.

It was McDowell. His cheeks were red and his hair disheveled. His eyes revealed that he hadn't had much sleep since I'd seen him last night outside of Bascomb's. He was wearing the same outfit, minus the stocking cap. Maybe the cap was only for muscle work.

"You should be happy, Tiger," he said.

"Tiger?"

"Unless he called you," he added. "He call you? He called the fuckin' press, this guy."

Now he even sounded like one of the Mangos. "Who?"

"Villa. We made him," he said proudly.

"Made him for what?"

"For the Salgado broad."

I looked at him. He was serious.

He said, "They found books of hers, plays, in there. You saw her place, everything neat and in a row. He took them when he killed her. Right out of the bookcase. Obviously."

He smiled at me with his perfect little teeth.

Danny Villa stole books from Sonia Salgado. Sure.

"You're free, Tiger," McDowell announced as he slapped me on the sleeve. "Tommy says you can go home." He let out a low chuckle. "And you thought it was black magic. Heh-heh . . ."

"OK," I told him. Then I continued to press forward through the crowd, nudging the Fox camerawoman as I shuffled by.

"Hey," McDowell protested. But it was too late. The crowd had closed behind me. His voice faded, disappeared.

As I arrived at the doorstep, I saw Villa standing in the middle of his waiting room. Flanked by two detectives, he wore a spotless blue suit, a white shirt, a blue-and-silver striped tie. In his lapel was a gold pin of an unfurled American flag and a Cuban flag, their poles crossed. As one of the detectives reached for his elbow, Villa stopped him by raising his arms, and the handcuffs, dramatically. He tugged at his French cuffs, damped down his silver hair and pronounced himself ready to go. Two uniforms came from Villa's inner office; one carried three hardcover books in a plastic evidence bag. From here, I could see the titles: *Cuban Theater in the United States. Cuban-American Theater. The Floating Island Plays.*

"Ah, Mr. Terry Orr," said Danilo Villa.

He stepped toward me and shook my hand.

"I myself have chosen to believe the contrary," he said with a politician's smile.

"And that would be?"

"You do not work for them," he said. "In fact . . ."

One of the detectives, the less tolerant of the two, came forward and told Villa to move.

Villa looked at the long-faced cop and said, "I am telling my friend here something."

"Talk to him at the arraignment," the cop sneered.

"Perhaps you, Detective Brooks, prefer I tell the cameras instead."

Brooks shoved his hands into the pockets of his black trenchcoat. "Go ahead," he grunted, nodding toward me.

Villa smiled as if to show his gratitude.

He turned to me and leaned closer. I could smell his woody cologne.

"Can you imagine," he whispered, "that all of this began with a ticket for running a red light?"

I stepped back.

"Ah, you know," he said. He waved a finger at me. "So you also are a clever boy."

Brooks said, "Enough." He turned to his partner and nodded: Let the perp-walk begin.

Villa dropped his arms and let them dangle. After wriggling his shoulders to get his suit to lie as he wanted it to, he turned sideways so he and Brooks could fit through the door frame. Villa wasn't going out cowering in shame. He wasn't going to miss a photo op or TV face time.

As they started to move into the crowd on Third, Villa looked back at me and said, "And to think I paid those damned tickets. Can you believe that?"

I stood in silence as I heard the crowd rush forward. Shadows disappeared as the TV crews went into action and the door frame filled with white light.

Villa did his first interview in Spanish with Telemundo 47.

I waited in the outer office for a few minutes until Villa, under a shower of still-camera flashes, was placed in the back of a blue-and-white, a cop's hand on his silver hair. The uniform with the three books, the ones someone would insist Villa had taken from Sonia's, had left and was replaced by two other young cops in blue who seemed for a moment not to be sure what to do next. I bet myself that they knew enough not to let me into Villa's private office. I wanted to see what else had been planted there: Sonia's statue of Santa Barbara, perhaps. A pair of her panties. What meager savings she'd been able to put together in Bedford Hills.

As I looked out onto Third, I saw McDowell. He'd hung his badge on a thin chain around his neck, and it bounced on his chest between the panels of his down vest. Pacing, he watched the crowd disperse. Like the uniformed cops behind me, he was waiting for instructions.

Finally, one of the uniforms asked me for ID. When I showed her my P.I. license, she nodded politely and told me to get out. When I started to protest, she told me to take it up with Brooks, whom I'd find at the 19th Precinct.

"What's Villa charged with?" I asked.

"Brooks," she replied.

I nodded amicably, not unaware that I had an unlicensed .38 in the pouch of my sweatshirt.

A man in a Burberry raincoat and a copy of *Barron's* under his arm stuck his head into the office to see what might happen next. When he was shushed away, he tsked his complaint, stiffened his thin neck and walked off.

When the last crew, the Fox team, finally packed up their van and pulled out, the last few people who'd been watching Villa's show drifted off, and this small stretch of the Upper East Side returned to Saturday-morning quiet. McDowell, who was standing at the rear of a blue-and-white, started across Third; then, when he realized I was still inside, snapped his fingers. He turned as I came out onto the avenue.

"You're going back downtown, right?" he asked as he crossed from light into shade.

I shrugged. I had a few calls I wanted to make. And I wanted to get off my feet for a while: My solar plexus ached like hell where Bascomb had abused it.

"I'll give you a lift," he said. "Maybe we'll go see Tommy. He'd like that now."

I looked at him. Out from behind the snappy patter, Officer McDowell had nothing to say. Villa had been hauled off in cuffs and somebody had told him that was a good thing. Tommy would be happy with him and he could now go back to doing whatever it was he liked to do.

"I got something for you, McDowell," I told him.

"What's that?" His question revealed no real sense of curiosity. He was still basking in his illusions, the satisfaction of the phony scenario. It was no wonder Tommy liked this kid. He was everything Jimmy wasn't. Watchful, trustworthy, obedient. All he needed was a tag, a collar and a leash. Maybe a bone too.

I told him to follow me to the corner. When we reached 89th and Third, I shaded my eyes and pointed to Bascomb's tow truck.

"What's that?"

"You were looking out for it last night," I said.

He froze; he didn't reply.

"That's Bascomb's," I added. "AB Towing and Repair. In Queens? Thirty-fifth Avenue?"

His expression changed and he bit his bottom lip. "I don't know what you're talking about," he charged.

"Last night you and Jimmy Mango were looking for Alfie Bascomb," I said. "There's his truck. You want to know where he is, ask Tommy. He might know by now."

He stepped back. He tried to conceal his surprise, his concern.

"Did you tell him Bascomb took off on you?" I asked. "That he left town? He didn't . . ."

He frowned. And then he seemed to get angry. "You—"

"Christ, Tommy is going to blow," I said, cutting him off. I gestured toward Villa's storefront. "He went to all this trouble because you told him Bascomb was gone."

"Aw, you don't know shit," he said finally.

I stepped out onto the avenue and stuck my hand in the air. Up at about 86th Street, a row of taxis waited for the light to change.

"The key's in the ignition," I said. "Drive it down to Elizabeth Street."

McDowell looked at the tow truck, looked back at me.

"You'd better get with it, kid," I added. "You're no player. You're being played."

The cab I thought I'd get pulled over for a fare at 88th. I got mine out of the second wave: one of those minivans designed for four people, at least. A poor substitute for a good ol' Checker.

I told the cabbie to go west at 97th and take Columbus south.

"Eventually," she said.

We left McDowell, who was somewhere between befuddled and furious, at the curb. After cutting across the Upper East Side on 91st, we entered Central Park at 85th and motored steadily to the West Side. As we cruised under new buds on thin boughs, I looked up and saw the singular towers of the grand buildings of Central Park West. And as I started to drift, I remembered it had been only Wednesday that I'd been trying to shake McDowell as he tailed me through the park on my way back downtown. Little wonder Tommy Mango wanted me to stay home. His problem: how to ensure that the link between his father and Sonia Salgado remained unknown. That he'd gotten a call on the case of Sonia's killing seemed to make it easy for him to handle it. Simple B&E, he said.

Then comes along this guy, this ex-jock, ex-writer, hothead fuck who barely knows what he's doing . . .

Or was it more sinister than that? Why did Tommy have to cover up a more-than-30-year-old link, a dubious one in a certain light? A bright lawyer would have no problem making it look like a coincidence, just a hardworking cop doing his job.

What was he thinking when I called him? "A fuckin' break." Or: "Not this pain in the ass . . ."

I heard a voice. "Your phone."

"Huh?"

"Your phone is humming."

"Thanks," I said. I felt a twinge in my lower back as I arched to undo the handset from my belt. The gun shifted in my sweatshirt. "Hello?"

"Lieutenant Addison wants you."

"Bella?"

"Dad, Saturday is my day to sleep," she complained. "Arrgh."

"You sound like you're sleeping now."

"In thirty seconds, I will be," she said. "Lieutenant Addison is home."

"Bella?"

"I sleep now. . . ."

———

"They found your friend," Addison said. "In Woodside. He was trying to get on a bus."

We were leaving the park at 66th. An egg truck was backing toward Tavern on the Green, and a bay horse and his carriage in the cul-de-sac had to move aside. The sluggish, thick-bodied horse, accustomed to anything, shuffled without lifting his head.

"He was probably trying to get to the LIRR," Addison continued. "He lives out in Far Rockaway."

"You would've found him sooner or later," I said.

"Not too hard to find a man stumbling around with blood all over his shirt, his face, his hands."

A nose broken twice is bound to make a mess. "Yeah, well, I appreciate it," I said. "I— Hold on."

I leaned forward and asked the cabbie to get on Broadway.

"What happened to Columbus?" she asked as she adjusted the pink frames of her glasses.

"It's all right," I told her.

She shrugged as I returned to Addison.

The lieutenant said, "You're in a cab. Where are you going?"

"Listen, Luther, thanks for—"

"Not so fast, son," he said. "What's it all about?"

"This is the guy that came at me on forty-fifth with the wrench. Bascomb."

"Now you're even. So?"

I said, "Last night, Jimmy Mango and one of Tommy's boys were looking for him."

"Interesting. But in and of itself, Terry—"

"He's done time, Luther, back in the seventies, for assault," I said. "Hit a cop."

"He did, did he?" I could picture him raising an eyebrow. Funny how that kind of news always interests another member of the fraternity.

"You've got enough to question him," I said. "If you need me to come in if you want to hold him, no problem. Press him on Sonia Salgado. They went to high school together."

Traffic started to bunch up ahead at 51st. I tapped a finger on the dividing glass. When the driver looked in the rearview, I told her to ease over.

"First Mango, now Sonia Salgado," Addison said with a touch of resignation in his voice.

"And you're going to hear that Danny Villa's been picked up," I said. "Tell him that."

"Danny Villa?"

"Right."

"He's in this thing too?"

"I think you're going to find that out, Luther."

"All right. Give me your cell number."

"I'll call you," I told him.

"Don't make me wake up Gabriella again," he said. "Payback would be waking *you* up."

As I stepped out of the cab, I said, "I don't sleep, Luther." Then I stopped myself. Once again, Addison had just helped me and hadn't needed to.

"Luther, I'll call later."


I was walking west on 45th, book-ended by visitors milling outside the Marriott Marquis, sinewy delivery men leaping from boxy trucks, red-eared optimists with the theater listings clipped from the *Times* on their way to the TKTS booth, steel-jawed cops on horseback, hard-hearted hustlers who sought to blend into brick and brownstone.

I hit the last few numbers and waited for a response.

"Hello?"

"Julie?"

"Terry," she said, "hi. Are we courting some sort of bad luck? To talk on the morning of— Or is there a problem?"

"No, no problem," I said.

"OK. Good." She sounded relieved.

"Julie, I need to come clean with you on something."

"Uh-oh."

"Something about Sonia Salgado," I said, as I approached the Aladdin Hotel.

"I see," she said, in her professional voice. "Go on." She was ready to hear confession.

I squinted as I looked east to cross the street. "I found something in Sixto's file," I told her. "A connection between Tommy Mango and the guy who might've been Sonia's boyfriend."

"What is it?"

"Mango's father wrote up Sixto two years before Glatzer was killed," I said. "Moving violation."

"I see."

"Tommy knows I know," I told her. "He's keeping me away from his old man."

"Well, Detective Mang—"

"He's been intimating to a few people that I was involved in this," I said.

"In the Salgado murder? How so?"

"Either he or his brother Jimmy are telling people that I'm working for them."

"Which is in exact contrast with the facts, I hope. . . ."

"Sure."

"Good, Terry," she said.

I nodded. "The guy I went at on forty-fifth? The guy with the wrench? Turns out Jimmy Mango sent him after me."

Pen scratching on paper: Even over the cell, with its occasional bark of static, I could hear Julie taking notes.

"He's been arrested, by the way. His name is Bascomb. They found him in Queens, his nose all busted up."

"May I guess how that happened?"

"And Danny Villa's been brought in too," I reported. "They found three books from Sonia's apartment in his office. It's a setup. Villa's not that dumb."

"No," she agreed, "Danny's far from dumb."

No, he's not. But he'd called me in to send me away from digging into Sonia's murder. Addison was right that telescoping a 30-year-old case was bound to be a distraction. I needed to know why Villa had done it, and how he knew Bascomb.

I stopped near the scoop of the underground garage and looked back toward the rising sun, toward Times Square. "Tommy's moving to wrap this up, Julie."

"Have you called Sharon?"

"No."

"I'd better."

"Why not?"

"Does anybody else know about this?"

I said, "It depends on how much Luther Addison gets out of Alfie Bascomb."

"Luther—"

"I called him when Bascomb shook me," I said.

I started heading west again. On the other side of Ninth, a yellow school bus was taking on passengers outside the Seventh-Day Adventist church.

"Where are you now?" she asked.

"Forty-fifth, on the West Side."

"So you can have another fight?"

"I owe a guy an update," I said. "He's the only one who showed Sonia any heart."

"I see."

I was outside the Avellaneda now. Reviews of a play that needed a sub-way station were behind me.

She said, "You be careful, Terry."

I felt the heft of the gun against my stomach. "I am. I will."

"Try to stay in one piece until tonight, OK?"

I told her I would.

## 15

I pressed the intercom buzzer a second time before I noticed that the Avellaneda's entrance was unlocked: A thin strip of bare wood was visible in the crack between the black door and frame.

I went inside and, choking back a desire to call out, I pulled the door shut tight behind me, turning the lock until the deadbolt snapped.

Something was wrong; I knew that right away. Hassan protected his theater. It was his life. He wouldn't leave the front door open. Unless something extraordinary had occurred.

Or someone forced him to.

Before heading down the steep stairwell, I stopped to listen.

I heard the sizzle of steam heat, water rushing through rattling pipes, the subtle creaking of the wood under my feet, the sound of my breathing, my heart beating.

*"A heart unfortified, a mind impatient, an understanding simple and unschooled."*

Claudius, that greedy fuck, might've been a bit less condescending to his nephew had Hamlet pressed a .38 to his ear.

I reached under my coat and into the pouch.

My fingers fastened on the gun's grip.

Fortified, I went down the stairs, patiently.

I could feel the subtle, persistent ache in the kidney where Bascomb got me, the moisture on my chest under the heavy sweatshirt, as I took the steps one at a time, leaning my weight against the black wall on my left.

I reached the bottom step, waited and then, with my left hand, yanked back the velvet curtain that led to the seats.

I moved fast down the carpeted aisle into the empty theater.

And I saw him. He was in the light of a single bright spot.

He wore his djellaba over a black turtleneck and black corduroy slacks. One of his embroidered slippers had fallen to the floor.

Probably when he'd kicked over the high stool.

The other slipper was still on his foot, which dangled some three feet above the stage.

Hassan's head had settled close to his chest, but the thick rope prevented his chin from resting against his body.

The other end of the rope was tied high in the flies.

He swayed slightly, in a small circle, hanging amid the subway station that *No Direction Home* required. He was downstage from the unseen tracks, from square pillars that seemed to be made of steel but were crafted of plywood and foam and painted to deceive.

As I came down the aisle, I saw on the proscenium his colorful half-fez. When I reached the stage, I saw a sheet of paper underneath it.

I slid the .38 into my coat pocket.

And in the cool silence I lifted the sheet of his private stationery: The name Safi Majorelle was in calligraphic script on the top right. At the bottom, the address of the theater.

On the paper, a note written by hand, carefully, deliberately:

To my brothers and sisters:

I have lived my life to educate, to entertain, and to provide enjoyment and enlightenment. To bring joy and to relieve sorrow.

To celebrate the creativity of the Latin American people, particularly the Cuban people who live in exile in America.

This theater that I have created, and that we have sustained together, is very strong now. Strong because I have had the honor of dedicating my life to it.

Whatever I may have done, I have done not for myself, but for the love of the spoken word, of actors and their craft, for collaboration, for the thrill of theater—the highest form of Art.

I suffer now, my friends, and I wish to suffer no more.

Life has become unbearable and it will never become better. Soon, I will cease to be me—which means I will no longer be able to join you in the pleasures we have shared.

I wish to leave you with a thought. You know me and what I have done. I am very proud of what I have created, whatever the cost. The kindness that I have shown has been repaid countless times by others.

Finally, I want to say to you all—

Viva los grandes escritores de Cuba—Gertrudis Gómez de Avellaneda, José Jacinto Milanés, Diego Tejera y Francisco Sellén y Manuel Martin, Dolores Prida, Edwina Acuñar-Gonzalez, Isolina Leyva y Héctor Pérez y Manuel Pereiras—all of you who live to show us what we must know and what we must never forget.

Adios,

He signed the letter with a flourish. Safi Majorelle.

When I lifted his little hat to slide the suicide note back under it, I felt something stiff inside, a piece of cardboard, perhaps, to help it retain its shape.

I turned the hat over. In the top was an old color photo, square with a white border, the kind taken with a small family camera. It was faded and bore vein-like cracks from years of handling.

Two boys in their late teens, early twenties. Standing on what was unmistakably a New York City street corner in bright daylight, they had their arms around each other's shoulders and they smiled broadly, comically, at the photographer. It was summertime: One boy wore a loud madras shirt with short sleeves, the other a skin-tight T-shirt that revealed a fit, sturdy body. Both had wild, unkempt hair, long sideburns, wide belts with oversized buckles, jeans slung low on their hips. The boy with the madras shirt had a cigarette in his left hand.

On the white border under his image was written a name: Safi Majorelle. Under the other boy: Danny Villa.

The names were written in the same ink he had used for his suicide note. I understood immediately.

I turned over the photo to see if there was anything written on the back. There was.

*I have been a good man.*


Before I left the Avellaneda, before I was back on 45th, I knew that whatever tolerance I'd developed for this fetid game, this depravity, this charade of life, had been exceeded. And now I was sick of everything: sick of taxis, of midtown, of the small whitecaps on the gray Hudson, of the scavenger seagulls; sick of stumbling across death while life continued for the corrupt who readily corrupt and, having done so, thrive. In this game, the dead were never innocent, and how they suffer for their flaws. And the corrupt: Where are they now? Lunch at La Grenouille, a drive to open the summer home on the Cape, a week of pampered luxury at the Hotel de Paris in Monte Carlo? Not this bunch. A corner seat at a greasy spoon in TriBeCa. A table in a ratty bar in Little Italy. A handmade suit, a closet full of handmade suits: that appointment necessary for the illusion of power, for power over an impressionable few.

And me? I was sick of myself, my endless meandering, my purposeless purpose, my inability to understand all the reasons why things happen as they do.

I left Majorelle tied to the rafters. Someone for whom his suicide note was intended would arrive shortly.

Saturday matinee.

I was on Tenth Avenue, heading south, and I passed a gas station, rundown tenements, abandoned buildings as cars and small trucks from the Lincoln Tunnel rumbled north. As I crossed 39th, I went past hotdog vendors and immigrants with bouquets of roses trying, though not very hard, to serve those who sat in the disorderly queue of vehicles headed underground. Meanwhile, the sun had made its way over the skyline; or at least, its rays squeezed between the tall buildings in the steel-and-glass jungle to my left. It warmed the vendors and it caused people in cars to turn down their visors. It did not a god-damned thing for me.

Einstein said, "God is subtle, but he is not malicious."

Sure he is. And for his own amusement.

From his perch deep in the cosmos, beyond the cosmos, he spots, down on the third planet from a sun in one small solar system, in one neighborhood soon to be destroyed in a city that lived to destroy, a young girl, not bright but hopeful—that deadly combination. This scenario, thinks God, needs a little something, a twist, that kind of special little zing that only a Supreme Being can conceive.

With a lift of an eyebrow, *deux ex deus,* it changes.

Enter a boy at school, charismatic, perhaps attentive. One of his friends, an exotic not from Hell's Kitchen, not from Cuba, but from Morocco, loves what she loves: the theater, where nothing is as it seems, where dreams are possible. When the friend, Ahmed, talks about theater, stardust dances before the young girl's eyes. And she sees a future for herself.

But the charismatic boy from Cuba doesn't love the theater. Nothing interests him, except immediate gratification of the dullest sort—the cheap thrill of petty crime, for example. This charismatic boy is clever. He's bold. He thinks he knows. He thinks he understands.

One score, he thinks, and I'm gone.

He meets a cop, with whom he shares a lack of scope. The proposition is interesting: diamonds, carried by a defenseless old man.

Luis Sixto rips off Asher Glatzer.

The thin edge of a sharp knife. Asher Glatzer is dead.

Luis Sixto runs off with the diamonds, stays away for a few years, changes his appearance.

I withdrew the photo from my coat pocket.

I looked at the boy with his arm around Hassan.

I put my finger over the boy's large nose, his wide nostrils.

I imagined his hair as silver and well-groomed, rather than the wild black mop on the boy's head.

A neat suit, a perfect suit. Handmade shirts, club ties, shiny wing-tips.

What else? An education. A diction that hides his roots but doesn't deny his Cuban heritage.

A change in temperament. A dignified, gentlemanly attitude. Maturity.

Lifts in those wing-tips.

I was still studying the photo.

New teeth.

What else? A little work around the jawline? In the photo, the boy's chin juts out ever so slightly.

Outside the Javits Center, a gaggle of men and women in business attire, cheeks red from the wind, all carrying the same royal-blue tote bag bearing a crestlike logo, waited impatiently for a shuttle bus, considered crossing Ninth on their own.

I'm in their old neighborhood, I realized: Some 30 years ago, Sonia and Sixto held hands here and, surrounded by tenements, Hassan dreamed. It was all gone now: tenements and dreams. So thoroughly and completely gone that it was as if neither had existed.

Christ, I was tired now. My kidney throbbed. It was better-than-even money that I'd piss blood when I got back to Harrison Street.

My knee was sore, from running hard on concrete, up stairs, skidding to a stop in the subway station. Choking.

Ghosts.

No, I won't quote Hamlet again. That fuckin' parlor trick. I took a two-credit course, aced it. I've seen it at the Delacorte, at the Public; hell, I almost saw it at the Old Vic. But Marina was worn out from the flight.


I made it to TriBeCa by 11:45 or so. Since my cell phone hadn't hummed, I knew Bella was still sleeping: no requests for jelly donuts and hazelnut coffee, "if you don't mind, Dad. And get something for yourself. My treat."

The green door was unlocked. Leo was behind the bar, reading Thursday's *Times-Picayune,* sipping chicory coffee. For some reason, he opened the blinds on the Hudson Street side of the bar. Little mites fluttered in the sunlight.

So that's the color of the Tilt's floor. Somewhere between murky gray and Creature-from-the-Black-Lagoon green.

Leo had something enticing burbling back on the hot plate in his office. The scent of nutty flour, thyme, and seafood filled the bar.

"Shrimp gumbo?"

He looked over his bifocals. "You got it. Be ready noon or thereabouts, if you ready."

I shook my head.

"Oh, yeah," he said. "Gotta squeeze into that tuxedo tonight."

"Tuxedo. You too?" I asked. I was still over by the door.

"D says you got him this girl your daughter tell him is pretty fine."

"We're going in as four," I said. "All goes well, we should walk out that way." I put my hand on the lock on the green door. "He here?"

"No," Leo said, shaking his head. "Probably trying to borrow some shoes."

I snapped the lock and walked over by Leo. Above him, Saturday-morning cartoons without sound. Something from Japan, frenetic, violent.

I dug out the .38 and handed it to him.

"This has been here the whole time," I said.

He took it.

" 'The whole time'?"

"Since whenever." I sat across from him on a wobbling stool. "Or I'm going to have to answer for pulling it on somebody this morning."

"Oh, yeah?" He took off his glasses.

"Addison had the guy picked up. When he hears I had that, he'll be all over me."

"No shit," Leo said as he wiped the gun on the well-worn white towel he wore on his straining belt.

He lifted himself off his throne and, with a thick hand on the bar, inched along toward the register. He leaned down and, biting his tongue as he groped for the slot, slipped the gun back in its hiding place, from which it had been absent for two years.

"You don't need it?" he asked as he edged back.

"I got no choice," I replied. I slid off the stool.

"It's here, you want it back."

I nodded thanks and rapped on the hard wood with a knuckle. "Tomorrow."

"Hold up," he said. He turned and reached to the top of his compact-disc player. He handed me his copy of Donizetti's *L'Elisir d'Amore*. The young, bearded Pavarotti smiled at me as Leo added, "There's magic in there."

I must've looked like I needed it.

# 16

"Dad!"

There she was; there was no confusion now: She was a young woman. Her soft brown hair framed her sweet face with its delicately applied eye shadow, rouge, faint traces of lipstick: the face of a young woman, with definition, strength. Determination. Her young woman's face, now in a fierce grimace. My 14-year-old daughter had her hands on her hips as she stood in her white, ankle-length slip, her legs in pantyhose with floral designs. Dainty white socks on her feet.

"What?"

She sputtered, "You— You look like you're just going, you know, like, *out*. To a restaurant. Or a play."

I was wearing a classic blue blazer—which I'd had dry-cleaned—a blue Oxford, black wool slacks and loafers.

"I don't want to feel self-conscious, Bella."

I felt fine. I'd taken a long nap, spoken to Addison—they were holding Bascomb; they'd charged him with aggravated assault, which might get busted down to simple assault, but what the hell, it'll put him in Rikers until Monday—hadn't spoken to any of the Mangos or

McDowell, since, to my surprise, none had called or come by to wave Villa over my head. Nor had I pissed blood. A steamy shower had brought back the feeling to my knee. I felt fine: I'd more or less figured out how I'd deal with this morning's fuck-up at the Willet's Point station.

"This is a special occasion," she said. "I told you."

"Bella, for a special occasion, I wear this."

Exasperated, she muttered, "You wore that for my fourteenth birthday."

"Point made," I replied. We went to Chanterelle, my favorite restaurant, where Marina had taken me for my 30th. Wonderful nights, then and last year. Bella had sipped Champagne demurely as we waited in the home-like, flower-laden foyer for our table.

Rebuffed, she turned and went to the stairs. "Ten minutes," she said.

"I'm ready."

She said something about a tie as she padded back to her room.

Ten minutes later, she came back down.

Her dress was a very pale baby-blue, long and full with a kind of frilly stuff at the bottom; bare shoulders with thin straps, the front cut modestly; and she wore a white, frilly shawl. The shoes were white flats with pert bows.

Instead of her customary two dozen rubber bands, she wore a silver bracelet. Falling to just above the neckline of her dress on a fine silver chain, a silver heart-shaped locket rested against her skin.

She saw me stare at the pendant. "You don't mind?"

I had given it to her mother a long time ago, when I was still at St. John's. It cost next to nothing, but it meant everything to me when Marina took it from my hand, then let me do the clasp at the back of her neck.

"Mind? No," I said. "Bella, you look fantastic."

She beamed.

I asked her to turn around and she spun slowly, her hands holding out her ample skirt.

"Perfect," I said. "Really."

"Thank you," she replied modestly.

"No rubber bands, though."

She bent down and tugged at her white socks, showing me the rubber bands around her ankle.

The sharp honk of a horn sounded as if it came from a car parked on our front steps.

"That's the limo," Bella said hurriedly. "Come on."

"Limo?"

"Yes, I ordered a limo. With my own money. Now, let's go."

"OK, but—"

"Dad, get the camera. Over there, the camera," she said, pointing, as she scurried to grab her white handbag. "Mrs. Maoli wants photos. Glo-Bug, too, and Daniel. Dad. *There.*"

The disposable camera was on top of Bella's manuscript.

"Got it."

"Come on," she repeated. "Your friend is waiting."

"Julie?"

"Dad, I wouldn't describe Dennis as *your* friend. Would I?"

She held open the front door.

"Go."

I stepped into the brisk night air and immediately skidded to a halt.

"Oh, Christ, Bella." A white stretch limo.

"Very *Spinal Tap*," she said as she squeezed by me.

A black man who weighed about 330, most of it muscle, stood beside the car wearing a black tuxedo with a gold embroidered vest. He smiled to reveal a glittering diamond in his front tooth.

"Good evening, Ms. Orr," he said. He tipped his black cap and bent at the waist.

Flecks of stars danced above us as Bella went down the steps toward the cobblestone, toward the open door of the limo.

"Perfect," she said.


Julie Giada lived on 28th Street between Second and Third avenues in Kips Bay, a neighborhood dotted with brownstones, short, four-story apartment buildings and thick caliper trees.

As the white limo cruised uptown, I stared absently at the gold spire of the MetLife Tower, at Madison Square Park, at lazing dogs sniffing in the dark run. Thoughts of Hassan returned as we left Sixth: the reaction of his friends as they took a frantic phone call, expressing disbelief for a moment before shifting to acceptance and understanding. Memorials were being crafted now, I thought, by people who knew nothing of Sonia Salgado, who would not believe Hassan capable of any kind of betrayal, who might credit him for his generosity of spirit in sharing books of plays with an indigent murderer. For perhaps the fifth time since we left Harrison, I tapped my jacket pocket: The photo of young Hassan and old friend Sixto was still there.

As the limo navigated the narrow crosstown street, I wondered how the press would play Hassan's death. A small box in tomorrow's *Times,* followed by something warm in Monday's Metro Section or in Arts & Leisure, I concluded. The *Post?* A screaming headline on the newsstands later tonight. Something like BROADWAY BIG FOUND HANGED IN THEATER. But what, I wondered, was a bigger story? Danny Villa, media star, professional rabble-rouser, *El Caballero,* is, says the NYPD, a suspect in the murder of a female ex-con. That's too good, I realized: Nothing pleases a tabloid editor so much as exposing celebrity hypocrisy. So the suicide of an artistic director of a cultural institution goes inside; page four, eight.

If that editor jumps the Villa story next to the piece on Hassan he'll be almost as cute as he thinks he is.

Meanwhile, Bascomb is an afterthought. "Blue-collar man brought in on an assault rap" gets nothing.

"Bella, how do you know where Julie lives?"

She sat across from me, her back to the driver, on the buttery black leather seat. She had a drink in hand—Diet Dr Pepper—in a heavy crystal tumbler. She was loving all of it.

"Darryl," she said, pointing over her shoulder with her thumb as the limo went east on 28th. "He's nothing if not prepared."

A diamond glittered in the rearview.

"Actually," she added with a smile, "I asked her."

As if to advertise the tenor of the neighborhood, two women bundled in cloth coats, their gray hair under thin, pink scarves, were on the front steps of the brownstone where Julie lived.

As Darryl edged the limo next to a hydrant, the glass doors of the brownstone opened and Julie Giada appeared.

"Oh, man," I said.

"Didn't I tell you?" Bella nodded.

She was dressed in a long, deep-purple satin gown with a plunging V-shaped décolletage. A matching purple shawl covered her bare shoulders.

As she stopped to kiss her flattering neighbors, Darryl came around and opened the door.

"Get out, Dad," Bella instructed.

I did. When I arrived at the steps of the brownstone, one of the women whispered, "That's him. Tall. Good skin."

"But not a tie," replied the other old woman. She expressed her chagrin with an irksome shirk that brought the shoulders of her coat over her large ears.

"Terry, this is Mrs. Sadler. And Mrs. Malone."

"Hello Mrs. Sadler, Mrs. Malone."

They smiled politely. Then Mrs. Malone whispered, "He's the one who—"

"Ssshh," snipped the other woman.

I took Julie's hand as her purple shoe touched the sidewalk.

"Hello, Terry," she said.

"Julie."

I led her to the limo. She bent gracefully under the low ceiling and joined my daughter, shifting her full gown as she eased into the soft seat across from me.

"So, finally, Gabriella," she said. "Hello."

Her fragrance left a faint, pleasing trail as Darryl closed the door and I sat with an accidental *oomph.*

"Killer, Julie," Bella cheered, "really. Dad?"

Taking her cue, I began, "Julie, you look—"

"Is it all right?" she asked, shifting her gaze from me to Bella and back again. "I'm not much of a rock 'n' roll girl."

"Julie," I said. "Excellent. Really."

Her round face shone in the glow of the small dome light and her brown eyes sparkled under soft traces of violet on her lids. "Thank you."

Bella took a satisfied sip of Diet Dr Pepper.

"And thanks for the advice, Gabriella." She tapped my daughter's hand.

"You're welcome."

Darryl took a left on First. The wide avenue was quiet below the flapping flags outside the U.N. building.

"Your father told me about your book, Gabriella." She sat with her hands and purple clutch purse on her lap.

"Really?" Bella raised an eyebrow, then looked at me.

"Mordecai Foxx. The name is so evocative," Julie said. "It's the eighteen-seventies, isn't it?"

Bella nodded. "After the end of the Tweed Administration."

I knew this: Mrs. Gottschalk, the school librarian, had told me that Richard B. Connolly, the subject of my *Slippery Dick,* played a role in Bella's book, as did several of the Tammany Hall regulars. Connolly, city comptroller during Tweed's reign, was the first of the ring to roll over on the others. A world-class vermin, he would've gotten along fine with the Mangos—father and sons.

"Will you let me read it?" Julie asked.

"Sure," Bella chirped.

"I'd like that."

My daughter slid her glass into a side tray and offered her right hand to Julie. "Deal."

They made a dramatic, arching shake. "Deal," Julie said as she smiled at me.

Big Darryl slid the limo behind a queue of yellow cabs at the entrance to Vanderbilt Hall in Grand Central Station.

No TV crews or photographers, no racks of groupies drawn to the buzz, however soft, of celebrity.

"There's Dennis." Bella tapped Julie on the knee as she pointed.

Diddio was waiting on the red carpet that led into the station. He shuffled nervously, anxiously, as he peered into each cab that came to the curb. I thought he looked good in his tux, with his scraggly hair more or less combed, his shoes shined. Almost healthy, though a bit undersized: The cuffs of his sleeves extended to the bases of his thumbs.

"He's going to win an award," my daughter added. Though she appeared calm, her foot was dancing on the limo floor.

As we pulled up and stopped at the lip of the carpet, I asked, "What's the protocol, Julie?"

"I think it's Gabriella, me, then you," she replied. "Not that I've done this before. . . ."

Darryl's ample hand jutted into the car. Bending carefully to avoid the roof, Bella came forward and stepped into the April air.

"Thanks, Darryl," I said as I got out behind Julie.

He replied with a smart, professional nod. "Anything for Ms. Orr."

The introductions were underway by the time I arrived.

"Glad to make your acquaintance," Diddio said nervously, formally, without looking directly at the four-star woman in purple standing next to him. He fingered a laminated badge that was clipped to a lanyard around his neck.

Julie nodded. "Hello, Dennis."

I pointed to the yellow badge. "That is who?"

The word "nominee" was embossed over the face of a round man with a floppy walrus mustache and a sneer that looked permanent.

"Lester Bangs," D told us. He lifted the badge for us to see. "Hall of Fame, our first inductee."

That told me nothing.

"This is the first— Is it the New York Rock Critics Association?" Julie asked. "The first awards ceremony?"

"Third," Diddio replied, holding up three fingers. He looked at the sky, then at a man in a tux and red socks who wore a baseball cap with the word "anarchy" above the bill.

We stood in silence as the opportunity for explanation withered. An empty double-decker bus wheezed to a stop, then made an illegal left at Park Avenue.

"Let's get inside," Diddio said finally. "If it's good with everybody, I mean." He looked at Bella, then me. "It's happening already, kind of."

Bella grabbed him and took his arm.

"Shall we?" Julie said to me. She tucked her arm in mine and we followed.


Separated by a sloping path that led to the concourse, Vanderbilt Hall was actually two magnificent foyers: Beaux Arts architecture highlighted by a row of gold, egg-shaped chandeliers above pink marble floors. Now, a black curtain blocked a view of the vast main concourse, the vaulted dome with its constellation, the Westchester- and Connecticut-bound riders of Metro North.

The hall was dotted with perhaps 30 round tables set for eight, and Julie caught the theme before I did. "Oh, cute," she said. "We're backstage after a rock concert." She pointed to the folding chairs, red plastic tablecloths, bowls of brown M&Ms, drooping daisies in soda bottles.

At the east end, about 70 men and women, mostly in ill-fitting formal wear accented with ornate jewelry and other mild flights of affectation, milled around a bar that seemed to serve only longneck beers and cheap California white.

I said, "Don't they all look—" But I stopped. Asking Julie if everyone in the odd lot in back resembled Diddio didn't seem like the way to go. I wanted her to like him, to see what Bella and I saw in him.

On a stage at the other end, a small combo with two horns played jazz with a Latin flair. It sounded pretty good to me, but no one was on the small dance floor.

"Somehow, I didn't expect this," Julie said.

"What did you expect?" I asked.

"I have my expectations," she said coyly, "but I'll keep them to myself."

"Well, this whole thing is news to me," I told her. "But I've got to stand by Diddio."

"Or?"

"Or Bella will kick me in both shins."

She asked, "Should I be calling her Bella?"

"Oh, no," I said quickly. "No, no."

Diddio and my daughter, her eyes locked on him in admiration, returned with drinks.

Brow furrowed, Diddio handed me a beer. "We're a little low on star power," he said as he sipped the cold brew.

I offered the longneck to Julie. She declined and took a glass of club soda from my daughter.

"Cock Michaels is here," Bella said cheerfully, hopefully. Her face was red with excitement.

"Well, every year we invite all the New York guys. But, you know, what are we offering, you know what I mean?"

Affixed with black tape to the station's walls were banners advertising the event's sponsors. Only a few local businesses had thrown in their support. I recognized the brown-and-yellow logo of J&R Music World on one wall, the blue box of *The Village Voice* next to it. Zabar's, Helmsley Hotels and the Humane Society of New York had also ponied up for the critics.

"No real big fish, D," I said, as I pointed toward a red-and-green flag from Ray's Pizza.

"We can't go to the record labels," he replied. "Conflict. Taco Bell? Not very New York. Wal-Mart? They spike stickered discs."

"There's a certain set of principles at work here, I suspect," Julie said kindly.

"Nah. We're just inept at anything other than rock 'n' roll," he replied, peering at his scuffed shoes. "If we had to get real jobs . . ."

The Latin band came to an abrupt stop, the sudden silence accentuating the awkwardness of the moment. People who had been shouting quickly shifted to hissing whispers, soft social laughter.

"I suppose you have to keep your distance," Julie continued, offering Diddio a gracious exit.

"They hate us," he said. He pulled at the wet label on the beer bottle.

"Cock Michaels likes you," Bella pointed out hopefully.

"Yeah, but . . ."

"I've heard of him," Julie said, over the din of conversation, rising now to take up the silence. "Is he still popular?"

Diddio said, "He's presenting the Doc Pomus Award for best New York song. Doc helped him. Michaels loved Doc. Loyal guy," he nodded. "Good guy."

"Then why do they call him—"

"His first name is Cochrane, Dad," Bella explained dryly.

"You know this guy, T," Diddio said. "You do."

"I do? From where?" Drinks in hand, people from the bar area were moving toward tables, shifting into folding chairs.

Bella answered. "From the plate. On my bedroom wall."

I thought for a moment. "That's Cock Michaels? Wow."

"What?" Julie asked, looking side to side. "What don't I know?"

I explained. When Bella had come home from the hospital, Diddio had greeted us with an enormous fruit basket—"Tangerines, man!"—and a delicate, handmade plate of cute little yellow stars against a sapphire sky. A large beaming star in the center bore the name "Gabriella." Underneath it were written a few lines from a song: "Remember you are as a star in the midnight sky: brilliant and never alone."

The music picked up again. "'Caravan,'" Diddio said, glancing toward the Latin group. "Dizzy's arrangement, 1954."

"I think I just saw somebody," Julie said. "Behind the band."

"Could be," D said, shrugging sheepishly.

"Dennis," Bella said. "Introduce me to somebody."

"You want me to?' he asked her.

"Yes."

Diddio turned to me. "Go ahead," I told him. "I'll get us a table."

"Number nine," D said, adding with childlike pride, "I'm a nominee."

Two pretty guys from some band called Precious Nina sat with us, giggling, playing with their teased-up hair, talking only to each other and staring down Julie's dress as we ate our theme meal, which was adorned with green salad awash in bottled Italian dressing.

We were given little bottles of Jack Daniel's on the side.

"In honor of Keith," Diddio explained.

Apparently, Keith Richards is one of the good guys. He put himself at a table near the stage and graciously greeted everyone who came by. He was beloved by the crowd. He got up three times to visit the john and each time he received a crisp round of applause. Maybe it was the chains on his boots that he wore under a tux that looked like it had been made for Zorro.

I told Julie I'd now been in the company of two Rolling Stones. "How many are there?" I asked her.

As she returned her plastic fork to her paper plate, she said, "Dead or alive?"

"There are dead Rolling Stones?" I asked. "Why wasn't I informed?"

"T," Diddio said, nudging me with his elbow. "I got someone you might want to meet."

"Me?" He hadn't spoken aloud in 15 minutes, instead spending the evening nodding at passing colleagues and whispering gossip to Bella, who drank it up with a perpetual smile.

"Sure." As he stood, his paper napkin fluttered to the floor. The pretty boys from Precious Nina tittered.

I looked at Bella, at Julie, at the two pleasant young women who filled out our table—they were from a P.R. firm that handled "women with an edge, Liz Phair types. Ani DiFranco before men."

"I'll be right back," I said, as Julie leaned toward Bella to resume their conversation.

As we went away from the now-quiet bandstand, I tapped Diddio on his bony shoulder. He stopped on the runner between the foyers and turned to me, his black hair flying into his face.

"D, what are you doing?"

"Doing?" He looked up at me. "Introducing— You mean, like, in general, like? I'm getting ready to hang my head. Or get my prize. What?"

"I mean with Julie," I said over the dinner din. "It's obvious you're smitten with her."

"Smitten? Man, I am smote."

"Are you going to talk to her?"

"Not yet, no."

I liked this about Diddio: no false claims, no fumbling excuses. A stand-up guy standing up for his misbehavior. "What are you waiting for?"

"'Til I get some leverage, man," he replied. "I win that award and I am the *bomb,* right?"

"Maybe she's not looking for a bomb, D. Maybe you ought to be a nice guy who talks to her."

He frowned quizzically. "You think?"

Julie had spent most of the evening listening to Bella's stories and sneaking glances at me, as I wondered where Bascomb was, how Sixto was explaining his fraudulent Danny Villa biography and who finally found Hassan. There was a lot I needed to tell her.

"Who do you want me to meet, D?"

He turned and started off again, pointing at a table not far from the back of the hall.

"That guy," Diddio said.

He pointed at a large man with floppy brown hair and a big brown beard. The man, who would've resembled a bear even if he hadn't been wearing a brown suit and a beige, open-necked shirt that revealed the top of a hairy chest, had a reporter's notebook in front of him. A vaguely familiar celebrity seemed eager to give her opinion as the man scribbled. She'd made herself up for photographers and her skin seemed a dull orange under her off-blond ringlets.

"Wait here," Diddio instructed.

I watched as he interrupted the interview and whispered to Bear, who nodded and excused himself to the celebrity as he closed his notepad. When the man stood, Diddio seemed to shrink, and as they came toward me I had the impression I was watching a big, burly ventriloquist taking his long-haired, tuxedoed dummy for a walk.

But Diddio was no dummy.

"Terry Orr, this is Tom Coombs. Of *The New York Times*."

As we shook hands, he said, "So you're Terry Orr."

"R. Thomas Coombs," I replied.

He tucked his notepad into the side pocket of his jacket.

We were the same height, but he had maybe 50 pounds on me.

"You're sizing me, Terry," he said. "Is that private-eye policy?"

"That's it," I replied. "I'm deciding whether to kill you now or see if the Sulzbergers will buy you back."

He laughed. "The union, maybe. You can't be that upset about the column, Terry. I seem to recall that you got off easy."

Diddio said, "Tom, I want you to tell Terry I wasn't a source for the piece."

Coombs looked at me. "He wasn't."

"Thank you," Diddio said, bowing slightly. "I've got to go now. It's almost time."

As Diddio went off, I said to Coombs, "This must be a gold mine for you."

He nodded. "What's the old saying? 'Writing about music is like dancing to architecture.' Something like that. But these guys are so earnest. Someone like your friend, he thinks the world revolves around this music. Everybody's life would be better if they could just hear the next song. Or understand the last one."

"So you'll cut them some slack," I said.

"Are you kidding?"

"I thought not."

"You're here for Diddio?" he asked.

"What else?"

We were both looking across the hall. Busboys were taking away paper plates, plastic cups and cutlery. They'd decided to cut out the middle of the operation by dumping the stuff directly into big black garbage bags. On the stage, instruments were being shifted around, chairs moved, microphones rearranged.

"What are you working on?" he asked.

I shrugged.

"Last time you didn't talk to me I got a column out of it," he said.

"You shouldn't have mentioned my daughter and the money," I told him sharply. "She didn't need that. She's a good kid and it's going to stay that way."

"You've worked my side of things, Terry," he replied. "You know how it goes. Besides," he added, "your daughter is what makes you interesting."

"What led you to think I want to be interesting?"

He nodded agreeably. "We have no choice, sometimes."

"No, I guess not."

"Is that her over there? Next to the woman in purple?"

I said yes.

"She's growing up. And the woman?"

"She's already grown up," I cracked.

"I'll say," he chuckled. "Do I know her?"

If he visited Sharon Knight at the office, he might. "I don't know. Do you?"

He looked at me. "No, I don't think I do."

Workers in gray uniforms were shifting the podium toward the center of the unadorned platform. A couple of potted plants might've helped.

"You got something for me?" Coombs asked.

I looked at the Bear. He wrote a widely read column for the city's most respected media outlet. What he wrote wore the mantle of credibility; that is, people believed what he reported, even if it was sprinkled with his opinions.

Coombs was the kind of guy I'd been searching for when I'd run through the microfiche at the Public Library: an influential columnist.

Onstage, one of the men in gray affixed a logo to the podium—the stylized photo of Bangs.

I turned to Coombs, then pointed to the soft black curtain that separated us from the great hall.

He followed me.

I dug the cell phone out of my pocket.

We were on the other side now, and the vast concourse was quiet. A few young people with campers' backpacks were sitting near the information booth, chatting affably, as couples in neat casual dress and copies of *Playbill* rolled up in their hands searched the overhead boards for the next train home. The bar at Michael Jordan's was packed, and the crowd spilled onto the stairs at the west end of the hall. From somewhere, the peal of laughter, the squeal and wheeze of a train easing into the station, a cart on wobbling rollers, all echoing high and wide.

"Ever hear of Sonia Salgado?" I asked the *Times* columnist.

He shook his head.

"Run a NexisLexis on her," I said, "whatever."

"A summary might be useful," Coombs said as he drew next to me.

I leaned against the shelf in front of an empty ticket window. "When you hear about Danny Villa's arrest and the suicide at the Avellaneda, she'll pull it together for you."

When I started tapping in my own number to recall the message Addison had left me, Coombs asked, "Is this going to be her?"

"Not unless they have cellular in heaven."

I handed him the phone.

"Keep me out of it," I told him.

## 17

They finally pulled Diddio and Bella off the Vanderbilt Hall ceiling and now it was time for everyone to celebrate, commiserate, dance. They were taking photos over by the podium where the awards had been presented, where Cock Michaels gave a waifish woman I'd never heard of the Doc Pomus Award for a song I'd never heard. To pose for their photos, the winners among the critics were grouped in a row of uneven clip-on bow ties, shiny rented tuxedos and awkward grins. Between snaps, they giggled and jostled to stand next to Keith, who either had saintly patience or had nipped at more than a few mini-bar Jacks.

The photographers—including the woman who'd won the regally named Best Picture Award—finished their assignments, and I watched from a distance as Diddio introduced Bella to his peers. No shrinking violet she, my daughter zoomed in on the Rolling Stone. Diddio snapped them together with our Fuji disposable.

The boys from Precious Nina had stumbled off and the two PR women had traded us for a couple of writers from *Entertainment Weekly*. The Latin band was playing something familiar that I couldn't place and then it suddenly shifted to a quiet number. I looked at Julie.

"Shall we?" she asked.

"Why not?"

I took her hand.

And when we reached the dance floor and I took her right hand in mine and brought my right arm around and touched her warm skin, I knew it was all wrong. Within one measure of the slow romantic song, I knew this wasn't my Marina in my arms. The hand I held wasn't hers, nor was the dark hair that brushed the side of my face. The scent belonged to someone else. And by the second measure, I was acutely aware, once again, that I would never hold my wife, *mei carissima,* ever ever again.

I looked over Julie's bare shoulder to Bella, who was chatting up one of Diddio's friends, a man her height with long blond locks.

"She's wonderful, Terry," Julie whispered. "You should be very proud."

I waited until the catch in my throat went away. "I am."

Julie looked up at me, then nestled her head against my chest. And we swayed to the pretty music and I tried to think of nothing and when we turned I saw Bella. She was looking at me and she waved and then she brought her fingers to the sides of her lips and tucked upward: Smile, Dad, she instructed.

I smiled at my daughter.

She nodded. She approved.

The saxophone player gave way to the trumpeter, who played low, as if moaning, and I knew that soon he would rear back and let out a cry.

It came to me clearly. Say it now: Julie, I can't do this. I've heard you, I understand. But I can't do it. Try Diddio, if you'd like. He's a better bet for you. He's got a heart of gold, like you do.

You're a good woman, worthy of passion, of honesty.

I felt her thigh against mine and I heard the rustle of silk as we turned.

Suddenly, she let out a low chuckle.

I pulled back to look at her.

"I'm thinking about the way Gabriella screamed," Julie said with a laugh.

The award for Best Feature had come in the middle of the program, tucked between Best Review (Concert) and Best Profile (Band). As some model read the names and subjects, Diddio had closed his eyes and I'd noticed that Bella was squirming in her seat. If I'd looked under the table, I would've seen her tugging at the rubber bands around her ankles.

"And the winner is Dennis D—"

"YAAHHHH!!!"

The startled model stopped and the room erupted in laughter.

Bella didn't care. She leapt from her folding chair and threw her arms around Diddio's neck.

Robust applause, the loudest of the night, followed the laughter, and it continued until Diddio finally wriggled out from my daughter's grip. As he went toward the podium, Bella came over and leaned against me. She was crying.

"I'm so happy for him," she said as I ran my thumb under her eyes. "Nothing good ever happens to him. He's so, so . . ." She took the handkerchief Julie offered. "I love him, Dad. And he won! He won!" She patted her hands together in a little girl's applause. Then, composing herself, she ran her fingers along her hair, a thoroughly feminine gesture the model at the podium might've used.

Diddio took the envelope and scratched his head, played with his long hair, shuffled from side to side. He pointed with the envelope toward our table.

"My friend," he said sheepishly. "Gabby, wave. It's all right."

When Bella signaled modestly with Julie's handkerchief, the critics and their guests laughed, applauded.

"And her Dad," Diddio added. "My hero. Terry, really, man."


Now Julie tugged lightly at the back of my hair. "Hero," she repeated.

"I think he was, I don't know, overcome by the moment," I told her.

"Terry," Julie began demurely, "it's not really my style . . . I guess I'm shy about some things . . ."

She wore a nervous, enigmatic expression of hope, anticipation, and she suddenly seemed younger than she had when I first saw her in her enticing purple gown.

"But, you know," she said, "sometimes it's not easy to—" She laughed. "I don't know why I'm so jittery."

Bella was looking into Diddio's envelope now and she frowned quizzically. The envelope, I'd wager, was empty. A prop.

Julie drew up. She was going to say it.

"Well, what I wanted to tell you—"

I cut her off. "Julie, what about D?" I looked into her brown eyes. "You
haven't told me what you think of him."

She slowed down. "Dennis?"

I skidded to avoid stepping on her. "I mean, he's a good guy, right?"

She let go of my hand and, as I withdrew my arm from her waist, she
lifted her hand from my shoulder.

"Julie?"

She looked up at me. "I'm sure he's a good guy," she replied, hesitantly.

The other couples on the dance floor drifted around us.

She stepped back. "I don't— What are you saying, Terry?"

"I mean, I can't . . . I don't want to stand in the way of anything promising."

"Oh, really?"

"I mean, the two of you, maybe . . . I don't know. Good people, kind.
You know."

The flute continued its flight, and I glanced at the bandstand as the drum-
mer signaled the other musicians. A flourish on the cymbals and the band
ended its song.

Over the modest applause, I said, "Should we join him over by the
Rolling Stone?"

"No, I don't think so," she replied sharply.

"All right. Why don't—"

"In fact, Terry . . ."

"What?"

"If you don't mind, I think I'll call it a night." She looked away. "I'm not
myself." She brought a finger to her temple. "A headache."

"Julie—" She was inching away. "Wait. Please."

"No, I really don't think so."

She turned and hurried toward the table to retrieve her wrap.

As I came up behind her, she said, "Will you apologize to Gabriella and
Dennis for me?"

Her cheeks were flushed. "Julie, listen, let me explain. I—"

"Please, Terry."

"OK. Of course. Sure." I moved the chair that was between us. "Let me get a cab for you, Jule."

"I can get my own cab, Terry."

She went quickly up the slight incline toward 42nd Street.



"I don't believe you. I mean, what were you thinking?"

She'd leaned over, pressed a button and sent up the partition that separated us from Big Darryl. On the seat next to her was a box that held Diddio's prize: a portable, anti-shock DAT player/recorder with a built-in microphone.

"She suddenly, out of nowhere, gets a headache just when you start to tell her she should be interested in Dennis."

"Bella, I know she didn't have a headache," I said as I looked through tinted glass to the white foam on the East River, to smokestacks and, in the distance, bolts and bridges.

"Dad, Julie has no interest, none, zero, in Dennis," she continued, accenting her words by pounding her leg with the side of her fist.

"And this you know how?" I shifted my foot onto the hump in the black carpeting.

"Dad, Julie is interested in you. In you. Y–O–U."

"I—"

"Go ahead. Frown. Make faces." Bella pointed to the top of my head. "That brain is not just in there so your head's not empty."

"I don't know what you're talking about, Bella."

"The dress, Dad, the hair, the makeup," she continued. "No one's going to do that for a blind date."

"Listen, Bella, I'm not completely—"

"And I was watching you when you were dancing. When you were dancing, she looked very happy. Very happy.'"

"Bella, how about you stop wagging your finger at me?"

"You better bring flowers."

"Flowers aren't going to get it done."

She shifted, bringing up her leg and tucking her white shoe under her. "She'll forgive you. Eventually."

"I doubt it."

"Eventually," she repeated.

As we approached NYU Medical Center, the big limo smacked into a deep pothole. Bella and I bounced. The crystal liquor bottles jangled.

"Don't just call," she added as she retrieved the box that had slid across the leather seat. "Go talk. Apologize nice."

"Bella, I mean, your expertise. Where does it come from?" I asked.

"I'm not an expert," she replied calmly. "But I know you."

"I'm not the issue. Julie is."

She shook her head. "You." She put the box on her lap.

The limo drifted into the right lane, moving us toward the Houston Street exit.


We thanked Darryl and he watched as I punched in the code and unlocked the front door. I heard him leave Harrison as Bella opened Diddio's prize.

"You sure you should be doing that?" I said as I hung my blazer on the newel post.

"He asked me to," she said. "He won't be able to figure this out by himself."

"Let me rephrase. Do you think you should be doing that now?"

The clock in the stove made the time 12:36.

She kicked off her party shoes. "Dad," she pleaded, "I'm having the best night of my life."

"OK, OK," I said, waving at her.

I could hear her humming as I passed her mother's paintings.

When I reached my study I hit the PLAY button on the answering machine to listen to Addison's message, as Coombs had. As I eased into my hard chair, his baritone filled the small space.

"Terry, Luther. Your guy Bascomb is a hard-ass piece of work. He wanted Danny Villa as his lawyer and when we told him about Villa's arrest, he tightened up. I threw Mango's name at him and he . . . No, he didn't like hearing it. And I guess you might've heard by now but Villa's got a story to tell us, something about a guy named Sixto. I'm going back in now."

"Press him on Ernie Mango," I said to the recorded voice. "You'll find why Sonia—"

"I'll catch up with you later," Addison said. The little tape beeped and I watched it rewind and the machine shut down.

"—had to be taken out now." Talking to the darkness, I added softly, "If the diamonds are gone, why did Sonia have to die now?"

When I returned to the kitchen, Bella had the DAT recorder out of the box. A Styrofoam cube rested on my chair and the box top lay on her manuscript.

"Don't lose any of that stuff," I said as I went to the refrigerator.

She rolled her eyes and went back to the directions.

"You want something to drink?"

"No." She looked at me. "You know, this is easy to use, actually."

I grabbed the water, let the door swing shut.

Bella took the microphone out of its plastic wrapping. "You see how happy he was?"

I came around the table, I lifted the directions. As I refolded the accordion-style sheets, I snuck a peek. She was right. Seemed simple enough.

Suddenly, she stood, pushing off the table. "I'm going up," she said.

"That's it?"

"I'm still happy," she smiled. "I want to do my journal."

"You can do it down here, if you want. In the living room."

She came over to me.

"You OK?" she asked.

"Me? I'm fine. You?"

"OK is not even close. I'm super!"

She went up on her toes and kissed my cheek.

"I'll put that away in the morning," she said, gesturing toward the DAT recorder, Styrofoam, plastic wrap.

As she reached the stairs, I called to her.

"Bella?"

Her white socks had slid down her white stockings, and the shoulder strap of her pretty dress sagged.

"You were great tonight, Bella."

She smiled at me. "Thanks." Then she turned and went toward her room, humming a tune the Latin combo had played.

I sat at the table and, sipping the cold carbonated water, listened as Bella went into her bedroom and then left it a minute later to pad down the hall to the bathroom. By now, her dress was on a hanger in the closet, her slip and undergarments were in the hamper in her room and she had on a mismatched set of pajamas or an old T-shirt of mine.

Minutes later, she went back to her room and I heard the door close, the knob catch, and in my mind's eye, I saw her dig out her marble-notebook journal, take a pencil from her cup, and jump onto her bed, landing in a cross-legged seated position. Words flowing on lined paper, the story of the best night of her life.

A sidebar: My father the blockhead.

And then it was quiet and I heard the kitchen clock tick and the refrigerator vibrate. Slipping the electronic equipment into their proper slots, I completed the puzzle and slid the Styrofoam into the box with a squeak that sent a shiver through me.

I set the box squarely in front of Bella's seat.

I took another sip of water. Then I looked at my watch, as if it would tell me something different than the clock in the stove had. As if it would tell me morning had arrived and no ghosts had appeared during the long, billowing night and that something as mundane as the sun would relieve me of the weight of my reflections.

I felt it coming on now; silence in the house. The prologue had begun: The trembling ceiling had flown away, the walls waffled, the floor caught fire. Alone, abjectly so, I was reaching for the lifeline, made not of rough hemp, but of sorrow, self-pity, torturing thoughts intended to make me feel better, to somehow assuage the burden of my own liability in creating this nightmare in which I live, in which Bella lives.

"*'Tis unmanly grief.*"

But Marina had come to me this morning in a train station in Queens, and again tonight as I held a fine woman in my arms. She had come in horror, screaming at the moment of her death. She had come in tenderness: Remembering I would never hold her reminded me of holding her, my hands on her warm, olive skin.

Right now, in this chair, I can believe she is about to touch my shoulder, about to lean down and kiss my cheek.

I feel her warm breath on my neck, my ear.

"Terry, the children are sleeping now," she beckons.

I rise to join her, to kiss her before we sweep upstairs to our bedroom—

I can't live this way.

It's been four years, for Christ's sake.

I am alive now.

There is so much to be done.

A desperate man in the auto graveyards of Queens. A community leader taken away in handcuffs. A man at the end of a rope. A woman in my arms. A daughter: "I'm super!"

I have to occupy myself at all times.

Yes, I do.

*Arrowsmith* is waiting in the living room.

Yes and I'd taken a nap earlier today. I'd be awake for hours. I could give it the time, the attention it deserved.

And then to my office: the early edition of the *Times* online.

A full night, without ghosts, away from the abyss, from the molten fire.

I turned and I saw Bella's manuscript.

# 18

There were two Roman Catholic churches within easy walking distance of Julie's apartment: the Church of Sacred Hearts of Jesus and Mary on 33rd off Second, and Our Lady of the Scapular and St. Stephen on 29th. I chose the former. The other one sounded to me like the result of a merger of two old-money companies, neither of which could afford to alienate its shareholders by giving up its brand name. Besides, I couldn't remember what a scapular was.

The mid-morning sun spread its rays on the East Side, and the accompanying breeze, too placid to be called wind, gently nudged the bare trees. Rainwater on the gray sidewalk rippled modestly. With all quiet on wide 33rd Street, I set up with my back to the Kips Bay Towers, a block-long slab of concrete that wouldn't have been out of place in Soviet-controlled Budapest. A blonde whose pajama top snuck out from under her waist-length jacket followed her plucky dog as it examined fire hydrants, NO PARKING signposts and tires for scents and information. Heading toward First, two young men walked together with a snap in their step, each with a copy of the fat Sunday *Times* tucked under his arm.

At 10:30, the church started to empty. The dour middle-aged couples who exited first, heading off in different directions, were followed by three women who wore white stockings and rubber-soled shoes under pale rain-coats and went east toward NYU Medical Center. A group of Asian women waited patiently behind two old, hunched women who navigated the church's four short steps by clinging to its aluminum banisters, hanging on as a handful of kids younger than Bella squeezed by. Finally, Julie appeared, accompanied by a priest in his vestments. He was petite, with lively eyes and an attentive gaze, and he shook Julie's hand as they parted.

Stepping between parked cars, I crossed 33rd and drew next to her as she headed toward Second, passing the Sacred Hearts rectory.

She wasn't glad to see me, but she was too polite to say it right out. She looked over her shoulder, back toward the church.

"Thinking about praying?" she asked.

"No."

"That's unfortunate."

She had on a long blue coat and gray-blue slacks. Her familiar gold cru-cifix, which she hadn't worn last night, lay atop her pale-blue turtleneck. She wore no makeup and her skin looked fresh and healthy.

"Julie, I'd like to talk to you. Can you spare a few minutes?"

"Terry, if—"

"Julie, give me a chance to make good," I said, cutting her off.

She gave me an impatient glare as she stiffened. I could see she wanted to rip into me.

She hung open her mouth and, annoyed, let her eyes drift. Then she said, "Fine."

"You have breakfast yet?"

"No."

I pointed toward Second. A coffee shop was tucked between a Duane Reade and Kips Bay Hardware.

We went west.


Julie ordered a cup of tea and told me she was due at her parents' place for their weekly family dinner. When the waitress returned with my toasted corn muffin, I cut it in half and pushed the small plate across the table.

She sat back. There'd be no intimate gestures between us.

As I retrieved the plate, I said, "Julie, first I want to apologize."

"For what?"

I stopped. "You know."

She stared into my eyes. "I'd like to hear it."

"For not being as alert . . . For not being alert." I put my hands on the table. "How's that for an answer?"

"Cute's not going to get it done, Mr. Orr," she said. "Not by a long shot."

"It's what I've got, Julie," I told her, as she sipped her tea.

She put the cup on the saucer.

"I'm here," I said, "and that ought to mean more than words. All right?"

"No, not really, but . . ." She shrugged.

I was going to tell her she could do a lot better than me. But if she was as smart in romance as she was at her profession, she'd already figured that out.

Julie said, "You look like you had a rough night."

"As a matter of fact, I had a remarkable night," I replied. "I read Bella's book."

"You did?"

I nodded as I swallowed a chunk of the buttery muffin.

"She said she didn't think you would."

"I did."

"And?"

"Well, it's a bit difficult to give a detailed critique of my daughter's book," I said. "She probably needs to spend a little more time with Edith Wharton and Henry James, and a little less with old newspapers and academia. Clearly, she memorized Riis and downloaded chunks of *Gotham*. And I'm sure her conclusions about—"

"Terry . . ."

"Julie, it's . . . It's, what? Amazing. And surprisingly insightful. Bittersweet. If I could get any distance from it, I'd call it unexpectedly spectacular."

"'Unexpectedly'? 'Surprisingly'?"

"Well, she was 12 when she started it."

There are sections where Mordecai Foxx, Bella's "unassigned" detective, is searching for eight-year-old Sophie, the abandoned Italian immigrant, in the squalid Five Points slums that—

"Did you tell her?"

I said, "She was still sleeping when I left."

"Will you?" she asked.

"Of course." I'd clipped a check for $400 to the title page—our original bet, I believe, was four-to-one against, as Bella proposed when I told her I doubted she'd stick with it—and I'd written her a note, telling her I'd be back or I'd call.

"You might want to omit the 'unexpected' part," Julie suggested. She squeezed a few drops of lemon into her cup. "Do you think it's publishable?"

"I've been avoiding that thought."

"Why?"

Because I knew it needed work and I knew she might ask me to do it, and after I did it, I'd have to contact my ex-agent, and I'd be back where I was. Without having earned the right to be there, without having taken Weisz down.

Even Harteveld would understand.

"I don't know," I replied. "I don't want to create false hopes."

"Terry, she doesn't care if it's published. She cares only that you are impressed. And proud."

And she wanted a little more than that. Never has a grievance been aired so abundantly, so thoroughly, for a single reader.

"I am proud and impressed," I said. I knew I was smiling behind my tired eyes. "Very, to both counts."

"You know, Terry," she said, "you'd be a sweet man if you didn't have your head up your butt all the time."

She nodded triumphantly. She was letting me off easy.

"Jule, I need to apologize for something else. About this Salgado thing, there's a few things I haven't told—"

She held up her hand. "Bascomb's been arrested, Villa too," she said. "And Tommy Mangionella is telling people you might've killed Sonia Salgado."

"Yeah, and Bascomb asked for Villa to be his attorney."

"That doesn't seem unusual. You saw them together, Terry."

"Julie, Danny Villa is Luis Sixto."

She sat back. "What?"

"Hiding in plain sight, more or less," I replied. "A bunch of cosmetic surgery. A phony bio."

"Are you certain?"

I nodded. "And Safi Majorelle was Ahmed Hassan."

I reached for an inside pocket of my leather jacket and withdrew the old photo of Hassan and Sixto. I pushed it across the table.

Julie studied it, then looked up at me. She tapped a finger on Hassan's footnote. "Majorelle and Villa," she said. "Their aliases."

"Seems so."

"My goodness," she said, shaking her head in quiet disbelief. "Can it be so?"

Now it was my turn to tap the photo.

She said, "Well, we'll know if it's true once Danny is printed."

"It takes days to match fingerprints, doesn't it?"

"A myth, at least since IAFIS opened in ninety-nine," she said, holding up two fingers. "Two hours."

I finished off the last of the muffin and downed the coffee.

"You know, I always wondered about Danny," she mused. "So *suave.*"

"*El Caballero,*" I said. "The Gentleman."

"Could it be he didn't want to get into the system?" she asked.

I shrugged. He was going to be telling his story to somebody. A man who had reinvented his life and gotten away with it for 30 years had a lot to say.

"So where does that leave things?" she asked as she lifted the photo and slipped it into her coat pocket.

"Well, if you guys play it right, in a couple of hours you'll know who killed Glatzer and Sonia."

"You're not going to get off that, are you? Idealizing Sonia Salgado isn't—"

"Julie, let's assume she didn't kill Glatzer," I said. "Can we do that?"

She arched an eyebrow. "Go ahead."

"She's out of Bedford Hills with a grievance, right? I mean, *she* knows she didn't do it."

"Are you saying she knows who did?"

"Doesn't matter," I said. "With her gone, that thing is closed."

"Yes, but now this . . ."

I sat back. "A simple B-and-E gone wrong. Could've been beautiful."

"But then you showed up," she laughed.

"Sonia had to go," I went on. "The question is why."

"And the answer is . . . Terry?"

"Sonia knows about the link with Mango. Maybe she doesn't know who killed Glatzer. But back then, Sixto had to tell her about the cop on the Bowery who chose the mark."

She shook her head. "This only works if Sonia didn't kill Glatzer. And the man's wallet was in her room."

"Jule, I never said she wasn't involved somehow," I explained. "She dipped Glatzer's billfold."

"Ah, Sonia isn't perfect," she said, with a sarcastic dig.

"I'm not idealizing her."

"You heard that? I wasn't sure . . ."

I nodded.

She leaned her arms on the table. "Terry, you don't have it. Sorry."

"It fits, Julie," I said.

"Not unless Bascomb gives up Sixto for Glatzer or unless Sixto knows Bascomb killed Sonia and tells us."

I realized that she was right. It might be her job, the NYPD's, the D.A.'s, to finish it off, but I was the one who was trying to pull it together. I had to keep working it until it was done.

"You think Bascomb will talk?" I asked.

"I don't know. I haven't spoken to him. I doubt Sharon will let me on this one." She smiled, nodded at me. "Because of you."

"What about Sixto?"

"Danny's too smart to talk without a deal," she replied. "He won't roll over on Bascomb until he has one."

"Maybe someone in your office will interview Tommy."

"All depends on what Danny and Bascomb say," she said. "We need a reason to talk to him or the PBA will come down on us. And once we bring him in, Internal Affairs will be involved. They have to be."

"I see."

She took a sip of her tea and pronounced it lukewarm. I noticed a lemon pit as it floated to the surface.

"You think someone might call in his brother Jimmy?" I asked.

"Why?"

"He's the one who hired Bascomb to keep me away from Hassan."

"Really?" she asked thoughtfully. "Does anyone know this?"

I learned it from Bascomb and hadn't told Addison. "No."

She paused, "An interesting way to find out what Tommy's been thinking."

"Maybe," I said, then added, "Couldn't hurt."

"Sure it could," she replied. "Could make big brother upset."

"And?"

"What are you saying?"

"Sooner or later, Tommy's going to be upset."

She nodded and, as I dug for the bills in the pocket of my jeans, she lifted a cell phone from her purse.

"Tell them to try Elizabeth Street," I said. "Either the old man's place or a bar up the block. Marco's."

She nodded as she pressed buttons.


I decided to go to Little Italy via Second, passing Stuyvesant Square and the East Village, avoiding the temptation to turn west on St. Mark's Place and revisit Sonia's now-silent apartment. I was still holding back something from Julie, from Sharon, and I wanted one more shot at it before I turned it over. I needed to do this part of it myself.

Taking my time to avoid running into blue that Julie and Sharon sent, I reached Elizabeth Street just before 1 P.M. and, since I came from the north, I went to Marco's first. To my surprise, it wasn't open yet for business. Inside, Lil' M was working over its terrazzo floor, slopping the heavy mop back and forth, a determined grimace on his face.

I kept going on Elizabeth. The street was quiet; fat meatballs, hot sausages, maybe a few *braciole* were simmering in the sauce in the deep, tempered pot. Fresh bread and a chunk of Pecorino sat next to a short blade, a curved grater with an old wooden handle. The old women, back from Mass and all wearing the same familiar apron, were cracking open heads of iceberg lettuce under rushing cold water over a tin colander; slicing tomatoes, draining jars of black olives; humming a song sung 60 years earlier by other women working in their kitchens as they'd gotten their family feasts ready, and by their mothers before them back in Naples, in Bari, in Foggia. Their husbands were wading slowly through the newspaper, waiting for their children to get back from the bakery with pignoli cookies, chocolate biscotti, a heavy cheesecake rich with ricotta.

That is, unless the old man lived alone, his loving wife gone to the grave, one of his sons prowling alleys trying to erase the remnants of his greed, of a decision made long ago that now had caused two violent deaths, and the other son at Centre Street, telling one of the D.A.'s bureau chiefs to go fuck himself. That old sorry man is staring at yellowed old wallpaper, dull, faded flowers in uneven rows, acid and liquor swishing around in his empty stomach, still flying on last night's fuel. He's wondering if he should bother to shave. Eat the *tonno* out of the can or scrape it onto a chipped saucer with a few crackers, maybe. Hair of the dog. I always drink out of a glass, he says to no one, and that—and *that*—makes me a *drinker,* a man who likes a drink. Not a . . . Four Roses, always out of a glass, sitting down. (Pause here as he throws back the liquor.) And I— Did I take my pills before? Ah, shit. Now I got to get up and go in the fuckin' bathroom to see if—

Now who the hell is that, knocking on the god-damned door Sunday afternoon?

"You remember me?"

He looked at me and hoisted his thin suspenders up onto his bony shoulders. He wore a sleeveless undershirt and baggy gray slacks. Slippers. He coughed twice and I could smell the liquor.

"No," he said softly.

"I'm the guy you have to tell it to, Officer Mangionella."

He swallowed and his Adam's apple bobbed beneath his gray stubble.

"*Sergeant* Mangionella," he said.

"We're going to sit down and you're going to tell me all about Luis Sixto and Asher Glatzer and Sonia Salgado—"

"Yeah?"

"—and then you're going to feel much better. Better than you have in years, Sergeant."

He didn't have as much punk and swagger as he did when he had his full load on. He looked every bit the old man far into his fall, a man whose life long ago lost its direction.

He hung his head, cocked an eyebrow. "Tommy says—"

"Yes he does," I nodded. "But it's me and you now."

Peering up, he studied me with his unsteady eyes.

I said, "And I know you didn't want it to happen this way."

"Listen you . . ." But he stopped and whatever remained of his natural defiance drained away. "No," he said softly. "No I didn't."

"You didn't kill anybody."

He shook his head. "No. Not really."

"OK if I come in, Sergeant?"

"This is *my* home," he answered.

I leaned against the door frame. "It's time you get this off your chest."

He looked at me, sagged, and then stepped aside.


I found in his cabinet a can of Progresso chicken soup with escarole and I heated it for him in a dented saucepan, using a stick match to light the gas flame. His favorite chair in the living room was the one that slumped in the center, the one with the cable box on the arm, the one that faced the old RCA TV. I put the push-button box back on top of the old brown TV, swinging the thin cable behind it, where it dropped among balls of dust on the hard wood.

"You sit, Sergeant," I said.

He did.

I set up the tottery TV tray in front of him. His heels and knees fell together under it between its thin gold legs.

The scent of the canned soup relieved the stale smell of sickness, of lethargy.

In the kitchen, I put away the pint of Four Roses and, using paper towels as a pot holder, poured the hot soup into a bowl. I put the bowl on a plate and brought it to the old man who, defeated by time, sat alone among faded memories and artifacts neither ancient nor antique but merely old.

I sank into the sofa and watched as he blew across the spoon before he sipped.

"Is this your wife?"

Ernie Mango had a stereo cabinet on spikelike legs, a gold waffle-pattern covering the speaker built into the front of furniture that held a turntable and maybe a few vinyl albums behind a sliding door. On top was the bleached color photo of a short, heavyset woman. She was in her mid-twenties, and she had on a black coat and wore a big, hopeful smile. There was snow in the background, piled at the curb across the street. The cars on Elizabeth Street behind her were models from the '50s and '60s, with snow on their roofs. The photo had been blown up to fill the 8 x 10 Woolworth's frame, but it hadn't held its focus and it was soft under the dusty glass.

"Yes," he said, as he blew on the soup. Steam rose from the bowl into his face.

"Rosa, wasn't it?"

"How do you know?"

"I know someone who knew her," I replied, thinking of Mrs. Maoli. "Said she was a lovely woman."

He nodded as I put the photo of Rosa Mangionella back in its place. Then he said, "I could use something to drink with this."

He didn't hide his disappointment when I returned with a glass of tap water.

As I sat again on the sofa I said, "So how do we do this, Sergeant?"

He shrugged impassively, though not defiantly.

And I realized I was close to playing it wrong. Kindness was anathema to hard men, a weakness. I'd had the edge when I hovered over him and he was on shaky legs. I had it still, but I saw it could get away from me, as he rested in his familiar chair and I sat on foreign ground, as the hot soup worked on settling his stomach, reviving him, sobering him. Instead of facing a weary man clamoring to flood his conscience with drink, I might be talking soon to the guy who sired Tommy and Jimmy Mango, who gave them the merciless values that governed their small, callous lives.

"Let me tell you how I think it went."

He made a gesture. He wanted something to dip in the *brodo*. A piece of bread, a cracker.

"I make it like this," I said. "One morning you see it clear: Twenty years and out with half pay isn't going to do it for you. You've got ideas, you and

Rosa, dreams, and you don't want to wait. Meanwhile, on the Bowery, where you spend hours every day, there are men with diamonds. So many diamonds . . ."

He took another taste. A sliver of escarole hung from the spoon.

"But how to do it? Everybody on the Bowery knows you. You're the man who helps them, protects them."

No reaction; then, he blinked and an eyebrow twitched.

"Then you meet Luis Sixto. A fantastic coincidence."

I was going to ask him who flipped who. I wondered if Sixto tried to talk his way out of the tickets in Alphabet City by offering Mango a deal—I could hear him, Spanish accent, lots of attitude, "Maybe we can work something out here, Officer. Man, what do you think?"—or maybe Mango gave him an opening: "There's a way to lose these, *chico,*" he'd say, leaning against Sixto's car, holding the tickets in the late-night crosstown wind. But I decided to press on. I knew this much: Asking one of the Mangos a question, father or sons, was giving them an opportunity to lie.

I said, "You knew when Glatzer went on his late-afternoon delivery runs, a few hundred K in diamonds in a pouch. You probably kept an eye on him every now and then."

"Damned straight." With a limp hand, he used the dripping spoon to point at me.

"He expected it, you at his back."

"Fuckin' Jews," he muttered.

"Worse when they're connected?" I led.

"Wouldn't give you sand in the fuckin' desert."

"Sixto could rip off Glatzer."

"Why the fuck not?" he said. "Wet my beak, you know what I'm saying?"

"He had enough."

"More than enough." He wiped at his nose with the back of his wrist.

"Sixto brought in his pal, Bascomb."

He frowned. Then he remembered. "Big kid. Liked to mix it up."

"They'd take him down into the station at Chrystie and Grand."

"That's the idea," he said.

"But the girl . . ."

"The dip," he said, as if correcting me. "Sixto's got her trained. She can lift a wallet from anybody, *anybody*, she wants to."

"But not diamonds from a pouch."

"No, not diamonds from a pouch."

"So they go back," I said.

"Glatzer, he had balls, this guy," Mango said. "Fought. A fighter."

"Having his wallet stolen wasn't going to chase him off his own street."

"'Cause I got his back. That's the job."

"Right. But they didn't have to kill him," I suggested.

He shrugged.

I tried it again. "He should've given up the diamonds."

"He— Yeah, right. But he *fights*." The old man punched at the stale air.

"It was your idea to put it on the girl."

"Yeah, my idea," he sneered. "Sure. Right."

"So it was Sixto—"

He dropped the spoon into the bowl. "Sixto," he said over the sudden clatter. "All of it."

"Sixto—"

He tapped his temple. "Smart kid. Very smart kid."

"You didn't hear from him."

"Oh, yeah," he laughed darkly. "Christmas cards. Hamiltons in a picture window. Yeah. Right. *Feliz* fuckin' *Navidad*."

"What about Bascomb?"

"He never got a dime. Not a dime. Nobody."

He tried to push aside the tray, but it wobbled as if it would tumble and he gave up.

I watched as he fell into his thoughts. Then he burped and looked at me.

"Sergeant," I said, "do you know Danny Villa?"

He frowned in confusion. "No. Who's that?"

"Tell me about Sonia Salgado."

"He put it on her. Sixto." He nodded, nodded, pointed with a crooked finger. "Him."

I scuttled to the edge of the sofa. "But thirty years . . . Thirty years and no one says anything."

"They told me she was, you know . . ." He put his thumb and forefinger at the side of his head and twisted his wrist. The Italian-American sign for someone who's not right upstairs, someone who's simple.

Hassan said Sonia wasn't bright. So did Villa.

"Besides, the Jews . . . Beame is mayor, Koch then. She don't see the sun, you know what I'm telling you? The parole board?"

I nodded.

"So what I am supposed to do? It goes like that," he said finally, letting his eyes slowly close, open. "Life. Everybody knows that."

"You'll have to explain it to me, Sergeant."

"Some poor, dumb . . . She's unlucky." He ran his tongue over his top teeth and, as his eyelids sagged, he said, "Who cares, right? I mean, I never got mine, so . . ."

"Your Rosa wouldn't let you get away with that talk, Sergeant."

He puffed up as if ready to come back hard at me. But he stopped and he looked away.

"Sometimes, they're our conscience," I said.

We sat. After a minute in the sepia glow from Elizabeth Street, the silence was heavy.

"Not sometimes," the old man said. "If it's sometimes . . ."

"I'm with you, Sergeant."

I watched as he ran an index finger under his eyes.

He said, "I didn't know this Sonia. I didn't ask for her. I didn't—"

"But you knew."

He sat still, then he nodded slowly.

"It's a huge burden, Sergeant, a secret like that. A secret you can't share with anybody."

The old man sank back into his favorite chair and he looked away from me.

"I got to make my peace," he said.

"That's right, Sergeant. We all do."

"I got to make my peace now."

I nodded.

"Thirty years . . . So I went to see her."

"You went to see Sonia? When?"

He thought for a moment. "I don't know."

"Where?"

"They put her in a halfway house," he said. "Over in the Village."

"What did she say?"

"She didn't know nothing. What I was saying, she didn't know."

"You told her about you and Sixto?" I asked.

"She didn't know. She thought he ran . . . that he ran because somebody was going to set him up for Glatzer. Like they did her."

"She didn't know he had taken off with the diamonds."

"She didn't know nothing," he said. "She's thinking love and he's going to come back, if he can pull it off. She's thinking he wants to, you know, 'cause it's love."

"Until you explained."

"She said I was wrong, I was crazy. She was going to call the cops."

"So you . . ."

He peered down into his lap.

"What did you do, Sergeant?"

He said, "What else could I do? I said I'm sorry. What I wanted to do."

"What did she say?"

"She told me to leave. She pushed me. Shouted. Screamed."

"That's it?"

He looked at me and held up his palms.

"After thirty years, you go to see her?" I asked.

"I couldn't go up to the prison. They would know."

"Thirty years . . ."

"She's out and the world's gone fuckin' wacky with the World Trade Center and, you know, good people, heroes, doing . . ." He hesitated, then he pointed to the faded photo on top of the old stereo cabinet. "And I'm here, looking at that picture. Rosa."

"Did you tell Tommy you went to see her?"

He thought for a moment. It was one thing to tell the man sitting across from him about a dark thing that happened a long time ago, about his obligations, memories of his late wife. It was something very different to talk openly about what was said to Tommy the Cop.

"Sure you did," I said. "You can't keep a secret from Tommy. He's got *your* back now."

"Let me tell you something about my Tommy," he said sharply. "My Tommy, he don't take shit from nobody. Tommy, he *knows*."

I stood. I'd heard all I needed to and I didn't want to listen to a testimonial for Tommy the Cop, not from an old fuck who let an enfeebled girl languish in prison for 30 years so he could play Mr. Big at the dinner table or buy a bungalow down the Jersey shore.

"I got to go," I told him.

He tilted his head. "Who are you?"

I lifted the bowl and spoon from the tray. "I'm the guy who's cleaning up."

He said, "Oh."

# 19

I closed the old man's door behind me and walked down the short hall to the stairwell. As I trotted down the stairs, I saw the pale curtain ripple on the glass below me and watched the front door open with a crash. Jimmy Mango stormed in and, without stopping, jumped the first few steps.

He looked up at me, first at my sneakers, then my face, and didn't try to hide his hostility, his disgust. He stopped, backed down the stairs, and waited for me with his left hand on the newel post.

"Who said you could hassle him?" he charged. He tapped his fingers on the wooden knob.

"Your asshole buddy McDowell," I replied as I kept coming down the stairs. "He gave me a note. After he planted the books at Villa's."

As he slowly moved his right hand around toward the small of his back, Mango let the wisecrack slide.

"You going to tell me how it went at the D.A.'s?" I asked. "Or do I have to watch you cry on tape?"

"Don't bait me, Four," he said through gritted teeth. "You got nowhere to go now and you are in way over your Ivy fuckin' League head."

I reached the bottom step and he came directly in front of me, his face red, his eyes in tight slits.

"Back, Jimmy," I told him as I moved down to the ground floor.

"You gotta answer for messin' with my old man," he spit as he continued to grope for whatever was stuck down the back of his jeans.

"Jimmy," I said, as I put my left hand on his chest, "fuck you and your old man."

"You son of—"

Before he could react, I shoved him and he stumbled backward toward the door and I dove at him, driving him hard as he crashed against the corner, his right hand pinned behind him. As he grimaced, I grabbed at his left arm with my right hand, held it firmly by the wrist and threw a looping left to the side of his face that caught him high on the cheekbone. I threw a second left, this one shorter, more compact, and caught him flush on the jaw. The side and back of Mango's head hit the wall behind him with an ugly thud and he went down, sliding in the corner until he was seated awkwardly on the hallway floor.

I looked down at him. He was out.

I reached down, pushed him over, and stepped in to get my hands behind him. The nine-millimeter pistol he had tucked away had landed beneath him, under the seat of his jeans. Which meant he'd gotten to it as I went at him.

I lifted the blue piece and put it in my jacket pocket.

Now I had a gun of my own.


The cabbie let me off on the wrong side of Greenwich and I jogged on glistening cobblestone toward my house, scooting across as cars, taxis and a red flatbed Ford moved south.

I entered to find Bella in the kitchen, sipping a Yoo-hoo, holding the $400 check I'd written.

"I'd forgotten about the bet," she said.

"Really?" I hung my coat, with my new piece tucked snugly in an inside pocket, on the back of the laundry-room door. "Why else would you write a book?"

"Very cute," she nodded, then added as she folded the check. "You're good to your word, Dad."

"You too."

She wore an oversized blue shirt with an Esso logo and the name "Bud" in script over the breast. The frayed cuffs of her floppy blue painter's jeans all but covered her scuffed bowling shoes.

"Well?" she asked.

"A full report. But later," I replied. I took a bottle of cold water from the refrigerator. I wanted to seem composed, unconcerned. But I needed for her to be ready to move. "You have plans?"

"Not really. I intended to sleep until three."

It was 2:06. "I think it's fallen through, Bella."

"If Julie didn't call three times, it wouldn't have."

I sat on the edge of my seat and took the slip of paper she slid toward me. A 917 area code; Julie was using her cell phone.

On the other side of the table, *Nursery of Crime* was back in a neat pile: Bella, I'd bet, had run through it to see if I'd line-edited the thing.

"She say what she wanted?"

"No, but I know you two made peace."

"Yep." I drank half the bottle of carbonated water.

She studied the Yoo-hoo label. "You are going to have to deal with it, Dad."

I cut her off. "We were talking about your plans."

"None now," she shrugged. "Homework. Why? You want to do something?"

"Sure. But I can't." I dropped my elbows on the table. "Bella, I need you to go out. Now."

She put down the Yoo-hoo bottle. "Are you in trouble?"

"No."

"But?"

"But Tommy Mango is coming and he's going to be angry."

"Tommy the Cop?" she said, inching up in the seat. "I think it's you who needs to go out."

"Bella . . ."

"I don't know where I can go." She paused thoughtfully. "Glo-Bug's not around—"

"Daniel Wu?"

"No. He's doing a big family thing. Sisters, grandmother, that stuff. And Eleanor's with her father and stepmother in Scarsdale." She stopped suddenly. "I could call Dennis."

"I don't think so." Who knows when his all-night prowl ended? He might've chosen to crash at the Tilt. "Hey . . ."

"'Hey' what? That's not a good 'hey.'"

"Let's go see Leo."

"Oh, no," she said. "Dad, no. Dad, it's demeaning."

"No, it's not."

*"Dad."*

"Get your coat."

She stared at me, let her eyes drop and then lifted herself from the seat.

"You can work on your *Hamlet* paper," I added, as I went to the laundry door to grab my coat. "The question of Claudius's greed—"

"Not Claudius's greed, Dad." Her chair caught on the floor as she pushed it toward the table. "Hamlet's. It's Hamlet's greed."

I stopped. "What?"

"Hamlet's the greedy one," she said without looking at me. "It's all *me, me, me.* He's just obsessed and bitter. All that stuff about revenge. That's greed."

I shrugged. "I thought it had to be about money."

"There's lots of kinds of greed."

She went to the stairs. Her backpack was upstairs, and her books, her music, her journal.

"You know, we used to do things every Sunday," she muttered.


Ten minutes later, we entered the Tilt.

Leo looked up from Friday's edition of the *Times-Picayune*. "Gabriella," he said, a lilt of genuine surprise in his voice.

"Hello, Mr. Mallard," she groaned as she shifted her gray fedora to the back of her head.

Grabbing his cane, he hoisted himself from his throne. Giraffes nibbled on leaves on the silent TV.

"You seen D?" I asked.

He said no. "He win?"

"He won," Bella replied dryly.

"No kiddin'? Ain't that something."

"Leo." I gestured for him to join me at the center of the bar. As I waited, I pointed to a booth in the rear of the room. Pouting, she grabbed her back-pack and dragged it across the floor as she passed the pool table.

Wheezing from the short walk, Leo whispered, "She don't like me."

There was a certain imperial streak in Bella. Something about the dank, musty bar, and Leo's aura of resignation, put her off. Marina would've re-acted the same way.

He added, "She used to."

"Leo, I got Tommy Mango on my ass and it's personal now."

"What happened?"

I told him.

"Yep," he replied, "personal. But you know maybe he comes here you ain't home."

"Yeah, but he's not looking for her."

"I can't see that's his style," Leo said in agreement.

I nodded. Not yet, anyway. What Tommy needed to do now was reach me before I could report what his old man had told me.

"How long you going to be?" he asked.

I shrugged. "I'll get back to you. You need to go somewhere, call D."

"Where do I need to go? Hell, I'm going to lock the front door and fin-ish my newspaper."

I tapped him on the arm.

"You need to carry?" he asked. His Smith & Wesson was back under the bar.

"I'm set."

I went to Bella, who sat in a booth next to the pool table. She was wad-ing through the contents of her handbag and thus far had removed her MP3 player, earphones, the instructions to Diddio's portable recorder, her marble-covered journal, an ad hoc group of pens in assorted colors and a well-thumbed paperback edition of *Hamlet.*

"*Give thy thoughts no tongue,*" I said, "*nor any unproportioned thought his act.*"

"Yes. Thank you for that."

Or maybe Polonius was greedy too. Maybe pragmatism is a form of greed.

"Ask Leo if you can mess around with the jukebox. D has a couple of crates of CDs in those cases for the empties back there."

I could see she was intrigued by the idea. Not that she would say so. "Maybe."

"All right," I said. "I'll be in touch."

As I turned to leave, she stood and said, "Dad, should I be worried?"

"No. Tommy Mango isn't going to bother you."

"No, I mean should I be worried about you?"

I shook my head. "I'm going to call Julie and I'll be back as soon as I can."

"Watch yourself," she advised.

"Got it." I backpedaled away from her, moving along the length of the pool table.

"Kiss?" A desolate smile crossed her pretty face.

I stopped, went to her and kissed her cheek. "Ask Leo about opera," I whispered. "You'll be surprised."

I could feel her watching me as I went toward the front door and pointed at the big bartender, who shook the head of his cane at me as I moved outside.


"Terry, where are you?"

"Back in TriBeCa."

"I've been trying to reach you," she said. The connection was good, but I couldn't tell if she was indoors or on the street.

"Yeah, I need to talk to you too."

"I'm on my way downtown," she said.

"What's up?"

"I think Tommy Mangionella is working his magic," she said. "Bascomb and Villa are both on their way to Central Booking."

"He's trying to get them together." I started walking south on Hudson. I'd take Chambers over to Centre. "You going there?"

"I'm in a cab right now."

"I'll meet you," I said as I hustled across to the shady side. "I talked to the old man. He went to see Sonia. He wanted to apologize."

"How did she take it?"

"Not too well, apparently," I said. "She threatened to call the cops."

"Which meant he had to tell his son."

"Tommy's up to his thick neck in this, Julie."

"We'll see," she said. "If the rubber guns can keep from putting Villa and Bascomb in the same pen, we might find out."

I was moving on West Broadway, passing the entrance to the uptown Broadway line. Our old station. A flash: Little Bella, aged four or so, holding on to the thick wooden handrail as she navigated the big steps one at a time.

Julie said, "I'll leave word with security. Meet me in the sub-basement."

I was moving fast along Chambers, passing under cast-iron trellises, empty-faced clocks, hand towels hung to dry, through sun and shadows, sun and shadows. If I pushed any harder, I'd be jogging. "We'd better go in together," I said.

"Why?"

"I'm carrying," I said.

She hesitated, then said, "Fine."

"I may get there before you."

"I don't think so," she said. "We just pulled up."


When I arrived, she came upstairs to get me and we went to the sub-basement, where cops were going through the mind-numbing exercise of fingerprinting and photographing the accused on their way to court for arraignment.

As I sat next to her, surrounded by industrial green walls as a stream of men fresh from a precinct-house grill came into the room, Julie said she'd been told that Bascomb and Villa hadn't seen each other, that they'd been kept in separate pens. But both were going upstairs, for interviews with someone from Morgenthau's team. In theory, Bascomb, sulking in a pen for assaulting me, didn't belong to Sharon, as the executive A.D.A. on Homicide, but Julie said she'd talk to him anyway. "This one isn't likely to die," she said. There was competition among the Bureau Chiefs and their deputies, she said, but it barely simmered on a Sunday afternoon.

"Could be interesting," she added as we crossed under the metal detector, as I rode in on her gold badge. "Danny Villa has friends down here."

"A political agitator who's friendly with cops," I mused as we went toward the elevator bank. "Surprising, no?"

"There are a lot of Hispanic cops," Julie said. "Danny's not necessarily a bad guy in their eyes."

Now we watched through glass as a dough-faced sergeant named Flam rolled a man's fingertips across black ink and onto a white form. The man had a big black eye and an ugly welt on his forehead, and he looked as compliant and regretful as a puppy who'd gotten caught staining the rug. Someone uptown had given him an orange jumpsuit, which, Julie said, meant he had been undressed when he was arrested.

"I'll bet you he roughed up his wife," she said.

"Think she gave him the shiner?" I asked.

She whispered, "I hope so."

Flam, who looked like he'd retire tomorrow if someone asked, shiftlessly pushed his customer through the long room toward a lanky photographer in blue. I watched as Blackeye edged into place in front of a wall that measured his height. Another cop, a fat guy who might've been at the academy with Flam during the Lindsay administration, prepared the board that would hold the wife-beater's name and docket number.

I said, "It's a dull factory you got—"

She cut me off. "Is that him?"

I looked to my right. Bascomb, at the front of the line, filled the door frame. His nose was swollen and packed with cotton, and the front of his work shirt was splattered and streaked with dried blood.

"You did that?" Julie asked.

Bascomb had run through this routine before. He came forward, let Flam remove his handcuffs and take his big right hand to get it done. Cooperating, moving slowly, steadily, Bascomb seethed: By now, he knew his trip downtown was about something more than trying to take off my head with a wrench. I'd given him half the story as we'd wrestled in his shop out in the auto graveyard. Somewhere along the line, he'd gotten the rest of it:

Hassan was dead and, in a pen down here well below street level, his old pal Luis Sixto was in custody. Bascomb had to know his old high school friend, now known as the lawyer Danilo Villa, would have the edge when it came to He Said/He Said. Bascomb had to know he'd be on the hook.

Flam slapped a paper towel in front of the big guy and Bascomb took it and rubbed it crudely across his hands, smearing the black ink. He looked for a wastepaper basket under the table, then let the ball of paper drop to the floor.

Which displeased Flam. The old cop yelled at Bascomb to pick up the crumpled paper. Instead of doing what the cop told him, Bascomb looked up toward Julie and me.

And as he did, I heard a door open behind me. As Julie turned, I looked to the right, where Blackeye and Bascomb had entered.

There was Villa, and the cop who brought him into the room wasn't the severe, gray-haired cop who had escorted the others.

It was McDowell, in his black sweatshirt and pressed jeans, his badge hanging on a lanyard around his neck.

As McDowell looked toward the glass, I heard Julie's voice:

"Detective Mangionella," she said as she began to stand.

I saw his reflection: the long leather coat, gray suit, white shirt and white tie. A look of cool, compressed composure.

And then it started in slow motion, misty and silver at the edges, acutely focused at the core.

Bascomb bent as if to pick up the ball of paper, but instead drove an elbow hard into Flam's kidney, knocking him against the table. As the old cop flinched in pain, Bascomb snapped his gun from his leather side-holster.

He turned on his heel and pointed the gun at Villa, who opened his eyes wide. His hands were still cuffed and he brought them up awkwardly, covering his face as he started to crouch into a ball. He muttered in Spanish: *"Ah, coño."*

McDowell shoved him and then backed away, retreating behind the door frame, bounding into the cop with the gray hair.

Bascomb did not hesitate. He squeezed off a shot, another, a third, and each caught Villa in his side, tearing through his immaculate suit into his flesh. As he tried to stand, Bascomb's gun issued a fourth bullet and it caught Villa in the side of the face and he went down as if his legs had been cut off suddenly at the ankles.

I dove and pulled Julie down just as Tommy the Cop fired two shots at Bascomb.

Glass shattered and fell in jagged sheets onto the dark linoleum.

With Julie under me, I turned and peered up at Mango. He had his weapon in his hand. It dangled at his side.

He stared at me.

He raised the automatic and pointed it at me.

I felt the air leave me. The Nine I'd taken from his brother was in Julie's handbag.

Mango closed his right eye and, training the gun on me, bit on his bottom lip.

"Get up," he said.

I put my hands in the air in front of me, palms up.

"Yeah," he said. "Bang. Just like that."

He put his gun back in the holster under his left arm.

"See how it goes?" he said slowly, deliberately.

He took the short flight of stairs and entered the room, nudging the photographer.

I stood and reached to lift Julie. She leaned her back and shoulders against the green wall and shimmied to stand. I retrieved her gold crucifix from among the shards of glass.

"You all right?" I asked, as I handed her the cross and its thin chain.

She closed her eyes, then nodded.

I turned toward the room, looking through the window frame. Sharp glass jutted from its corners.

Tommy stood over Bascomb. He'd caught him square in the temple and the big man's blood spread below him.

Across the room, McDowell was kneeling next to Villa's perforated body. As I watched, he looked over at Mango and, instead of shaking his head to indicate the lawyer was dead, he nodded.

Flam had his head down on the table where the fingerprint pads and white cards lay undisturbed. Mango put his hand on the back of the old cop's neck and gave it a curt squeeze. When Flam stood, he was shaking.

"Mother of God, Tommy," Flam muttered. "Mother of God."

"It's OK, Frankie," Mango said.

"I let him get my piece."

Mango looked at me out of the corner of his eye.

"Mother of God, Tommy," Flam uttered. "Could've happened to anybody."

"I said it's all right, Frank."

"Tommy, I know your old man," Flam pleaded. "Me and Ernie— We go way back, Tommy."

I felt a hand on my arm.

Julie said, "Terry, let's get out of here."

I followed her out into the long hallway. As we stood under artificial light, she looked up at me and, by putting her fingers on my chin, turned my head to the side.

"You've got glass in your hair," Julie Giadi said.

As I went to brush it away, she stopped me and I bent over for her to remove the tiny slivers.

I put my hand on her shoulder.

I took her in my arms.

She held me around the waist.

A moment later, she stepped back. "God, Terry, I was afraid he was going to shoot you."

Yeah, me too, I thought.

I said, "Maybe he doesn't know I went to see his old man."

Tommy had had this setup going without his brother Jimmy, who was now either grilling his father or looking for me.

"Let's go upstairs," she suggested. "Call Sharon."

I agreed and walked with her toward the elevator bank, toward the gathering crowd, mostly middle-aged men in blue, who had come to inspect the carnage.

Julie reached back and took my hand. As we squeezed through, I looked over the crowd and I saw McDowell. As the young cop leaned his head against the green wall, he seemed overwhelmed, as if in awe of the thoroughness, the finality, of Mango's deft solution.

If he had only looked to his left, McDowell might have seen why it wasn't as neat, as final, as it seemed. He would've seen the eyes of the stranger, the eyes of the only man left standing outside the Mango family who knew their secret. A secret that had once been shared with many outsiders—Hassan, Sixto, Bascomb—now was known only by me.

"I can give you an hour," I told her.

She looked back at me.

"I've got somewhere else to be."

# 20

I got to the Tilt at a little after five, as the sun had begun to slide behind the buildings on the other side of the river, casting a narrow orange glow over the Jersey Palisades. The thin bright light spread its rays across cobblestone, onto old brick and cracked sidewalks, and I covered my eyes as I crossed Hudson, jamming the change the driver had given me deep into my pants pocket.

I pounded with my palm on the thick green door and, seconds later, I heard the lock snap.

"Welcome home."

Diddio was wearing an old Ramones T-shirt and black jeans, black Chuck Taylors and Bella's fedora on his head.

"Hey, champ," I said as I squeezed in. We shook hands.

He locked the door behind me.

The lid of Leo's jukebox was open and my daughter sat in front of it amid stacks of CDs on the Tilt's grimy floor.

I must have grimaced because Bella said, "It's fine, Dad. Leo's cool with it."

"We're going Cuban," D announced as he locked the door behind me. "Los Van Van, Adalberto, Cachaito, Compay, some old Beny Moré . . ."

I turned to Leo. He was on the customer side of the bar, staring up at the TV.

"Watch this," he said, pointing with his cane to a sun-soaked veldt. "That tiger don't know whether to attack that antelope baby or go protect her kittens."

"Nobody called, Dad."

Everything was OK at the Tilt-a-Whirl.

I looked at Diddio and gestured for him to follow me. I went to the omnisex restroom and waited. A minute later, I came out and called to him by name.

"I wasn't sure," he said. He jogged 12 feet and he was winded. "I mean, I thought maybe you wanted me to go in here with you, but then, like, what if he doesn't and I walk in on him—"

"All right, all right," I said, holding up my hand.

"How's Julie?"

She's an aggressive, almost bellicose interviewer, I thought. But I was clearer now for her questioning. Once I'd looked over to Sharon for relief, as the eye of the video camera continued its relentless stare. She'd nodded in amusement, in pride.

"She's doing fine," I replied.

"I heard you guys worked it out," Diddio nodded. "I've got to tell you, T, I'm surprised. Happy, man, but surprised. I mean, in my mind, I got you a widower, seventy-two years old, playing shuffleboard in Kissimmee, black socks—"

"D, what's up with you tonight?"

"Tonight? I've got an Elliott Carter tribute at Saint Ann's. Or Bakithi Kumalo at S.O.B.'s, or Jonatha Brooke at the Bottom Line."

"Can you take Bella with you?"

"On a school night?"

"I've got to make an exception."

"Be great, T," he smiled. "People will think I got a date. Finally."

"A fourteen-year-old date, D?"

"Maybe, like, I'm doing that Jerry Lee Lewis thing." He punched my arm. "Only kidding, man. Hee-hee."

I reached into my pocket and handed him all the cash I had on me: $84. "Go nuts."

"I'm on the tit, man, at those clubs," he said. "You know that. If I got to start laying out green . . . Woof."

"Buy a decent dinner. Tad's. Blimpie's."

He took two $20 bills. "Maybe a movie first. *The Concert for Bangladesh* is at the Quad. Poor George."

"A classic," I nodded.

"Fat Clapton. 'I've forgotten Billy Preston!'"

"What are you two talking about?" Bella asked, as she stuck her head around the door frame.

"You'll have to ask him," I replied.

"It's me and you, Gabby," Diddio announced.

Bella frowned. "On a school night? What's going on, Dad?"

"We're going to have a visitor."

"Detective Mango?"

"Bingo."

"Oh."

"It's not that, Bella. We're finishing up, that's all."

Unconvinced, she started snapping the rubber bands on her wrist.

"Maybe we ought to take this out of the bathroom," I suggested.

As we reconvened at the pool table, I told Bella to give me her backpack, which sat, neatly filled, in the red booth.

Swiveling slowly on the stool, Leo said, "The tiger chose the antelope."

"Of course," Bella shrugged, as she passed the backpack to me.

"Tiger can't be nothing but a tiger," I added.

I looked at the clock above the cash register. Knowing Leo kept it 20 minutes fast let me calculate the time.

"I've got to rip," I said.

I took the fedora from Diddio's head and put it on my daughter's. "Keep him out of trouble," I told her.

"Who's going to watch for you?" she asked. She smacked the cue ball against a side bumper.

"You. Our angels. Horatio. Who knows?" I said. "It's not that big a deal."

"You're letting me stay out on a school—"

*"OK,"* I sang. "Call me when you're coming home. D, be good."

"Yes, sir." Now he was sitting on the floor, surrounded by little CD towers.

"Leo, thanks."

"What? She made my day."

I went around the pool table, pushed the off-white ball back to its center and went toward the door. "Who's going to lock up?"

Bella volunteered.

I looked out onto Hudson. No Mango, no McDowell. Taxis flowed south and, on the west side of the street, a woman with grape-colored hair and an old-fashioned peacoat paced in small circles, her tiny handbag hanging low on a gold chain. On the other side, in the fading sun, a teenage couple stole a kiss while riding Razor scooters, no easy trick.

In the distance, jackhammers continued to pound on Church Street.

"Be careful," she told me.

"Sure."

"I mean, you've got to tell me about my book."

"I'm going to," I said, as I stepped onto Hudson.

"A hint. *Please?*" she asked. "Did you at least like it?"

"Ouch. Whining . . ."

"All right: Please. Julie said you would."

"No chance," I said. "And I'm not being mean."

"It stinks, that's all."

"All that work requires a nice, long discussion."

"Yikes," she said, looking away.

"You want a quick review?"

"Er, yes?"

"Did Julie encourage you to ask?"

She nodded.

"Does Julie seem like the kind of woman who'd let someone walk into pain?"

She smiled as she leaned against the open door.

"How's Hamlet?" I asked. "Still greedy?"

"Sorry 'bout that," she replied, with sad eyes.

"Forget it," I told her. "A question: How old is he?"

"I don't know," she said. "Your age?"

"He's fat, out of shape and about seventeen," I told her. "You think an adult could be that indecisive?"

She started to say something. But she stopped.

"See you later." I pulled the bill of her fedora over her eyes and yanked the door closed. I waited until she did the lock, then I went toward our home.


I knew one of them would come when night fell, and, as the river rolled and small planes crossed the dark skies, as unblinking klieg lights shone on the devils' deed, he would suggest we talk about it. He'd come armed with the knowledge that what would work best with me would be the appearance of rationality, the possibility of addressing mutual interests. So I was betting on Tommy. If Jimmy came, he'd be carrying a cannon, expecting I'd stick the Nine in his ear. Not that Jimmy wouldn't come. He'd show someday, no doubt, and when he did, it'd be in a lonely place, and he'd do it swiftly, from behind. Which meant I needed to avoid such places and, if I stumbled upon one, I needed to remember never to turn my back; to put my back to the wall, always.

I took a bottle of Badoit and Bella's backpack into my office and sat in silence, with only the light of the desk lamp accompanying me. And as I read, I thought I heard the rubato of Sheila Yannick's cello: something modern, dissonant with long lines and few flourishes or filigrees. When I finished I went out through the living room, passing the soft chair where Dorotea Salgado had sat, passing Marina's luminescent green water and mottled limestone arch, and, with the kitchen lights low, I got ready for my visitor.


I was lost in the stars when the harsh knock on the door came 45 minutes later: a Weill recital at the Lowenstein auditorium, with Marina at my elbow. Startled, I got up, looked through the peephole. It was who I expected; yes. Nervous? No. Edgy; on edge. A nice rush. Let's get it done.

Before I undid the lock, I took another quick look around the kitchen. Under the somber glow of the lamp in the stove, I saw that everything was in its place—in shadows, gray corners, neat; all as it should be. And the nine-millimeter piece that, I'd discovered, had only eight rounds in the clip, sat in my pocket on the other side of the laundry door.

The persistent buzz of the refrigerator. The fading fragrance of Bella's apple shampoo. The creaking of old wood under uneven footfalls.

"Tommy."

The evening air was crisp and rich with the salty scent of the river. The streetlight flickered, as if sending code to the cobblestone.

"We've got to talk," he said, looking up at me from the bottom step. "No surprise, right?"

I stepped aside. He lumbered past me, pulling in the night chill, and he took off his long leather coat and put it on the back of the chair near Bella's *Nursery of Crime* as I sealed the door.

Mango made a big deal out of noticing the manuscript, rapping it with a knuckle.

"I heard about this," he said. "My nephew. You read it or what?"

"Sure."

"So . . ."

"Unexpectedly spectacular."

"No shit."

I shrugged. "None."

As he put himself in Bella's seat, away from his coat, her manuscript, he said, "Just what you need. More money."

I leaned against the sink, felt the cold porcelain through my jeans. "You want a drink, Tommy?"

"Maybe a little soup. *Escarole.*"

I smiled and kept my arms folded across my chest.

"What did he say?" he asked.

"Tell me what he told you," I replied. "I'll tell you if it's right."

"He emptied the bottle, Terry, so he's not talking to nobody. You know, he's an old, old man." Mango tapped the side of his head. "His melon, it ain't too reliable."

"He said he went to see Sonia. To apologize."

"Apologize for what?"

"Tommy," I said, "we both know what we're talking about here."

"Enlighten me." He ran his hands, his blunt, manicured fingers, along the edge of the table.

"He apologized for whipping up the scheme that got her thirty years in Bedford Hills."

He nodded darkly. "Oh."

"He wanted Sixto to rip off Glatzer and they'd split the take," I continued. "But Sixto went his own way. He got Sonia to dip for the wallet, got Bascomb to kill Glatzer, he set up the girl, then he took off."

"I see," he said, the two short words dripping with cynicism. "And how do you figure this?"

"I talked to Sixto."

"Nobody talked to Sixto."

"I talked to Villa," I amended.

"Hearsay is what they call it," he said slowly, as if calculating as he spoke. "Don't count for much."

"What can you do, Tommy, when your father goes to see her and he tells her what she never knew—that Sixto set her up? Her fantasy, that he's in hiding somewhere, afraid of being framed himself, that he's going to come back for her one day, is shattered. Gone. She starts screaming, says she's going to call the cops. Christ, what a nightmare."

"I can't let her take him down," he said, slap-slapping his thumb on the table. "You're saying that?"

"I'm saying if your father had stayed on Elizabeth Street, Sonia might've been able to salvage something out of her sorry-ass life."

He sat back. "So my old man killed her."

"Hell, no," I said. "Bascomb did. Jimmy hired him."

"And that's a fact?"

I said yes. "I spoke to Bascomb too."

"Well, neither of them is talking now."

"I've got to give you that, Tommy. Very effective."

He waved his hand. "You don't ever want to go to your last resort," he said dismissively.

"But they're not really silent," I led.

"'Cause you know?"

"Me. And Jimmy," I said. "Maybe McDowell."

He shook his head. "McDowell is back in Queens. He's a good boy. His eyes are open now."

"And Jimmy?"

"He says you took his piece."

I didn't reply.

"Jimmy always had a temper," he shrugged. "He has to learn to negotiate."

I said, "I walk down a dark alley, Tommy, I don't ask him to watch my back."

He leaned into the light and looked hard at me. "You think my blood is going to give me up? They could take his eye and he don't give me up."

"No, but maybe thirty years from now he tries to apologize to somebody."

He stopped and ran through it.

"I don't see he knows what you know," he concluded. "See, you know too fuckin' much, Terry. And the problem, worse, is that people believe you. People in the D.A.'s. And Addison, who you dragged in I don't know why." As he shook his head, a streak of light crossed his silver toupee. "Too bad you had to wake up, Terry. We were all better off when you were fuckin' *pazzo.*"

I was going to tell him I never was crazy, merely lost. But there was no point. I sensed he was headed toward where I wanted him to go. Why distract him now?

"So where does it leave us, Tommy?"

"I've been thinking about that."

"Soliciting ideas?"

"No," he said curtly. "It's time to lay it out."

I moved away from the sink to sit in my chair.

"The thing is," he said, "how to get you to keep your mouth shut."

"That seems right," I agreed.

"A guy like you, though, he has to talk."

Not necessarily, I thought.

"I guess I could tear down this house—your wife's pictures, your son's toys. Memories. This book," he said, nodding toward the manuscript.

"And that's going to do what?"

"Maybe it needs to be something more, Terry. Something terrible and permanent, like—"

"I'll burn down your fuckin' world, Tommy, and you know it."

"I'm saying—"

"Take away my reason to live and I burn down the whole fuckin' planet."

He frowned severely. "Now you're threatening *me?*"

"Looking at her wrong, anybody, will set me off. So you keep that in mind and you tell Jimmy. Tell him tonight. Nobody thinks about my daughter, nobody says her name. Not once."

"See, you're trying to edge me into a corner, Terry, and that we can't have. Ask Danny Villa. Ask that fuckin' dunce Bascomb."

He sat back into the shadows and now he folded his arms in front of his broad chest.

"What I got here," he began, "is a guy who knows my old man tried to hook up with Sixto to rip off the Jew. For thirty years he sat on it while your Sonia was in jail. . . . What a mess."

"Did your father know Bascomb killed Glatzer?"

He said no. "Look," he told me, "you don't know my old man back then. Believe me, all he's thinking is no diamonds. He don't give a fuck, I'm telling you."

"So what about Sonia?"

"Sonia? You should be happy, Terry. Them that fucked with her are gone."

"Bascomb, Sixto, Hassan—"

"Boom. That's it. *Finito.*"

"Yeah, except Jimmy brought back Bascomb," I nodded. "Symmetry. Sweet, in its way. What goes around . . .'"

"Terry, this thing has got to run its course. You hear what I'm telling you? You know a lot of stuff nobody can confirm. Not anymore."

"Like I said—"

He cut me off. "I'm thinking you make a lot of noise but it can't work out for you. It can't."

"No?"

"I'm thinking what you want at the end of this is Weisz," he said as he leaned forward and put his elbows on the table.

We were no more than a yard apart now. I could smell his breath, see the simmering fury in his black eyes.

"I think you'll do anything to nail that fuck, Terry."

I nodded slowly. He saw me in the shadows.

"I deliver Weisz in one year, by next April, and you keep your mouth shut for the rest of your life. And mine."

As he watched me, I bit my lip and closed my eyes. Then I absently scratched my head above my eyebrow.

"I bring him to you, Terry. Down here. You want him alone in an alley, you got it. You want me to bring you him in pieces, one finger at a time, an ear, no problem."

I looked at him.

"You like that, Terry," he said. "I know you do."

"Tell me, Tommy," I replied. "Did I have it? Bascomb back then, Bascomb now."

"I will say I don't know why he did it. Very aggressive guy, this guy."

"And the diamonds?" I asked.

He ran his fingers around his face. "Villa. Every cent, plastic surgery. That and to buy his way back to New York."

"If he's one of the bad guys, why did he call me?"

"What else could it be?" he shrugged.

I thought for a moment. "Get me to focus on the Glatzer murder."

"Bingo," he replied, pointing at me. "You'd wind up looking for Sixto. Which should've been a long-time dead end."

I shifted in the hard chair. "So you're telling me your father had nothing to do with framing Sonia?"

"You and this Sonia . . ." He shook his head. "No, not a thing."

I stood. "All right."

He looked up at me and then he stood too. "We got a deal."

"I got to do what I got to do," I said, putting it as he would have.

He reached for his coat and carefully hung it on his arm.

"Who would've thought crazy Terry Orr would've become a pretty good P.I.?" He rapped the table with a knuckle. "Some day, huh?"

He opened my front door and went out to the salty air, to flickering lights, to rounded cobblestones, to the relative silence of a Sunday night in TriBeCa.

————

I went to the phone and dialed her cell number. It rang several times and I expected a recorded voice, but then she answered.

"Julie Giada," she said officially.

"Where are you?"

"Terry?"

"Terry."

"Home, recharging my cell. Watching TV."

"I thought you might still be at Centre Street," I said.

"Where are you?"

"Home. You want a nightcap?"

She hesitated, then said, "Let me get dressed."

"No purple gowns."

"Funny man," she replied.

"I got something for you."

"I hope so."

She said she'd be here in a half-hour.

That'd give me enough time to see if this god-damned thing Diddio won worked.


We were sitting at the kitchen table, espresso cups empty, the cookie plate littered with crumbs. All the lights were on.

From the seat that faced the white front door, Julie Giada stared at Diddio's prize, his silver DAT machine. "I can't believe it."

I nodded. "The sound quality is remarkable."

I'd put the thing on top of the refrigerator. And to back up the built-in recorder, I stuck a mike on top of Marina's "The Cliffs of the Gargano." Triangulate, the instructions said, a phrase I hadn't heard since the Warren Commission's report.

"No, I mean, how badly he played you," she said. She wore a magenta turtleneck over black slacks and under a black vest with embroidered patterns that for a moment brought Safi Majorelle to mind.

"You don't think it appealed to me: Weisz on a plate?"

She looked at me. "You're a good man, Terry."

Maybe so. Maybe not.

"He'll come after you," she added.

"Tommy? Not after today. He does that and what happened at Centre Street doesn't look too righteous," I said. "Besides, it's too late to turn back now."

"Or his brother," she nodded.

I smiled. "I know you guys," I told her. "You guys will work over McDowell until he gives up Jimmy."

"For?"

"For overexuberance," I said. "For putting Bascomb close enough to Sonia to kill her. Whatever."

I heard the front door move, as if struck by a gust a wind. Then it opened.

Bella, happy, tired, fedora tilted to the back of her head, entered, then suddenly stopped. Behind her, Diddio peered in cautiously. He looked over at Julie, then at me.

"What's this?" Bella asked.

"What?" I said. "We're having coffee."

"Hello, Dennis," Julie said.

He nodded.

I knew him. He was thinking: Could've been me. His brain was racing: Julie Diddio, running with him along a beach, back to their loft near the tunnel, 2.5 kids, a summer place in Portsmouth, retire to Arizona, the moon-faced grandkids visit. A memoir, "Greasy Fries: Ramblings of an Award-Winning Critic." I'm not feeling too good, Julie. Oh, oh no. Forty great years, honey. I love y— St. Peter; hey man, what up, dog? Where's Hendrix at?

"No, I mean, you're using our DAT," Bella said. She slipped out of her denim jacket, put it on the doorknob to the laundry room.

"Yeah, and it works."

"Sure it works," Diddio said, as if challenged. "It's the best thing ever invented. Period. Better than air conditioning."

"Which reminds me, D, are you going to shut the door or leave your ass out on Harrison?"

"Ass on Harrison," he replied. "Going to S.O.B.'s. South African funk. Julie?"

Nice move, I thought.

"I'd better stay here, Dennis. Thanks, though."

"Yeah. Right. Bye."

"Wait," Bella said. "Kiss, kiss."

They made exaggerated motions as if to kiss each other on the cheek, European-style, then intentionally missed by several feet.

Bella closed the door. "So?"

"How was your evening?" I asked her. "What did you wind up doing?"

"Burgers at Walter's," she replied and, with a bad British accent, added, " 'I've forgotten Billy Preston!' "

"Is somebody going to tell me what that means?" I asked.

Julie shrugged.

"Now I'm beat," Bella said, "but what a weekend."

You're telling me, I thought.

"Leo's not so bad, Dad," she added. "He told me how to shoot nine-ball. And make a Cuba Libre."

She went to the refrigerator, withdrew a half-filled container of cranberry juice and started to hoist it to her lips. But, anticipating my criticism, she stopped, went to the cabinet and filled a jelly jar.

"Bella, can you make a copy of this DAT tape?" I asked.

She squeezed by me and lifted the small machine. "See this?" she said, pointing to its side. "I can patch it to my system. You want a CD or a cassette?"

"Three cassettes."

She put the machine and the little tape in a pocket of her baggy blue painter's jeans. "No problem. I'll do the first one while I'm in the shower."

"Bella," I said, "I don't want you listening to it, all right?"

She frowned. "Well, now I want to, but OK. Fine."

"Thanks."

She kissed me on the cheek with her sticky cranberry lips. " 'Night, Dad."

I tapped her hand.

She put her jar in the sink and smiled at Julie.

"Good night, Gabriella."

She went toward the stairs, put her hat on the newel post and carried the bottle of juice up toward her bedroom.

After a moment passed, Julie said, "It must be nice to come home to her."

I nodded. "We're doing all right."

We sat in silence for a moment. We'd have to wait until Bella, fresh from a shower, powdered, bare feet padding down the stairs, gave us the first cassette for Julie to deliver to Sharon. To pass the time, I was going to ask Julie to join me in the living room. There had to be something on TV; maybe she had a favorite program. Who knows? Maybe she had a little Sunday-night routine: lay out the clothes, TV with a snack, something not too . . . Or maybe we could talk about Sinclair Lewis. There were magazines under the coffee table.

But to go to the living room, I'd have to take her past Marina's paintings and she'd want to talk about them and I didn't want to do that. I was tired, I had been frightened, I needed to get through the next few days, I needed my head to be clear. If I wanted to go to Foggia to sit in Rafaela's fragrant garden and swell once again with the intoxicating feeling of acceptance, the warm, unfamiliar satisfaction of family; or stroll in platinum twilight near the Medina Azahara outside Córdoba and suddenly take Marina in my arms; or to ask her over a chilled Ostuni what she knew of the Majorelle Gardens in the Gueliz; to taste her fingers as I took a bite of the plump fig she offered—

"Terry, I have to say something."

"Julie. Yes."

She stood and ran her hands along the back of the chair, then squared it to the table.

Upstairs, the shower water ran. The pipes under the sink behind me hummed.

"Terry, I think I know a good thing when I see one."

I turned to face her. She was blushing.

"Julie, it's not there," I said, tapping my chest. "It's not you. I think you are a very special woman. But I don't have it anymore. It's gone."

"I can't believe that."

"Believe it," I said. "I wish it weren't so."

She stared at me and I saw the beauty in her eyes, the integrity; and I saw she was groping for the right thing to say.

But there was no right thing. I can put everything back to how it used to be, but without Marina, I am empty where my heart once was. Without my little boy—

"I can wait," she said finally.

"I wouldn't, Julie. Please. You deserve so much more."

She came toward me. "That you said that tells me I'm right."

She leaned down and kissed me on the lips. I did not reciprocate.

"I've made up my mind," she whispered.

I said OK. I nodded. I think I smiled.

I felt nothing.

## 21

The cabbie, a brawny Nigerian who crammed for his INS quiz at every red light, dropped us off at 65th and Broadway, in front of a bus stop surrounded by Juilliard students on their way back to Yorkville. The sun was behind us now, lingering above the murky green Hudson before it would slide behind the Jersey Palisades, and it cast a vivid light on the buildings on the east side of the busy intersection. The pale stone of the Church of Jesus Christ of Latter-Day Saints shone as if in a celestial spotlight.

Bella looked up at me. "So?"

"Yeah," I said, as I lifted her backpack that strained with textbooks, notepads and CDs. "I'm OK with it."

But I knew it was a different thing to be underground than to be in the golden light surrounded by laughing college kids, preening white-haired widows in fur, busboys jogging toward their restaurants after making quick deliveries, a harried man with a disorganized ream of newspapers who was late for an Iranian film showing at the Walter Reade Theater.

"What's in this thing?" I asked as we started toward Alice Tully Hall, crossing wide, lumpy 65th. "Cinder blocks? A bowling ball?"

"Idle chatter, Dad?" she asked as she squinted, shading her eyes with her hand.

"That obvious, huh?" I felt an unfamiliar nervousness in my stomach and knots of tension in my shoulders, my neck: the slow, insidious version of the crushing attack of anguish, of dread, that I'd suffered last week on the platform at Willet's Point.

"It's going to be fine," she said with mature assurance. "Really."

"You've done this before."

She hesitated. "No, but I wanted to. Daniel said he would go with me."

"But . . . ?"

"We should do it together," she told me firmly.

"Says Dr. Harteveld."

"No. Says me."

On the island between Broadway and Columbus, a green, post-industrial pagoda held an elevator that descended to the platform for the downtown trains.

With Davy in the stroller, Marina would've used that elevator to go underground.

I was listening to NPR when my daughter came down for breakfast. As she handed me the two cassettes, I asked her if she'd listened to the terse, cryptic conversation I'd had with Tommy Mango.

She came around behind me, pushed a Pop-Tart into the toaster, dug with her index finger for a vitamin in the white tube. "What did you tell me?"

"You always do what I tell you?" I asked.

She went to her seat and tugged the front page of the *Times* toward her.

"So this is what it's all about," she said as she read a story below the fold. "Tommy the Cop killed two guys, including Danilo Villa." She looked up at me. "Isn't he the guy—"

"He's the guy."

"I think he spoke at my school. When I was in the sixth grade."

"It's a long story."

"Summarize," she said.

"Fly right. Be good to your friends. Money is worth less than you think. Secrets are a myth. And always do what your dad says."

"Instead of what he does . . ."

"Exactly." Then I said, "Maybe that last one wasn't part of it. No, not really."

A man takes an oath, even a man like Ernie Mango, and he must mean what he says, he must do what he says he'll do. Held against the value of a man's word, diamonds should be an easy temptation to avoid. Held against a man's honor, all temptation ought to be.

I told Tommy the Cop this: "I got to do what I got to do."

He found out a little after 3:15 A.M. that we didn't have a deal.

I looked across the table at the archive photo of Danny Villa in the *Times* and I thought of the old snapshot Hassan had given me, of two boyhood friends hanging their arms on each other's shoulders. I thought of the terror in young Sonia's eyes in the *Daily News* photos I'd seen on microfiche.

The toaster popped behind me. I waved Bella back into her chair and got her breakfast, scorching the tips of my fingers as I flipped the fruit-filled pastry slabs onto a plate.

"Juice," she instructed.

I looked at her. She wore a navy-blue hoody with Japanese characters across the chest, black jeans, her Cons. I thought I noticed she'd reduced the number of rubber bands on her wrist. There was a system at work, but I couldn't fathom it.

"I believe you took the bottle upstairs."

"Empty now, but we have more."

And we did, on the top shelf, in back.

As I handed her a glass of cranberry juice, I said, "Give me the original tape."

She clucked her tongue and reached into the pouch of her sweatshirt. "Here."

I dropped the tape into my shirt pocket. Into my safe-deposit box it would go.

"Why do you need three?" she asked. "I mean, we gave one to Julie. . . ."

"One for Luther Addison—"

"You're talking to him? That's encouraging."

"Bella—"

"I'm observing. That's all."

"And the other is for a reporter at the *Times.*"

"Coombs."

"Yes."

"Symmetry," she said. "I like it." She crammed a corner of the Pop-Tart into her mouth.

"What time do you get out today?" I asked.

She chewed, swallowed and said, "Two."

"I'll pick you up."

"Why?"

"I want to do something."

She drew up. "Dad, I'm a little, you know, too old for my daddy to be—"

"I thought we'd go to Lincoln Center. To the subway station."

She stopped as if dumbstruck. "Really?" she said finally.

"It's time." There has to be an end to greed.

"Well, it's actually past time, but yeah, sure. Count me in."

"And we can talk about your book. Your very good book."

Chewing again, she merely nodded, as she considered what it meant to visit the place where her mother and brother were killed. But I could see that the compliment pleased her.

NPR now had us in Uruguay. The government wanted in on the Declaration of Paris about 150 years too late.

I turned to look at the clock in the stove. "We gotta go."

She passed her plate to me. "You're taking me to school too?"

"I'm going your way."

"I'm seven again." She slipped her arms into her denim jacket. "Goody. I should've asked you to cut my breakfast into teeny wittle pieces."

I had to go to the bank, to Midtown North to find Addison, to the *Times* on 43rd.

I was going to find Dorotea Salgado. I owed her the story. She deserved to know. She wouldn't have her daughter to hold, but maybe, before her world became a torrent of confusion brought on by Alzheimer's, she'd sleep better knowing her Sonia's hands were clean.

Maybe then a few minutes with Mrs. Maoli. Something about approval, about external validation. About extended family.

Then I'd catch up with my daughter at Walt Whitman.

"Ready?" I went for my coat. The Nine was still in the pocket.

"Ready," she replied as she hoisted her backpack onto her shoulder.

I opened the door and we went out into the morning chill.

Outside Alice Tully Hall, glass-encased posters were set like dominoes ready to tumble. One announced that it was the year of Rachmaninoff.

In a better world, Raymond Montgomery Weisz might be performing—

"Let it go, Dad," Bella said.

"What?"

"You're staring at the poster," she said, "and you're thinking about the wrong stuff."

As I nodded, she pointed north. "After, let's go and spend some money. Buy you some clothes. I'll treat you to a new blazer."

On the east side of Broadway was an Eddie Bauer, a Gap. On this side, Tower Records, a Pottery Barn. Midtown Manhattan, a mall on the outskirts of Boise, Idaho: the same thing. Welcome to the cultural capital of the world.

"I need clothes?" I asked.

A sarcastic smile was her reply.

"I dress better than Diddio."

"Hey," she said sharply. "Leave him alone."

I wondered which direction Marina had been coming from. Maybe east, from the Park. Or maybe she'd been strolling Davy through the Lincoln Center campus. It was modeled after the Piazza del Campidoglio in Rome, designed by Michelangelo. The fountain in its center, with the breeze off the Hudson, made the plaza a pleasant stop on a summer's afternoon.

There was a concert that noon in Damrosch Park. The music of Niccolò Castiglioni.

"Let's take the stairs," she said. "And, yes, for Julie, you'll need new clothes."

I took a breath and followed her as she held on to the cold banister in the

center of the steep stairwell. I stared at her hand, compelling myself to remember when it was pink, pudgy and little.

I felt fine. Just a bit nervous, a little tense. Natural.

When she reached the bottom step, she turned to face me. "Clean, no?"

That it was, and well-lit. New gray tiles, shining silver turnstiles, readable
maps in frames. Graffiti? None.

A subway station outside of Boise.

"Come on, Dad. We'll go stand on the platform."

"I— Sure. Why not?"

She took a MetroCard out of her denim jacket. After she swiped it, I hesitated, then passed through the turnstile, pushing its blunt bar with my
knee. She followed.

We were alone.

The familiar scent of stale air, of the mire between the tracks, cleaning so-
lutions, disinfectant. A woman who had either boarded the last train or just
left the station wore too much sweet, candy-like perfume.

"You look good, Dad. Pretty steady."

Rita Santiago was standing over there. She was closest to the shadowy alcove where Weisz had been hiding. Gerald Schaber, who was reading *Town
and Country*, was over there, more or less, by the trash bin, using the overhead fluorescent lights to illuminate the magazine. He'd said he heard Marina scream before the stroller went over the edge. Maurice Bock, the piano
tuner, said Marina didn't scream until Weisz, arms outstretched, hissed angrily as the stroller went over the edge. Sylvia Barron said Marina didn't
scream, but a startled Bock did.

Sylvia cried when I visited her, notebook and diagrams in hand. She
sends us Christmas cards.

But she didn't try to help Marina. Neither did Santiago, Schaber, Bock,
the two Benjamin kids on their way to shop in the Village. Healy, the ex-
cop, did nothing. Bum leg, my ass.

"Dad, maybe we can take the train back home. Start a new habit."

I looked across the platform where other Juilliard students waited for an
uptown train, their instrument cases at their heels. A security guard, headed
north for the four-to-midnight shift, had his lunchbox under his arm as he

studied his thick shoes. Five years ago, Jean-Pierre Coceau was over there, not far from where the guard stood, according to Santiago. A resident of Breil, France, who was in the States on business, Coceau was the only one I hadn't spoken to. But he must've seen it all.

The lighting here is better than I ever imagined. Here, in this surreal subway station, with its medicinal scents, its spotless tiles, gleaming trash cans. Surprisingly normal. Calm, almost tranquil.

My palms were damp as dishrags, and my stomach leaped.

I could feel my skin under my clothes.

I focused on my running shoes, on the dark pillars between the tracks.

"Dad?"

"Yeah, sure," I said, too quickly. "We'll take the train back home."

It had to be right there, to my left. Weisz came from behind that post, banged into Marina and shoved Davy and the stroller before she could react.

As Marina dove onto the tracks, the white light of the express train bearing down on the station, Weisz pivoted and scrambled wildly toward— Toward where I was standing now. Bobby Circati said he hurdled the turnstile. Rondell Robinson said he fell and crawled frantically under the silver bar. (I believe Robinson. A calm, reasoning man. Repaired Xerox copiers. Had it not been for his arthritic hip, I believe he would've helped my wife save our boy. I've always felt that. Meanwhile, Circati thought he had attained celebrity because he'd witnessed a deadly crime and was on *Eyewitness News* and in the *Post*. A punk. I wasn't wrong to smack his head.)

Robinson said, Bock said, Rachel and Zalman Holtz said, Marina tried to lift the stroller up onto the platform, but it was coated in the oily muck that seeped between the tracks. She panicked—who wouldn't?—and then, desperately, tried again.

Meanwhile, the train, roaring, klaxon blaring. Brakes squealing?

Yes, said Robinson.

No, said Donna Benjamin, then a cynical 17-year-old.

I can't be sure, shrugged Muhammad Sarwar from Kew Gardens, Queens.

"Dad?"

What would I have done had I been here, in this clean, well-lit station, with my wife and son?

Bella was in school.

I was doing nothing, walking around TriBeCa, killing time. I could've come with them.

Why hadn't I?

"Hey, Dad . . ."

Weisz wouldn't have run at me. I'm too big, too obvious.

But if he had?

I could've gotten Davy off the tracks.

I was working out four, five times a week, playing B-ball nights. I was strong, quick.

If Weisz had somehow gotten around me, I could've jumped off the platform down onto the tracks and, with the train bearing down hard on me, I could've gotten Davy to safety, to his mother's arms. My little boy, frightened, bruised, but alive.

I would've rolled up onto the platform, seconds before the train reached me.

Would've been nothing but a story to tell. A New York story, one with a happy ending.

"Dad, here it comes. I think it's an express."

I looked down at Bella. She was just a kid back then, 10 years old, very bright, precocious but curiously, wonderfully naive. The world is a sanctuary for a 10-year-old like that, a girl embraced by a loving mother, a gurgling, contented infant brother. It goes like this: She leaves for school, she returns and all is what it was before, perhaps even a bit better. The world is a rose yet to blossom.

There are no police cars in front of the house, red lights whirling, Mrs. Maoli in tears and fighting hysteria, as Bella walks home as planned with Eva Figueroa and Glo-Bug, chatting about schoolwork, pop culture, goofy boys. Bella, innocent for the last time. All she can be, for the last time. My Bella . . .

If I had been there—if I had been *here*—all the pain she's endured, the loneliness, heartache, anxiety, alienation, would've never occurred.

But it has. Of course, it has. All because I was not here.

"An express, yep," she said, over the growing noise.

I see the light, I hear the train. Students behind us, passing through the turnstiles. A tall, thin woman who'd yet to remove her sunglasses.

The concrete floor beneath us rattles, rumbles.

Bella takes my hand.

The train rushes violently toward the station. It's not going to stop.

I feel its power, its relentless energy. I hear its grinding wheels.

Sparks, sulfur.

My head is spinning and my knees buckle. The walls wobble and shake.

"Bella . . ."

"I got you, Dad."

The train explodes past us. I feel it, car after car, sucking air from the station, pulling air into the station, fracturing, destroying. Its ferocious forces shove me aside, knocking me away from my daughter, who holds tight onto my hand.


And then there was a kind of silence, disrupted only by the clicking of steel wheels on steel tracks, the jangle of the cars as they rumbled off into the distance.

"Dad, open your eyes."

I saw the back of the silver train as it disappeared into the tunnel blackness.

I turned and I saw Bella. Tears streamed down her perfect cheeks.

"You did it, Dad," she told me.

Her voice melting to sorrow, she said it again.

"Dad, you did it."

**Songs performed during the Beatles' $500 million reunion concert at Madison Square Garden:**

*First Set*
Get Back
With a Little Help from My Friends
Something
Ob-La-Di, Ob-La-Da
Boys
I Saw Her Standing There
She's Leaving Home (with the Eos Orchestra)
The Long and Winding Road (with Eos)

*Intermission*

*Second Set*
"John" medley, performed by Eos:
    A Hard Day's Night/Strawberry Fields Forever/Julia/Across the
    Universe/Norwegian Wood/Lucy in the Sky with Diamonds
Because (performed by the Harlem Boys Choir)
Here Comes the Sun (with the Harlem Boys Choir)
Yesterday
If I Needed Someone
We Can Work It Out
In My Life (sung by Paul and George)

*Intermission*

### Third Set
Yellow Submarine
Penny Lane
While My Guitar Gently Weeps (with Eric Clapton)
Back in the USSR

### First Encore
All You Need Is Love (sung by Paul and Jeff Lynne)
Let It Be

### Second Encore (with Eos, Harlem Boys Choir)
Imagine
Hey Jude

Diddio had the set list signed by Paul, George and Ringo as a gift for Bella. It's now in a sealed envelope in Terry's safe-deposit box. Neither Bella nor Terry knows what's in the envelope.